Praise for Corrina Lawson's
Phoenix Rising

"A touch of the X-Men with a smattering of coming-of-age legend, *Phoenix Rising* certainly keeps the reader's attention. Lawson effortlessly switches points-of-view, from Alec to Beth and back again...The edge-of-your-seat plot keeps the story rolling along."
~ *Library Journal*

"Put *Phoenix Rising* on your keeper shelf, it's an amazing read. I absolutely loved it, especially the characters. Once I started reading I did not want to put the book down."
~ *Night Owl Reviews*

"I was very attracted to the continued stream of action sequences that never let the story flatline... Readers looking for an adventure into a paranormally complex and political world with a quite literally hot hero, will want to check this out."
~ *Long and Short Reviews*

Look for these titles by
Corrina Lawson

Now Available:

Freya's Gift
Luminous

Phoenix Rising

Corrina Lawson

Samhain Publishing, Ltd.
11821 Mason Montgomery Road, 4B
Cincinnati, OH 45249
www.samhainpublishing.com

Editing by Jennifer Miller
Cover by Kanaxa

First Samhain Publishing, Ltd. electronic publication: November 2011
First Samhain Publishing, Ltd. print publication: October 2012

Dedication

For the four minions, Erin, Joseph, Kyle and Cassandra, the best cheerleaders and supporters that a mother could ever have.

Chapter One

Beth Nakamora settled back into the cushions of the chair and put her notepad on her lap. She debated sliding forward to perch on the edge of the chair but decided that would make her appear too eager. She suspected her new client would come in literally breathing fire. Better to let whatever storm was brewing wash over her before trying to get through to him.

And she needed desperately to reach him. His life depended on getting him to trust her, though he was unaware of it. Perhaps seeing her nearly lost among the oversized cushions of the chair would help. It emphasized her small—and hopefully unthreatening—stature.

The door flew open, and Alec Farley strode into the room.

He didn't make eye contact or acknowledge her existence. Instead, he paced the temporary office, scowling, sizing her up in silence.

Beth doodled on her pad and watched him watch her. Alec was taller, stronger and, well, far more grown-up than she'd imagined. Somehow, she'd mentally slotted him in with all the adolescent teens she counseled. No doubt because she thought of Alec as needing her help.

But this was no boy.

Alec was a full-grown *man*, every inch a soldier, and a very attractive one, or would be once he stopped scowling. If God reached down to create a superhero, he would look much like Alec Farley. His shoulders were wide and strong and his dark blue T-shirt hugged his flat stomach.

She'd expected to be fascinated by him but not to be so *impressed*.

He moved like a dancer, in perfect balance, and his wavy dark hair half-hid an unnerving gaze as his blue eyes seemed to notice everything all at once. She wondered if Alec was using his telekinesis to explore the room. From what she'd been told, he was capable of using TK to poke into corners, check under objects like the two chairs and even under the carpeting. Something beyond his pacing definitely seemed to be happening. She could practically feel power oozing out of him.

If he's like this now, what is he like when he's calling fire?

"Hello, Alec."

"You don't belong to the Resource," he said. "You don't belong here."

Belong. An interesting word choice. "What makes you say that?"

"You're not armed. You're not adhering to the dress code for the lab techs. And you're so tiny. You almost like a little kid with that dark hair, except that, well, you've got nice bre—I mean, you have the shape of a grown woman. Just how old are you?"

She pushed her dark hair out of her eyes. Well, score one for breasts, even small ones. At least he was convinced she was an adult. "I'm old enough to have a master's degree in psychology." And mature enough to sit still until he settled. And not so young that he could intimidate her.

"Why did you take the desk and couch out of the room?"

"They were both big and ugly. The chairs are more comfortable."

"So we're supposed to sit down and have a nice little *chat?*"

"If you like. You don't have to sit."

There was fury in his question but also fear, if her years of experience of dealing with defensive patients were any indication. The fury she understood and was typical of many people forced into counseling.

But Alec's fear didn't make sense. As far as he knew, she was here to help him learn how to work better with outsiders. She didn't see why he perceived danger. Had he or someone else seen through her cover story?

"Are you from outside?"

He said "outside" like being from there made her an exotic. That was at least an interesting change from being considered exotic because of her Japanese ancestry.

She put the pad down on the table, pencil neatly on top, and stood. "I'm Beth Nakamora." She held out her hand. "What do you mean by 'outside'?"

He refused the handshake. "I meant will you be living here?"

He lived at the complex, as did all the scientists and guards. "I have my own home." She took a step back. "So, yes, I guess I am from outside. Does that surprise you?"

He paced the room again, putting his back to her. She matched his silence. It certainly was no hardship to watch him move. She tried to keep her professional detachment but couldn't help noticing that his backside presented an awfully nice view, especially in the tight jeans.

He finally turned and pointed a finger at the coffee table. Her notepad rose from the table into the air. The pencil rolled to the floor while the pad flew into his hand.

She gasped. *Argh. Focus. You know what he is.* But seeing him in action was entirely different from hearing about it. Again, power seemed to crackle in the room. Did he suspect why she was really here?

He narrowed his eyes and focused. "What are these? Some sort of Japanese language symbols?"

"Why not just ask me what I was writing?" She crossed her arms over her chest. Was her voice shaky?

Taking a deep breath, Alec pointed a finger again. He frowned, concentrating harder. The knot in her red patterned scarf unraveled. She tried to grab it, but his telekinesis was faster and the scarf flew to his hand.

Her face grew warmer. She let her hand rest on the spot where the scarf had been. Her hair brushed against the back of her hand. She wanted to rush forward and grab the scarf out of his hand. *No.* He wanted her to get angry.

Alec looked down at the scarf and fingered it. "It's still warm from being around your neck."

"This is not a good way to prove that you don't need help working with people outside the Resource." She rubbed her neck.

He clenched the scarf tighter and dropped his head. So that accusation had hit home.

"Look, I don't need you."

"Why not?"

"I've heard all about psychologists from Daz, about how they spin your head around, find ways to twist words and declare people unfit for duty."

She breathed an inward sigh of relief. He objected to her being a psychologist. He didn't suspect what else she was. "Who's Daz?"

"F-Team's leader, my commander." Alec stepped closer, tapping the notebook against his hip.

She backpedaled automatically, then wished she hadn't given ground. Still, avoiding confrontation was right until she had the full story behind his hostility. No surprise that Alec's assault team commander didn't like psychologists. Few soldiers did.

"Ah. And does Daz approve of trying to bully people who are shorter and obviously less gifted than you?"

Alec backed up, giving her space again.

"You don't look too concerned."

"Why would you want to intimidate me? Obviously, I can't hurt you." She rubbed her neck again.

"Yeah, you can. You write a bad report and recommend me out of F-Team, then I'm out."

He thought she had the power to do *that?* No wonder he was hostile. "Who told you that would happen?"

"I was ordered here. I can read between the lines." He covered her scarf with the notebook in his other hand. "Besides, you're a shrink."

"So I'm going to make your head smaller?"

He smiled, despite himself. It was a charming smile. "No, I just—"

"Have an aversion to psychologists? Or to small women?" She pointed at his hand. "Or to silk scarves?"

"How about people who manipulate me? Like you're doing with all these questions. Like—" He shook his head and let the sentence hang in the air.

Had he been about to say "like Richard Lansing"? Lansing was the head of the Resource, and Beth guessed he was behind Alec's hostility. Lansing had been furious that the CIA had used its leverage with the Resource to order Alec into counseling. What would be the best way to sabotage that counseling? Exactly this, by making Alec too angry to listen to her.

No wonder Alec had a thing against people who manipulated him.

Alec tossed the notebook back onto the coffee table. It hit with a clunk and slid several inches. He kept the scarf wrapped around his hand. She kept her chair between them.

"You're operating under a false impression," she said. "I can't force you to work with me. You don't have to do this."

"Of course I have to do this." He leaned over the back of the other chair.

"Why?"

"Lansing thinks it's necessary."

She'd guessed right. Lansing had set her up. "Your foster father? He can force you into things?"

"Yes. No. I mean, sorta."

"What things can he force you into?" Good, Alec resented his situation. As well he should.

"Look, he's got my best interests at heart."

Beth was sure that Lansing had *Lansing's* best interests at heart. But Alec needed to find that out for himself. "What makes you believe that?"

"He raised me. He taught me to use my fire as a child, when it was out of control. He made me what I am."

She nodded, hoping to encourage more conversation.

But Alec broke eye contact and stared at the bowl of M&Ms on the coffee table between the two chairs.

"So you're saying that I can just ask and you'll leave and I'll never see you again?"

She nodded again. "You're my client. I can't treat you without your consent, no matter what Director Lansing wants. If you decide that you don't want my help, this will be our only session, as much as that would disappoint me."

Disappoint didn't begin to cover it. She *needed* to help Alec get out of his lifelong prison. But she couldn't force this on him. That would be exchanging one prison for another.

"We'll see." He flopped into the chair and tore a piece of paper from her notepad. "I was just fooling with the scarf." He held up his hand. "Watch."

13

He crumpled the paper in his hand and concentrated. It erupted in flames. Power seemed to burst outward from him. Her face flushed. A second later, the fire went out. He opened his palm and let the paper's ashes fall on the table.

My God. Beth was reminded of the original meaning of "awesome". The inspiration of awe. During that demonstration, Alec had looked like a god come down from Mount Olympus, smiling as he showed off to lesser mortals.

"The power you have is frightening to a lot of people, I imagine. I can see why their reactions would bother you." Did everyone sense that burst of power when Alec used his fire? Philip hadn't mentioned it. He wouldn't let her walk in blind. That meant he didn't sense it.

So why did she feel it?

"The idiot CIA liaison on the last mission freaked about my fire," Alec said.

"And you didn't handle that well, which is why I'm here."

"You didn't freak."

"Why should I? Your fire seemed perfectly under control."

"It was." He frowned. "You're not being straight with me. You have orders from Lansing to treat me, no matter what. So you have to do that, no matter what."

She shrugged. "Orders or no, Lansing already knows that I can't treat you without your consent. I only wish—"

"Wish what?"

She glanced away from him, just for a second, to the camera hidden near the window, cursing again that this couldn't be a real session. But there had been no choice. No cameras, no getting to Alec at all.

"Um, I'm a little out of my element," she said. "As you said, I'm from outside. I'm used to working in my own office."

"We have to meet here. I need security around me for my protection."

"So I understand. The security procedures to get inside this complex are impressive." They'd done everything but body-search her.

"Where's your office?"

"Not far. About forty minutes away, in Montclair."

"That's a little south of here? Closer to New York?"

"Yes," she said. "Alec?"

"Yeah?"

"Have you decided if you want to work with me?"

He tapped his fingertips on the armrest. "Assuming I agree to be your client, what exactly would we be doing?"

She came around from the back of the chair, sat and leaned forward, resting her elbows on her thighs. Now, they were getting somewhere.

"My plan is practical application. Role playing, anticipating future situations, like how to defuse personal issues without violence." Such as finding a better way to show annoyance than burning paper to intimidate a psychologist half his size.

"For a start, we can go over the situations where you've had trouble in the past and sort out where you could have made different choices." She crossed her legs, relaxing back in the chair, trying to appear more in control than she felt. "But before that, you need to give me back my scarf." She put out her hand.

"Don't you want to probe my confused psyche? Ask me a bunch of how-do-I-feel questions?"

"Would you like me to do that, Alec?"

He narrowed his eyes, then smiled as he realized she was kidding.

"Role playing sounds like simulated training. That's okay. But I want to know more about you."

"I'm close to my doctorate in psychology and I mostly work with gifted teens and young adults." *And I'm here to help you, even if you wouldn't think of it as help yet.*

"You don't look old enough to have a doctorate," he said.

She smiled. "I'm two years older than you are."

"I'd have pegged you as twenty, not twenty-five."

"I get that a lot."

"Can I call you Beth?"

"Beth is too informal."

"You've been calling me by my first name."

He noticed everything. "You have a point. All right, try 'counselor'. It's close enough."

"Okay, then, counselor."

He unwrapped the scarf from his hand and held it out to her. His

15

larger, stronger fingers brushed against her shorter, more delicate fingertips as the silk slid from his hand into hers.

The nerves at the base of her skull exploded, sending what felt like an electric current through her spine and down to her toes. It enveloped her like a living thing, a concentrated stream of the same power she'd sensed from him the entire session.

Save that this power aroused her. Every nerve seemed blown wide open, raw with longing.

More, please. No, wait...

Alec jerked back abruptly into his chair, his shoes scraping against the carpet, and rubbed his palm.

She froze and wasn't entirely sure she could have moved if she wanted. She tried to breathe normally. What the *hell* had he done? Judging by his reaction, Alec didn't know either.

"Is something wrong?" The scarf still dangled from her hand. Her voice worked. Surprising, especially since the rest of her felt completely stunned.

He darted a glance at the camera. "No, nothing's wrong, other than that I didn't expect you to have such soft hands." He grinned. "And you're very pretty. Such a cute little button nose. Nice eyes too."

She got the message. Play this down for Lansing and his watchers. "Thank you." She sat back in the chair, the energy from their touch fading. Good. Being aroused by a client was right up there on the list of things that shouldn't happen. Ever.

But she'd never felt that alive before.

"I bet you compliment all the girls."

"You've got nice legs too."

She tied the scarf back around her neck with trembling fingers, her flush fading.

"So, are you ready to start now?"

"Sure." He clapped his hands. "Let's go."

"Good." She picked up her notebook.

He popped a few of the dark chocolate M&Ms in his mouth, perhaps to cover his own discomfort. She'd brought them here to make herself feel less nervous. They'd been her mother's favorite candy. Silly, but it was like part of her mother was there because of the candy's presence.

Alec wiped his palm on his jeans. Some of the candy coating must have melted in his hands.

"What's first, counselor?"

She outlined the problem that he'd had with the CIA liaison on his last mission with F-Team. Throwing someone across the street with telekinesis was not a good response to verbal insults.

He listened intently, as if he was memorizing every word. He soaked up everything, she suspected. Which made it more of a tragedy that he was locked here, only let out to use his gifts as a weapon.

Alec, I'll help you see the bars of the prison, I'll help you see what is possible beyond this. Trust me.

The video on her laptop started, the camera angle canted to the right. Beth tilted her head to see better and tightened her hand on her foster father's shoulder.

She took a deep breath, inhaling the scent of the peppermint tea that she'd brewed, comforted by the familiar surroundings of her home, especially the Buddha cabinet in the corner. She'd tried to add some warmth to that lifeless Resource office for Alec but that had been almost impossible. At least he'd liked the M&Ms.

Most of all, she was grateful for Philip's presence. Nothing could ever harm her while he was around. She was aware they were mismatched, with Philip tall, broad-shouldered and gray-haired, while she looked very much like her native Japanese mother: short, small-boned and with dark hair. But they'd always understood each other perfectly.

He was her father, in every way that mattered.

He reached up and patted her hand. His large, muscular fingers engulfed her smaller, thinner ones. He adjusted the video controls with the mouse. "This is about five years old," Philip said. "Your firestarter would be eighteen, then."

At first, there was only a fuzzy impression of a clearing in some rural area, with a stand of evergreens surrounding it. There was no sound. The blurriness cleared, the film focused and soldiers appeared, rushing across a field to an entrenched position. Though she knew it was a training exercise, it looked real.

In the middle and just back from the main group was a soldier without a rifle. She recognized Alec, though he was a few years younger, not yet at his full height, and lacked the broad shoulders that she'd admired just a few hours ago. The regular soldiers raised their weapons, aiming at where their enemy was hiding. Alec raised a hand and dirt exploded in front of the trenches, showering whoever was in them with dust. None of the dust fell toward the oncoming soldiers.

Her eyes widened. She'd no idea his telekinesis was that powerful. Picking up her legal pad or grabbing her scarf was one thing; controlling thousands of dust molecules like that, entirely another. She bent down to look closer, practically breathing in Philip's ear. How had Alec learned such control when her own talent, telepathy, had been so wild and unpredictable, even before it went latent?

After a few seconds, the dust cleared, and Alec appeared at the top of the embankment, his hands outstretched. The camera zeroed in on his face for the first time. Even with his helmet on, she could see his intent stare, so unlike his mostly confused expression during their session. His mouth was frozen in a near smile, as if he was having the time of his life. It was very similar to his smile when he'd burned the paper for her.

He was spectacular.

Clearly, this was his world. No wonder he'd been uncomfortable when confronted with her, so outside the rules of his very controlled life. No wonder he'd wanted the upper hand.

Alec yelled something to his ostensible enemy. A simple warning or something with more flourish, to match his mood? Fire erupted around him, circling him. The close-up remained on his face. He grinned. He actually grinned as he was encircled in flames. But maybe it was the destruction, not his gift, that brought Alec such fierce joy.

She hoped not.

In the video, men scrambled from the trench, throwing down their weapons in defeat. Alec waved his hands, as if holding a wand, and the fire disappeared. He jumped from his place on the top of the embankment to the defeated "enemy", and raised a hand in victory. The rest of the assault team arrived, crowding around him, all smiles, giving him claps on the back.

They must be his F-Team, the Resource's elite private assault squad.

Alec pointed and they parted for him, all of them staring into the clearing. The camera panned away from the soldiers and focused on the grass in the clearing.

The grass burst into flames, racing in perfect straight lines, making specific shapes, as natural fire never did. Her jaw dropped open as she realized the flames were spelling out words. The fire vanished, leaving charred grass that spelled *Ready to Roll.*

My God. He could have easily killed her with only a quick gesture in that office. She backed up and smacked her calves on her table, spilling her tea from the cup to the saucer.

The video cut back to Alec. He high-fived a few of the soldiers but they backed off when an officer approached. The officer glared at the others with unspoken authority. Alec immediately stopped grinning and saluted him. The officer saluted back, then flashed a smile, making his face come alive. This had to be Daz—Commander Daz Montoya of F-Team.

An older man walked in from the shadows, a tall, thin man wearing a sport coat and bowtie. Richard Lansing. The director of the Resource. Alec's father in all but name, the man who'd turned Alec into an obedient weapon.

Lansing gruffly nodded to Alec, signaling approval. Alec dropped his head, yielding to his foster father. Though, whatever else Lansing had done to Alec, he hadn't made him afraid of his gift. That put Alec one step ahead of her.

"How did you get this?" she asked Philip.

"With great difficulty."

Philip stood from her desk chair and disconnected his thumb drive. "I can tell you over and over how dangerous he is but it has more impact if you see it."

Philip was as grim and tightly wrapped tonight as she'd ever seen. The lines on his face were deeper than last month, when she'd first insisted on helping Alec, and Philip's hair seemed to have gone completely gray overnight.

"The video doesn't completely mesh with the person I met." Alec had been more carefree in the video, less tightly wound. Less wary.

"Of course not," Philip said. "Farley's fully grown now, much more of a seasoned soldier." With exaggerated care, Philip pulled down the roll top of her desk, covering the laptop. "Remember, his first instinct was to intimidate and attack you."

"Intimidate, yes, attack, no. He was careful. He didn't want to hurt me."

"This time. What if you push harder?"

"He won't hurt me." There'd been no malice in Alec, only fear of the unknown and frustration at having no control. Given the situation, he'd responded with a lot of maturity. He'd *listened*.

Philip grunted and walked to the window, staring out at her balcony and the paper lantern that she'd lit for the *Obon* Festival. The odds on her ancestors traveling from Japan to Montclair were slim but the effort made her feel less alone. At least she had Philip. Who did Alec have?

Philip began pacing, shedding some of his coiled energy. "How long do you think it will take to get Farley to walk out of that damned place willingly?"

"I'm not sure." She crossed her arms over her chest. "He's well overdue for some rebellion. He senses his cage and I suspect he's becoming less tolerant of Lansing's reasons for keeping him so under wraps. He definitely resented Lansing's orders to see me and that's why he came in literally breathing fire. Classic displacement. He couldn't go after Lansing, so he went after me."

"So Alec is under the impression that you work for Lansing and not the CIA?"

"Yes. Alec thinks Lansing is my employer. Or, at least, he did. Now, I think he's willing to believe that I might be a free agent."

"Typical of Lansing. Instead of admitting that he was strong-armed by the CIA to get Alec counseling, he lies to make it seem like his decision," Philip said.

Beth sat on her couch, needing the comfort of the oversized cushions. "I think Lansing is a manipulative bastard, yes, but you've dealt with many dangerous men over the years, Philip. What's so different about this one? You talk about Lansing as if he's the devil."

"That's close enough. Lansing doesn't give a damn about Alec, just Alec's power. You'll notice he was careful to demand submission from Alec in the video, rather than showing any approval." Philip stopped pacing and knelt in front of her. "Beth." He took her hand. "Now that you've met Alec Farley, are you sure you're not risking your life for a junior version of Lansing? Is Alec worth the danger?"

She squeezed his hand back. "Yes, he's worth it." *I like his face. A good strong face. A hero's face.* And that smile. That would make anyone melt.

"And when did you decide that he was worth the trouble?"

She stared at her statue of Buddha and the offering bowl of M&Ms, in memory of her mother. Philip asked a good question. When had her worry *for* Alec finally overcome her fear of him and the danger she faced trying to help him?

She knew. The change had started when he'd smiled at her joke about making his head smaller. And it had sparked into something stronger when they'd touched hands and she'd gotten the shock of her life.

She couldn't admit that intense physical desire, so strong it had seemed nearly a compulsion, to her *father*, especially since her attraction to Alec violated every professional ethic in the book.

"You know, if Alec accepts the truth, he could do a lot of real good with that fire," she said. "He doesn't need to run around playing soldier all the time."

"Oh, I'd say he's doing more than just playing." Philip stood and began pacing again.

"You're practically jumping out of your skin tonight, Philip. What's changed since you let me go in? Is something else wrong?"

"Yes." He stopped and faced her. "My superiors in the CIA gave me a time limit to get Alec out or eliminate him."

"They'd kill him?" She clenched her hand into a fist.

"Yes, they'd kill him. They'd rather use him but they'd eliminate him if they had to." Philip picked up her teacup from the table. The teacup was the perfect size for her. In Philip's hands, it looked like a child's toy. He raised an eyebrow for permission. She nodded and he drank the last dregs of her tea.

"And now we have to walk the tightrope," he said. "When can Alec stand on his own? And if he can't, I have to decide if he's better off at the Resource or with the CIA."

"Both choices are still slavery for Alec."

"Both are better than dead."

"You said you could save him. What's this all about if we can't do that?" She hugged a pillow with gold fringes to her chest. The fringe tickled the back of her hand.

"I said I'd do what I could. I can't guarantee anything."

"Slavery or death are not good options."

"Exactly. That's why I came to you in the first place." He started ticking points off on his fingers. "One, I needed somebody outside the CIA that I could trust. Two, I needed a psychologist who would understand Alec. And three, I needed someone who would have his best interests at heart. But—"

"But nothing. I'm glad you came to me."

"I'm not. I regret it." Philip sank into her armchair and closed his eyes, hiding from the light of her corner lamp, covered by shadows. "Death has a way of spilling over onto anyone in its path. Alec's life is one of violence. I don't want you in the way. This was a mistake, a serious mistake."

His quiet worry scared her, far more than Alec had. She pulled the pillow tighter to her chest. "It's not a mistake."

"How much time do you need with him?"

"Maybe three months. If I see Alec once a week, I can get him to demand more privileges from Lansing, more time in the outside world instead of being locked up in that place. But I have to build up some trust with Alec first. That's key."

"Push too hard with Alec, and Lansing will sense you're a threat, eliminate you and cover it up. The CIA has leverage on the Resource because of their contracts with them but that protection only goes so far. And if Lansing found out who you really are, well, he'd love to get his hands on a telepath." Philip slapped the armrest.

She swallowed hard, sick to her stomach at the idea. No, she didn't want to be a prisoner again. Ever.

"You can stop Lansing if needed?" She flexed her fingers, waiting, hoping for reassurance. Her father could protect her from anything.

"I can't stop Lansing completely or I would have long before this," he finally said.

Oh.

"Lansing wants to build his own empire and he's got the patience to take years to do it. You think the Resource compound is his only facility? He has a regular mercenary operation centered in upstate New York, one that is pulling in millions from government contracts. Not to mention his business operations. With that kind of money comes influence, which Lansing will use to leverage more power, until he gets it all." Philip's voice became lower, more intense.

"How are you so sure about this? You make him sound like an evil villain out of a comic book."

Another long pause. "You'll have to take my word for it."

She punched the pillow, angry that he wouldn't tell her everything, as usual. But she believed him. "Of course, I trust you. You know that."

"Good." He tapped his fingers on the armrest. "I have to ask, Beth. Is there any chance that your telepathy might reach Alec to make him see reason? If you could order him outside, you could treat him away from the Resource. If the CIA believes Alec is a free agent, they'll back off, at least for a while."

"I don't think so." Her fingers dug grooves into the pillow. She'd been grateful for years that her telepathy was gone, that she was normal. Until she saw Alec use his abilities with such joy. "My telepathy is permanently blocked off. I've tried but it's been gone since the kidnapping. Trauma, probably, but I can't sort it out and there's no one to ask for help." She bit her tongue. "Recovering telepathy is not something any doctor specializes in."

"Calm down." He leaned forward, bringing his face into the light. "I'm sorry to have asked. And even sorrier I couldn't help you with it."

"Not your fault. You saved me, remember?" She shook her head. Did the idea of regaining her telepathy disturb her more than not having it? Perhaps. "I might be able to go faster with Alec, though if he's absorbed his values from Lansing, that's a problem. What is Daz Montoya like? Alec's obviously bonded to him. Are his values different?"

"Montoya is a decorated former Navy SEAL with a clean service record. He started as a noncommissioned officer, went to college and came back into the Navy as an officer. He has outstanding personnel reports."

"So you'd say he has some moral values, at least compared to

Lansing?"

Philip frowned. "Montoya's taking money from Lansing and he's intelligent enough to realize that Alec is being kept prisoner at the Resource. Those are two strikes against him. But his past record suggests a, um, honorable man."

"That's promising." Beth took a deep breath. "It might make my work easier. But my worry is that Alec could switch his dependence from Lansing and Montoya to me. That's not what Alec needs."

"Too damn bad, if it keeps you safe."

"But Alec needs to be safe too, secure in his own self. That's why I went in there. Everyone else is manipulating him. I can't add to it." She stood, dropping her pillow.

"It's better than him being dead."

"You're trying to scare me away, Philip. Why did you let me do this in the first place? When you told me about Alec, you must have known that I'd want to help him any way I could. Why not just keep it from me, if this was so dangerous? And don't tell me it's because I fit your mission parameters."

Philip stood and bowed to her, a traditional Japanese bow, with more grace than she'd ever managed.

"I swore to a little girl I rescued that I'd give her a normal life, as normal as possible after her mother's murder." He cleared his throat. "And that means letting you make your own choices even if they terrify me." He nearly choked on the last words. "If I kept things from you, like Alec, things you'd want to know, or lied to you about them, I'm no better than Lansing, am I?"

She crossed to him and hugged him, tight. He had so much essential kindness hidden behind that scary exterior. Often, she wondered if he showed it to anyone but her. "I couldn't have found a better father, Philip Drake."

"I should have sent you into foster care after I rescued you, and faded away from your life."

And take away her lifeline? "You didn't because we need each other. And Alec Farley needs us now."

"Yes, my fondest wish has always been to expose you to mortal danger to save a brainwashed firestarter." He kissed the top of her head and rested his chin there. She fit perfectly in the comforting circle

24

of his arms. His soft sigh warmed her hair. "If my instincts feel this going wrong, I'm going to pull you out, immediately, no questions asked. Understand?"

"And Alec?"

"You're my first priority. Always."

Meaning that he would sacrifice Alec to keep her safe, if necessary. She was tempted to let him. To be prisoner again, helpless, maybe drugged and out of her mind...

But I can't abandon Alec.

Chapter Two

Alec took a deep breath to calm down before going back into the room. His counselor had taken complete control of their first meeting. If they were going to have weekly sessions, that had to change.

She was from outside. He needed an ally to get long-overdue privileges out of Lansing. He wasn't a boy anymore. His team, especially Daz, knew that. It was past time that Lansing learned it.

Beth Nakamora needed to learn it too. She had seemed smug during their first session, at least until that jolt of power between them. More than anything she'd said, that had made him want to see her again. He wanted to repeat the experience and make it last much longer the next time.

He smiled. Hey, it was justified. He didn't know what caused it, so he had to experiment and find out.

But he'd have to be careful and bide his time with the cameras watching. Lansing might have shrugged off the first incident but a repeat would raise suspicion.

Alec stepped inside the room. Beth was sitting in the chair again, waiting for him. The M&Ms were on the coffee table again along with a glass of water. A bucket of ping-pong balls sat next to Beth's chair.

"Why do you have ping-pong balls?"

"Trust me."

She was trying to get the upper hand again and draw him out. Two could play that game.

"Do shrinks usually use props?"

"Occasionally. You struck me as someone who learns best by doing. I wanted to illustrate something to you about proportional response."

"So?"

"Do you want to sit or stand?"

He remained standing, instinctively falling into parade rest. This was manipulation again. And he could take a page from Daz's book and see where patience got him.

Besides, it wasn't like she was a physical threat.

"Ready?" she asked.

"Sure."

She shoved her hand into the M&Ms and tossed a handful at him.

"C'mon," he said with disgust. Some test. He twitched a finger and grabbed the M&Ms in midair with his TK. They hovered, unmoving.

He could toss them back at her but why waste M&Ms? He twitched his finger again and formed the candy into a line. He let them fall into his mouth one by one.

"Mmmm..." he said, swallowing the last.

She hadn't moved, her mouth set in a line, but there was something about her expression that made him think she was amused. That wasn't what he was going for, though that half-smile was awfully attractive.

"Was that a proportional response?" he asked.

"Oh, definitely."

She grabbed the bucket of ping-pong balls and tossed the lot at him.

Like the M&Ms, he took hold of the balls with his TK with little effort. They were so light, it was easy to keep them hovering.

He let his hands fall to his sides and began juggling with his TK. The balls zipped around his head and shoulders, faster and faster with each second. But he wasn't watching them. He was looking for some reaction from her.

Her eyes widened. And her face started to flush. Interesting. Did she get turned on when he used his power? She wasn't built like the girls he saw at the strip clubs but she was all in proportion and she had such a beautiful face.

He let go of the balls and they hit the carpet, bouncing to all corners of the office. He stepped closer to her.

"You've got nothing left to throw. So what lesson—"

27

She picked up the glass and threw the water at him, ice cubes and all.

"Hey!"

Cold water soaked into his black T-shirt and trickled down his arms.

"Son of a bitch."

He spit out the water and concentrated, agitating the air around him until it began to warm him up.

"You're steaming," she said. "Literally." She set the empty glass back down on the coffee table.

She thought this was funny? "Why the hell did you do that?" Had she known or just guessed that water wasn't something he could easily grab with TK?

"There's a point if you let me explain."

"Not yet." He waved his hand and all the ping-pong balls in the room rose at his command. He grouped them together and held them over her head. He could simply drop them on her but, no, if she wanted to see what his power could do, he'd show her.

He took a deep breath and set the ping-pong balls on fire. Her eyes widened again and she started to get out of the chair.

Not yet, counselor.

He sent the fireballs swirling around her, wreathing her head in flame but being careful not to set her hair on fire. They swirled between her head and shoulders and zipped down in front of her breasts.

He watched her face carefully for a reaction. She flushed again. That could be from the heat. Her hands gripped the chair tightly but she seemed to be fighting a smile.

It was possible she was turned on. Not what he was going for, but good.

He pointed his finger and the balls flew to him. He waved a hand and the fires went out. The ashes fell harmlessly to the carpet. She stared at him for a few seconds and then she put her hand over her mouth. He saw shadows of a smile as she took the hand away.

"Now that is a proportional response."

He collapsed into the comfortable chair, settling in. Damn, she was pretty, especially now that he'd gotten her to unbend a bit.

"Explain," he said.

She sat back in her chair, the calm mask descending over her face. But now he knew it was just a front.

"You've trained long and hard with your power, obviously. You're built for a fight and trained in hand-to-hand combat. No doubt that you know what's a physical threat and what isn't. Even when I tossed water on you, you knew it wasn't an attack."

"But I did attack back."

"Playfully."

"With fire."

"But you weren't trying to hurt me."

"Of course not."

"Similarly, you don't need to toss someone yelling at you over a fence or throw someone insulting you into a wall, any more than you needed to hurt me for tossing the water on you."

So they were back to that again, his supposed lack of control. Point of fact, he'd been in perfect control of his abilities both times. "Both guys were being assholes." They'd thought his fire was out of control. He had showed them out of control.

"Yes, I have no doubt they were being assholes," she said. "But you didn't have to react that way."

"So I should have just let it go?"

"There's a wide range of choices between ignoring them and using your power to physically abuse them."

"Lansing didn't care." Lansing had seemed amused. At least until the CIA had complained, anyway.

She frowned. "We're talking about you, not him. Besides, what did Commander Montoya think?"

Alec sighed. "He thought I went over the top. But he was pissed at the guys too."

"You're going to have to work with hostile people in the future. You're going to face this situation again. You need to know how to handle it better."

She pointed to the ashes of the ping-pong balls. "Basically, you took the verbal equivalent of a ping-pong attack and used a gun instead."

"Not quite. The TK didn't hurt them. If I'd used my fire on them, it would be more like using a gun. So instead, you think I should lift assholes off the ground and juggle them?"

"Well, that's probably less painful than what you did." She smiled. And he was tempted to lift her off the ground to see what happened. Too bad she wasn't wearing a skirt today.

"You're a clever man, Alec. You have options. You could insult him back. You could have a verbal argument instead of letting it get physical. Or you could do something with your power that's more, um, subtle."

"Like stealing your scarf?"

She frowned. "It was better than grabbing me with your TK. It's not so much what specific way you react, it's more that you think before you react. Remind yourself not to use a nuke when a ping-pong ball will do the job instead."

"You're forgetting something. If someone breaks rank and slows down an operation because they're freaked about my power, someone could get killed, including me. We don't have time for anyone to decide they're in charge when they don't know jack shit about what I can do. That's exactly what the guy I threw into a wall did. It's a lot more 'proportional' than you think it was."

"You may have a point."

Aha. "Then can you put in your report to the CIA that they need to assign people who can handle my power and don't go foaming at the mouth because they're scared."

She nodded. "I can." She put up a hand. "But—"

"But what?"

"But you're going to increasingly come into contact with people who don't understand your power, who are afraid of what you are. You have to plan how to react to that, in any situation."

"You mean when I go outside, even when I'm not on a mission."

She nodded.

"Then it would be a good idea if I get outside more," he said. "To practice."

"That is an excellent idea."

I know.

"Good." And he suspected she would take him to far different places than F-Team. She didn't seem the type for strip clubs.

Now to seal the deal. He concentrated on the M&Ms, picked up a handful with TK and presented them to her, letting them hover just above her lap.

She put down her pad and held out her hand. He dropped the M&Ms into it.

"Thank you."

"You're welcome." They were on the same page.

Step one, accomplished.

Chapter Three

The door to the office that Beth had used at the Resource for the past six weeks was wide open. She peered inside. Strange. Alec wasn't there, even though he'd been arriving early to wait for her.

She stuffed her hand into her blazer pocket, fishing for the bag of M&Ms. Philip said the device inside the bag couldn't be scanned, that it would look like just another peanut M&M. But if it had been detected, maybe the emotionless security guards that prowled this place were moving in on her right now.

"Good afternoon, Ms. Nakamora."

She spun on her heel toward the voice, her face hot with guilt and fear.

"Good afternoon, Mr. Lansing," she said and hoped that she sounded calm.

The Resource Director wore his customary black bowtie and tweed jacket. His arms were clasped behind his back and his manner gave no indication of his mood. Beth fought a swallow. Her fist nearly crushed the M&Ms.

"Is Alec all right?" she asked. "I expected to see him today."

"Plans have changed," Lansing said.

"Changed to what?"

"You have an irritating habit of asking questions, Ms. Nakamora. I've noted it during your sessions with Alec."

"That's what psychologists do." If Lansing had any morals, he wouldn't be listening to those sessions in the first place. "Alec is my client. Any objections should come from him. And what is the change in plans?"

"That I speak to you first." Lansing's lips twitched. "I've noticed you seem overly close to Alec. We need to talk about that."

"I don't understand your implication." Was her first impression of being found out correct? She glanced around. There was nowhere to run.

"Alec's half in love with you," Lansing said.

What?

"That's not part of your job description," he continued. His voice turned harder, his body straighter and more menacing. "I realize he's probably intrigued because you're different from what he's encountered before. But that doesn't excuse your part in this."

Lansing was stupid for someone who should be so smart. She clicked her tongue, knowing it would annoy Lansing and not caring. "Alec's infatuation is a common side effect at this stage of therapy. Right now, he thinks I have answers. When he realizes that only he has the answers to his problems, it'll wear off, as these things do."

"It won't wear off if the object of his desire feels the same as he does."

That was closer to the truth than she wanted to admit. Each time Alec used his power, she felt it at a deep and sensual level. And she liked the feeling. That he resembled a sculpted god didn't hurt either. "I have the same affection for Alec that I have for all my clients."

"Lucky clients, then." Lansing snorted. "Every session, you draw closer, physically. Last time, your knees were touching. And you keep smiling at each other."

She shook her head, relieved that was all the evidence he had. What century was Lansing from that knees touching bothered him? "Did you rewind the tape to count the smiles?" She couldn't keep the sarcasm out of her voice.

He shook his head. "I didn't have to. Alec attracts women. That's natural, given his looks and charm. Those who work for me are under strict orders to steer clear but some of them have tried anyway. I've taught Alec better manners than to take them up on it. He seems to view you differently."

Beth crossed her arms over her chest, her fear dissipating. If Lansing knew about the device in the M&Ms or who she really was, he wouldn't be probing about Alec's crush on her. "Alec is my client. Your

33

suggestion is absurd. Where is he?"

Lansing's eyes narrowed. He stepped closer and loomed over her like a homicidal giraffe. "Alec is preparing for a mission. It came up suddenly or I would have called and canceled your session."

She fought the urge to step back from Lansing or do anything subservient. He wasn't the first man to try to intimidate her with his height. "I'd like to see his preparations. Watching Alec at work would definitely help in my evaluation of him."

"I have no doubt of that. However, I don't think you have the stomach for seeing what he really does. Women rarely do." Lansing shrugged. "It won't matter. If all goes well on this mission, we can dispense with your services. The CIA can't very well complain if there are no problems. I'll extol your virtues, how you managed to help Alec so quickly and everyone will live happily ever after." He clasped his hands behind his back again. "Separately."

He meant for this to be the last time she ever saw Alec. No wonder he was letting his façade crumble and trying to scare her. He'd decided she was a threat and was tossing her aside. *But I need more time.* Only remembering Philip's oft-repeated instructions to never lose her temper with Lansing kept her calm. Her heartbeat sounded so loud in her ears that she wondered if Lansing could hear it.

"That's not a good idea, Mr. Lansing. Alec has—"

"Wasted enough time with you. However, he seems to want to see you today. Since arguing with him about it might distract from the mission, you have ten minutes." Lansing raised a hand and snapped his fingers. From around the corner of the corridor, a guard appeared. "Take her to Alec's quarters. And wait outside to escort her out of the facility when they're done."

She was as much a prisoner right now as Alec.

Lansing smirked. "I can't say I'll miss you, Ms. Nakamora. Make it fast and don't trouble him. His life depends on focusing tonight."

"Suppose Alec wants to continue as my client?"

"That's not up to him." Lansing loomed over her again.

"It should be." She stood her ground. "It will be."

Lansing curled a hand around her upper arm. "When you speak to Alec, you will not let him sense anything out of the ordinary. I'll be listening. I'll know."

Lansing's fingers dug into her arm. She winced, fighting anger, and tried to tug her arm away. Lansing held fast.

"If you do or say anything I don't like, then it will be more than your services that are dispensed with. Remember, the CIA can't watch you all the time. And the Resource and Alec are more valuable to them than you are." Lansing dropped her arm and walked away.

She rubbed the arm, wincing, and watched as Lansing turned the corner at the end of the corridor. Lansing was a bully, a garden-variety bully. No wonder Alec was ready to rebel. But if Lansing was angry enough to threaten her, then maybe she was getting through to Alec.

She smoothed down her blazer and made eye contact with the guard. "Lead the way."

He took the direction opposite where Lansing had gone. She kept blinking during the walk, adjusting her eyes to fluorescent lights that seemed to grow brighter with each step. They went down one level, using a staircase of white walls and steel mesh steps that continued down several more flights past the first level. She'd thought the Resource only had one basement. Now she wondered exactly how big it was.

"Here." The guard stopped beside a nondescript white door and assumed a position to the side of it. "Ten minutes."

This was Alec's prison, then. No, he'd call it his home. He must be thrilled at the idea of a new mission, a chance to do something useful again. She shook her head, remembering Lansing's smirk. The joke was on him. Lansing had wanted the image of a hero to present to the rest of the world. Instead, he'd gotten a real one. She wondered if Lansing realized he'd done his work too well. Maybe he never would, if Alec didn't learn the truth.

She knocked.

Alec opened the door. "Hey, counselor. Lansing said he'd send you. Sorry about missing the session. Duty calls."

If Alec in jeans and a T-shirt had been attractive, Alec in uniform was even more so. "Hello, Alec."

He wore military boots, camouflage pants and a dark green shirt. The rest of his mission gear lay on the black couch—body armor, jacket, guns and a helmet—all neatly arranged. She recognized most of the gear from Philip's training video. Only Alec's hair was different, longer than the military cut from his training days. His one small rebellion?

The entire living room was the same, in perfect order. No rebellion there.

"That's quite a stare, even for you." Alec tilted his head and frowned. "You can't be that mad I'm missing a session. What's wrong?"

Everything is wrong. "Not wrong, Alec, so much as confused." She felt around in the M&M bag and found the right one, with the little grove on it, and pressed. Philip said it would scramble all the electronic listening and video devices within about twenty feet. *It better.*

"I'm sorry for staring. I've haven't seen your equipment up close before."

"Hah!" He sat in an easy chair to lace up his boots. "You know you can see my equipment anytime you ask."

"Um, that's not quite what I had in mind." Alec had charmed her. Lansing had been right about that. She hadn't counted on him being so genuinely interested in her.

At least she'd had the willpower not to touch Alec's hand and risk that intense jolt of energy a second time. Just being around him was seductive enough.

Alec shrugged at her refusal, walked back to the bed and loaded a clip into his handgun. Some sort of pistol, though she had no idea exactly what kind. Philip would have known. Alec's eyes narrowed as he double-checked the weapon. For a moment, he was completely the competent military officer.

Satisfied, he set it down and turned to face her. He frowned, on uncertain ground again.

"Did anyone ever show you a life without guns?"

He raised one of those perfect eyebrows, oozing more confidence than ten men. Who wouldn't have that confidence, if fire literally danced to their command?

"You know, I thought Lansing agreed too quickly to send you. Did he want you to check up on me?"

"No." But it would be like Lansing to say that he had.

"Hah. I think you're a bad liar, counselor. A life without guns? That's the kind of leading question that he uses to test me."

"I'm not lying." Not about that. "No, it's the first time I've seen you prepare for a mission. It worries me." She looked down at the dark carpet and scuffed her feet. "I have doubts about what you're doing. I think you're not seeing the big picture." *Like how your foster father is using you to gain power and influence, at the risk of your life.* "You don't have to put your gift to this use. There are so many other things you can do that don't involve violence."

Or the possibility of being killed.

Philip had been terrified at letting her walk into danger. Looking at Alec, she knew how Philip felt. Just how dangerous was this mission tonight?

"Only I can do what I can do," Alec said.

"Which is all the more reason not to risk your life so recklessly." She was pushing too hard, out of fear. No choice now. She'd run out of time.

"I'm not reckless," he said. "I'm as careful as I can be."

"With weapons and body armor? If you're doing something careful, you don't need them."

He buckled on the body armor and walked over to her, so that they were only a few feet apart. He towered over her, even more than Lansing, but she didn't feel the least bit afraid of him, not since their first meeting. He wouldn't hurt her. Despite his work as a soldier, there was no meanness in him. She rubbed her arm, remembering Lansing's anger. Alec wasn't like him at all.

"I like doing this," Alec said. "I make a difference. It's what I'm trained for."

"Yes, I know. But you never had a say in any of that training. You've told me that."

"Fighting the bad guys is family tradition." He straightened. "Lansing's too old now, so it's my turn. It happens all the time. Daz has the same deal, on both the American and the Filipino sides of his family."

"Daz didn't grow up isolated in this place."

"Yeah, well, Daz didn't have to worry about accidentally burning down the schoolyard as a kid. I did." He shook his head and crossed his arms over his chest. "Are you seriously trying to talk me out of going tonight? C'mon."

"I'm trying to get you to reconsider what you've been forced into

37

doing for your entire life. There's a whole world out there you haven't seen."

She walked over to the coffee table, reached down and brushed her fingertips over the gun. Her hand trembled. The gun looked like the same kind that her kidnappers had used, years ago. If he stayed with the Resource, Alec might become like those men, using any ends to justify the means.

"Hey! What's with the nerves? Where's my competent, no-nonsense counselor?"

The gun rose from the coffee table, floating in air. She turned and followed its flight. He snatched the gun out of midair with a smile and holstered it.

"See?" he said. "I control the guns, not the other way around."

"And who controls you?"

His chest, Kevlar vest and all, rose and fell in a deep sigh. "I know someone in this room who's trying to control me. What's wrong, Beth?" He walked to her and lifted her chin with two fingers, his dark eyes crinkling around the edges.

"This is not a life you chose, this is a life that's been imposed on you, from birth."

"And?" His fingertips moved along her jaw, in a soft caress. *I should move away. It feels too good. But he's listening.*

"I'm scared. About this mission, about you being locked up inside the Resource forever." Deathly afraid, so afraid her stomach felt like a heavy lump of coal. "There's so much you don't know about the Resource and about Lansing, so much you don't understand. And you need to know it before it kills you."

"Hey, I know Lansing can be a bastard. And that he's overprotective and controlling. I'm working on it. But it doesn't change the fact that this is my job." Alec leaned closer to her face. "We can talk about that another time."

"Do you really think there's going to be another time?" Her voice rose, almost panicked now. She wasn't getting through. "What if you get hurt tonight?"

"Look, this cell might have a dirty bomb. They need to be stopped, and I'm the one who can do it. I have to do this, right now."

"Just that simple?"

"Yep. I walk away, people get hurt. I do my job, people are saved. That's the deal, that's my life. You analyze things too much." He cupped her face in his hand. "But if it took this mission to find out you care, then good."

She shuddered. Wrong, wrong, she shouldn't let him touch her like this. Yet it felt like he touched her somewhere far deeper than her skin. A shiver, like the one from their first meeting, traveled from her neck to her toes, setting her nerves jangling. "This is wrong."

"The mission isn't wrong," he said, misunderstanding her. "Relax." His face was less than an inch from her lips and his breath fell on her cheek. Her skin felt inflamed, sensitive to the slightest movement of his hands.

He kissed her.

His lips were softer than she had expected, tender, not at all like his casual, even macho, confidence. She closed her eyes and wrapped her arms around his neck, feeling those strong muscles and pulling him against her, intensifying their contact, even as her mind screamed in protest. *This is not what I came for!*

Her body became enveloped in that strange energy, alive as never before. It was like the kiss had a second level, one which she responded to instinctively, creating a living connection between them. He drew her lips apart with his tongue, still tender, still allowing her the chance to back away. But she opened her mouth to him instead, her whole self consumed with wanting to touch him, her face flushed with desire. She grabbed the buckles of his body armor for balance, her equilibrium lost along with her reason.

He crushed her against him, no longer tender, a bruising kiss demanding conquest. She allowed him full control, despite the buckles digging into her shoulder. He lifted her completely off her feet and brought her up to his eye level.

"Beth," he breathed, brushing his lips against her neck before moving back to her mouth.

Her mind whirled, too lost to remember that she should stop him. She *wanted* him too much. The air heated up, warming them. The papers on the coffee table began to smoke.

Startled, she broke the kiss. There was a momentary disorientation, like a soft mental slap. The tingling stopped. Her skin went cold.

She let her head fall to his shoulder and closed her eyes. Her last chance to reach Alec and she'd blown it. More, she'd crossed all ethical boundaries. Yet his arms around her felt so right.

Alec spun around and set her into his easy chair. He swallowed, breathing heavily, his face and neck flushed. Staring at the papers on the table, he reached out a hand and they burst into real flame. He twisted his wrist, calling to the fire. It came to him, wrapping itself around his wrist like a bracelet. He smiled, blinked, and the fire vanished.

He whistled through his teeth. "Wow. You are some kind of hot, counselor, to set me off like that. I usually have to think about creating fire."

"I've noticed that." Her muscles seemed to have no will of their own, unable to move, unable to stand. "I'm sorry you lost control."

"Hey, don't be. It felt good. All of it." He picked up the rifle. "If I didn't have to report now, I'd never have stopped."

She nodded, drawing her knees up to her chin. What a mess she'd made. Unethical. But that connection between them, almost a compulsion, didn't feel like anything even approaching normal. She'd kissed men before. This was far different. This was *alive*.

I want more. Ancestors damn me, I want more.

I can't have it. It's wrong.

"So if the farewell is like this, what will my welcome home be like?" He put on his jacket, tension in his short, sharp movements. He didn't know what to make of her. With all her mixed signals, he had good reason.

"Your welcome home?" she repeated. Would Lansing change his mind if Alec insisted on seeing her when he got back? Maybe, maybe. "Well, when I see you again, I definitely need to talk to you more." She sighed. "But I shouldn't have kissed you."

"Why not?"

"It's unethical."

He grinned. "It didn't feel unethical."

"No, I guess not."

He put his hands on the arms of the chair, looming over her. "You really hate what I do, don't you?"

"I don't hate it, I hate that you've been forced into it."

He frowned. "No, I haven't."

"The fact that you think it's voluntarily is just a symptom of the problem."

"Then we'll talk about it in our next session."

"And if Lansing doesn't want you to continue with me?"

"After tonight, he'll owe me. No worries." He smiled, his easy confidence still flowing. "It's nice that you're afraid for me."

He kissed her cheek, brushing his soft lips against skin that tingled with renewed desire. "Meantime, remember, F-Team and I can handle ourselves."

He took the rest of his gear, slung the rifle over his shoulder and walked out of the room, whistling.

She reached into her pocket and switched off the scrambler. Great. What a total cluster fuck, as Alec would say. She'd crossed the line and kissed her client, she still had no idea if Lansing would let her back in to see Alec, and she certainly hadn't convinced Alec that Lansing was truly dangerous.

Of course, all of that would be immaterial if Alec didn't survive this damned mission tonight. His team only received the hardest missions, the ones that government teams found too high-risk.

And a dirty bomb was extremely dangerous.

Plus, looming over everything, there was the threat from the CIA. Philip was not Superman. He couldn't guarantee Alec's survival forever if his superiors decided against it.

She snapped out of her chair, her nerves still on fire. In a normal situation, she'd stop being Alec's counselor after kissing him. But she was the only outside contact he had. She might be his only hope to survive.

She wandered in his living room, among his things, looking at the little pieces of his life, searching for some clue to reach him. No photos, no little knickknacks and no signs whatsoever of his individuality sat on his bookcases. Alec had told her during one session that he'd lived in this room since he was twelve, with breaks for various military training, and then had permanently settled into it when he was sixteen, when F-Team was brought in to train with him. She never would have guessed that from how little of his personality was reflected in the room.

He did have CDs, a strange combination of classical recordings and rap music. Classical from Lansing's influence and rap from Daz and F-Team, probably. They were alphabetically stacked, Biggie Smalls to Eminem to Mozart and Schubert. But the classical CDs had dust on them. F-Team was winning the music war. Who would Alec choose, if forced: Lansing or F-Team? Or was that really a choice, given that Lansing was the ultimate boss of F-Team? It depended on whether there was a difference between Daz and Lansing.

The built-in bookshelves held more titles centered on the British Empire than she expected, particularly on events of the Victorian age. Lansing's influence again. Empire building would be like him.

She put her face in her hands, stilling tears. When Philip had talked about the cost, she'd thought it was about doing bad things. Now she realized he'd talked about mental cost, about always having to remember how much truth you could reveal to any one person at any given time, never being able to be yourself. It could drive a person mad. It explained a lot about Philip.

She had to tell Alec the truth about her. And soon. If he lived through this mission.

Alec was thirty seconds late to the briefing. He slowed to a walk to appear unhurried. No sense giving Lansing an excuse to question him about Beth's visit. As he turned the corner to the briefing room, he passed Lansing whispering to one of the Resource security people.

"You're certain those cameras went down?"

The security officer mumbled something that Alec couldn't hear.

"Normal interference? No, you double-check everything. Now."

"Yes, sir."

Good. Lansing was too worried about a screw-up somewhere else to question him.

Commander Daz Montoya stepped out of the briefing room into the hallway. "Firefly, good, you're here," he said to Alec. "It's time."

The rest of F-Team was already seated in the briefing room. As always, they'd turned their chairs sideways to have the room's only exit in view. Alec had learned they did this out of long habit—they had to have their backs protected. Even Kowalski, the CIA agent who was about to give the briefing, kept the door in sight. Alec turned his chair like everyone else.

Daz sat straight, military posture, as always. A perfect soldier, even down to his cropped hair. Alec could only hope to be as good someday. Beth thought being a soldier was a bad thing. She didn't understand. What he did *mattered*.

Kowalski cleared his throat and started the briefing. Alec banished all thought of Beth from his mind. This was work. No distractions allowed.

The briefing was a quick slideshow given in Kowalski's dry style. No emotion seeped through. He might as well have been talking about a widget and not a dirty bomb. Alec's heart started hammering in his chest as he realized this mission was more serious than any of his previous ones. He took a deep calming breath and wondering if he was the only one nervous or if everyone else was hiding it like he was.

Their objective was to stop a transfer of radioactive materials from arms dealers to a terrorist cell gathering components for a dirty bomb. The exchange was to take place tonight at the Newark docks. F-Team's job would be to secure the radioactive materials. Getting the cell and the arms dealers would be gravy.

Gabe, the lanky tech officer, raised a hand. "So are we likely to deal with the fanatics or the pros tonight?"

Good question. Members of the cell would fight to the death, no quarter given. Arms dealers would surrender if defeated. Pros were always preferable to fanatics. They were predictable.

"We don't know," Kowalski said. "They could both be there."

Everyone in the room groaned.

"This cell is a mystery," Kowalski said. "From what we can tell, they've mixed mercenaries in with their fanatics."

He clicked to a close-up of dark-haired man with droopy eyes, thinning hair and a potbelly. "This is Hans Ulrich. He's a German national and well-respected mercenary, which means he fulfills his contracts perfectly. We don't know where his true loyalties lie and he's never shown up with religious fanatics before. He's the cell's liaison with the arms dealer."

Hans looked ordinary and unremarkable. Alec would never give him a second glance. Just as well that he didn't do intelligence.

Another photo replaced Hans. By contrast, this man was immediately striking. His mouth was set and his dark eyes seemed to be looking out from the photograph in what could only be a death stare. Not someone Alec wanted to meet in combat.

"This is Demeter, full name unknown, the leader of the cell. We think he's a Turkish national. He's a fanatical Sunni Muslim, known mostly as a trainer of suicide bombers. He'd be happy to blow himself up for the glory of Allah while striking against us. His cell shares that goal, save for a few that Hans brought in."

"So what the hell are Hans and Demeter doing working together so closely?" Daz asked.

"We theorize that Hans is handling the money and arrangements," Kowalski said. "The other mercenaries are his back-up against betrayal by Demeter. Once the cell has the radioactive materials, we figure Hans and his people will drop off."

"Meaning you don't fucking know," Jimmy said from the back table.

"Cut it, corporal." Alec glared at Jimmy. They didn't have time for this if they wanted to get going. Jimmy knew that and should be controlling his nerves better.

Jimmy shrugged and subsided.

"Last thing," Kowalski said. "If possible, we don't just want these guys dead. We want someone left alive to talk."

"You said the radioactive materials were priority," Daz said.

Kowalski took a deep breath and rubbed his bald head. "And it remains priority. But we get the cell too, and we don't have to worry about them finding more nukes. And we get Hans, we find out who's got the purse strings on this one. There are a lot of questions about this operation and we want answers."

Daz nodded.

They spent a few more minutes reviewing the layout of the docks and the warehouses. Kowalski glanced at his watch and ended it. Alec took a deep breath. His heart wasn't hammering anymore. The nerves were fading, as they always did.

Lansing grabbed Alec's arm on the way out.

"Something that you want to tell me, boy?"

Alec shrugged the hold aside. Obviously, Lansing was referring to

Beth's visit. "What are you talking about?" *Back off.*

Lansing's bushy eyebrows came together. "I want you to concentrate tonight on the *mission.*"

"I'm doing nothing but concentrating on the mission. Go watch in mission control," Alec said. "You'll see."

"I expect no less." Lansing scowled and walked away.

Daz stepped to Alec's side. "What bug is up his butt?"

"Who knows? Let's go."

Chapter Four

F-Team loaded into the van that would take them to the Newark docks. Daz tapped Alec's shoulder as they stepped inside. "Good slap-down of Jimmy in the briefing," Daz whispered. "You're learning command."

"Thanks," Alec mumbled. He took his seat and dipped his head to hide a smile. Daz was stingy with praise. *I better not let it go to my head.* Alec closed his eyes and ran through the briefing one more time in his mind. He braced himself as the van started moving.

Some of F-Team whispered among themselves, small-talk, to stave off nerves. One of them mentioned a girl and that was enough to bring Beth back to Alec's mind. He flexed his hand and thought of her small but very adult body wrapped around him, so hot that it felt like his insides had been burning, never mind the papers. He'd nearly ripped off her clothes, pushed her against the wall—

Daz elbowed him. "Hello? You with us, Firefly?"

"Yeah." He leaned back, resting against the side of the van. The body armor pressed against his skin, banishing thoughts of naked Beth. Her breasts might not be large but they certainly looked perfectly formed from what he could tell.

"Why'd Lansing feel the need to give you that last warning?" Daz asked.

"Maybe he's got Alzheimer's," Gabe chimed in. The rest of the team laughed. Alec smiled.

"Lansing doesn't like Beth. He thinks things between us are getting too personal."

"Aha," Daz said. "Well, Lansing's got a point. Girls can make you stupid."

"Not this one." Try jazzed. Hot. Incinerating.

"The shrink get to you?" Daz leaned forward. The dim light made his brown face appear darker than normal. "Dammit, you're grinning."

"I'm not." Alec thought of Beth's legs wrapped around his hips, his erection pressing against his pants. If he'd kept going, she wouldn't have stopped him. She'd been as into it as he had. "Beth came to talk to me right before I left. Got me thinking, that's all."

There was a snort from the other side of the van.

"She mess with you?" Gabe fiddled with the radio in his helmet. His long fingers made short work of some adjustment.

"Mess with him? I bet that's what he wanted," Daz said.

Alec choked back a laugh. She'd wanted him. Finally, he'd gotten under her skin. Now he needed to get under her clothes.

"Spill." Daz poked him in the ribs, not that he could feel it under the body armor.

Alec dropped his head, feeling his face flush. What was he, twelve and looking at his first naked photos? Daz was only teasing to pass time and keep everyone mellow.

"*That* kind of send-off?" Daz asked, voice filled with amusement. "No wonder the old man was uptight. He hates you playing around with the staff."

"She's not staff. She's from outside. And Lansing hates a lot of things I do lately." Alec shrugged. "It was only one kiss."

"So instead of the shrink screwing with you, you're screwing the shrink?" Gabe grinned.

The team laughed. Several more shouted suggestions on what else he could do with the shrink. At least one suggestion was anatomically impossible. Or so he'd thought. Alec tried to picture Beth in that position. Hey, he could use the TK with her. He didn't have to hide it, like with the girls he'd met through F-Team.

I could find out what the TK could really do.

He sat back and let the teasing roll over him, running positions in his head, picturing her reaction. Beth was so little, almost child-size. But there had been nothing tiny or child-like about that kiss. She was definitely a *woman*. No wonder his fire took on a mind of its own for a second back there. He'd better squelch that next time. A room on fire wouldn't do much for their sex life.

And there would be a next time and it would be more than one kiss.

Unethical, my ass.

The van started to slow.

"Okay, team, check through the equipment one more time. Full stealth mode. Gabe, you stay with Firefly until we set up a perimeter. Our target's the warehouse closest to the dock. At least, so the intel says. We know how wrong that can be."

"Damn straight," Jimmy said.

"It's not an excuse to screw this up. Got it?"

"Got it," Jimmy mumbled.

Maybe Daz had had enough of Jimmy's attitude too. The rest of the team nodded.

"Remember, *complete* radio silence," Daz said. "We can't chance being picked up by anyone. Only I can break it or give orders to break silence. Got it?"

Alec nodded with the rest.

The back doors to the van opened to darkness. The smell of the sea, mingled with oil fumes, flooded into Alec's nostrils. The only discernible noise was the distant lap of waves against the docks.

The team lowered their infrared goggles over their eyes and filed out in silence, leaving him and Gabe for last. Daz gestured with his hand to the team. They split up into two groups, five each, one headed right, one to the left. The only sound was the quiet slap of their boots.

Alec rolled his shoulders and centered himself, closing his eyes to call the TK. Gabe would watch out for him. That was the deal. F-Team protected him physically, he took care of them his way. Since he was hanging back, Alec had time to go deep with the TK. He took several long breaths, forcing himself into something resembling a trance, and unleashed his TK, the energy flowing out of his body like an unseen hand.

It was exactly like fumbling in the dark for a light switch. Likely he wouldn't hit anything. But the TK could go faster than F-Team could walk and he might find their targets first, save time, maybe save lives.

Dark, black, empty. Nothing.

Not helpful. He gritted his teeth and went deeper. Wait, something moving but he couldn't get how big it was. Damn. A hand shook his shoulder. He opened his eyes.

"Time to move. Follow me," Gabe said.

They walked in the darkness. Five steps, listen. Another five steps, listen again. He winced at the sound of his own footsteps, much louder than Gabe's quiet tread. He'd improved over the past two years but he wasn't up to Gabe's level yet. If he wanted command, he would have to get better.

Gabe held his M-4 carbine with ease, despite the fact he looked more like a scarecrow than a soldier. Alec only carried a handgun. He left the rifle in the van. Something that bulky would slow him down tonight.

This would be much easier if he could just light up the sky with fire but, no, stealth mode.

I hate stealth mode. C'mon, let's get this started.

Gabe stopped. Alec studied the area again. Long, large warehouses loomed over them on both sides, all the way to the edge of the piers. Metal shipping containers as big as his apartment were stacked outside the warehouses and even on the docks. Cranes and other heavy equipment used for loading and unloading hovered above them, silent.

There were a ton of places for their targets to hide. Recon would have helped but there hadn't been time.

Likely, Daz was weighing whether to go into one of the warehouses or hunker down and wait to spot their targets in the open.

Movement flashed out of the corner of Alec's eye. A small shape. He reached out his hand, to grab it with the TK. Gabe raised the M-4.

The shape meowed.

Alec relaxed and dropped his hand back to his waist. Gabe lowered his carbine and tapped him on the forearm. They started walking again.

"We should have found them by now," Alec whispered.

Gabe nodded. "Yeah. F-Team's moving forward ten yards at a time. We'll go all the way to the dock, then backtrack until we've got something."

That was standard procedure with unknown target locations. Alec nodded. They edged closer and closer to the docks. The sea smell grew stronger. They stopped again. Impatient, Alec sent his TK rolling forward and bumped right into F-Team, almost slapping Daz's helmet.

A docked tugboat, with its running lights on, came into view at the end of the third pier.

"Damn," Gabe whispered.

Fuck it. Alec pushed his night goggles up. Intelligence had said nothing about having to deal with a water transfer. The cell must have sensed discovery and moved. Shit, F-Team didn't have water back-up.

But they had him.

Alec closed his eyes, concentrated and surrounded the tug with his TK like an invisible hand, to hold it in place.

It was too big to hold for long. Crap.

The tug bounced in the waves, making it harder to control. The engine revved in neutral. Once it shifted into gear, Alec doubted he could hold on to it. A wave splashed against the tug, sending it bouncing higher, and Alec lost hold.

If he were closer, he could grab the bridge controls and shut down the engine. A bad idea from this distance. He could easily hit full throttle instead of stop. He couldn't use the fire, either. If there was a bomb on board, that might set it off.

Even without radioactive materials, that would make a hell of a mess.

Fuck. I have to get closer. Now.

The distinctive sound of machine gun fire rang out, along with the nastier sound of the bullets pinging off concrete.

Sniper!

He and Gabe scrambled for cover behind the nearest metal shipping container. Gabe was nodding, listening to whatever came through his radio. Things must be dire if Daz was breaking radio silence, even if only to quickly contact Gabe. "Came from above," Gabe said. "Not sure where."

"Shit," Alec said. If he used the TK to find the sniper, he wouldn't be able to grab the tug if it left the dock. If he used fire to locate the sniper, he'd light up the whole sky and the sniper would have a clear shot at F-Team too.

"Screw the sniper," Alec said. "I'm headed to the tug. The TK will keep the bullets off me."

"Don't be stupid," Gabe said. "There could be more than one sniper. You'd never see bullets from another direction in time. Let the team do their job."

Alec punched the container in frustration.

Gabe spoke into the radio and nodded at the voice in his ear. "Okay, Firefly, Daz is going to get you an opening. You see it, you go. We'll cover."

He nodded. F-Team would risk their lives for him. *I hate that.*

Alec took a long breath, smelled his own sweat, the plastic tinge of the Kevlar armor encasing his chest and the salt of the ocean, all mixed with the smell from the bullets.

The sound of heavy footfalls from F-Team rushing to the dock mingled with the tug's engine noise. Terse, yelled instructions from Daz buzzed through Alec's radio. Yes, things were not going well.

Shots from above again.

The crane.

A muffled cry of pain. Someone hit the ground with a groan.

Man down. Shit.

Screw the tug.

Alec threw the TK at the crane and bumped into the metal so hard that he stumbled. He braced himself against the shipping container for balance and fumbled up the crane with the TK. He found a foot, knees and then a rifle.

Gotcha, you fucker.

The tug's motor roared. Alec swatted at the sniper, intending to knock him off his perch. The sniper braced himself and held steady.

Screw subtle.

Alec twisted his hand and loosed the fire, letting the energy flow out of him, twisting the air, agitating the sniper's skin molecules until—

The sniper's face burst into flame.

There was a horrific scream. A fireball in the shape of a man glowed at the top of the crane, fell, and hit the dock with a thud and a hiss. The fire spread outward from him.

Alec took a deep breath, smelled the burning flesh and knew he should want to puke but all he could think was that the man deserved it. One of his team was down because of him. The fire rose around Alec, wanting to break free, responding to his joy at not being held back anymore.

He reached out a hand and the flames flew to him, surrounding him, embracing him. He closed his eyes, feeling the heat, lost in it. This was more like it. Screw stealth mode.

Gabe knocked his shoulder with a rifle butt. "Get the tug!"

Right. Tug. Bomb. "Got it." Alec sent the fire raging out from him, rising into the sky. The blaze flew up fast, almost without conscious effort. So easy.

He held the fire over the tug, menacing it. *Turn around, now, or I'll burn you!* He walked into the open for line of sight, letting the flames wrap around him.

Several men on the tug shouted and surrounded a large, square container in the stern. Alec recognized Hans by the droopy eyes and potbelly. Hans motioned to the others on deck and pointed past the docks. The others calmed down and the tug started moving away again.

The fire screamed at Alec, rolling into a ball of raging heat, wanting to consume what was in its path, more powerful than any fire he'd handled before. It wanted to incinerate the entire tug, including the bomb. But he had control. This is what he'd trained to do all his life.

He created a wall of fire on the far side of the tug, trying to make it retreat. More shouting. Again, Hans calmed the others down and the boat kept moving. Alec had to let some of the fire spin away, lest it hit the bomb. They'd called his bluff. *Shit.*

The tug chugged into the harbor, taking it farther from Alec's range and closer to a big, shadowy shape out on the water. Another ship. No way he'd be able to stop the bigger ship if they loaded the bomb on it. Sweat poured down Alec's neck and back. His breathing grew quicker, his eyesight blurrier from the smoke of the burning dock.

Hans was the calm one. Get him and the rest would panic. Alec broke off a small ball of fire from the flames above the tug and sent it crashing into Hans' chest.

Hans screamed, stumbled backwards and fell into the water. Steam hissed and was quickly snuffed by a wave.

The tug stopped moving, dead in the water. *Yes!*

A shadow fell over the tug. Their pickup. The transfer wasn't at the docks like intelligence said, it would be on the water. Kowalski, who'd berated them for their mission questions, had been wrong. If Daz didn't go after the CIA fuck, Alec would.

Daz yelled out loud. Alec ignored it. Daz's voice buzzed in his ear from the radio. Alec tore off his helmet. Tears ran down his face from the smoke. His knees grew weak. The fire almost escaped from him, almost roared into the bomb.

Dammit, I can control this. What was wrong with him? He knew better. He dropped to his knees and pushed the fire back to the tug's bridge. Another man was yelling now. Alec saw the face illuminated in the firelight and recognized Demeter, the fanatic. He should crisp him too, but if he let the fire go even a little, he'd lose it completely. *Hell.*

He raised a hand and created a roof of flame over the boat. There! Let them try to move the bomb with that there. He grinned, panic gone, and stood. He blinked and saw the flames around him had grown.

They whispered to him, embraced him, until he was weightless, free, just like the fire. Nothing could hurt him, nothing could defeat him, especially not some second-rate terrorist cell.

"Firefly!"

I'm busy, Daz. Alec blinked and finally registered the twenty-foot wall of flames directly around him. The fire he'd created had joined with the flames from the sniper's body and grown into an inferno.

F-Team was trapped between the warehouse and a shipping container and the flames were closing in.

They'd be incinerated.

In the distance, a horn sounded, close to the tug. *Fuck!* Daz yelled his name again, voice more desperate. Okay, easy. Take control of both fires. He could finish the mission and save F-Team at the same time. Piece of cake.

He spun around and around in the flames encircling him, pushing them upward, away from F-Team, sending them into the sky, where they'd have no fuel and would sputter out on their own. The metal of the crane above twisted and buckled from the intense heat.

His throat felt like dust. Heat enclosed him, baking his skin. He shouldn't have made it so damn hot without realizing it. He knew better. What the hell was *wrong* with him?

He waved his hand. The flames around him started to sputter out. Good, F-Team was safe. The roof of flames above the tug disappeared.

No, shit, he didn't mean *those* flames. He reached out with his TK toward the boat. He felt something fuzzy, like a figurative cotton ball in the air. He had no idea what the hell that was.

An explosion rocked the night air, splitting the tug in half. Alec fell face-forward to the dock. He spat out ashes, cursing. What had happened?

The fire around him leapt high again, its flames a vivid blue color. He couldn't have exploded the bomb on the tug—he'd been careful. So what the hell had done it?

He pushed himself up with his arms, bit his lip and the fire around him stole the air from his lungs and took control of him.

He closed his eyes, joined the flames, felt them rise up around him, like he was flying high with it, flying to the water, flying to consume that big ship out there. Who needed control?

This was all he needed. He could *be* fire.

A sharp pain stung his neck.

He blinked and looked down. Tranquilizer dart? The fire engulfing him started to falter and die around him. No, he couldn't lose the flames. He needed to *fly.*

He looked up and saw Daz dimly through the smoke, aiming a rifle with a weird-looking barrel. He reached out and another dart stung his hand.

He collapsed to the docks.

Chapter Five

"Congratulations. Demeter is still free. He has the final dirty bomb components. Bonus: Hans Ulrich is dead and whatever brakes were on this cell are gone." Kowalski crossed his beefy arms over his chest and glared at everyone in the briefing room. "Nice job."

Alec winced and looked down at the gray, colorless floor of the Resource's briefing room. His fault. He'd screwed up so badly that Daz had to tranq him. He hadn't lost control of the fire like that since he was fifteen.

Now Demeter had the radioactive materials and a bomb to use with them. Jimmy was dead, shot through the eye by the sniper. And the explosion set off by the terrorists after transferring the radioactive materials to the larger ship had destroyed the tug and erased all clues.

All because he had lost control of his fire.

"We're a specialized assault team." Daz stood. "We took your intel and planned a land assault. It was a water transfer. The mistake is yours, spook."

"You have a man who can call *fire* on your team," Kowalski said. "How the hell do you explain Demeter getting away?"

I can't control water, you asshole.

Daz slammed his fist on the table. "Look, you wanted them so bad, you should have held up your end of the mission and provided the right intel. Because of you, we lost a man."

Kowalski clasped his hands behind his back. He glared at Alec. "I suggest you let us worry about the lapse in intel and concentrate on getting your shit together, Commander, before you lose more team members."

Alec snapped to his feet. He waved a hand, calling the TK, intending to slam Kowalski into the wall. Daz elbowed him, breaking his concentration.

"Enough, Firefly," Daz whispered.

Alec sat back into his chair and crossed his arms over his chest. Okay, hitting Kowalski with the TK wasn't a proportional response. He tried to remember what Beth had said to do when he got this angry. *Distract yourself until you can think logically.*

He looked straight ahead but deliberately tried not to hear the remainder of Kowalski's debriefing. He didn't need to relive all that had gone wrong. He'd done that enough in his head over the last two days.

Three enemy bodies recovered: Hans Ulrich, crisped and waterlogged, another cell member from the water, and the badly burned body of the sniper. Forensic people were looking at them for clues. Alec doubted they would find anything. No one had any explanation for that fuzziness he'd encountered just before the explosion either. Part of that was his fault, he couldn't describe it properly because he'd never felt anything like that. Lansing had suggested stress had caused his TK to glitch. Alec didn't believe that but he had no better explanation.

F-Team had brought Jimmy with them back to the Resource. Jimmy's family now had to make funeral arrangements.

I didn't pull the trigger but it was my fault. I should be better; I should have spotted the sniper sooner.

He'd *failed.* Some hero he was.

Kowalski finished and stomped out, ending the briefing. Lansing appeared in the doorway as Alec filed out with F-Team. Lansing let F-Team go past but he stepped in front of Alec.

Alec clenched his jaw, anticipating another lecture.

"Director," Daz said, "we've got the training exercise in thirty minutes."

"You'll start the exercise when Alec is available, Commander, and not before," Lansing said. "That's an order."

Daz looked at Alec, then back to Lansing and nodded. "Yes, sir."

Lansing waited until Daz was well out of earshot to speak. "He's coddling you."

"Daz is protecting me, like he does any team member." Though

Daz backed down to Lansing often enough. The protection had limits.

"Neither of you protected Jimmy very well."

Alec dropped his head.

Lansing put his hands behind his back. "Casualties are part of being a soldier, Alec. Unfortunate, but expected. My primary concern, as I've said, is that you lost control of the fire. How often have we worked on that over the years?"

"Every day since I was three." Alec stared at the tile floor. Around F-Team, he felt like a soldier. Around Lansing, he still felt like that fumbling three-year-old who let flames run free.

"And now you lose control?" Lansing pointed a finger into Alec's chest. "I think it has something to do with Beth Nakamora."

Alec pushed Lansing's finger away. "What do you mean?" How could Beth be the problem?

"Psychologists are good at creating self-doubt. Your power works on mental ability. If doubt is created, control is lost. She created doubt in your mind."

"Beth doesn't make me doubt anything." In fact, Beth seemed to almost pull the power out of him. Look at the way those papers in his room had caught fire.

"You wouldn't notice if she did. That's how psychologists work. I thought she'd be the solution to your issues in working with others. Yet this happened on the first mission after she started treating you."

"One's got nothing to do with the other. The intel was bad, the—"

"Bad intel did not make you lose yourself in the fire. And the flames were blue, Alec, not yellow. You know better than to raise their temperature like that."

Alec met Lansing's gaze. "She has nothing to do with it."

"Protecting her does you credit. But she doesn't need it. I've asked Ms. Nakamora to watch your training exercise today. I plan to speak to her about this matter. If I don't like what I hear, she's gone."

No. "I want to keep seeing her."

"Prove to me that you have control in the training exercise and I'll reconsider my decision."

Beth clutched the metal railing, looking below at the gymnasium that was now disguised as a warehouse for the training exercise. As when she'd been brought to Alec's apartment, she'd been escorted to this location by one of the Resource security guards. She estimated they were down two levels from Alec's apartment.

Just how big is this place? She'd passed an entrance to a wing marked *restricted.* There could be thousands of square feet behind that entrance. It seemed the gymnasium was only the tip of the iceberg. All this seemed overkill just for Alec. Lansing must be doing something else here or planning to do something else in the future.

F-Team filtered in from the side door. Beth wrapped her hands tighter around the railing and looked for clues in Alec's manner. The terse CIA report that Philip had given her about the mission had given no hint of Alec's state of mind.

If she had burned a man alive, she would have been horrified.

But to Alec, the sniper had been an enemy and burning him an acceptable response. Alec probably felt guiltier at his failure to save Jimmy.

If Alec was nervous or doubted himself, he currently gave no physical sign of it. He looked the perfect soldier save for the hair that escaped from under his helmet. He stood straight and listened intently as Daz gave orders. F-Team's mission was to take down a sniper.

She leaned over get a better look, squinting. It was half dark down there, to simulate real conditions. The sniper's nest was at the top of one row, about twenty feet above everything else.

Inside the nest, Lieutenant Gabriel held a paint gun at the ready, silently waiting for his "enemies" to come into view. Gabe was wearing an asbestos suit, in case Alec's fire grew out of control again. She wondered if that precaution bothered Alec.

The team split into two. Alec stayed with Daz's group.

Beth bit her lip. The soldiers behind Alec kept glancing at him, almost afraid. That couldn't be normal, not the way Alec talked about how much he loved to be part of F-Team. But now, after what had happened at the docks, they were finally afraid of Alec's fire. She hoped Alec didn't notice.

The point of this exercise was for Alec to prove he still had control of his power. In a way, losing control might be the best thing for him. If he couldn't be used as a weapon, the CIA would back off from the order to either kidnap or assassinate him. And Alec wouldn't be exposed to the danger of future missions.

But failing would break Alec's spirit. And as much as she wanted him safe, she would never wish for that.

The team crept through the warehouse. Nothing had gone wrong. *Yet.*

Slowly, they worked through the rows of shelves in the mock warehouse below. If she still had her telepathy, she'd know what Alec was thinking, what he was feeling, if he was in the right state of mind. It seemed so strange to wish for it, given how often she'd been satisfied that it was gone forever.

Alec was probably calm. This tense, dangerous game was nothing new to him. Would he believe her if she told him that this kind of upbringing tended to breed paranoia and could create a kind of post-traumatic stress disorder? No, probably not.

Quiet footsteps echoed behind her. She refused to look up. It was likely one of the Resource guards, watching her.

"Find the exercise interesting, Ms. Nakamora?"

Lansing? She turned. His big hands closed around the railing like large deadly paws. Paws that could easily cover her tiny neck and squeeze the life out of her. No one would ever find her body in this cavernous facility.

"Alec looks to be in his element," she said. *Neutral. Stay neutral.*

"An element of which you disapprove." Lansing kept his attention on the action below.

"It helps if the soldier has a choice about fighting." She turned her face away from Lansing. How much did he know? Philip said last night that his greatest fear was that Lansing did know who she really was and he'd allowed her back into the Resource to grab her.

She'd come today anyway. Philip had been livid.

Below, Daz gestured to his group. The team surrounded Alec as they rushed from one aisle to the next to get closer to the sniper. Gabe unsuccessfully fired a round of paint balls at them.

"Dammit, boy," Lansing said.

"What do you mean?" The team looked like they were doing fine to her. No one hit so far.

Lansing shook his head. "They're going too slow. This should be a quick, easy exercise. Montoya is being protective and overly careful. He should have put Alec in charge of the second team." He turned to her. "And he's not the only one coddling Alec."

She bit the inside of her cheek, trying to control her anger. "Alec lost a friend for the first time. He burned someone to death for the first time. He failed on a mission for the first time. It's perfectly appropriate that he needs help to recover." She put her hands behind her back, hiding clenched fists. Had she gone too far? Avoid a direct confrontation, Philip had said. He'd nearly been ready to toss her in a closet and throw away the key to keep her from coming today. Instead, he'd taken other precautions.

"I sent Alec from my residence at a young age in order to toughen him up for his role in life. And I hired Montoya to teach Alec command, not protect him. Alec must stand up for himself and not wallow in failure."

"Acknowledging an emotion is not the same as wallowing in it."

Alec used to *live* with Lansing? Alec hadn't mentioned where he'd lived before he was twelve and moved into that room on the lower levels of the Resource. She'd assumed he'd been raised mostly in a laboratory or a safe room to protect himself and others from his fire until he learned control. But, thinking on it, there were shadows of a strong bond left in both Alec and Lansing that only continuous close proximity would explain. Alec definitely wanted to please his remote father figure, while simultaneously resenting him. A classic father/son paradigm.

"Emotions need to be channeled to the right goals, not used as leverage to stop fighting." Lansing's dark brown eyes narrowed and his lips turned into a thin line. He straightened and stepped closer, his large frame throwing her entire body into shadow.

"Fighting is not always the right goal." She turned to face him, keeping one hand on the railing for balance. *Here we go. I hope you weren't right, Philip.*

Below, F-Team regrouped. Unexpectedly, Alec glanced up and made eye contact with her. Startled, all she could do was nod. His curt nod back showed more tension than she liked. Alec turned back to Daz.

"Ms. Nakamora, his life depends on training for when he's in combat. You're distracting him."

"You invited me to watch."

"I wanted to assess you. The CIA said they needed someone to help Alec integrate better with outside agents. I don't think they'd approve of you wanting him off combat duty completely. You're a lousy therapist if you want Alec to give this up. He lives for this."

"Because he doesn't know another way."

"You have an agenda of your own and it's not to help Alec. I'm looking into it. Carefully."

Looking into it?

Lansing turned his back on her and stared down at the mock warehouse again. She swallowed, her legs too leaden to move. What had Lansing found? Perhaps he was probing her, trying to find out what she knew. Better to say nothing.

She craned her neck to see what was happening below. The team rushed the sniper's nest from different directions. Alec stayed in the rear of Daz's group, hanging back from the line of fire.

The sniper fired. She tensed and flinched, as if the shots were directed at her. But the paintball stopped dead in midair and fell to the floor.

Excellent!

No fire. That was only Alec's TK and appropriately used. Alec seemed to be focusing better than she was. She also noticed that at this distance, she couldn't sense Alec's power as she usually did during their sessions. Interesting.

The sniper fired more shots, in quick succession. Alec mimicked catching the paintballs with his outstretched hands. The projectiles stopped in midair, changed direction, and splatted harmlessly into the far wall. Alec was playing catch. She shook her head, almost grinning.

Then Daz went down to one knee, swearing, a paintball smudge bright yellow against his green uniform. Oh, hell, one of them had gotten through Alec's guard. Her grin faded.

Alec raised his hands, locked them at the elbows and shouted something. The paintballs coming at him burst into flames.

Uh-oh. The whole point of this exercise was for Alec to hold control and not use his fire. *Alec, calm down.*

F-Team scattered, avoiding the fiery paintballs. This would only reinforce their newfound fear of Alec's power. The boxes around the sniper erupted into flames. Alec dropped to one knee, breathing heavily. The flames engulfing the boxes grew higher, covering the top of the nest.

Gabe stumbled out of his nest, half-climbing down, half-falling. His body was completely covered in fire. *Stop, Alec, stop!* She held her breath.

Daz snapped to his feet, grabbed a fire extinguisher from the wall, and sprayed Gabe with it. Alec rushed forward and dropped to one knee next to Gabe. He waved a hand and all the fire went out, from the flames licking at Gabe, to the boxes on the sniper's nest, and the paintballs.

Beth let out a deep breath, leaning over the railing as far as she dared. How badly had Alec hurt his friend?

Gabe sat up, coughed, and knocked away the hands offering help. He stood on his own and glared at Alec. Alec dropped his head and backed away.

His team, the team that he loved, would be more afraid now. Like everyone who'd known about her telepathy years ago had been afraid of her, except Philip.

"He's not lost control like that in years. Years!" Lansing pounded his fist on the railing. "You're the only new element here. This must be because of you. It has to be."

"Excuse me?" She backed away, looking for the exit.

"I know that you somehow shut down my surveillance in Alec's room before the mission," he said.

Oh, hell. "I don't know what you're talking about."

"I'm going to find out what you are." He reached for something in his pocket.

"She can't really be CIA. They won't protect her. I'll take her and find out what she really is."

The intruding thought slammed into her brain. She grabbed her head and doubled over. Where had *that* come from? It was Lansing's voice but he hadn't said it.

She'd read his mind. Her telepathy had worked for a brief second.

She didn't know whether to cry or laugh. How typical that the first thing she heard telepathically in years was a threat. No wonder she'd hated hearing thoughts.

She closed her eyes and whispered a prayer for her mother's spirit and those of her ancestors to protect her. She heard Lansing take another step toward her. She lifted her head and opened her eyes. Lansing leveled a gun at her, one with a strange barrel.

"Tranquilizer will keep her out for hours. And we can get to work on her."

No escape, no escape. If only he would just put the gun down, turn around and leave her alone. Yes. That would be perfect. He should put the gun down, turn around and leave her alone.

Impossibly, Lansing lowered the gun and turned around.

Her hand fumbled for the door handle. The door opened, she slipped into the corridor outside and slammed the door shut behind her. She ran, glancing behind her, wondering when Lansing would follow her. Around a turn, she slowed to catch her breath, hope draining away.

Lansing had to know exactly where she was; he had cameras everywhere. He could follow her every move.

She slowed. Lansing must be toying with her, seeing how she'd react. A master playing with a puppet. No matter which way she went, she couldn't get out. They'd stop her when they felt like it.

Alec.

If she found Alec, perhaps they would let her walk out, so as not to alarm him.

And maybe she could save him too.

Chapter Six

Daz took off his helmet and slapped at the yellow paint on his leg.

"Daz, I'm sorry," Alec said. What could he say that would excuse that screw-up?

"At least you got the sniper, Firefly. In combat, that's what counts."

"That wasn't the objective." Alec looked away, back to the burned boxes. He'd failed. Again. He'd let the fire get out of control. It had felt so good too. Until he realized that Gabe was burning up.

"Look, I'm no scientist but it seems to me—" Daz leaned against the warehouse wall, "—that your fire's hotter than it used to be, which is causing the problem. You been eating your Wheaties or something?"

"What do you mean?"

"Never seen you make fire go crazy like you did on the docks. It was fucking hot. Lots and lots of blue flame. That was new."

"I don't get what you're saying." Did Daz mean he was even more dangerous?

"I used to train new recruits. Sometimes, the younger ones would get a growth spurt in the middle of training and the extra inches or extra strength would screw them up in hand-to-hand or on the gun range. You've grown several inches since we started working together. You have to be up to six-two by now. Maybe other parts of you have grown too."

Alec frowned but his stomach unclenched. "You're saying I've had a growth spurt with the fire?"

"Yep. You go to your techs, ask them to test the temp of your flames. Betcha I'm right."

"So what? I still set Gabe on fire." He punched the wall and hardly felt the pain. "I almost killed him."

"That's what he gets paid for. Anyway, 'almost' doesn't count." Daz clapped him on the back. "Ask me, a good day is when somebody doesn't end up dead."

Like Jimmy. "I freaked the team out. They're scared of me now."

Daz snorted. "You think Patton's soldiers weren't scared of him? Or Alexander the Great's Macedonians?"

"F-Team isn't scared of you."

Daz shook his head. "Yeah, they are, Alec. You just haven't noticed because *you're* not scared of me. Having soldiers under your command a little scared of you is a good thing."

"You're kidding."

"Look at how much Lansing accomplishes because his people know what the consequences of failure are. Though creating too much fear of failure causes other problems, like crushing initiative or making your people press too hard. That's also part of this. Lansing pressures you too much."

"I'm doing the best I can." Alec ground his teeth.

"You're tense and it's part of the problem." Daz put an arm around his shoulders. For the first time, Alec realized he and Daz were the same height. Funny, he'd always thought of Daz as taller. "Alec, look, no one can do what you do. We need you for round two with Demeter and his crew, especially if they're planning to use that bomb."

"You think I'll get another chance at them?"

Daz nodded. "Now that they've got the components, Demeter won't go underground for long. He'll poke his head out to use that bomb and then it'll be our turn again."

"I won't screw it up."

"I know. I told you, it's a growth spurt. Go to the techs, get tested and sort your gifts out. That's an order."

Alec nodded. "Okay."

Footsteps echoed down the hallway. Pumps, not work shoes. Daz turned and raised his eyebrows as Beth came into view.

"Remember what I said, Firefly. And, hey, relaxation might be good for you." He walked past Beth, whistling.

Alec straightened and ran a hand through his mussed hair. Beth had seen the whole exercise. Did it scare her too? Then he remembered. She looked fragile but she was more like steel than some hothouse Japanese flower.

"You got a lousy show today, counselor."

"Oh, I don't know," she said. "Your TK is really impressive, especially when it's not being used against innocent silk scarves or ping-pong balls."

He smiled at the warmth in her voice and felt the tension ease out of him. "So where do we talk?"

She blinked and her gaze flitted down the hallway and back again. "On the grounds, maybe? It's a beautiful day."

Was that his imagination or did her voice sound a bit shaky? Maybe she *was* scared of him and hiding it. "Sure. Follow me."

He led her back up the metal stairs and into the first floor of the Resource complex. Below ground held all the good stuff: his apartment, the training rooms, the gym, F-Team's rec room. Above ground had all those sterile offices with pastel colors.

Outside would definitely be better. He could take her to a spot where they wouldn't be seen and follow up on that kiss. Daz had practically ordered him to do it and, hey, a good soldier followed orders.

He pointed to a side door. She nodded and followed him, her gaze flicking back and forth at the miniature cameras that lined the hallways.

He blinked once they stepped outside, trying to adjust to the twilight after the bright fluorescent lights inside. Not total dark, not yet, but it would get there. Didn't girls think night strolls were romantic? He'd read that somewhere. Better Beth feeling romantic than scared of him. He put his hand on her shoulder.

Surprisingly, she leaned against him. And she didn't say anything about it being unethical, either. He took the lead, slowing his pace to her small steps. He could almost feel her skin under her light cotton blouse.

"Where are we going?" she whispered.

"Trust me."

"Okay." She looked around, squinting. "Which side of the Resource are we on?"

"East."

She nodded, as if satisfied with something.

They picked their way around a wall of scrub trees that hid the hill just past the exterior fence of the Resource. He used the TK to keep the branches away from her face, branches she hadn't seen in the dim light.

"Thank you," she whispered.

"You're welcome." Only one camera here and he'd use the TK to delay it from scanning this area. He was supposed to work on TK control. In theory, he was doing exactly what Lansing said. He wished he dared pull Beth tighter against him. She felt *so* good. But he didn't want to risk her backing off again.

He stopped in front of the chain link fence.

She glanced backwards. "Do you think anyone is following?"

He closed his eyes and sent his TK back to the trees. Nothing moving. "If they are, they're not close. Stop worrying. Daz knows where I am. They'll leave us alone."

"I hope so."

"You worry too much." Besides, if they did send anyone after him, it would take a while. They were effectively hidden from all the cameras. "Watch this, counselor."

He reached out a hand. A people-sized section of the fence parted in front of them, creating a hole big enough for them to slip through one at a time.

She sucked in her breath. "You had a way out and didn't take it?"

"Hey, I've been outside the grounds before. It's not that interesting."

"That's because—never mind."

"Good, because I don't want to argue."

He went through the hole first. Her sweater snagged on a bit of metal for a second, then she was free. They were *free*.

"You parted that fence very quickly," she said as they walked down the hill. "And with no noise."

Should he admit that it had been quiet for a reason? "I figured out the cameras have a small gap right there. I played with the fence a long time, pulling it apart, putting it back together, just to see if I could. It doesn't look like it's broken, but it is."

"That's amazing."

He clasped her hand. Once again, that weird electric hum between them clicked into place, though not as strong as when he'd kissed her. At least not yet. "I can do other impressive stuff."

"I'll bet."

"There's a clearing where we can talk." He squeezed her hand, gently. Such a tiny hand, it felt so fragile. If he squeezed too hard, he might break it. "A little stream too. No cameras, just us. I found it the last time I came this way. I liked it."

"It sounds lovely." She sighed. "I think you might be a romantic at heart, Alec."

"Maybe."

"Alec?"

"Yeah?"

"How would you like to go farther than the clearing?"

Was she asking him to her place?

"That could be good." He put his arm around her shoulder as they reached the bottom of the hill. The connection between them was a steady hum. He was close to full arousal and wondered if she was too. But she seemed more distracted than anything else.

Gravel from an old service road crunched under his boots. "How would we get to your place? It's too far to walk."

She paused, as if thinking hard about the answer. "A friend left me a car around here," she said. "At least, I think it's around here."

"You're kidding."

She leaned against him. He pulled her close. "You want me to go home with you?" He held her out from him, searching her face to see if she'd object. This was better than he hoped.

"In a way. The house where I want to take you belongs to a friend but he lets me use it." She put her hand on one of the large pine trees, looking around, squinting. She took two steps, and banged her knee into something that made a hollow metallic clunk.

"You okay?" he said. "That was no tree."

"No, it's our ride." She rubbed the knee. "This way, we can leave without anyone following. I wanted to surprise you."

"I'm surprised." He knelt down to look closer, and dropped her hand. She'd walked into the front fender of a car that was covered by a green tarp.

"Cool camouflage." He peeled back the tarp. A Honda. He'd been hoping for a sports car. But at least he was leaving with Beth to go to her place, where they could be alone with no watchers.

"Thanks." She punched in a code on the driver's side lock.

He got in the car as she pulled the rest of the tarp off. She dropped the tarp in the backseat, sat down behind the wheel, picked up the keys from the driver's seat and turned over the ignition.

"Wait, how'd you get a car out here?"

"Just lucky, I guess." She reached down into a side pocket on the door and slipped something into her hand.

His back stiffened. This whole thing was weird. He hadn't been seduced many times but this suddenly didn't feel like it should. He grabbed her right hand.

"Counselor? What's really going on?"

She turned, eyes wide. "I—" Her hand closed over whatever was in her palm. "I work with the CIA on occasion, so I've learned to be careful and plan ahead. The car was left here by a friend in case I needed it."

"Plan ahead for what? Why would you need to hide a car from the Resource? It can't be just to have sex with me." He gripped her hand tighter.

"The Resource isn't as benevolent as you think, especially its director."

"What exactly are you afraid of?"

She tried to pull her hand free. He tightened his grip. Lansing had warned him the CIA would like to get hold of him. Maybe that's what she was doing. And he'd walked right into it because she'd let him put his arm around her shoulder. Daz would never let him hear the end of that one.

"Alec, it's complicated. It'll take too long to tell it here, especially given how quick they'll miss you. As soon as we get where we're going, I'll tell you. But I swear, I will not hurt you."

"Not good enough." He dug his fingers into her wrist. "Talk to me now, before we go anywhere."

She tried to pull her hand free. He let her pull him closer to her, intending to pin her to the seat and get some real answers. But she twisted and her left hand came forward. He caught a glimpse of something sharp just before she plunged it into his shoulder. He jerked backward and hit his head on the rearview mirror. He looked down at his shoulder. A syringe was stuck in there, just above his collarbone.

Oh, *fuck*, another tranq?

"You—" He grabbed the syringe and pulled it out. Blood trickled down his T-shirt. Lethargy started to spread through his arm. Drugged. Again. "Why? I *trusted* you!"

"I'm sorry. We need to get away from this place. Fast. I won't hurt you."

"Yeah, well, this needle doesn't scream harmless." He jerked away from her and banged his back against the passenger door. He took a deep breath. Already, his arms and legs felt twice as heavy. He fought to keep his eyes open. "I'm out of here."

He fumbled for the door lock. Bad enough to have Daz drug him but now he'd been fooled by someone half his size. And Lansing had been right again. He couldn't trust people from outside.

Alec set his jaw and pushed Beth against the driver's side door with his TK. She let out a muffled cry of pain. His vision started to go blurry at the edges. Okay, let's see how she liked a fire show, close-up.

Something shifted inside his head, like a finger scraping against an open wound. He put his hands over his ears to block it out, almost doubling over. What drug did *this*?

He felt the car lurch into gear as he lost consciousness.

Chapter Seven

He had no fire.

Alec smashed his fist into the wall and stomped across the musty room, his combat boots making small thuds that echoed off the pipes above him. A basement. Beth had locked him in somebody's fucking basement.

There was a small kitchen area but it held no food. A couch, a coffee table and a recliner sat on top of a solid blue rug but there was no gaming console or TV in sight. The whitewashed walls were lined with empty metal shelves. The only thing that looked remotely interesting was the bomb shelter sign above the kitchen sink. Someone had a sick sense of humor.

Though, come to think of it, the basement did look like photos of the old-style bomb shelters from when everyone had been sure a nuclear war was imminent. There were no windows and only one door at the top of the steps that was locked solid.

Whatever else it was, it was his prison now.

He flung himself in the threadbare recliner, bringing forth a layer of dust. He coughed and wiped the dust from his eyes. This place could definitely use the Resource's cleaning crew.

All right, try again. The fire would work this time. It had to. He relaxed his muscles, letting himself sink into the recliner until he could feel the springs against his back. He closed his eyes and formed an image of the wooden coffee table a few feet in front of him. He imagined the grain of the wood underneath the polished varnish, imagined glowing embers and smoke rising, and pictured the glow flashing into blue flame. In his mind, the table was reduced to ashes in a matter of seconds.

Burn, baby, burn.

When he opened his eyes, the table was intact.

Fuck.

He kicked it. It wobbled. He snapped out of the chair, dropped to his knees, and pounded on the table with his fists. He pounded until his little fingers went numb. The table jolted back and forth from his abuse. Pain shot up his elbows from the force of his blows. Breathing hard, he stood and kicked the table over with as much force as he could muster.

It flipped over and skidded across the rug. He stomped over to it and kicked at the table legs, again and again. The wood splintered under the steel toes of his boots. He kept kicking until the legs were completely torn from their screws, until he began to feel the force of the blows through his boots.

He stopped, breathing heavily. Sweat rolled down his back, making the T-shirt stick to his skin.

Alec Farley, destroyer of tables.

Idiot.

All his flailing around had done was make his feet hurt.

He sat on the floor and put his head in his hands. What would Daz do? Get composure and start acting like a man, for one. Daz told him if he ever hit a stalemate, stop, think and review.

Review. He remembered sneaking out with Beth. He remembered getting in her hidden car. He definitely remembered that she drugged him. It had been more than a regular tranq too, because he'd felt something very strange inside his head before passing out. That was the second strange thing he'd felt this week, with the fuzzy weirdness the night at the docks being the first.

His best guess was that this drug had affected his fire. That meant once it wore off or he got the antidote, he'd have his fire back.

He stood, brushed the hair out of his face and fought to breathe slower and easier. Beth was the one who'd drugged him, she was the one who could get back the fire. Step one, get her, and then get the truth and the antidote from her, whatever it took.

Good plan, except he was locked in this basement and he had no idea where she was or if anyone would let him out. Presumably, if someone wanted to kill him, they would have. So likely someone would come for him at some point.

He stared at the heavy wooden door at the top of the steps. The locks were metal but it was a wooden door. Yesterday, he could have burned it to ashes in a few seconds or blasted it off the hinges with his TK.

Today he was completely useless. He closed his eyes, trying to avoid losing his cool again. Maybe there was something in here that he could use as a weapon against whoever came to talk to him. Or something he could use to pick the lock on the door. Maybe he could take the empty metal shelves apart.

A creak echoed down the stairway. The door began to open.

He rushed forward, tripped on the debris from the table, and fell. He cursed and skidded a few feet, burning his palms on the carpet. *Dammit, I knew I was gonna regret that.* He scrambled upright but his foot had only touched the third step before the person at the top of the stairs shut the door behind her.

Beth turned to face him.

"Counselor." He clenched his hands into fists and began stalking up the steps. She damn well better have an explanation.

"Alec." She put her hands up, as if to fend him off. "Your hands are bloody. What happened?"

"Like you don't know."

"Alec, I don't—"

He bounded up the remaining steps and trapped her between his body and the door. Her hair was completely mussed and her yellow T-shirt was so thick with sweat it was almost a second skin. He could clearly see her breasts through the cotton. Her jeans were grass-stained and torn. The laces of her white sneakers were undone.

She didn't look like a kidnapper. She didn't look threatening. Of course, she never looked threatening to him since she was half his size.

He didn't understand any of this.

He framed her head with his fists and leaned down to put them at eye level. She flinched, shrinking against the door, and bent her knees so she didn't have to look at him.

If that wasn't a confirmation of betrayal, he didn't know what was.

Fuck.

"Open the door, Beth."

He controlled his voice, just barely. His guts seemed twisted in a one horrific knot. He leaned in close to her delicate face, fleetingly thinking of how he'd found it the most beautiful thing in the world. He held his lips near hers in a mockery of the kiss they'd shared.

Her face flushed.

"Open sesame." He slapped his hand right next to her ear.

"You have every right to be angry but, please, get control."

"Oh, that's rich, coming from a jailer."

"I closed the door so we could talk safely. You're not a prisoner." Her eyes widened. "Is that what you think?"

"The hell I'm not."

"You couldn't get out? I thought you'd be able to use your TK on the locks, if you needed to." She swallowed hard.

"Stop taunting me and open the damned door!"

"Okay." She raised her hands to separate them. "Back up and give me room."

Wary, he backed up just one step, anger still at a boil. She couldn't really have thought he could open it. That had to be a lie.

Unless this was a test.

Lansing had played with his head before. Maybe this was a test of some drug that could control his fire more effectively than a temporary tranq. Lansing could have used Beth to set him up for it. She could be following Lansing's orders, just like he usually did. His anger cooled a little. He unclenched his fists. Beth pulled a tiny plastic box from the back pocket of her jeans. The box made a low humming sound, the lock tumblers clicked, and the door swung open, as if by magic. An electronic door, with an electronic lock. Someone had planned ahead to hold him. That supported the test theory.

Well, he'd had enough. Lansing would pay for this one. Let's see how he liked seeing that gorgeous oak desk of his reduced to ashes.

Alec rushed through the doorway, looking around for anything familiar. Instead, he was in a small, non-threatening hallway painted a pale blue, with a ceiling low enough that he felt claustrophobic. There were paintings of flowers hanging on the walls.

Flowers? Who decorated a prison with flowers?

"What is going on? Where are the cameras?"

She shook her head. "There are no cameras here, Alec."

He brushed past her, walked through the doorway behind her and ended up in a bright, cheerful living room. Two huge windows, floral curtains and pale blue painted walls.

This was the weirdest prison ever. Was she going to comfort him to death?

"This isn't a test for the Resource?"

She shook her head. "No, this was all me."

He walked through the living room into a smaller room. It turned out to be a bedroom, with that same pale blue color on the walls and another big-ass window. The bed was covered by a yellow quilt.

This was too damn girly for a prison.

"What did you do to me?" he said through gritted teeth.

She shrank back from him, retreating from the bedroom to the living room, her eyes wide. "I put you to sleep while I brought you here. I wanted to save your life. I understand you're angry about being drugged but if you'd just listen for a minute—"

"Listen?" He stalked to her and leaned in to her face. "You drugged me. You took away my fire. How is that saving my life?"

"Took away your fire? What do you mean?" She hugged herself.

She was scared.

Good. That made two of them. Maybe he was being a bully. But she could be playing on that, using her supposed weakness to manipulate him.

"What did you do to me?" He grabbed her upper arms, his fingers gripping her tight. She gasped and he let her go, annoyed that it still felt wrong, despite the fact that she'd been the one who'd hurt *him*. She wasn't an innocent.

He stalked past her again, out of the living room to the other end of the hallway, and ended up in a kitchen with light brown cabinets and white counters. This had a window too. Sunlight streamed into the room. Under other circumstances, it would have seemed, well, pretty.

This room also had an unlocked screen door to the outside.

"I don't understand," she said from behind him. "What do you mean, I took away your fire?"

He walked to the door. What would he find outside? "I can't use my fire or TK. I had it before you drugged me. I don't have it now. That means you did something." He stopped at the door and turned to watch her reaction.

Her dark eyes widened, her body slumped backward, needing the kitchen wall for support. Her mouth twisted in a grimace, as if he'd physically struck her.

"You can't use your fire or the TK? That's *impossible.*"

It could be an act. But she looked genuinely freaked. "Tell me what you did."

"I didn't do anything!" She straightened and looked at his hands. For the first time, he realized his knuckles were still bleeding from his assault on the coffee table. He'd gotten blood on her shirt when he'd grabbed her. He swallowed. Hey, it was partly her fault.

"You kidnapped me. You locked me in. And I don't see anyone else around to share the blame."

She winced. "Yes, but, God, Alec, your fire, I didn't, I've no idea how that could have happened. That was the last thing I wanted."

"And yet, the fire and TK are gone." She still sounded sincere. But her words and what had happened to him didn't add up.

"I let you out of the basement."

"After you locked me in."

"No, I locked it to keep out anyone who came after us. I thought if you woke up, you'd be able to open it."

"That's a neat lie, seeing as how you knew I didn't have the TK."

She shook her head vehemently. "I don't know how to convince you." She paused. "If I wanted to keep you prisoner, why did I let you out?"

"Because you were scared of me."

"But I could have had a gun or a weapon to defend myself when I came down there. I didn't."

"You locked the door behind you."

"So we could talk and not be interrupted. The basement is safe." She took a deep breath. "Look, I screwed up by drugging you. I know that. I can see why you don't believe me. Maybe you should just go."

"Go? Just like that?" Where the hell was he, anyway? "And go where?"

"Anywhere you want. The door's open." She crossed her arms and hugged herself. "There's a road in a mile or so. You'd probably find it and go wherever you like. Find a phone. Call the Resource. Go on walkabout, even."

He walked back to the door. The latch clicked and he pushed the door open a few inches. He *could* walk out.

"You're not making sense. First, you drag me here. You tell me you're saving my life. Then you let me go."

"I'm not going to keep you here if you want to go. That would just make a bigger mess of this than I already have. I'm sorry." She dropped her head.

He turned, keeping his hand on the latch. He wanted to believe her. "Why not just talk to me in the woods back at the Resource?"

She gritted her teeth. "Lansing was after me. He pulled a gun on me at the end of your training session and threatened to take me prisoner. He blamed me for whatever happened to make your fire go out of control at the docks. I had to escape but I didn't want to leave you there alone. There are things you have to know about how you were raised. Your life depends on it."

"Yeah, that's the third time you've said my life depends on it." He turned back to the door and opened it several more inches. He took a deep breath and smelled sea air. She'd definitely taken him somewhere new, different. The air smelled fresher and cleaner than at the docks. No oil or gas fumes.

"Did you take my power away?"

"Take away what you love most? No."

He shut the door and turned around. If he walked out, he'd never get answers. He could drag her with him back to the Resource and sic the scientists on her. But then Lansing would take over and he'd get Lansing's version of the truth. Plus, Lansing might hurt her. She didn't deserve that if he was wrong. And she needed to explain what she meant by his life being at stake.

"Okay," he said. "We'll talk."

Chapter Eight

It was entirely possible that she'd just lied to Alec. *Again.*

She could have done something to Alec's fire, though she had no idea how. There had been that fleeting moment in the car when it felt like her telepathy had flared. Worse, if she had done it, she had no idea how to *undo* it. Even when the telepathy had worked, all she'd ever been able to do was hear and project thoughts. Nothing like this had ever happened.

She'd taken one step to free Alec, to save his life from both the Resource and the CIA, and she'd made the situation infinitely worse. Alec would rather be dead than without his fire. And he might be dead, if he didn't have the fire and TK to protect himself.

But if she admitted that she might have taken the fire away, Alec would never listen or believe that what she told him about the Resource and Lansing was the truth. He'd go back there in a second.

She looked out the window over the kitchen sink, trying to relax by concentrating on the curtains she'd so carefully chosen last year for Philip. He'd smiled and said the summer flowers reminded him of her. He wouldn't be smiling now. He'd given her explicit orders to let him handle the situation with Alec. Considering how she'd messed this up, she should have followed those orders.

Alec stared out the window beside her. "Where the hell are we, anyway?"

"Maine. We're on a hill overlooking a small harbor."

He slapped a hand down on the counter. "You haven't made sense yet."

"Probably not." But he'd stayed. She had a chance to talk to him.

The closer she stayed to him, the better the chance that she could figure out what happened to his fire. And the longer he was away from the Resource and its director, the better chance he had of seeing the truth.

"What did you mean when you said I needed to know things about how I was raised?" he asked. "Why did you say that you wanted to save my life?"

"I'll answer but not with your hands bleeding all over the place." The cuts had to hurt. She reached up, opened the cabinet and pulled out a first-aid kit.

She could fix his hands quickly. She suspected she didn't have much time to fix anything else. Even if the Resource didn't find them first, Philip would show up. Alec didn't trust her. He certainly wouldn't trust Philip. Philip didn't trust anyone but her. A confrontation could easily turn violent. It seemed all her choices were bad or worse.

"My hands don't hurt," Alec said.

She twisted the top off the bottle of hydrogen peroxide with more force than necessary, spilling some over her hands. "At least let me clean the cuts."

"No. I want answers."

"I'll tell you as I'm treating your hands."

He shoved his hands over the sink. "Fine. So talk and bandage at the same time. Start with the problems about how I was raised."

He flinched when she grasped his wrists but didn't pull away. She poured the peroxide over the cuts and it immediately bubbled up.

"You were raised by Lansing to be a weapon, Alec. That's the way he sees you. That's the role he's given you. Nothing more."

"It's not nothing. F-Team is needed."

"You're not like F-Team. You're more like a sentient weapon that Lansing pulls out at need and locks up when the crisis is over." She pushed his hands under the running water.

"So that's all I am to you? You think I'm just a sort of tricked-out weapon?"

"No." Argh. He didn't want to believe what she was saying so he was not grasping her meaning. "I want you to be treated right. I want you to have a life. That's what I meant by saving your life. It's Lansing that views you as a tool, a weapon."

She turned off the water. Alec glared at her. "Yeah? Where did you get that from?"

"I truly am a psychologist who treats gifted children and young adults." She looked to his face for some sign of softening but he stared out the window at the ocean. "Mentor figures often manipulate their protégés so well that the one being manipulated doesn't notice."

She dried off his hands with paper towels.

"I'd say kidnapping me was manipulation. You did that, not Lansing. He raised me." He stepped back from the sink. "I know him. I don't know you. And you're CIA."

"No, though I've occasionally helped the CIA with a few things."

She dried her own hands, not daring to look at him. They were at a crossroad. Either he would keep listening or he'd walk out right now. He had never seemed so far away. Even that odd connection between them, the one that had produced the fire when he'd kissed her hadn't flared up when she'd washed his cuts. She couldn't feel his power at all.

"I thought with our sessions, that you'd eventually realize the situation on your own and gain independence. But Lansing was watching, contrary to all decency, and he didn't like my influence on you." She put out her palm. "Let me check if there's anything caught in those cuts."

He offered her his hands again. "Yeah, I got that from him. Lansing thought you were a bad influence."

"Do you agree?" She pulled out several splinters from his knuckles and waited on the answer.

He closed his eyes.

"You have soft hands." His voice was lower, quieter. He flinched as she spread antibiotic on the cuts. "Go on."

"After what happened on the docks, Lansing became more distrustful of me. It didn't help that the CIA forced him to allow me back into the Resource. So he pulled a gun on me after your training session."

"If he pulled a gun and didn't use it, he was just playing mind games with you," Alec said. "He does that sometimes. He wasn't serious."

"Even if that's true, listen to what you just said. You just admitted that your authority figure likes to play mind games involving guns with you. This goes back to what I was saying about Lansing viewing you as a weapon, not a human being. That is not the least bit normal."

"I'm *not* normal. I don't want to be."

"But you are human and you deserve to be treated like a person and not a weapon. When do you make your own choices? When do you choose your own life?" She laid a bandage over his hands. "Hold still a minute while I tape them up."

"I do make my own choices. I just happen to agree with Lansing."

"Right." She ripped off several pieces of medical tape. He grunted and pulled his hands back as she finished applying the bandage.

"You're leaving out the part where Lansing showed me how to use my gifts and you took them away."

"I didn't—" She bit down on her tongue. That sounded far too panicky. "I screwed up. I should not have forced you to come with me. But I didn't take your fire."

She straightened her shoulders and waited for his reaction.

"Nice story, counselor. Almost a fairy tale, even. The beautiful princess comes to rescue the gifted boy from a prison and saves him from a life of slavery. They live happily ever after. And it's probably just as phony as those fairy tales." He put both hands on the kitchen counter, bracing himself against it. "What I should do is have the Resource pick us both up and let them sort out the truth."

She wiped her still-wet hands on her jeans to prevent them from shaking. For the first time, she felt intimidated by his physical strength. "Yes, you could do that. Or we could eat and try to sort out what could have happened to your fire."

"I'm not hungry."

He walked through the door and let it slam shut behind him. She watched for a few seconds out the kitchen window to see if he would leave. But he stopped in the middle of the patio and stared at the ocean.

He was thinking about Lansing. He was thinking about his life.

Or, being somewhere new, he was simply too curious to leave yet.

Hands still trembling, she took a platter out of the cabinet and arranged crackers on it, finding calm in organizing them. Her mother had always organized something whenever she'd planned to discuss a serious subject. Beth added fresh grapes, apples and cheese to the plate. Philip must have been here recently if there was fresh fruit. He had planned ahead, as he had by leaving her the car. She poured a pitcher of water, grabbed a couple of plastic glasses, set everything on the platter and carried it to the patio.

There. At least one thing was normal.

Alec stood looking out over the view. She took care to set the plate down with as little noise as possible, not wanting to disturb him. Maybe he found it as compelling as she did or maybe this was the first time he'd seen the ocean like this.

The cottage was perched on a high hill with a soaring view of the jagged cliffs that overlooked an inlet used by the local fishermen. The sounds of the waves echoed up to them. Seagulls cried overhead.

The fall wind blew into the patio, caressing Alec's thick, dark hair. He crossed his arms over his chest, staring, brooding. God, he was so beautiful. And yet she'd dented him, perhaps damaged his very essence. The road to hell was truly paved with good intentions.

"This is not like New Jersey. Maine is northeast, up the coast, right?"

"Yes." She pointed to the food.

He shook his head, his mouth in a grimace. "I'm not hungry."

"You're dehydrated and hungry. I hate to mention it, since I'm the one who administered it, but maybe the drug messed with your system, upset some delicate physical balance that you need for your gift. Drink, eat and maybe part of that balance is restored. It can't hurt and it might help."

He narrowed his eyes at her and slowly took a cracker. She poured water and he drank it down in one gulp. She poured another glass and he did the same, so she poured a third. He picked up an apple and bit into it.

"How'd you get the drug that you used on me?"

"It was left in the car by a CIA contact. I told him no guns, I wouldn't permanently injure anyone. So he left me the syringe." She swallowed hard.

He munched on the apple. "How'd I get in the basement?"

"I carried you."

"You carried *me*?"

"More like dragged you. You were semi-conscious. I would have stayed with you but I went upstairs to get something and made the mistake of sitting down and that's when I feel asleep."

"Leaving me locked inside the basement."

"Leaving you locked safely in the basement in case someone broke into the house. I thought you could get out, if you wanted."

He tossed the apple core on the plate. "Let's assume I believe you. What's your take on how I can get my fire back?"

I wish I knew for certain. She drank more water. "Rest, maybe. You had a very rough time at the docks. You could be suffering from shell shock. Well, they call it post-traumatic stress now. The early term is more direct and accurate."

"So we're back to your hating my being a soldier again." He stood and paced the small patio. "Shell shock. Sounds like bullshit to me."

He'd done this in sessions, argued with her when what he was really doing was chewing over her words. "Think. You've been drugged before and not by me and locked up your whole life and not by me. Think about the people that did that to you. Do you really want to go back? At least take this time to look around at the world. You may never have that chance again."

"Even if I like the waves, the ocean isn't going to help me get my fire back. The Resource is the place that knows about my fire and how it works. They'd help me."

"Oh, sure. They want their weapon in working order and under their control."

He scowled.

To her, power had been a curse. To him, it was his life. What a gulf between them. *Analyze yourself, Beth. Have you been resenting him for it?* Deep breath, deep breath. Just because her power had stayed totally latent for years, it didn't mean his powers would stay latent too. Psychic abilities had to be at least partly based on subconscious desires. Look at how she'd heard Lansing's thoughts when he pulled the gun. Her fear cut through whatever block she had about using her power.

She bet if Alec wanted his fire back, back it would come, once he relaxed.

"What I'm saying is that your power is centered in the mind.

83

Maybe you need balance for it to work."

He uncrossed his arms from his chest. "You figure pacing on this patio will get it back? I don't think so."

Maybe if she wanted him to know normal, she should show it to him. And it would buy time, time for him to think, time for her to figure out how to fix his fire. "I recommend that we do normal things. Grocery shopping. Cooking. Laundry. Walk around the town here. Or go sailing. Surf the internet. Get bored. Read. Anything to relax."

His face went blank, as if she'd spoken a foreign language. "Sailing?" He glanced over at the water, his eyes wider. She'd finally hit a subject that interested him. She held her breath.

He flopped back into his chair.

"It is your *choice*." She dug into her front pocket and offered him the car keys. "Or you could leave, now. I won't hold you."

For some reason, the offer of the keys made him scowl again. He shook his head and she tossed the keys onto the patio table.

"How long would this relaxation program last?"

"That's your choice. Just as I said." She walked back to the table and tried to nibble a cracker but her stomach was lead.

"Daz said maybe I hit a final growth spurt and it threw my fire out of whack." His voice was almost a whisper. "Maybe I scared myself when I lit Gabe on fire. Is that what you mean by trauma?"

"You felt guilty about not only Gabe but about letting Demeter and his cell get away. And you think your fire's out of control. Maybe your subconscious shut it down until you can work that out." *Please, let that be true.*

He poured himself another glass of water. She kept quiet. She'd said and done enough to him. She'd given him plenty to think about already. He looked down at his bandaged hands, raised his head and stared at the bloodstains he'd left on the shoulders of her shirt.

"Okay, I'll stay a day or two." He stood. "But not just because you want me to relax. I don't know what game you're playing, counselor, but I want to find out. People don't always need guns to play mind games." He looked away, back at the ocean.

At his agreement, Alec expected instant action. But Beth insisted on taking a shower before going into town. That's not what happened at the Resource. No one wasted time there. No one left him alone, unwatched, either.

She did look a mess. Not that much of a mess that he hadn't wanted to seize her while she fixed his hands, though. They were alone. No reason not to do what he'd wanted when he left the Resource with her.

No reason, except he didn't trust her.

She showed him to the guest bedroom first, the one painted light blue on the first floor. There was a yellow quilt on the bed and curtains with sunflowers framing the windows, confirming his girly impression. But she opened a drawer in the bureau and pulled out a man's T-shirt and jeans.

"I think these will fit, if you'd like to change," she said. "Your shirt is sweaty and dirty. And there are bloodstains on it."

"Who do these clothes belong to?"

"A friend, the person who owns this place." She turned and left for her shower.

Probably her mysterious CIA contact or a boyfriend. Though she'd never mentioned a boyfriend.

The jeans fit. The shirt was a little tight. At least that meant he had bigger and stronger shoulders than her "friend". Had they done anything on this bed? He ground his teeth. She'd upended his life. He intended to do the same to hers. No way were they going back to this counselor/client business. If she was telling the truth, he had a much different relationship in mind.

He went back into the hallway, out the kitchen door and grabbed the car keys on the patio table. He jingled them in his hand as he walked to the front door. The car was there. He could go, he really could. She'd been telling the truth about that.

Except he couldn't drive.

Lansing's rule. No driving.

Alec had asked a few of the Resource employees to teach him to drive on the sly. No one dared, not even Daz, who wasn't scared of anything. That hadn't seemed strange then. It did now.

Lansing claimed driving was too dangerous. But, of course, not being able to drive prevented him from getting very far if he ran away. That supported Beth's story. In fact, he would have believed her completely if not for what happened to his fire. Lansing had done plenty lately to piss him off.

He looked at the keys in his hand. Driving couldn't be that hard. He could do it. F-Team needed him. Daz had said that Demeter would surface soon with the bomb. He had to be stopped.

Though how to stop the bomb without his fire, Alec had no idea.

If he left this place without Beth, she might disappear before he came back and he'd never get answers from her. He flexed his bandaged hands. What a soft touch, almost feather-light. He wanted those hands a hell of a lot lower on his body.

Who could he trust?

Daz said a soldier only knew what he could accomplish when he was completely on his own. Time to find out what he was made of.

He put the keys in the pocket of the jeans and went back inside, poking around. He walked about halfway up the narrow steps that Beth had taken to the second floor and heard a shower running. He retreated. Seeing her naked would be great, but what he really should do was search the rest of the house while she was preoccupied.

He pushed the living room sofa out from the wall, looking for anything unusual, especially signs of wires that led to cameras, but there were only baseboard heaters.

He put the couch back and checked the nature prints on the wall. Nothing behind those. The wall looked clean too, no sign of holes for small cameras. The bookcase was too heavy to move but the floor around it seemed clean. He pulled a few books out and flipped the pages. Just books. To be sure, he checked all four shelves, making sure they were books and not hidden cameras or listening devices.

So far as he could tell, then, this little house was what she said it was. He tried to use his TK to tap against the walls for hidden spaces.

Nothing, just that weird empty feeling in his head again.

He heard footsteps and turned. She stood in the hallway, her hair still wet from the shower. The simple blue v-neck T-shirt made her look younger, more attractive and more natural. He fought the desire to find out what kissing her would be like a second time. Lust is fine, Daz would say, but that doesn't mean you have to be stupid about it.

He had to be smart.

"Ready to go?" she said.

"Sure." He followed her out the front door, to the car, thinking of their kiss, wondering if that had been play-acting. He didn't want to believe that.

She opened the driver's side door of the Honda and shook her head. "I'm an idiot."

"What?"

"I forgot the keys. I'll go back around to the patio."

"No need." He pulled them out of the pocket of the jeans and tossed them to her. "You're not a very good spy to leave them lying around."

"I'm not a spy at all." She grabbed for the keys but missed and they bounced into the stone gravel of the driveway. She bent and picked them up, staring at him as she straightened.

"Thank you, Alec."

He shrugged. "Sure. Let's go shopping."

They got into the car. She kept turning to look at him out of the corner of her eye. Hell, this was worse than all the cameras. Those were just silent observers. They didn't pass judgment and he sure didn't find them sexy.

She plugged her iPod into the cassette adapter. The first chords of a quiet, beautiful song flowed from the Accord's crackly speakers. She hummed as she drove, going down a dirt road that he guessed led to a main road. The Honda swayed as its shocks attempted to absorb the potholes. She was mouthing the words to the song.

"Just my imagination...running away with me..."

"That's nice," he said. "It's nothing like the classical music that Lansing likes."

"Or the rap music that you have in your apartment."

He shrugged. "It's what F-Team likes. I've never heard this song before, though. It's a little like hip-hop but more soulful. There are songs like it in some of the movies I've watched."

"This song and others like it were an influence on hip-hop and rap." She tapped her fingers in rhythm.

"What's it called?" She'd never seemed this relaxed before and was treating him more like a person than a client.

"It's called 'Just My Imagination'."

"Trying to tell me something?" he said, voice bland.

She shook her head. "No, no. I just like the song."

"They don't play this in the clubs." Too slow for some of the strip clubs, for sure. There, it was mostly music with indecipherable lyrics and drumbeats. Not that he usually paid attention to the music. And action movies didn't slow down enough to play this quiet song.

"The song's over thirty years old and not the style they'd want in a strip club." She twisted her mouth into a small grin. "Did they ever give you a music course at the Resource?"

"Lansing taught me composers: Beethoven, Mozart, Schubert, some Vivaldi. And opera. I had to learn Italian for that."

"Did you like opera?"

"Italian is an interesting language. And I went to the performances." He'd liked the tux and being out in a crowd for a change. Of course, Lansing always had a pack of guards with them.

"I'm glad you saw opera live, at least. Did Lansing talk about the context in which opera developed?"

"No, he talked about the musical composition and some of the character arcs. Like Carmen. She never changes, even though she ruins lives. Maybe like someone else I know?"

She laughed. "I'm no Latin temptress. And that's a good analysis of Carmen. Did you learn anything else about music?"

"Lansing taught me to play piano."

Beth raised an eyebrow. "Did you like it?"

"Not really. He was good at it. I wasn't. He cut off the lessons when I started using my TK on the keys. He said that wasn't the point."

Beth smiled. "You were trying to get out of the lessons by annoying him."

"Well, yeah. It worked, didn't it?"

He stared out the window at the trees lining the winding road. Pine trees. Forever green, like the ones he'd torched for practice a few years back. He hadn't noticed then how majestic they were.

The song ended and a new one started, a little louder and with more of a back beat.

She turned onto a two-lane road, still heading downhill. No other cars were in sight. The sun beat down, light streaming through the fall foliage, bright reds and yellows. He didn't see any sign of cameras or surveillance in the trees.

"We really are out in the middle of nowhere."

"No, we're someplace where people aren't squished together like ants." Keeping one eye on the road, she reached down and changed the song.

"Hey, I liked that."

"You have good taste. That's Marvin Gaye." She stared straight ahead. "It's a seduction song. It didn't seem appropriate, just now."

He picked up the iPod and began to read the play list. It identified the new song as "We're Having a Party" by someone named Sam Cooke. That sounded like the name of a Beastie Boys song, so he picked it. Unlike the Beastie Boys, this party song was smooth, just like the others on the playlist. "So, it's all in my imagination and we can't have a seduction song but we can have a party?"

She cleared her throat. "There's no secret message in my iPod."

"Ah." He grinned. "Well, you are trying to seduce me, in a way. Seduce me away from all the evil." He lowered his voice. "The evil Resource led by the evil Lansing."

"Not seduce," she said. "Give you information. Teach you about what life should be like."

He shrugged. "I bet seduction is more fun than forced re-education."

"I'm not forcing you. You're here because you agreed."

"And because I want to regain my fire. I didn't agree to it being taken away."

She turned left, from the country lane onto a larger road, one marked with a highway number. He shifted in the passenger seat, holding the iPod up to eye level, continuing to scroll through her playlist. When in doubt, study the opposition. The artists listed included The Temptations, The Four Tops and The Supremes. The album cover shots showed African Americans. Strange names, though no worse than 2-Pac or C-Lo.

"Are these all the same style?"

"It's mostly Motown on that playlist. They were a small studio in a Detroit suburb but they had a unique sound. They were the first all-black record label to really cross over to the white audience."

"Like Eminem crosses over to the black rap audience."

"Exactly."

A McDonald's arch came into focus. Then another sign, this time for Wal-Mart. Those signs he'd seen before, on the drives to and from the Resource to a meeting or even on the way to the strip clubs.

He looked at her again. The steering wheel was slick with sweat from her hands.

"This doesn't look much different from New Jersey to me."

She nodded. "We're on the outskirts of the actual town center. Unfortunately, money is tight for most people here. The chain stores have better prices. To stay vital, the center of town has turned into the quaint tourist place that most visitors expect from Maine. But the stores there are too expensive for the locals."

"You make it sound grim."

"This is happening to small towns all over. Sometimes I'm convinced it's as much a threat to America in the long run as the terrorists you fight."

"I'm shaking in my boots at the thought of McDonald's conquering the world," he said with a grin. "Though it is kinda scary to think of that strange Ronald clown running the county."

"When did you go to McDonalds?"

"After the strip clubs. The drive-thru windows are open all night. Great fries and apple pies, even if they do burn your mouth. It's a nice change from the dinners that Lansing serves me. You need like a whole drawer of silverware for those."

"No doubt." She sighed. "You should tell Lansing that you want a course in economics and world trade if you decide to go back."

He rolled his eyes.

"Really. It might give you an understanding of the motivations of the rest of the world."

"Motivations aren't my job. Winning is."

"How do you know what's part of your job if you don't have all the information? Don't you want to know what conditions created people like Hans Ulrich and Demeter?"

"Why would I want to know that?"

"If you learn under what conditions people choose to be terrorists, you can change the conditions before they become terrorists."

"That sounds farfetched. How the hell can you tell who's going to turn out to be a terrorist and who won't? You can't know that. You just have to fight them and stop them."

"That's what you've been told. How do you know if it's true if you lack the information to judge?"

They stopped at a red light. The car ahead of them ran the light and barely missed being sideswiped. He winced. When the light turned green, she turned into the nearly full parking lot. "You can have control over your life. Why give it up to someone else?"

"If I spent all my time researching, I wouldn't have time to do what I've been trained to do." He stared out the window.

"Exactly. It's easier for Richard Lansing to keep you in ignorance because then you won't question orders. You were trained as the weapon. You're so much more than that. You can take charge."

"Lansing does just fine in charge."

"Mmm..."

He bit the side of his tongue with his teeth, going back over his words. No wonder she'd kept silent, with him just admitting he'd rather have Lansing run his life than try to sort it out himself. Lansing had good reasons for being in charge. At least, he'd *thought* Lansing had good reasons.

She cursed under her breath as she started to turn into what looked like an empty parking spot and saw it was blocked by shopping carts.

"Urban warfare?"

She snorted. "Unfortunately." She went onto the next row, tapping her fingers on the steering wheel. She wasn't even close to his in-control counselor, more of a nervous mess. Maybe she was what she said she was and he didn't want to believe her because that would mean everything Lansing had ever told him—every word of praise or comfort, even Lansing's gruff affection—it was all smoke and mirrors, all illusion to get him to use his powers in whatever way Lansing wanted.

If Beth was right, everyone at the Resource viewed him just as a freak, a weapon to be used and not a person. Did F-Team think that way? Daz was supposed to be his friend. Was that a lie too?

She pulled the Honda into an empty slot, far from the front door. He unbuckled his seatbelt.

"So far, this doesn't seem like it will help get my fire back. Not very relaxing."

She nodded. "It's a distraction, I suppose. And we do need some things, including food, to get your metabolism back on track."

"Can I drive on the way home?"

"Sure." She tossed him the keys. He caught them in midair.

No hesitation, no nothing. She didn't know. She really didn't know. "I, uh, you'll have to give me directions."

"It's an easy enough drive back, just a few turns."

He curled his fingers around the keys, digging them into his palm, feeling his face blush red. Damn. "I meant, I need you to tell me how to drive."

"You don't *know*?"

He shook his head, angry, but not at her.

"They didn't teach you to drive? Those—" She took a deep breath. "I'll teach you. Promise."

"Excellent." He tossed the keys into the air and caught them again. The world suddenly seemed much, much bigger.

Chapter Nine

"Driving is easy," Alec said. "I'm better than anyone in F-Team at the NASCAR game."

Beth rolled her eyes. "Except in real driving, you can't click the reset button. C'mon, Earnhardt. Let's get some food."

He followed at her heels as she negotiated the parking lot. She moved gracefully, light on her feet, but navigating all the cars and people reminded him of a military obstacle course. Some of the drivers paid no attention to those walking, even to the little kids with their parents. He glanced up at the big Wal-Mart sign. He'd seen them all over the place but had never been inside. There had been no reason. Anything he wanted, the Resource supplied.

Except the freedom to go inside Wal-Mart if he wanted.

They walked through the automatic doors. He blinked and stopped.

So. Much. Stuff.

Food. Clothes. Jewelry. Electronics way in the back. Signs to the right that said "home goods" and "garden tools". People bustled around, barely avoiding other shoppers. The women were too focused on shopping or keeping track of their kids to pay attention to anyone else. The men were mostly alone, intent on whatever they wanted.

Oddly, despite all the stuff here, no one seemed that happy, except an old woman wearing a Wal-Mart nametag and a smiley face button. She said, "Hello, welcome to Wal-Mart." He nodded back. She looked so frail, as if any movement would topple her.

They walked past her and Beth pulled a shopping cart out from a row.

"Why is that old woman working here?" he whispered. "Isn't someone taking care of her?"

Beth shrugged. "Maybe she needs the money. Maybe she likes working. Not everyone has the Resource to provide them with every material want."

"They didn't get me a car."

"That's hardly necessary to everyday survival."

"Says you."

He looked up and down the middle aisle and scanned for all the exit and entry points. No visible ones in the back or the sides. Video cams were placed above the front doors but they were cheapie cameras. Not very effective. They'd be easy to get around.

He looked up. Fire-resistant suspended ceiling and sprinklers. It wouldn't be that easy to burn. He might even have to start with melting shut the pipes that fed the sprinklers. After that, the paper would go up quick. And he bet there were flammables in those areas marked garden supplies and hardware. How much time before it was rubble? He'd never flamed something this big. He'd start small, with little fires in several areas and grow them, rather than trying to hit everything at once. It had worked with the small piece of skin on the sniper, thought it failed earlier with the table.

"Alec."

He blinked. "What?"

"You're doing recon, aren't you?"

He shrugged. "You said that you locked me in the basement to keep me safe in case someone was after me. I figured I'd better be alert for any threats."

He lied because he didn't want her to know that he'd been casing the place instinctively. She'd see that as more evidence of his being conditioned as a weapon.

She looked over her shoulder, eyes wide. "I should have thought of that. Did you see anyone?"

She'd bought his lie. Excellent. "No." But he'd be on watch now, since she seemed so alarmed. "So what are we buying?"

She pointed to the back of the store. "First, music, then DVDs and a bunch of food that's very bad for you."

And he could pick them himself. Anything he wanted.

"Are we buying M&Ms?"

"Sure."

"Do they have cognac or port?"

"Cognac?" She frowned.

"Lansing serves it after we have dinner. It's good."

"Even if Wal-Mart carried alcohol, you wouldn't find cognac here. I think I saw beer in the fridge at the cottage, if that helps."

He wrinkled his nose. "Beer's okay if it's not watery. What brand is it?"

"A local brand, I think."

"You didn't buy it? Then your mysterious *friend* did."

"It's his house."

She set off down the aisle. So much for getting the full story from her. He followed, craning his neck to see up on the high shelves. She was taking the long way around to show him the entire store. He should be annoyed that she was leading him by the nose but he wanted to see it all: the people, everything in stock and the layout. When he spotted the back exit, he felt better, less trapped.

He heard the distinct thud of army boots coming around the next aisle and tensed. Instinctively, he tried to use his TK to reach ahead of him but felt no sign of his power, just the empty feeling in his head again.

His hands closed into fists. He needed a weapon. That big bottle marked "Tide" looked promising. Nice and heavy. He reached out and closed his bandaged fist around it, ready to attack.

A young man in an army uniform holding a baby turned into the aisle, followed by a woman leading a toddler.

Alec snatched his hand back from the bottle and ducked his head. Beth was right. He was on a hair trigger. He'd been reacting like a weapon, not a person. If his fire had been active, he might have torched the guy. His stomach twisted. Even if he wanted to leave the Resource, even if Beth was telling the truth, where did he belong? All he knew how to do was fight.

"Ever watch *24*?" Beth held up a DVD box set. The cover showed a determined man holding a gun, with explosions and a sexy woman in the background.

"Jack Bauer, right? I heard Gabe mention it. He thinks the tech stuff in it is very, um, stupid."

"It's a fantasy version of what CIA does," she said. "You might like it. Lots of explosions, fighting and bad guys." She tossed it in the shopping cart.

To needle her, he picked up a DVD with a photo of an unbelievably gorgeous woman with big boobs. *Lara Croft, Tomb Raider.* Excellent!

"That's predictable," she said.

"You said I could pick. And I'm really good at the game." He grabbed a few more titles that looked interesting, wondering if he'd have time to watch them. They had a lot of movies here. He recognized many of the action movies, like Aliens and the Die Hard stuff, but there were other movies, starring a shitload of people he'd never heard of. Who the hell was Meg Ryan? Or Kate Hudson?

None of the documentaries Lansing had made him watch were on the shelves, however. Though some of the movies looked like disaster footage, including earthquakes, volcanoes and shipwrecks. He'd watched a few of those.

They walked to the CD section. He tried not to look surprised at how many different CDs there were. He knew there were all kinds of music from the different songs in movies and video games. It just hadn't hit him exactly how much was out there. There were soundtracks—he recognized *Lord of the Rings* and *My Fair Lady*—rap, jazz like Louis Armstrong, CDs labeled "pop" featuring scantily clad women and covers under "classic rock" that featured men with big hair, and that was just a start. At least he recognized Metallica.

He picked up a few of the classical CDs and noticed the orchestras were ones he'd never heard of. No sense wasting time on those. He found box sets of hits from the 1960s and 1970s, saw that they had some of the same groups as on Beth's iPod, and grabbed them. When in doubt, study the enemy.

She looked at his choices, smiled and headed to the food section. She filled their cart with cookies, chips, soda and chocolate. Eggs and butter came from a glass-front fridge. He'd never heard of most of this food but he bit back questions. He didn't want to look like an idiot.

What he really wanted was stuffed mushrooms or steak with béarnaise sauce but there was nothing like that in the store's fridge.

He knew that soldiers didn't eat the kind of food that Lansing served. F-Team preferred pizza and burgers. He hadn't realized that most people didn't eat like Lansing until their first pizza night.

His stomach rumbled. He should have eaten more at the house. Maybe it was that simple, that he was too depleted to even access his fire. Maybe it would just take him a day or two to recover. Hell of a lot of "maybes".

"Better get more," he said. "I'm hungry."

"Aren't you supposed to avoid junk food?" she said, her voice dry. "Part of training, yes?"

"I'm on vacation."

They lined up to pay. It was like the check-out lines inside McDonalds. She paid cash where Daz had given the cashier a credit card. It added up to much more than he'd thought, especially for a discount store.

The cashier, a woman about his age, winked at him. Startled, he smiled back. As Beth put away the change, the cashier leaned over and whispered to him. "If you ever want anyone full-size, find me."

Not knowing what else to say, he grabbed the bags from the carousel. That's what everyone else seemed to do after they paid. "I didn't realize all this would cost that much," he said to Beth as they walked away.

"Did you ever handle money? Set up a budget?"

He didn't hear any sarcasm in the question, so he answered her. "No."

They walked back to the parking lot and he put the groceries in the back of the Honda. "When do I get to drive?"

"Wait until we get to the dirt road. That way you won't have to worry about other cars."

"That's bullshit."

"Most people learn in an empty lot, not one full of drivers fighting one another for parking spots."

"Remember, I'm not normal."

"You have a special ability to drive perfectly the first time?"

He stared ahead, wondering whether to grab the keys. Then he remembered the near crash at the stoplight just before they'd pulled into Wal-Mart. Driving must not be as easy as it looked.

"Okay, you drive until we get clear."

They settled into the car, and he concentrated on watching her drive. "What's driving feel like?" He had always wanted to ask that but it seemed like a stupid question.

She took him seriously. "It's hard to describe. The movement's the same as being a passenger but more. As the driver, you have the power and the control." The light turned green and the car zipped forward. "At first, it's scary, because you're not sure how much strength to use for the steering and the accelerator. But after practice, it becomes second nature. It's like—"

"Like holding a gun. Squeezing the trigger seems easy but it takes just the right touch and lots of practice."

She nodded. "Just like that. And a car can kill too, if you do it wrong."

"If you do it right?"

She smiled. "It depends on the car and the speed. If it's safe, there's nothing like a fast car and an open road. Pure joy."

"Like my fire. When I let loose, when I don't try to hold it back, it's like I'm flying. Or like I'm falling and knowing I'll never hit bottom and it's all good." He sighed and stared at his bandaged hands. "It feels great. Felt great."

"I don't think driving quite lives up to that." She set her mouth in a grim line. "I'm sorry."

"Not as sorry as I am."

She flushed. From guilt or worry? He let it go and asked a question about stick shifts. This Honda didn't have one; it was an automatic. He kept up the questions until they hit the dirt road leading to her house. Well, her *friend's* house.

He studied the terrain, wondering if the house could be defended from attack. If the Resource found him, would they come up and knock on the front door and ask for him? Like hell they would. They'd treat it like an assault operation.

They'd surround the target before moving in. And, as far as he could tell, they'd have no trouble doing that. The only place to hide might be those woods to the left. The trees ran all the way to the cliff. If you could get across the clearing unseen, it might be good cover.

If the Resource attacked and *if* he didn't decide to go back with them voluntarily. He still had doubts about what Beth had told him. He should call them. He should at least call Daz.

"Will my little cabin hold up to assault?" Her voice was dry, not angry.

"Not even close. You don't care?"

"I never intended to use force to hold you."

If she was telling the truth, Lansing had pulled a gun on her to take her prisoner. Maybe he'd put off calling Daz. Daz reported to Lansing, after all.

She turned off the Honda and left the keys in the ignition. "Your turn."

She got out, gesturing to him. He jumped out, rushed to the driver's side and settled in. He shut the door with a flourish. The steering wheel felt perfect under his hands. He grinned, probably looking like a fool. His palms were sweaty.

"You're really amazing, Alec."

"Why?"

"Because one minute, you're the trained soldier, always on the alert. And the next minute, you have this enthusiasm for learning that's rare, almost singular. I think that makes you as special as your fire."

He blinked, not sure what she meant. "So, you going to get in or what?"

"I didn't know if you wanted me to."

"Sure. I need a witness. And if I screw up, I need back-up."

"See, I was thinking in case of screw-ups, I'd be safer outside the car."

"Hah-hah, 'fraidy cat. Some big, bold kidnapper you are, scared of a driving lesson."

She climbed into the passenger seat and shut the door. "Do your worst." She closed her eyes and relaxed back into the threadbare seat cushion, smiling. "God help me."

"You're gonna pay for that." He turned the key. The engine roared to life. *Success!* "That was easy."

"That was turning a key."

"You're a killjoy, counselor."

"You said you wanted the company. You didn't say you wanted

happy company."

I want your company. He also wanted his fire back. He took a deep breath and located all the controls and displays. "Hey, could you put on some more Motown music?"

"Shouldn't you be concentrating on learning to drive?"

"I like music when I'm training. I learned to first control the fire when listening to Ode to Joy. It was fun. I made the fire dance."

"That must have been incredible to see. But, um, don't make the car dance." She turned on the iPod. In a second, *"Get ready, 'cause here I come"* roared through the speakers.

"Perfect." He looked around. His legs felt cramped. "Why doesn't the seat adjust for me?"

"Because it's a less expensive car and a much older model than you've apparently used before. Pull the bar just under the seat to move it back."

He reached down, found it, and pushed it back until it felt right. He put his foot on the brake. He knew that much from watching Daz and the others. Some cars moved if you didn't apply the brakes, even if you didn't hit the gas pedal.

His heart started beating harder. Not as much as before a mission but as much as it did before a training session.

"Here we go."

He put the Honda in drive, as he'd seen her do. There was suddenly pressure on the brake pedal. A jolt of adrenaline shot through him, all out of proportion to that one small change. He was suddenly glad that she hadn't let him drive in the parking lot. Not that he'd tell her that.

He pressed the gas pedal. The car lurched forward with a jerk and he nearly lost hold of the wheel.

"Too much at once."

"I got that." He gripped the steering wheel tighter. He hated that she could see his nerves. He backed off on the gas, but only a little bit. The ride grew smoother, though this seemed way slower than when she'd been driving.

But he was driving! Hah! He tapped his fingers on the steering wheel, keeping time to the song. He pressed harder on the accelerator. They sped up. She clutched the door handle.

"C'mon, it's not that bad," he said.

"Not yet."

He slowly gained speed, trying to find the right touch that allowed small increases without that jerking movement. He relaxed his grip a little bit and rolled his shoulders to relieve the tension there.

He hit a pothole. The steering wheel pulled hard to the left. The car bounced. He squeezed the steering wheel, vying for control. This was not like a video game.

"The steering is being difficult."

"Not really. You're just not used to it."

"It felt smooth when you drove it."

"I had practice."

The Honda hit another pothole, a bigger one. Startled, he almost lost his grip on the wheel. He slowed, not wanting to do that again. That was not fun.

"Don't bother," she said.

"With what?"

"Going very slow to miss the potholes. We're going uphill, so you want to maintain speed. And the shocks can't get much worse. Just go steady and take the bumps as they come. You'll learn more about the steering that way."

He nodded and added pressure on the pedal. Their speed doubled. Beth winced.

"Hey, have faith. Watch this." He pressed harder. The Honda responded with a burst of speed, pushing his body back into the seat.

He glanced over at her. Her face had gone pale. He'd scared her, a little.

Okay, this *was* fun.

It was very like squeezing the trigger of a gun. Both required slow and steady movements. Too fast, and a jerk. Too slow, and the car didn't move enough. As for steering, the car went the way he pointed it but the movements were wider and more out of control than in the video games. It took more finesse and patience.

He could so get used to this.

Except he was running out of road. The house looked close.

"Hit the brake," she said.

He stomped on it. They bounced forward, and the seat belt

tightened to keep him in place. He swore and eased off on the brake.

"Apply it more gradually next time."

"I figured that out."

He took his foot off the brake, hit the gas again, slower, and rolled to the end of the driveway. This time, he tapped the brakes. They stopped, nice and easy.

He leaned back, grinning. Sweat was running down his back. He couldn't have driven more than a few hundred yards. It felt like he'd been in a real NASCAR race. This was nothing like the video game. It was better.

"Put the car in park, put the emergency brake on, turn off the ignition and take out the key."

He moved the stick to park. "So, where's the emergency brake?"

She tapped the lever between the seats. "Press the button and pull it up."

He did and was greeted with a grinding noise. "Is it supposed to do that?"

"Yes."

"Okay." He turned the ignition and took out the keys. The engine died.

He got out of the car, tossed the keys in the air and caught them again. Probably dancing was overdoing it.

"Next time," he said when she climbed out, "we go faster."

He was certain that he wanted there to be a next time, and not just with the car.

Chapter Ten

Beth opened the trunk to get the bags. "You really didn't see anyone that alarmed you in Wal-Mart?"

"No. But you're right, Lansing will come looking for me. Hell, I should call him except that I'm useless in a fight right now. Even if they find Demeter, I can't do a damn thing about it." He picked up several bags from the trunk. "If you're worried that I'm going to do something behind your back, you could always lock yourself in the basement or call your mysterious CIA friend to watch over you."

She turned, her face lost in shadow in the twilight, her hands full of grocery bags.

"It's not that I don't want to tell you about my friend. It's that I can't break a confidence. But he's not an enemy, Alec."

"Is this guy your boyfriend?"

She opened the door, the bags still in her hand. "No, he's my foster father."

"Ah." Good. Wait. "Your foster father is a CIA agent?"

"It's a long story."

"We have peace and quiet and time."

She opened the front door. "That's all I can tell you. Anything else would endanger him."

A CIA foster father. Huh. It did explain why she had CIA connections, perhaps why she'd been approved by the CIA to go into the Resource.

But it also meant that she still hadn't told him everything.

She put the food away in the cabinets. The sea breeze blew through the open window, bringing the sound of surf against rock.

He'd never heard that exact sound before, never knew it existed.

She tapped him on the shoulder. "Want to help cook?"

Cook?

She pointed to a cartoon of eggs and a gallon of milk on the counter.

"Okay."

She gathered a glass bowl, a fork and a pan from underneath the stove. He peered over her shoulder as she turned the burner knobs. How did you cook eggs if you weren't a fire starter? At medium heat, apparently.

"I'm guessing you haven't spent much time in the kitchen."

"Lansing has a kitchen in his penthouse, where I lived until I was eleven. But a cook prepared all the food. I wasn't allowed anywhere near it."

"Bet you snuck food anyway."

Alec frowned. "No. That would have been very bad manners."

"Ah." She broke an egg open, neatly dropping the runny yolk and white into the bowl. She threw the broken shell into the garbage under the sink.

"Why are you breaking the yolks?"

"How do you usually cook them?"

"I don't cook them. But I usually get them served poached on English muffins with sauce."

"You usually have eggs Benedict?"

"Sure, especially when I have brunch with Lansing."

"This is going to be a lot less formal than a dinner with Lansing."

"You mean like with F-Team. They use the microwaves in the rec room a lot. Sometimes I cook eggs for them in my hands."

"Really?" She put down the egg she'd been holding and gave him her full attention. "How long does it take to cook one in your hand?"

"About one minute. I don't have to make the fire that hot either. But you can't eat it right away because it has to cool. I burned my mouth the first time."

"It takes practice this way too. Here." She handed him an egg. "Break it and add it to the bowl."

"No problem." He knocked the egg against the side of the glass bowl, trying to imitate what she'd done. Instead, the eggshell shattered and the goo oozed all over his hand.

"Ick!"

She turned her head but it didn't hide her smile.

"If you think it's funny, here, have some." He grinned and slapped the remains of the egg all over her shirt.

"Gah!" She jumped back.

He shrugged and tried not to laugh. She pulled a shell fragment from her shirt and tossed it at him. He ducked, caught the shell fragment and threw it back at her. It hit her smack on the nose and she went cross-eyed just for a second, trying to find it. He laughed.

"I win." Damn, she looked cute all mussed up.

She strode to the sink. Figuring she wanted to clean up, he stepped away. She took the water nozzle from the sink, aimed it at him and fired.

"Hey!" He put up his hands to protect his face from the spray of cold water. Squinting, he stepped forward and tried to wrestle the nozzle from her. But she held on tight and the water sprayed all over both of them. He spat water out of his mouth, let go, and turned it off at the sink.

They stood there for a few seconds, staring at each other, water dripping from them to the floor. His wet hair hung in his eyes.

"Well," she said, "this is not getting us food."

"We have cookies."

She laughed. Her shirt, wet with egg and water, was plastered to her body. The shirt and bra were both thin material and now sheer because of the water. He could see her nipples. He was hard in an instant.

She kidnapped you, remember? Her foster father is a CIA spook, remember?

But she has such cute nipples!

She looked down at her shirt and noticed what he'd noticed. She flushed. "I need to change. I'll be right back."

"I'll be here," he called after her.

He used paper towels to wipe up the floor but his shirt was soaked, so he took it off and tossed it over one of the chairs.

F-Team took him out to clubs every now and then. The girls there had been impressed with his chest. He grinned. They had been impressed enough to show him how much they liked it. He must look pretty good to regular girls too, even with clothes on, or else the Wal-Mart cashier wouldn't have hit on him.

He peeled off the bandages on his hands because they were soaked too. The cuts looked a lot less angry now. He flexed the fingers. No pain, either. Good.

"Are they better?"

Her dark hair, like his, was still damp. She'd put on a sweatshirt, hiding those nipples. *Damn.*

"Yep." Hell, he felt better. And that weird feeling inside his head seemed almost gone.

"I'll get you a new shirt." Her glance slid away from his bare chest.

"Nah, I'm fine." Lansing would kill him if he ate dinner without a shirt on. Tough. He wanted Beth to look at him. "It's warm in here anyway."

She dropped her head and shrugged. "Suit yourself." She walked past him to wipe up the small bits of shell still on the countertop. "Well, it's a good thing we're having scrambled eggs."

"Scrambled seems appropriate for us." He leaned on the counter to look into her face.

"True." She sidestepped to the right, away from him, and broke several eggs into the bowl. He watched her cook. She was so careful in her motions, very precise about even the stirring. Five clockwise strokes with the fork, five counterclockwise, then five more clockwise and so on, until she was satisfied. She liked order. In that, she was like Lansing.

She poured the eggs in the pan. While she was distracted, he stared at the now empty bowl and the fork. Clenching his jaw, he concentrated on the fork, remembering to breathe in and out, slowly and carefully, just as he'd done when he first learned how to use his TK. When his eyes were almost cross-eyed from staring, the fork shifted about a quarter-inch to the right.

Yes!

He opened his mouth to shout, the elation too great to keep in.

He didn't make a sound.

Beth didn't have to know.

He needed an edge and this was it. Besides, the TK was weak. At full strength, he'd be able to send the thing flying around the room, not slide it around a measly quarter-inch. But Beth had been right. Relaxation worked. She hadn't taken away his fire. It was only a matter of time before full power came back.

She turned to him. "You're quiet. Something wrong?"

"Nope. I'm watching you cook." He took a few steps and peered over her shoulder at the stove. "It smells good, like breakfast at a diner." She smelled good too. He breathed in a honeysuckle scent from her hair. "Beth?"

"Yes?" She flipped the eggs with a spatula, ignoring him, as if he weren't literally breathing down her neck. Well, a little higher than her neck. She was short.

"I never cared about being stuck at the Resource before. Why not?"

"You accepted the world around you. Most people do. And you did care. You love going out with F-Team, for instance. You craved freedom, even though you didn't realize exactly what it was. A fish can't envision life without water until it's on dry land."

"Yeah, but then the fish dies out of water. Are you trying to kill me?"

"I'm trying to *save* you." She shook her head vehemently, as if he'd made a serious accusation. "But I agree, the analogy needs some work."

She scraped the eggs from the pan and divided them between two plates. She put bread in the toaster and picked up the butter from the fridge. He stepped back, watching her move around with that innate grace of hers. She still didn't look directly at him, which said a lot about how much she *wanted* to look at him.

The toast popped up. She buttered it, placed the slices on the plates and put the plates on the table. "Dinner is served." She bowed, like a servant.

"Awesome."

The eggs tasted fluffier than at the Resource. He wondered how she'd done that. Whatever it was, he gulped them down. The bread was whole grain, crunchy with a nutty taste, and was heaped with melted butter. He let it sit on his tongue, wondering why Lansing only liked white bread.

I need to learn to cook.

He grabbed the chocolate chip cookies while she finished her portion. Cookies tended to disappear fast in the rec room. He never got enough. He rolled the cookie crumbs around his tongue before he swallowed. He'd no idea why Lansing sneered at cookies. They were so good.

She ate in small bites, her head mostly down. Her damp hair framed her face and hid her expression. Her table manners were formal except he caught her sneaking a look at his bare chest. He made eye contact and smiled.

She swallowed and looked away. Her face flushed red.

"Hey, I was staring at your breasts. It seems fair that you stare at me." He brushed cookie crumbs off his abs.

Her face turned beet red. She dropped her head. For someone so grown-up, she seemed shy about sex. Or, at least, *talking* about sex. Their kiss hadn't been shy.

He helped her clean the plates after dinner, brushing up against her as they loaded the dishwasher. He closed his hand over a plate at the same time she grabbed it and their fingers met.

She froze.

"If you haven't noticed, counselor, I'm trying to hit on you." He set his hand over hers. That odd tingle he'd felt at their first meeting jolted his arm, all the way up his shoulder, though it wasn't as strong as during the kiss or as steady as it had been on the walk to the Honda when they left the Resource. His erection stirred again. Hell, it had never really left.

She glanced down at his pants and set her mouth in a thin line. "I know you're hitting on me, Alec. But this can't happen." She tried to pull her hand away.

He held it tight.

"You're interested. I know you are." The club girls had never said no. Why should they? Sex felt good.

"It has nothing to do with that." She sighed. "I know, I owe you an explanation. Just please let go of my hand first."

"Fine." He snatched his hand away, scowling. More evasion. Was this another way to control him?

She set the plate in the dishwasher and slammed it shut. He

crossed his arms over his chest, waiting.

She finally looked him in the eye. She had to tilt her head upward to do it. "It's one of the basic rules of therapy not to get in a relationship with your patient. There's too much possibility of manipulation even if the intentions are good. You're just figuring out what you want in life. I want those choices to be yours, not mine."

This again, as if he were a baby. He held up his hand and started ticking off points on his fingers.

"One, I think kidnapping violates the whole spirit of non-manipulation, so you've already blown it."

"I needed to do that to show you a new life."

"So you say. Two—" he took a deep breath, "—I have a mind of my own. Three, if you didn't want to break the rule, you shouldn't have kissed me in the first place."

"You kissed me," she said, her jaw set, determined to oppose him.

"You kissed back. Very well too."

"That was a mistake." Her voice went up an octave. "I'm trying not to repeat it."

He took her by the shoulders. "I know you must have gotten as juiced as I did from the kiss. Hell, I bet you felt something like that just now. Don't give me this bullshit. We're connecting, and it's not like any of the women at the clubs, and I *like* it." He pulled her against him. "Unless this attraction is part of your manipulation or some master plan you haven't told me about."

"No, of course not!"

She put her hand on his chest, right over his heart, trying to keep them several inches apart. If she wanted to chill him out, that was a bad move because her hand felt soft and warm on his skin and only made him want her more.

They were close enough that she must feel his erection.

"You want me, I want you. It's simple." He tightened his grip on her shoulders.

"It's not," she hissed the words through her teeth. "Let me go. Please. I can't."

His mouth hovered over hers. He had her trapped against the counter. He had no doubt she could feel his erection. He kissed her. She didn't respond, didn't open her mouth, didn't tremble and didn't do anything similar to what she'd done the first time they kissed.

She turned her head away.

"Look at me," he said in a low voice.

She did. She took a deep breath, her mouth closed, her jaw clenched. She bent backwards to gain space between them.

She wanted him. He knew it. She knew it. He stared into her eyes, looking for some message in them. She stared back. He could take her right here and she wouldn't be able to stop him. She knew that too. The only power she had was what he gave her. And he was getting sick of letting her call the shots.

She kept eye contact, still challenging him.

He let her go.

She backed away several steps, rubbing her shoulders, taking deep breaths. Her hands were trembling. He supposed it was possible she was right about the whole "counselor/client not getting involved" thing.

His penis disagreed.

His head agreed with his penis, especially now that he knew she hadn't taken his abilities for good. He paced the kitchen. He could grab her again, overpower her, make her understand that whatever was between them was *real*. That would be simple. He'd show her. He stopped and turned to her.

"Alec?"

One word, his name, and he could hear the fear in it. She was *afraid* of him. Not because of his fire but because he'd grabbed her and she couldn't physically stop him.

I'm no rapist.

"You're wrong about us."

"That's possible. But I won't change my mind."

"So now what?"

"Let me show you the computer." She pointed to the living room. "You can surf the internet tonight. There's a whole world out there for you. I won't limit it. Right now, I'm your fantasy. You need reality."

He could look anywhere he wanted on the 'net? He was only allowed to visit preselected sites at the Resource. Lansing had blocked everything else. Beth was trying to distract him from what was going on between them.

She'd picked a damn good distraction.

He sighed and rolled his shoulders to ease the tension out of them. "Let me see the computer."

It was in the roll-top desk in the living room. She got him online and backed out of the room.

"You're leaving me alone?"

"You want me, Alec, but you don't trust me and you're smart not to. Research on your own. Learn to trust your instincts and think for yourself."

"I am thinking for myself. I want you and you're stopping it cold."

"That's my choice," she said.

"It's a stupid choice."

"That happens, sometimes."

"It feels like you're making a stupid choice for both of us." She might still be setting him up for something. He ran his fingers along the edge of the monitor, looking for a hidden webcam. He didn't find one.

"There are no cameras here," she said, as if reading his mind. "Good night, Alec."

"Okay." He swallowed, staring at the screen as she left the room. *There's the entire internet out there!* Hey, maybe he could find porn. At least that would ease his frustration.

A breeze came through the window, bringing the smell of the sea. He was right about their connection, therapist rules be damned. Something was going on and he bet it was related to his TK and his fire. Whatever it was, it had made her lose control once. All he had to do was find the right moment for it to happen again, and then she'd change her mind.

Then she'd see that he was perfectly capable of making his own choices.

Chapter Eleven

"What's up this morning?" Alec asked at breakfast. "More shopping?" He popped a little chocolate donut into his mouth.

"I think one chain store is enough. First, we'll get a breakfast that includes things other than donuts and then maybe a walk."

She poured a glass of orange juice for him. Alec looked more relaxed than yesterday. He'd let his hair fall naturally around his face rather than trying to tame it, though those circles under his eyes told her he hadn't slept much. She remembered when her life had changed irrevocably after her mother's death. She'd been a prisoner for some time before Philip's rescue. It had, quite frankly, sucked, and she hadn't been properly functional for months. Philip had had patience with her meltdowns and her fears. Now it was time to pay that forward.

Alec was in better shape than she had been. He was an adult—that helped—and he wasn't in mourning for someone close to him. Still, he'd been kidnapped, told his entire life was a lie and forced to confront some awful truths. She'd have curled up in the fetal position. Alec, however, had approached it all with an optimism that seemed heroic, not to mention getting enjoyment from the little chocolate donuts.

He was far stronger than she would ever be. And, though it was petty, she couldn't help admiring the way he filled out his T-shirt.

"Anything new with your fire or TK?"

He ate another donut and looked at the ceiling. "Nope."

Damn. "How did you like the internet?"

"It's a bit overwhelming."

"Find anything out about me?" She put the carton back in the fridge. If he was smart, and she knew he was, the first thing he should have done was run a search on her.

"That'd be telling, counselor." He washed down the donut with the juice. "I thought of looking up the Resource."

Oh, shit. For all she knew, the Resource tracked all the searches about it, which could lead them straight here. *I should have thought of that last night.* But she'd been too rattled and off-balance after his kiss. "Did you look them up?"

"Nope. I wanted to learn something new, not read about something I already know."

She let out a deep breath. One bullet dodged. "What else did you look for?"

He flipped one of the chairs around so he could rest his arms on the back of it. "Did you know this house doesn't exist on any maps?"

A loaded question. "I'm not surprised."

"Because it belongs to a CIA agent?"

"Because it doesn't have a residential address. All the mail goes to a post office box."

"That makes a difference?"

"It does for internet search engines." Would he buy that? Google Earth could probably find this place and it had to be on the tax rolls, unless Philip had done something funky there, which was entirely possible.

She poured brewed tea from a teapot decorated with lilacs into a matching cup. Morning tea usually relaxed her. This morning, she'd need several pots to even approach relaxed. Hell, she needed to spike it.

"I think it's more likely that your foster father hid this place." Alec jumped to his feet.

She flinched, flashing back to the memory of how he'd grabbed her last night. The teacup slipped out of her hand, headed for the floor. "Dammit!"

The cup stopped an inch from the floor, safe, hanging in midair.

"Alec?" she asked, swallowing, looking at him.

He knelt very carefully in front of the teacup, his mouth taut in concentration. The cup settled quietly on the floor, intact.

Alec let out a deep breath and stared at the cup again, frowning.

He must be trying to lift it up. Beth counted the seconds, trying to disappear into the woodwork so as not to disturb him. Thirty seconds passed, though it seemed much longer. The cup didn't move. He stood up with a sigh of disgust.

"Weak. Too damn weak."

She reached down, picked up the cup and set it on the counter. Why wasn't he more excited?

"Alec, your TK worked. It worked!" *Thank God.*

"Only for a second." He slapped an open hand on the counter. "Damn."

"But it worked. You saw."

"No, it didn't, not really."

"You saved my teacup. You grabbed it in midair."

"It's a cheap trick. It was all instinct. I'm back to where I was when I was five." He turned away, rubbing the back of his neck.

But it *had* worked, if only for a moment. Not a simple push of something either, he'd been able to move fast enough to save the cup from shattering. She hadn't damaged him beyond repair. He would get his gifts back. This wasn't her fault.

Her heart felt immeasurably lighter.

"Your gifts *are* there, and you can access them if really necessary." She smiled, almost giddy with relief. "And, thank you. That was my favorite teacup."

"You're welcome, I guess." He stared at the teacup. "So when do you think the full control will be back?"

"We don't have any parameters, so I can't say for sure. But it couldn't hurt to repeat yesterday."

"I want to practice driving. And I want to see the beach."

"Yes, all that, but breakfast first. You'll get a chance to see the town too. We'll do as much as we can today. We might not get another chance."

"Because you think the Resource will find us?"

"Soon, yes."

"And that scares you?"

"Of course it does."

Yesterday, she would have insisted that he run, that he had to go with her. But after last night, she wasn't certain any longer that she had any moral high ground. The Resource had manipulated him, she had manipulated him. Hell, she'd kidnapped and drugged him. And she couldn't even tell if he really cared about her or if he had a patient's fixation on her.

Time to let go of the fantasy that she'd save him.

She was no savior, only a scared bumbler. He had to decide what to do next. Unfortunately, considering how he was bound up with F-Team and their work, she bet he'd choose them. At least now, he had truth of how he'd gotten to that point. Once he got his fire back, he could even stand on his own. Perhaps she'd given him the tools he needed to survive.

"You sure it's the Resource that scares you? Or do I scare you?" He stared at her for a long time. "Are you going somewhere on me, counselor?"

There had been a moment when he'd truly scared her last night, though she couldn't tell if she'd been more scared that he was going to kiss her or more scared that she *wanted* him to kiss her.

"I understand you're frustrated." She swallowed. "But I also know that in one day, your TK is back. Another day and your fire might be back. And then you'll be gone, one way or another. Likely, you'll go back to the Resource, to see if there's news about the terrorists that escaped with the bomb."

"Last night, I thought about how I let them get away. I screwed up the mission, you know. I have to fix it."

She nodded. "I know. I should have realized that about you sooner."

"You hate me being a soldier."

"No, I wish you didn't have to be a soldier. There's a difference."

She looked down at the small puddle made by tea that had sloshed from the cup. Once Alec stepped inside the Resource, she couldn't follow. The best she could do was show him his potential aside from being as soldier, as fast as possible.

He stepped closer to her and lifted her chin. She shuddered, feeling that strange vibration between them again, so very powerful. It had taken a lot of willpower to turn it away last night. But it had been the right thing to do.

Her toes curled from his touch. She backed away and reached for a paper towel to clean up the tea. She knelt in front of the spill. He leaned down next to her, hands resting on his knees.

"You really don't want to hold me here, do you? You've been telling me straight."

"Yes." She stood and tossed the dirty towel in the garbage.

They walked to the car. As she drove, he talked. He had a lot of questions and not just about driving. From the roundabout way he approached a few of them, she thought he'd found some internet porn last night. How refreshingly normal.

"Have you dated, Alec?" She doubted it. Lansing wouldn't have let him.

"I wouldn't exactly call it dating. When I turned eighteen, Daz took me out to some clubs and, well, um—"

"I see." And she did. It made perfect sense with his mentions of the strip clubs. Daz had taken his honorary little brother out to get laid, probably on a regular basis. At least his first sex had been a normal enough experience. But it also meant Alec had no experience with relationships. Another thing Lansing had robbed him of.

"Anyway, I was curious about what was on the 'net but some of what I found just confused the hell out of me. For instance, what's 'slash' and why is it so popular?"

Great. He'd found slash. Whatever happened to guys who simply looked up nude photos? "Where did you see the word?"

"I Googled Harry Potter. There were a bunch of hits that came with it."

"I bet." She kept her eyes on the road. "Slash means a homosexual relationship between two characters, usually in fiction, who aren't homosexual in the original work."

"That's sorta what I thought. Lansing believes being gay is bad. Unnatural. Wrong."

"Is that what you believe?"

He shrugged. "Gabe's gay. Nobody on F-Team cares, except for the ribbing he gets at the strip clubs. I don't think they told Lansing, though. But, anyway, Harry Potter isn't gay but they paired him up with guys anyway, like Draco. And Snape. I don't understand why you'd hook up straight characters."

"The number one rule of the internet: if it exists, there is porn of it. How did you end up with the male slash?"

"I was trying to find something on Hermione."

Hermione. Good choice. Alec had taste in his fantasy women. "When did you read Harry Potter?"

"Lansing thought he would be a good role model for me," Alec said. "It was a nice change from the nonfiction that I had to read for two hours a day."

"Find anything else in your 'net search?"

"Lots and lots of girls."

Whew. "No doubt."

"But I found one other weird thing."

"Just one?"

"A reference to furries. What are they?"

Furries? "How the hell did you find that?"

"I followed a link after I was, uh, looking at Halle Berry as Catwoman. F-Team has that movie in the rec room."

Catwoman and Hermione. Not so bad, for fantasies. It could have been a lot weirder, given Alec's isolation. "Furries are people who like to have sex while pretending to be animals. Some wear costumes. Some don't."

"Some of these furries like more than like it. They crave it. I found this long story about how this woman couldn't stand her new boyfriend because he could only get it on if she dressed like a cow."

She laughed, almost missed the next corner, and had to jerk hard on the wheel. When the car was straight again, she glanced at Alec. "Another lesson: Don't discuss furries dressed as cows when driving."

"Gotcha."

He lifted the iPod and picked some Motown. Her shoulders relaxed a little.

"It's impossible to not like this music," he said.

"I know."

"Did you listen to it growing up?"

She put a hand above her eyes to shade out the morning sun. "No. It's well before my time. I found it a few years ago."

"I could really dance to it."

She took the left at the intersection, heading into town. "You can dance?"

"Sure. Lansing said every proper gentleman should learn. First, I learned ballroom, then the Foxtrot, the Charleston and the Tango. And some dances that Lansing said dated from the Victorian age."

"Those group dances that everyone does at once, changing partners all the time?" There was the Victorian age again, the era that was all over Alec's bookshelves. It must have some hold on Lansing.

"Yeah. Lansing was good at them. One time, he pulled all the research techs together and made them dance like that. I think he was a little drunk at the time." Alec tapped his fingers on the dashboard. "Daz taught me some hip-hop. I picked up more in the clubs. Do you dance?"

"No, I never learned." Images of slow dancing with Alec came to mind, with her hugging him as tightly as those jeans. She swallowed down the lump in her throat. That should not happen.

"Why not?"

She blinked, trying to remember what he was referring to. He certainly hadn't read her mind. Ah, he'd asked about dancing. "Good question." They passed the Wal-Mart, heading down the main street. "I never felt comfortable dancing, I guess."

"Then that'll be something I can teach *you*." He sat back in his seat, arms crossed, smug.

"Yes. You can." At least in her dreams.

The buildings closed in on them as the street narrowed and they entered the original downtown, about five blocks of two- and three-story wood and brick buildings. It looked so tiny next to the big box stores and the strip malls. Once, it had probably looked authentic too. Now, it had far too many shops specializing in barely passable antiques or high-end jewelry and clothing. Sadly, the locals shopped at Wal-Mart.

"Kinda claustrophobic, isn't it?" Alec said.

"Most downtowns were built this way, at least in New England." She turned down a narrow alley that opened into a small parking lot. Alec twisted in his seat, trying to see everything at once.

"Aren't these just more stores?"

"Partly." She stepped out of the car. "But we need to eat, then we'll walk to the harbor and anywhere else you want to go."

"Great." He made a complete turn once outside the car, taking in the small bank across the street, the back entrances of a toy store and a jewelry store, and the delivery entrance to a restaurant that wasn't open yet. "Nothing very tall here. What's on the top floors?"

"Either offices or apartments."

"Do all small towns look like this?"

"Most of them in New England do. Some are bigger, some are pretty derelict by now. It's the same basic design, though."

Alec fell into step behind her as she headed for the local bakery. They walked a block, past the closed stores. Alec glanced at the jewelry store. He stopped for a second to look over the antique store.

"That's Queen Anne furniture, right?" he said.

"I think so. I don't know a lot about antiques."

"I'm sure it is. Lansing has a set in his dining room."

"Lansing has upscale taste." Cognac, eggs Benedict, authentic Queen Anne furniture and opera. She wondered what Alec would be like in an upscale setting. He'd picked up F-Team's casual habits, to assimilate better. What had he been like before then? A younger version of Lansing?

She shuddered at the idea.

Alec stopped again to peer into the toy store window, almost pressing his face against the glass. But he didn't say anything so she kept silent until he was ready to go. She suspected he hadn't had many toys as a child. Lansing didn't seem like he would be big on toys. As a father figure, he would have been a distant one, not one to indulge his foster son in play.

The small country bakery had a line stretching out the door. The wooden display case took up one side, and two small, round tables and a refrigerator took up the other. The tables were occupied, one with businessmen in suits and another with a mother and her young son.

"Smells great in here," he said.

She took a deep breath. Fresh bread. "It does."

She watched him watch the crowd, seeing it with his eyes. Mostly, the customers seemed to be on their way to work. Alec seemed particularly interested in the little boy at the table. The boy must have been about four and he kept up a constant, if somewhat incoherent, chatter with his mother while stuffing a blueberry muffin in his mouth. What Alec didn't notice was the two younger women in the line who were checking him out. Beth couldn't blame them. There was the great body, strong shoulders and the gorgeous hair. What was not to like?

"Have you had much experience with kids?" she whispered to Alec.

He shook his head and switched his attention to the bakery case. His gaze settled on the stack of apple turnovers.

"You could try eating something that's not full of sugar," she said.

"Why? I get enough stuff that's good for me at the Resource. I want something new. Anyway, it has fruit."

There was no way to argue with that, so she made no objections. She stuck with a bagel and cream cheese. Not exactly good for her but it would be filling and it was better than donuts.

The girl behind the counter briskly handed over their breakfast, the turnover in a bag and the bagel wrapped in wax paper. As they turned to leave, the little boy knocked into Alec and a bottle of lemonade flew out of the boy's hand.

The bottle froze in midair. So did the lemonade spilling out of it.

Alec grabbed the bottle and the liquid went back inside without spilling a drop.

"Hey," Alec said, staring at the kid. "Be careful."

The boy's mouth fell open in disbelief, exposing his lack of front teeth. Beth froze, having no idea what Alec would do next. She glanced around, checking to see if anyone else had seen Alec's trick, but nobody was staring.

The boy's mother rushed forward, yelling "Kyle!" and the boy hung his head. He walked the two steps to his mother looking so dejected that Beth wanted to hug him. His mom took his hand.

"I'm so sorry," the mom said.

Alec nodded. "It's okay. No problem."

Kyle's mom leaned down and whispered something in the child's ear. He nodded, solemn, his blond hair falling over his messy, blueberry-muffin splattered face.

"Kyle, tell him you're sorry," she said.

Kyle said, "Sorry," still hanging his head.

Alec leaned down so he was eye level with the boy and held out the lemonade. "Hey, no problem. You just startled me."

The boy's voice dropped to a whisper. "How'd you do that trick with the bottle?"

Alec smiled. "Magic."

The boy giggled and took the bottle back.

Alec straightened. Beth stopped holding her breath as she watched the mother and boy retreat out the door. She and Alec followed close behind. When they had walked far enough to be alone, she stepped closer to him.

"Alec, that's twice now that your TK worked!" She controlled the impulse to jump for joy. "And with liquid too. I thought you couldn't grab liquid."

"Sometimes I can grab small amounts." Alec pulled out the apple turnover and started munching. "It's not there yet but it's getting stronger."

"So why aren't you more excited?"

"Because I'm thinking, and because it's not my fire yet," he said. "Where's the harbor?"

That was a pretty clear signal to stop asking questions, so she did. "This way."

They walked a couple of blocks to the closed visitor's center and sat on a bench overlooking the half-circle-shaped harbor. There was no beach here, only a rocky shore that had been exposed by the low tide. Seaweed covered the rocks. Seagulls flew overhead, cawing.

Alec frowned. "This doesn't look like any harbor I've seen in books."

"It's a small harbor and a working one." She pointed to a couple of boats at a pier on the right. "Those are fishing boats, not recreational vessels."

Alec leaned back on the bench. He appeared nonchalant but he glanced right, left and behind him.

"Is someone following?"

He shrugged. "Not that I can tell. It can't hurt to check."

She nodded and tried to relax, respecting his silence. She'd been so focused on Alec that she hadn't realized that she'd blown up her own life with this stunt. If Alec went with her, she'd have to start a new life with a new name. And if he went back willingly to the Resource, she'd have to hide from them.

A new life, a new name, like last time, except now she would leave so much behind. No, she wouldn't think about it. She'd made her choice and that was that. No regrets.

"What you said, you're right." Alec brushed crumbs off his hand. "I have to go back to the Resource and soon. If the TK is working, even by instinct, I can help F-Team. They might be able to handle Demeter and his cell but I'm the only one who has a hope of keeping them from setting off the bomb when we attack."

She bit into her bagel, enjoying the feel of the soft morning wind around her face. "What will your reception be like if you go back? Will you be punished?"

He glanced around, on alert again, as he finished the last of the turnover. "If I have full power back when I return, they won't have the ability to tell me anything." He turned to her. "Come with me."

"What?" She swallowed. "You mean, come to the Resource with you?"

"Yeah."

"Alec, they'd make me a prisoner."

"Still think Lansing will hurt you?"

"He pulled a gun on me. I know he would."

Alec leaned forward and rested his elbows on his thighs. He'd picked a black T-shirt today, along with a pair of weathered jeans. He could have belonged here, could have been one of the fishermen, save for his smooth hands. She also doubted fishermen were this handsome. Very few men were. She finished her bagel. A seagull landed near them. She kicked out and it flew away.

"You paid for everything again. You know, I never have cash, just credit cards. And they're company credit cards. They'd know if I used them, wouldn't they?"

"Definitely, they could track your purchases. That's why I've stuck to cash."

"I never noticed not having cash."

She nodded. Why hadn't she thought to mention this to him before? It would have been the perfect way to show him that Lansing had no intention of letting him run his life. "Money is power and it's one way to control you."

"Anything I ask for, I usually get."

"It's not the same. You should be earning a very high salary. Akin to at least what Daz gets. The Resource pays well. And you should have control over that money."

He tilted his head up at her. "How much does the Resource pay you?"

She named her hourly rate.

"I don't know if that's a lot. That's good?"

"It's a lot. And I'm just an independent contractor. For combat, for what they ask of you, you should be getting twice that, at the very least. Let's put it this way, you should be paid enough to afford a place on your own in New York City or to buy a sports car like Daz."

"Now that's something I'll have to take up with Lansing." His face brightened and he straightened. "So, off to the beach?"

"Let's take a roundabout walk to the car, so you can see more of the town."

She stood and led him past the main drag to a secondary street filled with houses. There was a family—mom, dad, two kids—playing on a swing set in one of the yards, their weathered house looming over them.

"Where's your family?" Alec said.

"My mother died long ago. I only have my foster father."

"Your mother was the one who loved the M&Ms?"

"Yes."

"How old were you when she died?"

"Eight," she said.

"I'm sorry."

"Thank you."

He stuffed his hands into his pockets. They walked past another house, larger than the ones that overlooked the harbor. From the numerous cars in the driveway, she guessed it was a multi-family home. The white paint on the windows and the pale blue on the slats was peeling. This town had seen better days.

On the street, cars zipped by them into the post office parking lot. The day had definitely started.

"What about your real father?" he asked.

"He apparently never wanted to be around," she said. "My foster father *is* my real father."

"I never knew either of my parents," Alec said. "Just Lansing."

"He seems like he would be a demanding parent. Did you give him trouble growing up other than cheating at piano lessons?"

Alec shook his head. "No. Like you said, he can be pretty scary."

And young Alec had probably wanted to please him. That was his nature. He wanted to do the right thing. Beth stuffed her hands into her pockets too. "I know how hard it is to feel all alone, to think of yourself as an orphan. I know the Resource gives you a family of sorts. And I think F-Team really does care about you. That's what makes so hard to rebel. However, most people go through a rebellious phase with their families. You're overdue for yours."

"I seem to be overdue for a lot of things." The houses ended and Alec stared across a large lawn to a long, one-story brick building. "What's that?"

"An elementary school."

"Ah." He stared at the empty playground for a while before moving on.

"So how many good friends do you have?"

She cleared her throat. He sure knew which buttons to push, didn't he? "I have friends that I'm close to, but not as many friends as I'd like, and not as close as I'd like. Studies say that orphans have trouble forming bonds. I guess that's true."

He nodded. "So even if I was raised in the normal world, I might have trouble fitting in?"

She frowned. His mind was so quick. She'd underestimated him again. "I don't know. You were so young when Lansing obtained custody, too young to know what you'd lost, I think. You might have bonded to a new family."

"Maybe. And maybe I would have killed them or myself. My earliest memories are all of fire all around me, uncontrollable. Sometimes it scorches me too. I remember a lot of coughing, a lot of oxygen masks around my face. My first good memory is taking control of the fire and making it all go out."

She stopped. He turned to look at her.

"How old were you, Alec?"

"Four, I think," he said. "Lansing talked me down, that time. There are still some scars low on my back from before I really knew what I was doing. Lansing said I instinctively shielded myself from the fire with the TK but I was so young I forgot about my back."

"That must have hurt a great deal." *Oh, Alec.*

"It was incentive to learn control, that's for damn sure. Lansing gave me ice cream that night for dinner. I liked that."

She glanced at the school. No, that probably wouldn't have been a good place for Alec. "I think you might have a point. As much as I'd like to say you don't."

"Lansing did right by me." He started walking again. "First, I learned to not be a danger to myself. Then I learned how to control it. And none of the Resource techs ever made me feel like they were afraid of me."

She nodded. "Okay, they did all this. But that doesn't give Lansing total control over who you are, any more than any parents are allowed to dictate to adult children what path they should follow in life."

"Hey, isn't that what parents do?" He glanced over at her, watching her face for a reaction.

"No, I think good parents teach you independence, so you can make decisions on your own. They let you make your own mistakes."

"Is your foster father that way?"

She nodded. "I was young and scared. He pushed me out into the world. But I did know if I ever floundered, he'd be there. That helped."

And Philip had never pulled a gun on her friends. *That I know of, anyway.*

Alec stopped again in front of the town's library. He stared at it for a while, glancing from the sign to the library. It had three large floors, plus an attic, all done in a Victorian style that told her that this used to be a home before it became a library.

There was a stately wrap-around porch encased by white railings, like something out of a history book. All it needed was a swing.

Giggling could be heard from the back of the building.

"If I go it alone, leave the Resource, will you be there for me?" Alec asked.

He crossed his arms over his chest, challenging her. She tried hard to reach for her professional poise, elated at the possibility that he might choose to break with the Resource, against all odds.

"Alec," she said, her voice a hoarse whisper, "if you decide to leave the Resource. I will be there to help."

"Whatever I decide? Wherever I go?"

His stare unnerved her. What was he really asking?

"I can't follow you to the Resource. I also can't be your counselor. I've crossed a boundary there and can't go back. But I am your friend. If you want help, all you have to do is ask. I promise."

Her heart felt like a hand held it tight inside her chest. She could barely breathe.

"That's a hell of a promise. Why you made it, I'm not sure. I hope you can keep it." He turned back to the library. The morning sun glinted off his hair, giving it shine. He put up a hand to shade his eyes. "Lansing has a private library. A whole room. He used to read to me in it."

"What books did he read to you?"

"The *Iliad* and the *Odyssey*. Dickens."

"Classics," she said.

"I guess. I had to learn to sit quiet and just listen. Sometimes the suit he made me wear itched."

"You had to wear a suit?"

He shrugged. "Men dress up for dinner and after dinner, Lansing said."

"Not many anymore."

"I found that out from Daz. I haven't worn a suit since. Anyway, Lansing's library is a good size but nothing like this one."

She could almost see his thoughts on his face. Books. Made of paper. Easy to burn.

"Alec."

"What?" He turned to face her.

"The world is not kindling."

His face went blank. "The world looks different to me."

She backed a step away from him. "True."

"I'm going to see what those voices are."

He strode around to the back of the library. She had to struggle to keep pace and almost walked into him when he stopped abruptly under an oak tree. In front of them, there was a gathering of about ten young children seated on blankets on the lawn. She spotted Kyle, curled in his mother's lap.

Beth took a step to the side to see around Alec, having no idea why he found this so interesting. Alec crossed his arms and leaned against the tree trunk. He raised an eyebrow at her, challenging. She shrugged and watched the children with him.

A young librarian with long brunette hair tied back in a ponytail stepped down the back stairs, carrying several picture books in her hands. This must be a children's book hour. Wonderful. What a perfect place for a story. The trees provided shade and privacy but allowed the children to feel less confined. She smiled, remembering how her mother had often read her stories on long summer mornings, both cuddled together on their porch swing.

The librarian opened a book and began to read. Beth couldn't catch the words but when the kids began clapping in rhythm, she knew what it was. "Bingo". They were singing "Bingo". Kyle was a beat late, but he giggled and smiled just the same.

Alec watched Kyle and even tapped his foot to go along with the hand-clapping. She shuddered, thinking of Alec as a little boy, sitting rigid and careful in an uncomfortable suit while Lansing forced him to listen. No *Goodnight Moon* or *Thomas the Tank Engine* or *Little Engine that Could* for Alec.

The kids ended the song with a flourish and a lot of giggles. Alec's face lightened but, in a second, he scowled. He turned away from the story time and began walking back to the street, almost stomping. His mouth was set in a firm line. She wanted to rush to him and hug him, give him all the affection he'd never received when he was Kyle's age. Instead, she clasped her hands behind her back.

"Do all kids know that song?" he said when he reached the street.

"Bingo's very common."

"I never learned any kid songs."

"I'm sorry for that."

"Don't pity me."

His walk grew faster and she struggled to keep up.

"Where's the car?" he said.

"End of the street, turn left, and we'll come to the parking lot the back way."

Chapter Twelve

Alec thought he saw someone duck around the corner of the alley as he waited for Beth to unlock the car. And he could have sworn someone was watching them while they ate breakfast. He'd seen nothing concrete, only a flash out of the corner of his eye—something that shouldn't have been there. It could be either the Resource or the CIA.

I'm not paranoid if someone is really out to get me.

"Let's go to the beach now," he said. "I'll drive."

She shook her head. "You don't have a license. That's a problem if we're stopped."

Cops. Yeah, he wanted to avoid them. He looked around again. Two dark blue vans were parked in the bank lot across the street. If he'd had his TK and fire, he'd have walked over and confronted whoever was inside. But not now. Wait and see, until he knew the right moves, until he was at full power.

"Looking for someone?" she said, her voice trembling just slightly.

The Resource really did scare her. He shrugged. "It's almost automatic, like casing the stores or thinking of books as kindling. Okay, you drive for now."

As they pulled into the street, he watched the vans. They didn't make any move to follow. But he kept a close eye on the rearview mirrors. Beth headed away from the center of town, away from the stores and the traffic. But instead of descending, they seemed to be climbing. The beach should be at the lowest point.

"Sure we're going the right way?" The houses had faded to maybe one or two per mile. Empty fields and small woods took up most of the view.

"It's just a little farther." She turned onto a dirt road that ended in an informal parking lot with a wooden fence as a boundary. It was surrounded by huge trees, with no sign of the beach. No other cars were there.

"This doesn't look like the beach."

"We have to walk from here. There's a path."

He hoped it was a path and not a trap. But he couldn't see why this should be a trap, so he followed her down a narrow dirt trail that wound between exposed rocks and tree roots. It turned left, then right, but it went steadily downhill. The air was full of the scent of pine and the sea, a combination that seemed strange. It was definitely different from the industrial smells of the New Jersey docks. Gulls squawked overhead. That was the same.

The sound of waves breaking grew louder. They must be close.

"How much farther?" He tried to peer through the dense leaves.

"Just around the next turn."

He took ten more steps and the world opened up.

They were at the edge of a small, curved beach. It wasn't like the beaches Daz had talked about, the ones with white sand and crystal blue water.

This beach had sand but it was full of rocks. The biggest one dominated the beach and had to be the largest damn boulder he'd ever seen, about the size of a monster truck. It looked painted with stripes too. Weird.

Beth stepped forward, careful to avoid slipping on the smaller, slimy rocks. She stopped at the boulder and leaned against it. She crossed her arms and looked out into the ocean. For the first time today, she seemed relaxed.

He leaned against the rock next to her, looking at the white-capped waves and the water that seemed to go on forever. There must be boats out there but he couldn't see them. No wonder sailors said that the sea called to them. It offered the promise of something never-ending, adventures just over the horizon.

He'd never known this place existed before today. Never known it *could* exist. He'd seen videos. He'd even visited a geological museum once. They didn't compare to reality.

And he owed this to Beth.

"This is the most amazing thing I've ever seen."

"Well, that's a change, given your gifts are one of the most amazing things that *I've* ever seen."

He grunted and looked more closely at the boulder. He'd been right, it had stripes. They were caused by rock layers, not paint. Gray, yellow, black and some white. He'd read about geological layers. But seeing them out here instead of inside a stuffy museum was different.

"We grow good rocks here in Maine," she said.

He pointed to the different layers. "How did it get here?"

"The glaciers carved it out from wherever it was and dumped it here." She shivered from the cold breeze and hugged herself tighter. "You must have seen some of the outside world. Didn't you train in the wilderness?"

"Yeah, but that wasn't the same. I mean, I knew I was in the woods but I was running tactics and scenarios in my head. The woods were just window dressing. I wish I'd paid more attention."

"More of us should do that. I haven't been down here in ages. After all, it's just sand and rock and waves." She ran her hands over the rock. "Until you see it through fresh eyes."

"I want to get closer to the waves."

She nodded. "I'll wait here."

The sea smell grew stronger as he walked closer to the water. He knelt at the edge of the waves and dipped a hand in. It was cold, far colder than he'd expected, but he held his hand under for a long time before. When it was almost numb, he lifted it out and licked his finger. The water tasted salty and had a fishy smell, like clams or the caviar that Lansing served.

He wandered, picking up rocks colored black or pink and everything in between. All of them were smooth, dumped here by the waves over many years. He examined the broken seashells. He laid out the shells in a row to see how many different kinds there were, wishing he knew all their names. It wasn't until the water lapped at his boots that he realized the tide was moving in.

He felt the cramps in his knees as he stood. A wave splashed over his shells, taking most of them away. A strong gust blew into him and he felt a chill for the first time. He turned and saw Beth huddled against the monster rock, waiting patiently. The wind had blown the long strands of her hair around her face. Somehow, it made her seem more attractive.

He headed back to her, shivering, holding in his hand the one rock that he wanted to keep. It had some sort of green and white swirls through it and had been smoothed by years of exposure.

Beth had settled in a little depression that protected her from the wind. She shivered again. If he had his fire, he could've warmed them both up.

Well, hell, might as well try.

He huddled next to her. "Sorry, I didn't mean to take so long."

"No problem. I should have brought a jacket. I forgot this beach is mostly in shade."

He slipped the rock into his pocket and set his hand against the boulder. He put his other hand around her shoulder. "Here, let me warm you up."

She stiffened. "Alec, I thought we'd been over this—"

"Quiet. I'm concentrating." He closed his eyes, felt her against him, her head barely reaching his upper arms. He thought of his other hand and the giant, ancient rock beneath it. He imagined agitating all the little molecules inside, making them spin, move faster, heat up. Faster, faster.

She gasped. "You're heating up the rock."

"Yep. Warmer now?"

She hugged him, almost jumping for joy. "Then your fire is back! That's fantastic, Alec."

Her last word was torn away by the wind. "Not yet. I can't melt it, just warm it." Though even at his top strength, melting it would've taken a huge effort. Rock was rock. "And I can only warm this small area under my hand."

She put her hand on top of his hand and stopped shivering. "That feels good."

"Yeah."

He bent his head and kissed her.

Whoa.

This time, it was no small jolt of electricity. It was a full-on, powerful electric current that passed from him, to her and back to him again. He felt like he'd plugged them both into a live wire. No, that was too tame. More like they'd been hit by lightning. He couldn't have let go if he wanted, and he definitely didn't want to.

Neither, it seemed, did she.

He pulled her closer, tasted the sea salt on her lips, teased them apart and inhaled her sweet breath, all the time pressing her body closer. She seemed to collapse, as if she could melt into him. He kept kissing her until the connection grew so intense that it drove out everything but her. No wind, no waves crashing closer, no trees. Just her and the sky.

She broke the kiss.

He drew back his head and swallowed hard. She stayed huddled against his chest. The current had died down to a small buzz between them. He suspected it would come back at full strength if he kissed her again. Hell, what would it do if he made love to her?

Let's find out.

"You can't say this is normal, counselor. You had to feel that."

"I did."

Her voice was so low that he almost didn't hear her. She kept her face turned downward.

"Did that hurt you? Are you okay?"

"I think that remains to be seen."

There was enough dry sarcasm in her tone to reassure him. "Screw your theory about client crushes on therapists. This is something different, something way beyond it. It's related to my fire, somehow."

"I think—" she huddled tighter against him, "—I think you're right."

His erection pressed against his jeans. As close as they were, she must feel that and she wasn't moving away like she had last night. He bent down to kiss her again. This time, he wasn't going to stop.

"There's something you should know," she said.

"What?"

"We're the same age."

He pulled back so he could see her face. *"What?"*

"I had to swap schools after my mother died. They did some academic testing and I tested two grades ahead and then they got my age wrong. I never corrected it." She tilted her head to look at him. "I'm twenty-three. Just like you. In fact, I think you're a month older, if the birth date on your records is correct."

He studied her face, looking for any sign that she was teasing. "Well, damn. That means I should be in charge, right?"

"Oh, sure, the birth date changes everything," she said in that dry voice.

"I know something that will." He leaned down to kiss her again.

A seagull swooped down low. Something splashed on the rock, just above his hand. He flinched and snatched his hand off the rock. The heat died. "What the heck?"

She stepped back, though still within the circle of his arms. "It's bird poop. Good thing it didn't hit us."

"Blech."

She laughed. "Yeah."

He looked down at her face. She was trying hard to compose herself. But she couldn't fool him now.

"Let's shift over there, to underneath the ledge up there."

"*Here?*"

"It's perfect." He could almost see lightning jump between them. If his body could have burst into flame, it would have. She put her hands on his face. He let his mouth hover over her lips. "Tell me what you want."

"I want you," she whispered.

"About time." He had to show her, had to convince her how good it could feel between them. He pulled her a few steps to the right, so they were under the overhang.

He kissed her. She wrapped her arms around him. He slid his fingers under her shirt. She quivered. *No guts, no glory.* He reached for her bra. His hand unexpectedly found her bare breast. He closed his eyes, kissing her deeper. And he'd thought it couldn't get hotter.

"No bra?" he said, voice low.

"I'm small, so just the cami."

"It feels perfect." He squeezed softly and rubbed his thumb over her nipple. She moaned and nestled her head into his chest. He pushed her shirt and cami up to her shoulders, bent over and kissed her perfectly formed nipple. She bucked in his arms, making soft little sexy noises.

I have to have her now. But girls liked it better slow. The club girls he'd been with—they'd said most women would like it slow.

But he wanted her right this second.

She put her hand on his jeans, just below his waist, and pressed. She wanted him too.

I'll do slow later.

He pulled off his shirt. She unsnapped his jeans. She ran her hands all over his chest. Small hands, soft touches and fingers that teased the small curls of dark hair all made him nearly out of his mind. He pulled her pants off. In a hurry, she kicked them to the side. She slipped a hand beneath his underwear and took hold of his erection. He tossed off her underwear, barely registering that they were soft silk. All the while, the electric hum between them grew until it was almost ready to explode from him.

He pulled her off her feet, and she wrapped her legs around him, leaving only his boxers between them. Wait, wait, she was supposed to be open and ready and he hadn't done a damn thing for her yet. He had to do something.

TK.

"Hold that pose for one second," he said.

Her chest was heaving. Her nipples rubbed against him. He couldn't hold off for very long. Better make this good. He closed his eyes and buried his head in her shoulder, holding her tight. She was so damned light, it was like holding a feather.

He hadn't done oral before. He'd used his hands, once, but he'd fumbled it in the beginning. The TK would help him do it right.

Alec felt the way down her body with his TK, unable to resist stroking her breasts for a second. She gasped. Her arms tightened around him. His TK went lower, to her stomach. He brushed against soft dark hair just above her legs. She whimpered. Good to know he was doing it right.

With the lightest touch he could muster, he felt his way between her legs until he found the spot. *There.*

"Ahh..." Her legs gripped him tighter. His erection grew almost painful, demanding.

He added more force to his TK caress. She started making louder noises that he couldn't begin to interpret. All he could tell was that she seemed damn happy. Her whole body shivered. She almost jumped out of his arms but he didn't let go of her. She let out a long sigh. She ground her hips against him, almost making him come right there.

"You—" She drew a deep breath and raised her head. "You used your TK to do *that*?"

"It was good, right? It worked?"

"I think 'yes, yes, yes,' is the proper answer."

She let go of him to stand. She pulled down his underwear and grasped his erection. "Now, Alec, before I regain my mind and lose my nerve." Her voice trembled.

He braced himself against the rock and picked her up again.

"Just a little to the left," she said. "Ah, that's—that's it."

"I know." He found the wet, warm opening and pushed inside.

Tight, so tight. So good. He'd come right this second. No, wait until he was all the way in, they had time. Halfway in, he was slowed down by something. He thrust past it.

Argh.

Pain stabbed into him. He blinked, uncertain at first where it had come from. He tilted his head to see her face. She was wincing. She'd dug her fingernails into his chest and drawn blood. That must have been what he felt.

"Beth? What's wrong?" He'd screwed something up, he must have.

"Don't stop, it's okay."

"But you're in pain."

"Perfectly natural. I haven't done this before."

"You're a *virgin*?"

"Not anymore." She sighed and licked his earlobe. "I'm good. Finish it."

He didn't need to be told twice. He thrust again, then harder and harder. The living connection between them grew stronger, enveloped all his skin, made him forget about everything. It felt insanely good, better than when he let his fire go crazy, better than anything.

He came. It was an explosion inside, so overwhelming that it blinded him for a few seconds as the sparks spun around his face. They groaned together. Inside, she gripped him tighter. His orgasm felt doubled, like he felt hers and his own together, almost as if he was also inside her head.

It was so different than the other times. Maybe this was what people meant when they talked about being with someone you really care about, how it would feel different.

Thunder rumbled in the distance. She raised her head. Natural lightning lit up the sky.

"We should go back," she said.

He sighed. "Maybe."

Thunder rumbled again. Not dangerous but he couldn't use TK to keep them dry and still use it on her. Okay, back to someplace warm and with a roof. He lifted her off him and set her down. He noticed a little trickle of blood running down her leg.

"Beth! Are you okay?"

"Fine. Really." She snatched up her panties. He watched her put them on. He hadn't gotten a really good look before.

Perfectly compact body. The breasts weren't small, just in proportion. She looked so delicate, like one of her Japanese teacups with the lilacs and yet she acted anything but fragile.

She tossed his pants at him with a smile. "Get dressed, Alec."

He grinned. "Only until we get back to the house."

She dressed while he pulled his pants back on. He grabbed his T-shirt from the ground and shook out some dirt.

"Alec! Look at the rock."

He put on the T-shirt and turned around.

The rock had melted where he'd pressed his back against it. He reached out to touch it. Completely smooth and still a little warm. He could even see an impression of his bumpy scar, the one at the small of his back.

"Damn."

She put her hand right over the impression of the scar. "Are you hurt?"

"No." But he rolled his shoulders anyway. No pain. "Like I said, you really know how to turn me on, counselor."

Her face went blank for a second. "I see that."

Raindrops started to fall around them. He grabbed her hand. "C'mon, let's get back."

They scrambled up the trail, trying to beat the rain. She followed, her hand tightly grasped around his. He hardly noticed anything around them. All he could focus on was Beth, her hand in his. He started to grow hard again. If it hadn't been for the rain, he would have found a quiet place in the woods where they could make love again, slower this time.

"Hey, Beth?" They took the last turn to the parking lot.

"Yes?"

"How is it that you're, well, I mean, how come I was your first?"

"I've had boyfriends. I know how it works. But—" she took a deep breath and squeezed his hand tighter, "—it never felt right before. I had no idea it would feel like *that*."

"Neither did I. I've never melted rock without thinking, that's for sure."

They stepped into the makeshift parking lot. Everything looked the same. And everything looked different.

"I drive," he said.

She dug the keys out of her pocket and put them in his palm. Her hands were shaking.

"Yes, you drive."

Chapter Thirteen

"You can open your eyes now," he said.

Alec parked in front of Beth's house and took the keys out of the ignition. It hadn't been *that* bad. He thought he'd driven damn well, in fact. Not his fault that he'd had to hit the brakes hard around that turn. "I did fine."

"Since I'm just glad to be alive, I'll agree with you." She stared at the house and showed no signs of moving.

He walked around the car, opened the passenger door, and picked her up out of the seat.

"Alec!"

"I'm driving now, remember? And that was too damn short by the rock. I want more."

He carried her inside the house. She weighed hardly anything in his arms. For someone with such a hold on him, she should weigh more, be more substantial. She cuddled into his shoulder and he caught his breath. He could feel her heart beating so very fast, almost as if it would jump out of her chest.

She snapped her head up abruptly and pushed her hands against his chest. "Alec, stop. Put me down."

He laughed. "Not yet."

"No, I mean it." She frowned and tried to squirm out of his arms.

She looked scared so he set her down. "You okay? What's wrong?" Had he hurt her, despite what she'd said?

"I don't know. I-I think I saw someone or something on the dirt road in."

"Why didn't you mention it then?"

She rubbed her temples. "I don't know. Distracted, I guess. Thought maybe my mind was wandering." She smiled. He smiled back.

She grabbed his forearm. "But I thought I heard something right now too. There could be people hiding outside."

"I would've seen them." Okay, he'd used all his energy to watch the road. He could've missed something. She did seem genuinely scared, which was no good if he wanted to make love to her again. Plus, there were those moments in town when he thought they were being watched. He hadn't noticed anything since but he hadn't exactly been paying attention to anything but her for a long time. He could've missed a tail. If the Resource was out there, he had to make sure they didn't get anywhere near Beth.

"I'll take the car and go check."

"No, it's raining already and about to storm, Alec. I didn't mean—"

"It'll only take a second." He leaned over and kissed her, hard.

She dug her fingers in his shoulder, as if afraid to let go. "Stay here."

"Two seconds."

The sky was almost black now and the rain was falling harder. He backed the car out too fast and hit a pothole, knocking his body sideways into the door. He slapped the steering wheel, turned around and drove down the dirt road at a slow pace. Easy. A quick check and he'd be back with Beth. He fumbled around with his left hand, trying to figure out where the windshield wiper controls were hiding.

Something jumped out of the side of the road, about twenty feet in front of the Honda. Something *big*. He slammed on the brakes and started to skid. Eyes glowed in his headlights.

A moose, a freakin' *moose*.

The car kept sliding on the wet dirt, closer and closer to the moose. Too fast too close, he was going to hit it. His tires threw up rock and dirt behind them.

Damn, moose, move.

His forehead tingled, his eyesight grew dim and his TK practically exploded from him, flinging the moose aside. The Honda skidded to a stop. He looked right, to where he'd flung the moose. The moose swayed, almost fell, and regained its balance. It turned that big head at him, snorted as if to say, "What the hell was that?" and loped off, moving faster than an animal that size had any right to move.

Alec put the car in park and dropped his head, his forehead resting on the sweaty steering wheel. *Okay, so maybe driving isn't so easy.* He slowed his breathing. A TK move that big always left him a little drained.

A TK move that big.

That had been more than a trick. That had been more conscious than melting the rock too. Moving over a thousand pounds had been his limit, especially with something alive that pushed back. That's why he'd had trouble with that sniper. The moose had felt like child's play. The TK had exploded from him with more energy than ever before.

Maybe he was all the way back.

He looked down, grabbed the empty paper bag that had held the apple turnover and concentrated.

Flames exploded from the bag. He coughed from the sudden smoke and put the fire out. He punched the dashboard and raised his fist.

"Yes!"

Relaxation and sex, that was the ticket. Beth really did turn him on.

Wait. The first time that he'd kissed Beth, he'd burned the papers on his table without thinking. He'd shrugged it off as carelessness and distraction at the time. But during the op, his fire had been so powerful that he'd lost control entirely. Daz said he'd hit a new power level.

Maybe Beth had turned him *up*.

Thinking on it, every time that they'd touched these last few days, his gift had come back a little bit. Look at what had happened when they'd made love. He'd melted the rock around him without even noticing.

Now his fire was back.

No wonder it felt special between them. His gifts were sometimes unconscious, Beth said. They reacted to her because he felt so strongly about her.

But if it worked that way, then why had his fire disappeared when she'd kidnapped him? He was missing something. She'd have answers or know the right questions to ask.

He put the car in drive again, his heart pounding, and turned it around, back to the house. The rain fell in buckets now. No one was out here. She'd probably just heard the damn moose.

He drove only a few feet before he slammed on the brakes a second time at an obstacle in the road.

Daz.

In battle gear, holding out his hand in a "stop" gesture. *Fuck.* Alec rolled down the window. It hadn't been his imagination in the parking lot, then. They'd been following him.

"Firefly." Daz walked toward the Honda, blinking away the rain falling over his helmet. "We got a problem. You've been dealing with a telepath."

"What?"

Beth stared out the window, wishing Alec would return right this second. She should've stopped him but her mind seemed stuck in slow gear. She could hardly think through this headache. One minute, she'd been quietly in Alec's arms. The next minute, the voices had practically screamed inside her head.

She sat on the couch and rubbed her temples again. The crazed, insane, wonderful euphoria from making love to Alec had faded completely. Face it. Her telepathy was back. And it was out of control.

She had realized on the drive home that she hadn't screamed out loud when he'd taken her virginity. No, Alec had heard her mental scream. She'd unconsciously hooked them together, mind to mind. His gifts and her telepathy had created some sort of perfect storm. That was the intense connection between them, the lightning, when they touched.

And somehow, his power had flipped the switch on her telepathy too.

She had no idea how to control it or how to even interpret it. She didn't know, for instance, if the voices her telepathy had picked up were nearby or miles away. Alec had run off on what was probably a wild goose chase. If she had any idea how to use the telepathy, she could listen and try to find out, do something useful. But not through this headache.

Yes, good job, counselor, you have a client who's been brainwashed all his life and what did you do for him? First, you break all the rules and make love to him. To top it off, you unconsciously reach out and play inside his head.

Her whole body felt battered, as if Alec had slammed her into that rock. It would feel worse after she told Alec. Whatever his reaction, she'd have to face it. Alec had taught her one thing. Don't run, don't hide. She'd wanted to change Alec's life. Instead, he'd altered hers beyond recognition.

Her stomach rumbled. She ignored it and put her head in her hands and immediately felt dizzy. Her throat felt dry. Hunger, she could ignore. Thirst was harder. If she was dehydrated, that would explain part of the headache. She walked to the kitchen and pulled out the pitcher of water.

"Beth, we have to get the hell out of here. Now."

She closed her eyes and sighed, her hands tightening around the pitcher. "Hello, Philip."

Chapter Fourteen

Alec got out of the car. He extended his TK around him and it immediately bumped into several people, confirming Daz was not alone. Beth had been right. The Resource had sent an armed retrieval team. He sent out more TK feelers and counted twenty soldiers. Their moving around must have been what spooked the moose into the road.

Thanks a lot, Daz.

Daz stopped a few feet from him, illuminated by the headlights of the Honda. He didn't seem bothered by the rain pouring down on him. His gun was holstered at his waist. No sign of a rifle.

Alec crossed his arms over his chest. Because he felt like it, he kept the rain off of him with his TK. He let Daz get soaked.

"So talk, Daz."

"Firefly, you had us scared to death."

"C'mon, you never ran off with a girl before?" The circle of men was tightening around him. If he took them down now, he might miss one. Let them get closer, it'd be easier.

"I've run off with a girl more than once," Daz said. "But that's me, not you. You wouldn't, especially knowing we're waiting for intel on Demeter. I know you want in on catching them after what happened with Jimmy."

"Sure, I do."

"So I don't believe for a second that you forgot about someone who killed a team member and also happens to have a bomb with the power to poison a city."

Given the armed men surrounding Daz, it was not a good time to admit the reason he hadn't gone back was that his fire and TK had been near nil and he'd have been useless. "No, I didn't forget."

"Exactly. She snatched you."

"No." Daz took orders from Lansing. Lansing would say anything to get what he wanted. So Daz could be lying through his teeth and not even know it. "F-Team didn't have to go to this trouble to stop me from having sex. Christ, Daz."

"The assault team's not for you, it's for her. And it's not F-Team."

What? "Who? And, c'mon, they must have come for me."

"It's the Resource storm troopers. Lansing's personal goons."

"Twenty seems overkill for one shrink."

Daz cocked his head. The rain fell sideways off his helmet. "There was concern that you might be under the telepath's control and that you might attack us. She could be controlling you."

"Well, I'm not and she hasn't. She's just a little thing. No threat to anyone."

"She's a telepath and could have made you do all sorts of things and make you think that you *wanted* to do them." Daz stepped closer, studying his face. "How can you be so sure of what you're doing?"

Daz was so close now that it wouldn't be any effort for Alec to keep the rain off him. He didn't bother.

"Let's see, we came to a quiet home to relax, we went shopping, and, oh, she taught me to drive. It's been sheer torture."

"If she's a telepath, she could make you say anything, make you *do* anything. Or remember what didn't happen."

"And you've encountered how many telepaths?"

Daz frowned.

"If you got the info from Lansing, how can you be sure you have the truth?"

"I saw documents. Hell, Beth Nakamora isn't even her birth name. And she's definitely connected to a CIA agent who's so deep into black ops that he's probably gone rogue."

"Documents can be forged."

"Shit, Firefly, she's been with this black ops guy since she was eight. She could be so good that you'd never know she's messing with you and she probably wouldn't even need the telepathy for it."

Alec took a step back. His TK field faltered and the rain lashed at him. Beth had been raised by a CIA agent. She'd admitted that.

"Go on," he said through gritted teeth.

"I know you didn't leave the Resource on your own. No way that you planted the car she used to get away that day. Think, Firefly. Use your head."

"That's what I've been doing. More than at any time in my whole life." The men surrounding them closed in another foot. Alec let go of the rain so he could use the TK to keep track of all of them. One thing to bump them to see if they were there. It took more power to keep his TK on them constantly.

"It's illegal to grab private citizens with a commando team." It had to be against the law.

"She could be a rogue. She could be a player with people we don't even know about. She's not an innocent bystander."

No. This didn't fit Beth. She'd been a virgin, dammit. You don't send a virgin out to seduce someone. Hell, she was the reason he'd left the house. She'd heard something and worried. Why do that if she controlled him?

"Firefly, she lied to you, she kidnapped you. You're better off out of it. Stand aside and let the retrieval team move in."

Alec swept his arms and dumped every single soldier out there on his ass. The curses could even be heard over the thunder.

"She doesn't deserve this. And she's not controlling me."

A soldier stomped up to them, his rifle at the ready. Alec looked closer. A tranq gun. A fucking tranq gun. Never again. He waved a finger and the tranq gun flew out of the soldier's hands and up into a tree.

"Back the fuck off, sergeant." Daz chopped his hand in front of him.

"Commander—" the storm trooper sneered at the rank, "—you ain't in charge here. If he doesn't stand down, then it's up to us." He looked up at the tree. "And he sure as hell isn't standing down."

"And he sure as hell could reduce you to a cinder if you don't shut up," Alec said.

Daz put his hands on Alec's chest and pushed him back several steps. Startled, Alec let him.

"Firefly, stand down. I don't want you hurt."

"Get out of the way, Commander," the sergeant said.

Daz turned and drew his handgun. "You fucking back off, sergeant, or I'll be fighting *with* him, you got that? Take a step back and give me room." He held the gun steady on the soldier.

All right, Daz!

The sergeant backed up, cursing. Daz lowered his gun.

Alec stepped up to Daz.

"Thanks."

"That'll only buy us a few minutes." Daz shook his head. "If she's controlling you, she deserves whatever they're going to do to her. If not—" Daz stepped closer, whispering. "You really okay in there, Firefly?"

Alec tapped his head. "Yeah." He extended the TK to keep the rain off Daz too. The storm swirled around them both now. That should keep anyone from overhearing even if they talked in normal voices. "Daz, you can't let them go in there. She'll be terrified. This is wrong."

"If she's running an op on you, she's fair game."

"You on my side, Daz?"

"Always," Daz said. "But how do I know that you are really you?"

"You know me. You figure it out."

Daz nodded. "It seems like you. Your power seems in damn fine form."

And just in time too. "They plan to grab her no matter what I say."

Daz nodded. "That's why I came, to keep you out of the crossfire. I don't trust them."

Neither do I. Fuck. "I'll talk to her. She'll come out willingly with me." No, she wouldn't. It didn't matter. Stall these guys, get the truth from her. That's all he needed, the truth. Then if they had to fight, they'd fight.

"Negative. No getting in the middle of this. That's what I came here to avoid," Daz said.

"You don't let me go and get the truth from her, I'm going to fight. Now."

"Shit."

"We'll come out together." Yeah, that made sense. If Beth came quietly, there would be no chance she'd get hurt. He'd keep her close, protect her. He wouldn't let them be separated.

Unless she'd done what Daz said.

"You'd get her to come out without a fight?" Daz asked.

"Yep. Give me thirty minutes to talk her into it."

"Thirty minutes?" Daz lowered his voice to a hoarse whisper. "I don't know if I can stall them that long."

"Try, Daz. Please."

Daz nodded. "I can't promise. I'll try. Make it quick."

Alec nodded. "Thanks."

Daz smacked his shoulder. "As long as you're not under the shrink's control, you're team. We stick together. I told you that. Now get in the car and get moving before they realize what's going on."

Alec rushed to the car, mixing dirt with the rain and covering his movements. He shut the door quietly.

Daz stepped out of the road. He signaled to the sergeant who came stomping up to him. Alec put the car in gear and zipped forward. He gripped the wheel tight, expecting any moment to be shot at, but nothing happened.

Daz had bought him some time. He'd better make damn good use of it.

A telepath. That could explain a hell of a lot about Beth. And about why his power went crazy around her, like the melted rock.

Alec lost control on the slippery road and practically slid into the driveway. Rain battered down on the car. He had no idea what to say to Beth to convince her to go with him. Hell, she should be the one talking. Her story had a lot of gaps. If he found out she'd controlled him, he'd feed her to the Resource himself.

He saw a light around the back of the house, near the patio. The kitchen. He ran around the back, to check if the soldiers had gotten back there. Empty. He could try to take Beth out this way, down the hills and into the woods. There was a lot of clear ground, no cover, before the woods, though. It'd be easier to surrender and wait for a better opportunity.

Alec froze when he heard an unfamiliar male voice coming from inside the house. He crept up to the back door. The storm should muffle his footsteps. The man was talking to Beth. She sounded firm, decisive and seriously pissed. The man had a quieter voice, low and dangerous, like Lansing. *Shit.* They'd already gotten to Beth. Daz had either lied or not known about this. Alec crouched low, his finger on the door handle. The voices grew clearer.

"Do you have any idea of the danger that you've put yourself in? We have to go, now."

That didn't sound like the man worked for the Resource.

"I'm not leaving without Alec."

Thanks, counselor.

"The boy's already with them. He's made his choice."

"He's not a boy."

Alec wiped rain off his face. Who the hell was this guy?

"It doesn't matter. Forget him. We're leaving."

"I won't abandon Alec."

Alec swallowed. That didn't sound like she'd been using him or controlling him. It sounded like she cared about him.

"He's *abandoned* you."

"Let go of my arm."

That was enough.

Alec slammed through the door. The man and Beth broke apart. The man aimed a handgun at him. Alec flicked his wrist, casually knocking the gun out of the man's hand.

"Alec!" Beth said.

The man started to rush him. Alec smacked him into the wall. The man grimaced and fell to his knees but said nothing. He didn't even groan.

"Stay back from her," Alec said. "If you don't, I'll burn you alive."

"No, don't!" Beth said, her voice hoarse. "Alec, you can't."

"You all right, Beth?"

He kept staring at the intruder. The man stared back at him, not blinking, showing nothing in his face. His hair and eyebrows were gray but he didn't look old or frail or scared of being burned to death. This man had seen combat.

"I'll be fine if you stand down," Beth said. "Let him go."

"Let him go?"

She stepped between them, her arms wide. "Alec, this is Philip Drake. My father."

Her father!? "The black ops CIA agent who had you set me up?"

"If I'd set you up, you'd be dead," Drake said. "And we really don't

148

have time for this, not with the assault team outside. Unless you intend to do their work for them."

"You threatened her," Alec said.

"I grabbed her to get her out of here. And you're delaying her escape."

"No, I didn't—I came back to talk to Beth." Alec took a deep breath. "I need to know. Are you a telepath?"

Her face went pale. "I used to be. Not anymore, not until—"

"Until we kissed." Yes! Their powers were affecting each other. That's why his gift had jumped up a level so fast.

"That's all very nice." Philip scowled. "Sort it out when there aren't armed men surrounding my house."

Alec ignored him. He focused on Beth. "I got them to delay an assault. I need to talk to you."

"Alec, you'd—" She looked frantically toward the window, her eyes wide. "You'd give me to them?"

"No, I'm keeping them back right now. But I want answers."

She looked over at Drake, then back to him.

"Answers, okay." She sighed.

Drake cut in. "You want answers? She was a telepathic kid. A rogue eugenics group killed her mother to get her. The trauma shut down her telepathy. I rescued her, brought her up, made sure she was safe. She tried to do the same for you." Drake took a breath. "There, answers. We're going now."

"I'm the one who has you pinned to the wall, old man." Alec's eyes shifted from him to Beth and back. Those were a whole damned mouthful of answers and he still didn't have the ones he wanted.

"You only think you're in charge." Drake raised his other hand, showing a small revolver clutched in his palm. "If I'd wanted to shoot you, I would have. I palmed it the moment the Honda's lights flashed in the living room."

Alec winced. He hadn't been trying to be stealthy then.

"You didn't tell me," Beth said to Drake.

Drake shrugged. "I thought Alec might be a danger to you." He put the revolver in his pocket. "Since he's willing to stupidly rush an armed gunman for your sake, I've changed my mind. Now that we're all friends and he knows what is what, let's get out of here."

"There's no way out, that's why I need to talk to Beth before they get here." Alec said. "Look, Beth, c'mere."

She hesitated. "I—"

No time, dammit. He strode to her, pulled her close and kissed her, hard. She stiffened for a second and then wrapped her arms around him. Inside his head, something clicked, like a key fitting a lock.

He thought she'd screamed out loud in that split second where he'd taken her virginity. He'd been half right. She'd screamed inside her head and he'd heard it. If he could feel that, maybe he could feel whether she was telling the truth or not.

"I need to know if you're lying to me."

"Not-lying-telepathy-was-latent-only-worried-it-would-affect-you-then."

"Slow down!"

"I worried I messed with your gifts but they seemed to be coming back, so I stopped worrying but-something-happened-when-we-made-love-and-I-heard-you-in-my-head-their-voices-too-so-loud-so-loud—"

"Okay, that's enough. Easy."

"For fuck's sake," Drake said.

The paper towels on the counter burst into flame. Damn, it had happened again—he'd started a fire without intending to. He broke the kiss, kept his arms around her and extinguished the fire with a thought.

"You lied but not about the important stuff." He'd not only heard her, he'd felt what she felt. She cared about him. These few days had been real, not phony. "You're not controlling me."

"No." She nodded, her face flushed.

His every nerve ending buzzed from their kiss. "Then listen, fast. You too, Drake. Beth, you shut me off once. But you're also jacking up my power, and that means I can stand against anything, even Lansing. I can protect you."

Her eyes widened. She nodded for him to go on.

"And I think I'm doing the same thing to your telepathy. It was latent, now it's not. We'll need that edge while we're with the Resource to plan our next move. We can't fight them now, we're surrounded and I don't want you hurt in the crossfire. But we'll get our chance. Trust me."

"She's not going to the Resource. Ever." Drake scooped up his gun from the floor. "Follow me now before they get closer. There's an escape tunnel in the basement."

"But—" *That's not the plan.* He'd promised Daz to surrender with her.

Screw that. She was better out of here. But he had to stay. Daz had reminded him about Demeter. He had the power to fight now. And he owed Daz an explanation.

"Go with him, Beth. Find me when you get a chance. You'll be able to make contact, they won't be able to hold me now that I don't want to be held."

"Fine." Drake took Beth's hand. "Now, before we're trapped."

"No, Alec's coming with us." She grabbed his hand and held it tight.

"Alec-they-will-use-tranqs-you-won't-be-able-to-fight-back."

She really needed to think slower. That almost hurt. "No worries."

She grabbed his shirt, pulled him down to her and kissed him. The curtains over the sink burst into flame. He waved a hand and shut that down. He broke the kiss and rubbed her cheek with the back of his hand.

"I trust you," she said. "Be careful."

He nodded. Out of the corner of his eye, he saw a slim red beam of light. Drake smashed into both of them, sending them all crashing to the floor.

He heard the tinkling of broken glass. A tranq dart sank into the wall above them. *Dammit, Daz, you promised you'd give me thirty minutes!*

Something bigger smashed through the window, hit the counter and rolled to the floor. The hissing sound of escaping gas from the round container seemed unbelievably loud.

Tear gas.

Chapter Fifteen

Screw staying, Alec thought. Daz hadn't trusted him. He was going with Beth.

"Go, get to the basement," Drake said.

"What about you?" Beth said, coughing.

"I'm getting some firepower." He pushed her. "Go!"

Alec took her hand and they ran into the hallway. The house was so small that it was only about ten strides to the living room and then the basement door was on the left. Easy. No need to panic.

The living room windows shattered. Glass flew the hallway. *Shit.* More canisters of tear gas landed on the living room rug. He couldn't see through this, much less walk through it.

Beth coughed. "Hold your—"

"*—breath. Hold your breath.*"

They both started coughing. His eyes burned and started streaming tears. He'd underestimated these guys. He'd never had enough control to grab at gas molecules.

"*You never had control before, Alec. You said it, you're more powerful now, because of me. Try it.*"

"*Okay. You think about my controlling it too. Wish for it.*"

"*Will that help?*"

"*Can't hurt.*"

"*Hurry.*"

She fell to her knees, holding her hand over her mouth. Her eyes were closed tight.

He sent the TK out, trying to grab the gas floating around them. *Hell.* It was like trying to grab fog with his hands. For a few seconds, everything seemed the same. He couldn't take a clear breath, the gas stung his eyes, his nose and his lungs.

"Stop trying to grab it. Push it."

"You have good ideas, counselor."

"Ideas are all I'm good for right now."

She was lost in the middle of a coughing fit, curled into herself in a futile attempt to hide from the gas. He started pushing the gas, using the TK like a big shovel. His eyesight started to dim. His head grew heavier.

Beth scrambled to her feet and squeezed his hand. "It's working," she said, her voice hoarse.

He opened his eyes. He'd pushed the gas cloud up to the ceiling. He took a long clean breath, welcoming fresh air into his lungs.

"So my gift is good for something."

Her telepathic voice sounded just like her dry speaking voice.

"Let's go bigger, counselor." He clenched his teeth and shoved at the gas in the living room. He intended to throw it back through the broken windows and in the face of their attackers.

Drake brushed past them, holding a big-ass machine gun with a curved ammunition clip. A Kalashnikov, probably. How'd he get that?

"I think he was hiding it in the kitchen pantry."

"I'd hate to see what he keeps in his closet."

"I'll cover you," Drake said. "Quick. They're probably ready to come through the door."

As in on cue, the front door splintered inward. Alec instinctively threw his hands over his face to avoid the flying shards of wood. Beside him, Beth muffled a scream. Soldiers wearing gas masks rushed through the opening. He stepped in front of Beth and slapped at the lead attacker with TK.

The soldier flew backward and knocked over the guy behind him, sending both of them to the floor and temporarily blocking the front door.

Good. He coughed and blinked. *Fuck.* He'd let go of the gas. It descended around them again. *Easy. Calm.* He could fight and hold the gas if he could hold focus.

"It's just a few more feet, Alec."

Through the smoke, he saw the outline of the basement doorway.

He could get the gas to provide cover while Beth and her father escaped. He pushed with the TK and the gas cloud sparked. A fireball roared into existence, knocking him and Beth to the floor. He heard a muffled oath from Drake. Shit, he'd pushed too hard. He'd caused a fireball.

"Alec?"

Beth's thought was full of pain. He fumbled around on the floor to find her, trying not to panic, to remember to focus on keeping back the fireball. He found her slumped against the wall and pulled her against his chest.

Her head lolled forward. But she breathed.

"Stupid, stupid, my head hit the damn wall. Hurt, hurts. Dammit, we were almost there."

"We'll make it."

He stood, clutching her tight, throwing all he had at the fireball to keep it at bay. He shuffled toward the basement door and freedom. The fireball split in two and flew out the windows. One problem down. But the curtains and furniture had caught fire and so had the ceiling. The fire was too scattered, he couldn't hold it all back. His lungs began to burn.

He heard the familiar sound of machine gun fire. The smoke cleared for a second and he saw Drake standing at the top of the basement steps, laying down covering fire.

"C'mon," Drake yelled.

He and Beth rushed forward. Sharp pain stabbed his leg. He fell to his knees in front of the door, right at Drake's feet. He lost hold of Beth. He looked down and saw a dart sticking out of his thigh.

Not again. Not fucking again. He knocked the dart out with his TK. It had taken two tranqs at the docks to get him. They wouldn't get two this time.

"Ugh." Drake fell sideways against the doorframe. Blood gushed over the front of his shirt. He went down to his knees and stopped firing.

"Philip!"

Beth grabbed her father before he could tumble down the steps. She put her hands over the wound. They were quickly covered in blood. Incredibly, Drake opened his eyes and pushed her aside.

"Get out," he wheezed. He started firing again.

Alec looked up and saw a soldier carefully leveling his handgun at Drake. The gun fired. *No!*

Alec swatted the bullet away. He heard it ping against the metal chair near the computer at the same second another tranq hit his neck.

Drake pushed himself upright and started to move backward down the steps. He grabbed Beth's hand to get her to follow.

She hesitated.

"Leave me. I'll be okay."

"I can't leave you with them."

"You have to help your father. I'll find you when I wake up. Trust me."

Alec slumped to the floor. He focused one last time. Drake wasn't in sight anymore. Beth was at the top of the steps.

"It was fun while it lasted, counselor."

Beth blinked. She could think again, after God knew how long.

Her next to last memory was of Philip falling down the basement stairs, blood all over him. Her last memory was one of those damned Resource soldiers, reaching for her.

She curled her knees to her chin, wrapping the thin white sheet around her for more warmth than her flimsy nightgown provided. At least they'd treated her concussion, or so she assumed, since she had no headache or pain. She pulled the sheet tighter. The top of her right hand ached from the IV needle in it. She curled the hand in a fist. Her fingertips were ice cold. They'd kept the room temperature low, a subtle form of torture. Her reflection glared at her from all sides, flickering on the stainless steel walls of her prison. She looked broken and useless. She had owned a little porcelain doll as a child. It had shattered when she'd dropped it from her bed accidentally one night.

She felt somewhat like that now.

It was funny, in an odd way.

She'd been captured and taken prisoner again, presumably so her telepathy could be studied, just like when she was eight. The repetition of her worst nightmare should have left her a quivering mess. She should be miserable and tired. She should be terrified.

And she was, more than a little.

But she was also pissed off.

She'd been so close to getting away. But now that she could think again, she might be able to reach Alec. She closed her eyes, calling his name mentally.

Nothing.

Damn. She looked at her reflection in the mirror. She couldn't avoid how weak she looked, how much like a helpless captive she seemed. What had Philip told her in case of capture? *If you're ever taken, tell them what they want to know, if it's possible. Being cooperative will keep you alive long enough for me to get there. The truth is your best defense. The best lies start out with the truth.*

Of course, this assumed that Lansing wanted information from her. If he wanted to interrogate her, he'd taken his time about it.

The door opened. She froze. Two men dressed in green surgical scrubs walked in. She recognized them as the ones who'd had changed her IV bag earlier. Well, they were dressed the same, anyway. God knew what drugs they were pouring into her body. Something to keep her compliant, weak and confused.

The door opened again and Lansing walked in.

She swallowed down panic and watched him walk to her as if it was her first time seeing him. He was dressed as usual, in dark slacks, a white shirt, bowtie and a dark checkered sports coat. What was gone was the desire to appear friendly or normal. He scowled, making no attempt to hide his anger. When he'd pulled a gun on her, she'd gotten him to back down for a second. She thought he'd been testing her. Now she knew her telepathy had flared.

But *he* didn't know that. At least, she hoped he didn't.

He sat on the end of the bed, his thin fingers tapping on the metal frame, staring at her. She kept her head down. Lansing didn't think much of women. That's why there were no women in F-Team. Let him underestimate her, then. Besides, her knees would be knocking together if she hadn't been holding on tight to them.

"Akemi Fujii. You were supposed to be with me years ago. Things would be much, much better for you if Drake had not interfered and faked your death."

She snapped her head up to look him in the eye. He'd said Philip's name with such hatred. "I owe Philip Drake everything. And I am certainly glad not to have been raised by you." If he knew her birth name, then he knew everything. One less thing to worry about hiding.

"So your life was better spent by hiding your gifts, wasting your efforts on worthless people?"

She blinked. "What are you talking about?"

"You think you and Alec are the only ones who've ever had a gift? There are others. And most of them are like you—they don't have a clue what to do with their abilities." He switched to the chair at the side of the bed and put his hands behind his neck, relaxed. "You criticize how I brought up Alec. And yet you squander time on children who will accomplish nothing their whole lives. What a waste."

"I like helping children. They're not worthless." She hadn't hated anyone since her kidnappers. Now, she added Lansing to that list.

"Helping children? You mean the way you helped Alec, using sex to hold him? Is that the method you use with the teenage boys under your care?"

"Of course not!"

"But you violated your professional ethics with Alec. Why should it be the first time?"

She gritted her teeth. "What's between Alec and me is between Alec and me."

"Alec is still defending you. But I can read between the lines. You're scared of yourself. You're scared of your telepathy. That's why you can't use it."

Alec had kept her real secret. *Thank you.*

"You're a coward who is hiding from herself," Lansing said.

Ouch. Direct hit. She *was* terrified of her telepathy. At least, she had been. She winced and turned her face away from Lansing.

"If I'd raised you, you wouldn't be scared. Your telepathy wouldn't be gone, it would be powerful and under perfect control."

"If you'd had me, I wouldn't have a life at all." She turned to face him again.

"Alec's everything that you're not. No wonder that you needed to get close to him." Lansing stretched out his long legs. "You could have used your power to help him. Instead, Drake took you away to drab obscurity. Normal. Bah."

He wasn't asking her questions, he wasn't trying to get information. He must have come here to taunt her. Great. Was he going to do the maniacal mastermind laugh too?

"No, if I were with you, I'd be a slave." Philip had shown her that love was still possible. Her foster home, her teachers, her friends, they had all restored her faith in people. "Your control over Alec won't hold up any longer. He's seen reality now. He knows what you've done. He's finished with you."

Lansing sat up straighter. This time, *her* shot had hit home. "It's a phase. If you think a few days of sex plus a few counseling sessions will alter a lifetime's training, then you're a lousy psychologist." Lansing looked at imaginary dirt under his fingernails.

She flushed. Hadn't she herself told Philip that helping Alec was impossible? But she'd been wrong. Alec had seen the truth. More, he'd felt the truth from her, telepathically. Against all odds, she'd reached him. She'd accomplished that much.

"The boy has normal desires. Good for him. But you're not the only one who can satisfy them." He stood. "You know, what you should be doing is cooperating with me. This is your future now."

"Where am I?"

Lansing shook his head. "Your new home."

Never. She pulled the sheet tighter around her. "He doesn't know I'm here, does he? You haven't told Alec that I'm here at the Resource."

He waved his hand in dismissal. "Of course not. He thinks you're with Drake, that you both escaped. Alec doesn't need you or the distraction you provide."

Yes. She was at the Resource and not far from Alec.

"You're the one who's afraid. You're afraid that if we're together again, Alec will pick me over your lies. He already did, you know. He was coming with me."

Lansing set his jaw, angry for the first time. "You think this is a pissing match between the two of us, counselor? You're wrong. You're insignificant in the great scheme of things. You could have been part of it once. No more."

"What great scheme of things?" If only she could listen to Lansing's thoughts, she could find out a lot more. Years ago, it had worked on her kidnappers. It had worked briefly before with Lansing.

Why not now?

"No, I'm not answering that," Lansing said. "You had your chance."

She concentrated, trying to remember what she'd done to hear Alec. It was like opening a door with a broken hinge. She took a deep breath and gritted her teeth.

"She's scared, good. Alec would be appalled to see what a coward she is. Once he knows his future, he'll forget her. It's not like an Oriental is a proper mate for him, in any case."

It worked. She could *hear* him, like she'd heard that wordless scream of pain from Philip at the house.

"I don't want any part of your future. And I can't imagine you'll have a future when Philip finds me."

The force of Lansing's hatred for her father rolled over her like a physical blow. Lansing seized her and dug his fingers into her arms. "Philip Drake is dead."

She whimpered and tried to concentrate through the pain. She caught images from Lansing. Images of the house in Maine in ashes. Images of the retrieval team reporting that they hadn't found Philip's body.

He was *alive*. He'd gotten to the tunnel. "You're lying."

Lansing let her go and shrugged. *"She doesn't believe it. I hardly believe it myself. What a waste of life. My fault, I should have grabbed the boy when he was eighteen, or even at birth. I should have known he'd breed true. He could have been so useful. It must be the mongrel blood showing."*

Beth blinked. Breed true? Mongrel blood? What? Well, she knew one thing for sure now. Lansing was a racist, to go along with his other faults.

Lansing walked to the door. "Believe what you want. It doesn't change anything."

He couldn't leave yet. She needed to keep him here, to keep listening to his thoughts. "You say you care about Alec. Then why do you let him risk his life with F-Team? What kind of father does that?"

Lansing spun around. "Because Alec needs to learn to lead men, he needs to be forged in fire, so he can survive anything."

"And if he's killed?"

Lansing shrugged. "If he can't learn, then, well, he's not fit to lead. I'll miss him and then train another. There are others, you know."

"There will be many others. And they'll answer to me."

Megalomania. How nice. "Maybe what he's learned with F-Team is that you aren't the final authority on matters. That he can stand alone."

Lansing shook his head. "No, what he's learned from F-Team is that he should be in charge, that they rightly fear his power. He'll learn to make use of that fear."

God forbid. "He'll learn he can stand on his own, without you."

"He could be on his own but he'll be lost out there. I can offer him more than anything he'd ever find in a normal life."

"How?"

"I'm offering what he wants. A chance to be a hero. A chance to lead. A chance to be in charge of others like him and use their gifts to change the world. You could have been part of it." He shrugged. *"And your genetic children will be, as soon as I can sort out how to control telepaths."*

So, Lansing's racism didn't prevent him from wanting to use her or her future children, so long as they were under his thumb. Another type of slavery. "I don't want any part of you."

"That's not your decision any longer."

"Counselor this, counselor that. The boy's obsessed. He'll do better once he's taken care of Demeter's group, once he feels better about the failure. He'll stop insisting that he needs to leave to find her."

"If I'm so unimportant, if I'm a pawn, why are you bothering with me?"

Lansing smiled. "You need to know what you've lost. I wanted to be the one to tell you that." He walked to the door, put his hand on the doorknob, and looked around at the room. "This is your future. I hope you enjoy it."

"I will certainly enjoy watching you break, however long that takes."

She clenched her fist. Combined with that thought was contempt both for her being a woman and for being of Japanese descent. He'd use her if he could—he had no other telepaths available—but she'd always be a tool to him. Oddly, Alec did represent more than that to him. She wondered if Lansing had ever acknowledged his feelings for Alec.

Lansing turned and walked out of the room, his mirror images on the stainless steel walls winking out as he shut the door. The green-clad men moved in. One of them injected something into her IV.

The lethargy spread to her whole body before she could object. Her brain drifted back in time, back to when she was eight years old and all alone. No, not alone. Philip had come. That wouldn't happen this time, at least for a long while. Even if Philip wasn't dead, he was badly hurt. Alec wouldn't come—he thought she was already safe.

But, in a way, Alec had already rescued her. He'd given her back her telepathy and urged her not to be afraid of it. If he could stand up to the fact that his whole life had been a lie, then she could stand up to this.

I will rescue myself.

Chapter Sixteen

Beth?

Alec slammed down the intel report and stood. He closed his eyes and concentrated, listening. But he didn't hear her again. If she was trying to reach him telepathically, it wasn't working very well.

He paced the medical lab, wishing he were on the beach in Maine, huddled against the boulder with Beth in his arms. He shoved his hand into his pocket and fingered the rock he'd taken from the beach. No sky, no sea air here. Instead, only the sterile whites and chrome of the Resource's med lab surrounded him. He could read the CIA intel report on the terrorists again but he'd read it six times already. He nearly had it memorized.

The report claimed Demeter had time to assemble the bomb since that night at the docks and that he could strike at any moment. The CIA had finally tracked the origin of the radioactive elements of the weapon, concluding it had come from Russian sources and that it was highly possible the Russian government—read: Putin—was using terrorists to covertly attack the U.S. That was of serious concern to the CIA but it wouldn't help Alec in a fight against Demeter.

Alec was less worried about where they got the radioactive stuff and more concerned with that fuzzy something that he'd felt just before the tug exploded that night. If there was one telepath out there, there could be more. He had explained that to Lansing but the man said that was no consequence. Translation: if Lansing knew anything about it, he didn't think Alec needed to know.

Anyway, for all Alec knew, Lansing had concocted this report from whole cloth to keep him from leaving the Resource after the capture in

Maine. Oops. Sorry. Lansing kept calling it a *retrieval.*

Alec stopped in front of the med lab door. It was locked. For his safety, he'd been told. Beth had said that too, about the basement door in Maine. At least she'd unlocked it when he'd asked.

I'm sick of people doing things for my own good.

"We have to find out what she did to you, Alec," Lansing had said. Yet Lansing hadn't told him anything Beth hadn't confessed herself. Lansing just gave it a sinister spin. If Alec had known where Beth was, he would have walked out of here and to hell with stopping the damned bomb.

He poured a glass of water from the sink. Some of the clear, cool liquid slopped over his lips and down his chin, cooling his naked chest. They could have at least given him clothes beyond the sweatpants. Or let him stay in his room. Time to start demanding that, at least.

Lansing walked inside. He locked the door behind him. Naturally.

"You're up late again, Alec. Can't sleep?" he said, voice full of sympathy, falling into the tweed armchair next to the bed.

Alec shrugged. "What do you want now?"

"I was worried about you. I also wanted you to know I've gotten an intelligence update. I think we might be close to Demeter."

"Fine." Again with dangling the threat of the terrorists over his head so he'd stay.

"I'm glad you're back in time for the mission," Lansing said. "You'll have a chance to make up for your failure."

Lansing sure knew how to press the guilt button. What if they'd found Demeter while he was off with Beth and F-Team had failed to stop the bomb?

"Stop it, Alec. What could you have done? You didn't have your fire then, remember?"

Alec choked on the water. Beth? This was not a good time to make contact.

"Are you all right?" Lansing poured himself a drink of water from a pitcher at the bedside table and sipped, looking at Alec over the rim of the glass.

"Fine." He stared back at Lansing.

"I lived my own nightmare those days you were missing, Alec. I can't tell you again how glad I am to have you home safe."

"You're kidding." Alec drank more water and leaned against the sink. The old man *had* seemed eerily happy to see him.

"I'm not kidding. You should have called."

Alec jiggled the water glass in his hand, sending the ice cubes tinkling against the sides. "I didn't call because Beth was no threat to me and I decided I needed a break. I deserved one. I didn't expect you to send an assault team after me. It would have been a lot easier if Daz had just knocked at the door. Or, you know, phoned."

"So you've claimed, repeatedly. But the fact remains that when we descended on that house, you attacked us."

"You lobbed the tear gas first."

"Because the retrieval team saw a fire start inside the cabin."

Alec clenched his teeth, his temperature rising.

"Daz knew I was fine."

"Daz knew nothing of the sort. Have you thought or wondered why you set the tear gas on fire? That's stupid, Alec, and you're not stupid about your use of fire. The only explanation is that she controlled you and got you to fight back, only she didn't know how explosive your power is."

Hah. He knew something Lansing didn't for once. "I told you, all I knew right then was that I was being attacked. I defended myself."

"That was all you knew because that's all *she* let you know. I notice Philip Drake didn't have any qualms about killing to cover his escape."

"And you had no qualms about trying to kill him." Alec stared at the ceiling, counting the white tiles, an exercise that Beth had taught him in one of their sessions, to bring calm. He counted a vertical row of five, a horizontal row of seven. Thirty-five tiles in that corner. Better. Calmer. "You taught me that when someone attacks you, the best reaction is to fight back and sort it out later."

Lansing sighed and unfolded his long legs in front of him, relaxing or appearing to relax. "We've been over this. She was a CIA plant from that start. My fault, I should never have agreed. I'm sorry for that."

Alec tossed the glass in the sink. It shattered but he ignored the noise. Let Lansing get one of his staff to clean it up. He stalked over and put his hands on the back of the armchair, looming over Lansing. Under his hands, the upholstery of the chair began to smoke. Lansing jumped up, twisted to face Alec and pointed a finger at him.

"You see?" Lansing raised an eyebrow. "You've regressed since you met her. What does hurting me gain you, Alec?"

"Satisfaction." Alec crossed his arms over his chest. "Why don't I get a paycheck?"

Lansing blinked. "Excuse me?"

"Daz gets paid. You draw a salary, I bet. And even Beth got paid. Where's my money?"

Lansing rubbed the back of his neck, the command gone from his pose. For once, he seemed completely off-guard. "A paycheck? Alec, we can provide anything you want."

"Within reason. Within the borders of my cage."

"The Resource is to keep you safe, not to keep you prisoner."

"Does that mean keeping me a slave?"

Lansing shook his head. "If a paycheck means that much to you, fine, you'll get what Daz earns plus five percent more."

"Just like that?"

"The money's not an issue. You should have asked sooner if it bothered you. I'm not a mind reader, unlike your counselor."

"What about a car?"

"We'll discuss it."

"You mean no."

"I meant we'll discuss it. You'd need a safe car, an armored car, to protect against attack. Those take special driving skills to handle. Plus, I don't have one at the snap of my fingers."

"When do I get a chance to leave?"

"When I'm sure you're not a danger to others. If you lose control, like you seem perilously close to doing lately—" he pointed at the burnt back of the chair, "—you will hurt innocents. Remember what happened at the docks, when your team member died, when you also trapped the others in a firestorm. You would have killed them if Daz hadn't stopped you."

Alec swallowed. "I remember."

"Do you remember how the fire used to consume you, how dangerous it was? What if it goes back to that?"

"It won't." Alec reached around and touched the scars at the base of his back.

"Are you sure?"

"Yeah." *Maybe.*

Lansing crossed his arms over his chest. "Do you remember who was it that braved that fire, to help you gain control?"

"You did," Alec said in a quiet voice.

"We both could have been killed. All that time we spent together, all those years that you lived with me, all I tried to teach you and you say I don't care?" Lansing spread his hands in front of him.

"You wanted to use me."

"If that's all I wanted, I would have sent someone else to help you with your fire. I wouldn't have risked myself. I raised you. I've been here for you your entire life, Alec. You've only known this woman for less than two months. What makes you think she's right and I'm wrong?"

"She makes sense."

"When she talked, no doubt she did. But does it hold up?"

Lansing walked over and put his hand on Alec's shoulder. Alec almost pushed him away but he was too surprised. Lansing rarely got touchy-feely.

"You know people like Demeter exist. You've seen what they can do and you know what you can do to stop them, yes?"

Alec nodded, a knot forming in his chest. "Yes."

"And did your counselor want you to keep using your gifts to fight them?"

Alec shook his head. "She said there were better ways to use my fire than being a soldier."

"Did she name them?"

"No."

"I thought that you wanted to be a hero. But I suppose you'd rather shop at Wal-Mart and learn to drive."

"That's not—"

Alec pushed Lansing's hand off his shoulder and started pacing again. Beth hadn't lied, she'd offered love, but she hadn't offered a damn thing about what to do with his life, about how he could make a difference. In fact, she was completely against him being a soldier.

"Now you're beginning to think." Lansing shoved his hands into his pockets. "Would you like to see something?"

"If it gets me out of this room."

Lansing nodded. "We'll go to your home so you can get dressed, then follow me."

Alec put on his jeans, T-shirt and sneakers in record time. He shifted the pebble to the pocket of his jeans. Lansing said nothing while waiting. When Alec turned around to switch off the lights, he took a second to compare it to the cabin in Maine. Beth's place had had so much of her in it. This was his home but it looked so sterile. Like a coffin. Hell, not as fancy as a coffin.

Lansing led him down to a wall at the end of the corridor. A dead end.

"What do you think it is?" Lansing pointed to the painting on the wall.

"Monet's Japanese bridge," Alec answered. "It's a print, right?"

"Yes, but that's not what I wanted to show you." Lansing slid the print to the left, revealing a control panel, and punched in a code. Several seconds later, the wall slid away to reveal an elevator. Alec followed Lansing in.

"This goes up to your quarters." Alec must have ridden this elevator a thousand times. The scarlet paneling and the gold inlays were unmistakable.

"Yes. I should have let you know it was here on this floor and available to you. My mistake."

Lansing admitted to doing something wrong? "Why was it a mistake?"

"I distanced myself from you once I sent you to work with F-Team. I thought it was the right thing, for you to bond with your team. But I pulled back too much."

"It's not like we were close."

Lansing smiled thinly. "I'm all the father you have, Alec. I should have let you know that more."

Lansing was certainly in an odd mood tonight. Alec decided he preferred the usual dour, glowering Lansing to this one.

The doors to the elevator opened to the small hallway that led to Lansing's penthouse, which was perched on the top floor of the Resource building. Alec watched Lansing punch in the security code to the side of his metal door.

"Thought you'd have a different code by now, not the one I remember."

The door lock clicked. "I did," Lansing said. "I changed it back for you."

"Uh, thanks."

As they stepped inside, Alec really looked around Lansing's home for the first time in a long time. He studied the red oriental carpets, the Victorian-style sitting couches and the collection of wooden angel statues on the tables and shelves. Nothing cute about those statues. Grotesque, maybe.

He'd thought Lansing's home normal. After seeing Beth's cabin, it struck him as strange and more than a little creepy. No warmth here, not much sunlight either.

Lansing turned left past the kitchen, leading him down a familiar hallway. They stopped at the doorway to Alec's old room.

"It's smaller than I remember," Alec said.

"They always are."

Lansing hadn't changed his old room. The bed was still made with perfect corners. His glow-in-the-dark planets still hung from the ceiling. The hardcover editions of the Harry Potter books were still in the bookcase, along with all the history books. No little kid picture books, though, like the ones the librarian had read in Maine.

"Why did you bring me here?"

"To show you where you've come from. Does this look like a prison?"

Alec shrugged.

"I know I was harsh. You needed to learn to be tough, to survive. It was necessary. Now let me show you something else."

They went in the opposite direction, down another hallway and stopped in front of a heavy wooden door with a sword carved into the top half. Alec didn't remember this door at all. This was a wing of the penthouse where he'd never been allowed.

Lansing used a key that was six inches long with teeth about an inch long. The lock opened and they stepped inside.

It took a moment for Alec's eyes to adjust to the darker room. The lights on the walls flickered, casting weird shadows. "What kind of lights are these?"

"Gas lanterns," Lansing said. "I like them."

Weird but they fit the Victorian style in the rest of the place. Against the far wall, silent flames also flickered in the red brick fireplace. The mantel was a warm brown, which added some life to the gloomy room. Lansing went to a switch on the wall and the flames inside the lanterns and the fireplace blazed higher, chasing away the darkness and shadows.

Bookcases occupied the wall on both sides of the fireplace. Over the mantel was a crest with a skull in the middle, crossed by two red and white pennants. Under the skull was a banner that said "Or Glory." Death or glory? Um, okay.

The opposite wall was covered by a painting of a city besieged. The forces on the city wall flew the British flag and carried old-style rifles that were later than the Revolutionary War but before automatic weapons. Alec walked closer, studying the uniforms, and recognized the invading army as some sort of desert people.

Right. The siege of Khartoum, one of the most well-known battles of the British Empire. He'd learned about it during his studies of military tactics. The British soldiers had been overwhelmed after a siege and their General, "Chinese" Gordon, had been killed. Martyred, Lansing had said, with some anger. The painting was incredibly vivid— you could see the faces clearly, the lines of their guns, even the buttons on their uniforms.

"Why would you want to remember a defeat?" Alec asked.

Lansing linked his hands behind his back. "So it doesn't happen again. If the city had been resupplied in time, if the reinforcements had shown up just a few days sooner, there would not have been a defeat." Lansing paced away, stopping at one of the six waist-high tables in the room. All the tables held miniature recreations of battles.

"Bureaucracy always moves too slowly. That was the British Empire's undoing. Governments can only do so much and they get creaky and tired and hidebound. To get anything really done, you have to circumvent them."

"I wouldn't know. I haven't had much experience with governments."

Lansing leaned against one of the tables. "And that's deliberate on

169

my part. You don't need to know how government works. You just need to control it. Look at those soldiers. They followed orders at Khartoum. They died. They served well but they didn't reap the benefits of the empire. It teaches a valuable lesson."

"To be a better soldier?"

Lansing smiled. "To be the one in charge who reaps the benefits, not the one who dies."

Alec thought of F-Team and Jimmy. He crossed his arms over his chest. "Thanks, I feel very wanted."

Lansing straightened. Alec stepped closer to the table and recognized the Battle of Gettysburg in three parts, for the three days of fighting.

"You needed military training to know how to use force, Alec. It's one thing to learn about battles, another to be in them. Your courage had to be tested and honed." He pointed to the table, to the collection of Confederate soldiers under General Longstreet. "Lee ordered Pickett's men to charge the high ground. What would you have done?"

"That's easy. You shouldn't charge high ground, so I wouldn't give the order."

Lansing nodded. "But Lee was taking the human factor into account. His men had always won in a fight. So, given that you had men ready to fight and wanted to move forward, what would you have done?"

Alec leaned over the diorama. He lifted the figure of Jeb Stuart and shifted him to the very edge of the Confederate lines. "Have Stuart take his cavalry unit, circle around and attack the flank."

Lansing nodded. "Good. You take a weapon that the enemy doesn't have access to, in this case a mobile unit, and use it. In fact, that's what Stuart did but he was stopped. What Lee should have done is retire from the field, circle around and make the Union chase him." Lansing stepped over to a World War I setup and picked up a German biplane. "This eventually ended the need to assault high ground." He waved it over the Union lines at Gettysburg.

"And a nuke can take out the whole city with one plane," Alec said. "So what's your point? We need to go back in time and re-fight the Battle of Gettysburg with biplanes?"

Lansing grinned, looking almost young. "That might be fun, but no." He set the biplane back down. "Horses, biplanes, nuclear weapons. What do they have in common?"

"If you have them and the enemy doesn't, you win."

"Exactly." Lansing smacked his hands together. "They were game changers. And you, Alec, you're the next generation of game changer."

"You want me to be a general?"

Lansing shook his head. "You don't need an army. Assuming Russia's Putin is the one ultimately behind the terrorists with the dirty bomb, how would you deal with him, if you had to oppose him?"

"We're going to take out his proxies and render the dirty bomb useless."

"But Demeter's cell is simply a feint to cause destruction and confuse the enemy. Smart of Putin. If the cell succeeds, it will leave the United States in crisis without costing Putin a thing because there's no definite proof of his involvement. The end result is that he'll have a free hand in his corner of the world while the United States deals with a crisis. And if the cell fails, there's no downside for him. He's the one with the real power in all of this. He has control."

"So what would you suggest?"

"I think taking out Demeter is too slow. It drags out the game." Lansing stepped over to the chessboard near the fireplace. "What's the object of this game?"

Alec picked up the chess king with his TK and let it hover in the air. "Take the king." He frowned. "You mean, take out Putin?"

"Yes. You go right to the top and grab the king." Lansing crossed his arms over his chest. "You have the power to do this. And there's no reason you shouldn't."

"Or I could do this," Alec waved a hand and the chessboard burst into flames. He watched it burn, controlled the fire, careful. Let Lansing see who was in charge. He listened to the grandfather clock in the corner and counted ticks. When sixty seconds were gone, the chessboard was ashes and the metal pieces were half-melted. He shut down the fire.

"I could wreck the entire game," he said.

Lansing had watched the destruction in silence. He swallowed. "That's right. We write our own game."

"I write *my* game," Alec said, arms crossed over his chest, echoing

Lansing's pose. It would help if he knew what his game was. What did he want, other than making sure Beth was safe?

"In time. But with the Resource and its power and influence at your back, you can eliminate competitors, amass power behind the scenes, control governments, even."

"You want me to be president or something?"

"I considered it but presidents are immaterial in Western society. Money is the key, and the power to take it."

Damn, Lansing, I was kidding.

Lansing continued, lost in his little speech.

"With your gifts, with my money and with the backing of the Resource, we will find others like you. All you need is a handful of game changers like yourself and the world is transformed. With far less destruction than an atomic weapon too."

"You have others like me?" He had guessed after learning of Beth's telepathy that there must be others. He wondered if Drake knew about them. If he found Drake again, he might ask the CIA agent about that spongy thing at the docks. Drake would give him a straight answer. Lansing wouldn't.

"In time we'll have a full team." Lansing nodded. "Your counselor is one, or could have been one, if she wasn't afraid of her gift. And with all that power at your disposal, you'll never have to worry about anyone controlling you."

Except you. "That sounds ambitious." And a little insane. More than a little.

"It's not. It will be easy. You'll help train the others, help them appreciate their gifts, give them a destiny and a chance to help rule."

"And put them in a cage, as you did for me? Beth might have shut down her gift, but she controls her life."

"You're freer than Beth Nakamora." Lansing swept the melted chess pieces onto the floor with the back of his hand. "Let's assume she didn't consciously try to manipulate you with telepathy. Let's assume that she meant well and simply didn't have control over it. That means she could do things to your head on impulse. If she wanted to control your fire, for instance, her subconscious might reach out and do that."

Alec turned away and looked at the fireplace. Beth *had* turned his fire off.

"So?"

"An untrained telepath is probably worse than a trained one. And why is she untrained? Because she's scared of her gift. She's afraid. Is that a good thing?"

"No." Beth had been scared. It hadn't made sense. Why be scared of something that was so useful?

"She's locked in her own internal cage, scared of her shadow, not seeing the possibilities that you can, yes?"

Yes. "I don't know about that. She seems to like her work."

"And now she's given up her work to go into hiding with Drake. What kind of existence is that?"

"You scared her, sending the team to attack."

"And I bet she said she was leaving before that, didn't she?" Lansing raised a bushy eyebrow.

"None of your business." Alec turned away and stared at the painting. Beth didn't want this life. She didn't want him in this life either, but she hadn't offered a good alternative.

Become the person in charge, become the one who saved the soldiers from being killed by making the right decisions. Become the one who could change the game by going to those making the bombs instead of fighting the people who received them.

Lansing's plan had appeal.

He heard Lansing walk up behind him. The older man put a hand on his shoulder once more. That was twice in one night. Lansing must really want him to agree.

"You're going to change things for the better, you're going to have the leadership and the power to help people like yourself, and you're going to make decisions that will benefit the world." Lansing squeezed his shoulder.

"So why am I a prisoner here?"

"You are *not* a prisoner. We're taking safety precautions. It's the price you pay for greatness. Or you can decide to be like one of those soldiers in the painting. Normal. Disposable."

Alec shook his head. "Why do I have to choose between what you say and freedom?"

"You have the choice between obscurity and making a difference.

173

That requires sacrifice. Look what happened when you left. Drake could have killed you or kidnapped you for the CIA." Lansing dropped his hand away.

"Being locked up is not sacrificing to help others. It's being a slave with no choice."

Lansing collapsed into a parlor chair in front of the fireplace. "Perhaps it seems that way to you. It's natural for you to feel restless, locked up, hemmed in. Maybe keeping you here, waiting on word about the bomb, is only making it worse. Move back to your own bed tonight. And if you want rooms up here, I'll arrange it. A full apartment for you."

"Thanks." Wait, was he thanking Lansing for putting him in a different cage? But maybe he had a point about cages. He'd never been scared of what he was. Beth had.

"Also, you need some time outside."

"I want the choice to go outside when I want, where I want."

"You need bodyguards. F-Team would do."

He scowled. "I'd rather not." Daz should have given him more time in Maine. Instead, he'd joined in on the attack.

"You need some time with the team before going on another mission, to make sure there are no problems with team unity. A night out."

"Daz helped them attack me. He helped shoot Drake."

"Drake was shooting at him."

True enough.

"Well, if you don't want to have some time outside the Resource as you just claimed—"

"I didn't say that." A night out. It would give Beth or Drake a chance to contact him, assuming Drake was alive. In any case, it would get him away from his half-crazy mentor, and give him space to think.

What did he want? What was his game?

Alec stared at the flames in the fireplace. They leapt higher, responding to his unconscious desire for a massive fire. He could burn down this entire room. He could burn down the penthouse and Lansing with it. He didn't have to stay. But aside from finding Beth, where would he go and what else would he do with his fire that would make as much of a difference as what Lansing offered?

"Take the night. Go out," Lansing said.

"What about Demeter? Word could come at any time."

"Stay local. If we get something urgent, we can pull you back."

It was a nice carrot and stick. He'd get a night outside with his team and then Lansing expected him to come back to work and be happy under his thumb.

But what if he wanted the same thing that Lansing wanted? Sure, Lansing sounded more than a bit crazy. But there was nothing unreal about the money he had or how he'd built the Resource complex. Lansing had the muscle to follow through on this plan. Provided Alec went along with him. As Beth had pointed out, Alec didn't know enough about economics or politics or sociology to make an informed decision about what went on in the world.

"A night out would be good." Anything to get him out of this suffocating room.

"Good. Thank you for listening, Alec." Lansing's voice was gruff. He turned his back to Alec and stared at the fire.

"You sound like you really care, old man."

Lansing nodded. "You'd be surprised how much."

Chapter Seventeen

The strippers got down to their G-strings, waved to the crowd and sauntered off to applause.

The house lights came up. Alec slumped back in his chair. With the lights down, he could fantasize. With the lights up, the place just looked cheap and sleazy. The bar along the side of the club was half-full, unlike on a weekend, and the patrons ranged from a couple of dirty old men to scattered businessmen in suits. There was a group of college students sitting at the booth in the corner that had been jerking off during the show.

I'm never sitting in a booth again.

Daz had snagged the table at the front of the runway tonight, so they all had a nice view of the strippers. Alec had gotten into the show, like always, except this time, when he got aroused, he wanted Beth. If Lansing had wanted him to forget about her, it wasn't working. And if Lansing wanted him to make nice with F-Team, that wasn't working.

Daz grinned easily to the passing waitresses in the skimpy costumes. The girls grinned back. They always liked him, all of them— black, white, Asian, Latino. Alec had thought it was because he was so nice to them or because of his mixed-race heritage. But it wasn't that at all. It was the big roll of cash that Daz used for tips. He hadn't noticed the money before, and if Beth hadn't brought up money in Maine, he never would have.

Lansing paid Daz a hell of a lot of money. Now that he knew about that, Alec wasn't sure if Daz did this work for money or if team was more important, like Daz had always said. Daz had been with the goons in Maine, after all.

"Wait'll you see the new main event," Daz said.

Hoots and catcalls rang out as three women came out onto the runway that led from the stage. They wore black silk capes to cover whatever they might or might not be wearing. They set a cauldron down in front of them and circled it.

"Real art," Daz said.

Yeah, right. Nudes in a museum were art. A night at the opera was art. This was naked women dancing for money. The house lights went down again. The college kids whooped a bit, then settled. Alec straightened. He might as well enjoy it.

The three women on stage started chanting. He recognized the opening scene to "Macbeth".

"Double, double, toil and trouble..."

Damn straight.

The "actresses" quoted a little more from the play, then shifted to their own script, if you could call it that. The words lost any poetry and the strippers dropped their witches' capes. All three wore devil costumes. Well, if you could call bras with devils on the cups and red and black G-strings costumes.

The strippers began wriggling and writhing on the runway. The college guys hooted their approval and so did some of F-Team. Alec didn't. He didn't need an exhibition that left him horny and unsatisfied. He wanted Beth. Or a distraction from wanting Beth.

Let's make the show more interesting.

He concentrated and one of the strippers lost her G-string. She was smooth underneath. He preferred Beth's dark, curly hair. The patrons howled, figuring the loss of the G-string was part of the show. The stripper frowned, shrugged and kept going.

Daz elbowed him in the ribs. "Hey! Emo boy, don't do that shit here."

"Leave me alone."

"Stop brooding. There are plenty of girls in the world." Daz downed the last of his beer.

"Shut up."

"So you'd prefer a girl who drugs you and fills you with lies?" Daz twirled the empty bottle in his hand. "These girls will do that, if you pay 'em enough."

"Fuck you." Alec snapped to his feet, fists clenched.

Daz stood. "Get over it, Firefly."

Alec threw a punch before he consciously realized he'd moved. Daz swore and caught Alec's fist with his open hand. Using the fist as leverage, Daz pushed him backwards, almost knocking Alec off his feet. Alec blinked and called the fire. The air around them heated up. Daz, eyes wide, let go.

Three F-Team soldiers jumped between them, overturning the table and chairs and spilling the beer pitcher. Alec glared at Daz. Daz glared back.

The show stopped. The house lights came up.

"Back off." Daz shrugged off one of the soldiers. "I'm not gonna fight. It's Mr. Too-Good-for-This-Place that needs to chill."

"Yeah? I'm not the one who didn't back up his teammate during a fight." Alec gritted his teeth. He was about two seconds from making this whole place go up in smoke. *The world is not kindling.* That's what Beth said. She said he was better than that. Hell, even Lansing had said he was better than F-Team. At this second, he agreed with them.

He took one deep breath and looked away, anywhere but at his so-called friend. The others righted the table and chairs. The bouncer, a six-foot-six giant with a crew cut, sauntered up.

"Cool off and pay for the drinks or leave," he said.

Daz pulled a wad of cash from his back pocket and tossed it at the bouncer. "Take it out of that and tip the staff with the rest."

The bouncer nodded and the money disappeared into his pocket. "Good."

Gabe, who didn't seem to hold a grudge from being almost crispy fried last week, handed Alec a glass of water. But then, Gabe was always calm. And he wouldn't be distracted by the show like the rest of the team. The girls were not his type.

Alec took the glass but the water started to steam. Hell. He put down the glass before the steam burned his hand. He had to get out of here.

"Going to use the head," Alec said into Gabe's ear.

Gabe nodded. But Alec noticed that Gabe and Daz watched the whole time he was walking to the bathroom. F-Team might be smarter and better than the Resource goons but they belonged to Lansing, just the same.

Alec used the urinal and washed his face in the dirty bathroom sink. To hell with this. He'd stumble around and look for Beth on his own. The only problem with that was he wouldn't be available to fight Demeter and make up for Jimmy's death.

"Stay still, Alec, and do not turn around," a voice said from behind him.

Drake.

Alec grinned. That saved him a world of trouble. "No worries, Drake. Whatever you have to say, I want to hear it."

"You have plenty of worries," Drake said, his voice shakier than Alec remembered, "because unless you lead me to Beth, I will blow your head off."

"I saved your life in Maine."

A pause. "I know. It's why I didn't shoot you on sight."

"Look, you don't have to test me." Something had finally gone right, though how pathetic was his life that someone threatening to kill him was something good? "Take me to Beth. I need to see her." *And touch her, hold her and make love to her.*

"Seeing Beth is exactly what I had in mind. But your people are standing in my way. And so are you."

Drake spoke as if reading a grocery list, cold and blunt. Alec's grin faded. He dropped his hands to his sides.

"I've had enough mind games. Say what you mean. Or shoot me, if you think that's what Beth wants." Of course, no way would a bullet get past his TK.

"No, I need you alive to get my daughter back."

Alec turned around. Drake stared at him for a minute and then lowered his modified Glock. His other arm was in a sling. There were dark circles around his eyes and a deep purple bruise on the right side of his cheek. He didn't look like the confident spy Alec had met in the kitchen of the house in Maine. He looked like a man near death, with nothing to lose.

"What do you mean, get Beth back?" Alec's throat dried out.

"The Resource team took her from my house when they took you."

"And you *let* them?"

Drake winced and closed his eyes for a second. "I tried. I knew they wanted her alive, that I'd have another chance at it. But God knows what they've done to her."

"You're saying the Resource has Beth?"

"Didn't you hear me? Of course Lansing has my daughter." Drake scowled. "Think, boy. He lied to you again. That's what he does."

"How do I know you're not the one lying?"

"Fine." Drake sighed and leaned back against the wall. "If I wanted to lure you to somewhere else for some unknown purpose, I'd have brought my daughter with me. The person you trust. Who I don't have."

"Shit." Alec took a deep breath. Drake wasn't lying. He had no reason to lie.

Lansing had Beth.

Lansing had lied with a straight face. He'd said Beth was never coming back because she was afraid of her gift. And all the time, he had her locked up, exactly as she'd feared.

Alec's anger exploded, setting off his power. Clouds of hot urine-filled steam saturated the air. He shook his head, coughed and the steam dissipated.

"Save that for later," Drake said.

"Do you know where she is?"

"Somewhere inside the Resource facility. Lansing's best equipment is there."

Alec thought of the voices in his dreams, late at night. That had been Beth, just as he'd thought, but she wasn't trying to get him to listen, she was trying to get him to help her.

"Shit!" He unleashed a fireball to his left, just above one of the urinals. There must be a hell of a lot of alcohol molecules in the air for it to flare up so fast. He stared at the fireball, sweat pouring down his face, tempted to burn it all. But why use his power here when he could use it on Lansing and the Resource? He blinked, concentrated and the fireball disappeared.

"You might want to do something that will attract a little less attention until we find her," Drake said in a dry tone that sounded like Beth.

"We'll get her. Tonight. And if they've hurt her, I'll kill everyone inside."

180

Drake smiled. "Fine by me."

Alec nodded.

Someone pushed against the bathroom door. It only opened a crack before jamming. Alec looked down. Drake had stuffed a wedge of wood under the door.

"Alec?" Daz said.

Alec looked at Drake. Drake stepped forward and kicked away the wood. "Answer," Drake whispered.

"Yeah, Daz?" Alec asked.

Daz pushed and the door swung open. "Look, I'm sorry. I know you like the girl."

Drake jammed the wood triangle under the door again with his foot. He smashed his elbow into Daz's lower back, a kidney punch. Daz went down to one knee with a groan, and before Alec could react, Drake had a gun at Daz's head.

Alec blinked. And people said *he* was scary.

"Not a word," whispered Drake in that toneless voice. "Flat, on the floor."

Daz coughed, hesitated for only a second and did as Drake asked. His face touched the filthy floor. "Jesus, Alec, c'mon. It smells down here."

"You knew," Alec said. "You fucking knew all along about Beth. And you sat there smirking at me, making wisecracks and insulting her."

"That's past," Drake said. "He's going to help us now, aren't you, Commander? Give me the layout. Tell me exactly where she's being held."

"Alec, Drake's a psycho. His own people say that. You don't want to listen to him."

"He's making more sense than you." Alec cupped a hand and called the fire, just above his palm. It flashed into existence, close but not quite touching his hand.

"You don't want to do this, Firefly."

"Don't call me that!" He moved the fireball closer to Daz. "You think Drake's a psycho? How'd you like a pyromaniac?"

Daz swallowed and closed his eyes against the fire. "You believe him?"

"He didn't attack me. He's worried about his daughter."

"I'm worried about *you*."

"Bullshit. You're worried about your paycheck."

"That's not true."

"You helped them take Beth." Alec stalked forward, bringing the fire with him. He knelt down to Daz, the fire almost close enough to burn. "You either help us or I'm going to let Drake blow your brains out. And then I'm gonna take out the rest of the team and the ones in the parking lot, and then we'll have a nice fireworks party at the Resource as soon as I get Beth out."

Daz opened his eyes. "You can't do that."

"Yes, I can. Remember, I'm only a hair's breadth from going out of control."

"You're not. I know you better than that."

"Then why do you carry the tranqs on every mission?"

Daz sighed. "I've only used them once."

"You used them in Maine."

"That was the damn Resource goons! You think I wanted to go in there? I thought she was controlling you."

"I think all this stuff about team is garbage. You're just like those Resource guards. You take orders from Lansing, whatever they are."

"You're team," Daz said through clenched teeth. "That means something."

"You knew I was kept prisoner inside the complex. You never did anything about that."

"I thought you agreed to it, for your own safety." Daz closed his eyes, wincing.

"Bullshit. I complained to you about being stuck at the Resource a million times."

"I figured you weren't safe outside."

"You took Lansing's money, so you believed what he wanted you to believe," Drake said.

"No, I thought—"

"You could have tried to show me the truth," Alec said. "But you didn't." Beth had done that. Look what it had cost her.

"Okay, okay. I hear you. I fucked this up." Daz took a deep breath and nodded at the fireball. "Could you damp that down for a sec? It's burning holes in my eyes."

Alec blinked and the fire vanished. That had taken no effort at all. What the hell was he? A living weapon, of course. Thanks to Lansing. And to Daz. They'd gotten more than they bargained for now because now, thanks to Beth, he was incredibly powerful.

"You owe me a fucking explanation."

"Yeah, I do." Daz blinked, trying to clear his vision. "It's the job of a lifetime, you know? Elite assault team leader, save the world, work with a firestarter too. Such a fucking amazing thing, working with you. And, yeah, I like the money."

"Shows where your loyalty is," Drake said.

"Not anymore. I taught you about team, Alec. I meant it."

"You did squat to help me."

"That's why I'm going to help now," Daz said. "God knows I didn't want to turn your girl over to that goggle-eyed scientist. But she was hurt. Goggle Eyes said he'd fix her."

"You gave Beth to that freak?" Alec snapped to his feet. Lansing's pet head scientist liked inflicting pain.

"I thought that she'd made you fight back, call the fire. I thought— Fuck, I was wrong. I'll fix it."

"How?"

"By getting your girl back. Can I get up now?"

"Do you trust him?" Drake asked.

"I don't know," Alec said. "Get up," he told Daz.

Daz stood. Alec stared at the person who'd been his first real friend. Daz had also tranqued him twice and turned Beth over to Lansing.

Daz stared back. "I'll help. So will the rest of F-Team."

Alec frowned. Too easy. "Why?"

"You're my trainee, I'm supposed to take care of you. But instead, I took care of what Lansing wanted. He used me and I let him." Daz dropped his head. "I picked your shrink up off the floor in Maine. She was so little, so fragile. She babbled just before she went out, worried about you and her father." His voice dropped to a whisper. "Her face has been keeping me awake at night."

"I notice the guilt didn't make you tell Alec until I put a gun to your head." Drake was using the wall for support again. "Your conversion is a little late."

"Yeah, way too late." Daz stared at the floor. "Which is why I'm going to help now." He looked at Alec. "I taught you not to be a bully, to keep innocents out of the line of fire. And then I helped hurt her. Gotta fix it."

"I don't believe you," Drake said.

"You must have seen my service record, spook. You know who I am."

"I know who you used to be." Drake frowned. "You're not worried that Alec just threatened to kill you?"

"Girls make you do stupid stuff, telepaths or not." Daz shrugged. "Anyway, he seems more alert—more alive, not less. Must have been a hell of a couple of days in Maine."

"It was," Alec said.

"Enough," Drake said. "We're wasting time. We're going."

"Whoa, who said you were coming?" Daz said.

"I don't need your permission."

Daz grabbed Drake's forearm. "I'll help Alec. But not you, spook. You stay out of it."

"Get your hand off me before I break it." Drake didn't look tired any longer.

Alec stepped between them. Daz let go of Drake's arm.

"I'm not working with this *assassin*," Daz said.

"You've taken money from Lansing for the past seven years," Drake said.

"So?"

"He's murdered more people than I ever will. What does that make you, Commander Montoya?"

"Stop." Alec put his hands on Daz's chest and pushed him away. "Look, Daz, you're not exactly high on my trust list right now. I want Drake with me. Besides, would you rather have him with us or out there on his own?"

"He can't get into the Resource on his own," Daz said.

"Are you sure?" Drake said.

"You're not helping," Alec said.

"All I'm interested in is getting my daughter out."

"He wants to get Beth," Alec said. "You helped take Beth. You owe him."

"That doesn't make him any less of a psycho," Daz said.

Drake sighed. "What do you want? A pledge to shoot people in the knees?"

Alec smiled. Come to think of it, Drake did look a bit like the shape-shifting Terminator. Smaller ears, though.

"Do you know anyone more likely to get Beth out of there without causing a shootout? You said it yourself, Daz, Drake's a spook. This is what he does. He found us here, without bloodshed."

Daz relaxed. "Point."

"It should be a silent op," Drake said. "I don't want Beth in the crossfire a second time."

"Good enough for me." There was no way Alec was going back into the Resource with just F-Team, not knowing if he could trust them. He could trust Drake to protect Beth, no matter what. "Daz?"

Daz nodded. "We help get the girl out, yes. But if he steps out of line, I'm coming down on him."

Drake shook his head and bared his teeth. "I'm scared."

"Like I said, you're not helping." Alec wished there was some way to know he could trust Drake. "Answer a question for me, Drake."

"What now?"

"You rescued Beth when she was eight from her kidnappers under orders from the CIA. But then you made it look like she was dead instead of handing her over to Lansing. You disobeyed orders." Alec glared. "If you hated Lansing enough to go against orders and hide Beth, if you thought he shouldn't have kids for his program, why didn't you rescue me years ago like you did Beth?"

Something flashed over Drake's face. "I didn't know Lansing had acquired you for his program until recently. I didn't look. Lansing always suspected I'd hidden Beth. I wanted to stay as far away from him as possible so he didn't find my daughter."

Drake straightened. "In other words, I traded Beth's safety for yours." He looked Alec directly in the eye. "I don't regret it. I'd promised Beth I would keep her safe. And I'll continue to keep that promise."

Alec slowly nodded. "Okay." He looked at Daz. "Satisfied? All we're going to do is grab Beth and go."

"All right," Daz said.

Chapter Eighteen

Cold, cold, cold. It seemed never-ending. Even Beth's veins felt frozen. Her eyelids were heavy, but she couldn't sleep. If she didn't start moving soon, she might never move again. She pulled the thin sheet tighter around her. They'd stopped giving her the nightgown a while back. At least pretending to be more out of it over the last few days had resulted in less of the drugs that fogged her brain. She looked up at the IV hanging at the side of her bed. *I have to get the rest of that gunk out of my system.*

She could pull the needle out of her hand. That would hurt like hell and maybe open a vein. Or she might be able to tear the plastic tubing that led to the IV. Either way, a guard would come running and she'd have a chance to escape.

Yeah, one muscular, trained guard versus one drugged up, undersized psychologist.

Better odds than staying in bed.

She sat up and grabbed the metal IV stand. Set the scene, play to the cameras, turn them to her advantage. She stumbled out of bed and walked to the sink and toilet in the corner. They hadn't even given her a real bathroom. If she ever got out of here, the very first thing she was going to do was build a large private bath with fancy locks to keep everyone out. *And a bubble bath. I want a bubble bath.*

She pulled the sheet tighter around her shoulders. Cold sweat rolled down her back as she forced her numb legs to walk. She closed her eyes and reached out with her telepathy, in the hope that she might hear the guard. She'd practiced picking up thoughts from people inside the room when she could. But in Maine, she'd picked up thoughts from people she couldn't see. Of course, Alec had been there in Maine, somehow making her telepathy more powerful.

"They said she might be sick from some of the drugs. That must be it."

Yes. She'd reached the guard. She wanted to jump for joy but her numb legs prevented it. Keep watching, she thought, you'll see more. She dropped to her knees in front of the toilet and brought the hand with the IV attached close to her chest, to hide it from the cameras. She mimed throwing up, complete with the nastiest sounds she could make. She heard the faint voice think, *"Gross."*

For good measure, she cleared her throat and spit saliva into the toilet. Dizzy, she almost banged her head on the porcelain. She tugged the linen sheet over her head grabbed the IV tube and put it into her mouth.

Here goes nothing.

She bit down hard on the cold plastic. The drugs stopped flowing. She forced herself to count to sixty, to see if stopping the drugs would do anything for her lethargy. Drool dripped down her chin. No difference. It probably would take time but she didn't have any damn time. She twisted some of the tubing around her fingers, clenched down hard with her teeth, and pulled.

At first, the tubing seemed to stretch. She pulled harder. Her teeth felt like they were being dragged out by the roots and her fingers ached. No good. What the hell did they make this stuff from, anyway? All she'd done was put teeth marks on the plastic.

That left pulling the needle out. But not here. The closer she was to the door and escape when the guard rushed in, the better.

"She looks bad. Should I check on her?"

"Yes," she thought, *"you should."* She bit down on the tubing again and started to walk to the door. She smiled, thinking of how Philip would have liked her ingenuity. She kept the sheet over her head like a cowl and settled next to the door. Her limbs felt less heavy, her head less dizzy. Maybe stopping the flow of drugs had helped.

She braced her shoulder against the wall.

"What the hell is she stumbling around for now?"

"For this," she thought. She braced the hand with the IV against her chest, peeled off the tape and pulled the needle out of her hand

with a swift jerk.

"Damn!" Red blood gushed out of her hand as the needle came free. She looked at the blood, spots appeared before her eyes and pain wound up her arm like a snake.

Don't look, don't look, don't look. Her hand throbbed. She wrapped a corner of the sheet around her hand to stop the bleeding and grabbed the steel IV holder. Blood seeped out from under the sheet, coating the metal, making it slippery and hard to hold.

The door opened.

A uniformed guard stepped through the doorway. She straightened and swung the steel holder at his head. It smashed into the side of his skull, just above his ear. He toppled over and landed on his back with a cry of pain.

Huh. That had actually *worked.*

She jammed her bare foot in the door to prevent it from closing, wincing when the weight slammed against her toes.

The guard rose, cursing. The IV holder slipped from her hands, too coated with blood for her to grip it any longer. He was too close— she'd never get out the door before he grabbed her.

"Stop, stop, stop."

Miraculously, he did, just like Lansing had done the day they'd watched Alec together, though she hadn't intended this result either time.

My God. What am I?

"What the hell are you doing?" The guard looked down at his feet.

"Getting out," she said. *"Stay here. Do not move. Do not call for help."*

He blinked again and remained stuck in a weird half-hunched pose. She shot through the door and it swung shut behind her.

Freedom!

She took a step and something tugged at her. She turned and saw the trailing edge of the sheet was stuck under the door. She wrapped her hands in the sheet and pulled hard. The sheet was stuck tight. She dropped it in disgust. Great. Now she had to run around this place naked.

She tucked her bleeding hand against her chest and began running. The guard had come from left, so she went left. Her head seemed clearer and her legs no longer felt like lead, though her smashed toes ached. Even without the sheet, she was warmer.

Her feet slapped against the linoleum as she ran, a noise that seemed far too loud to her ears. Somebody would notice it, soon.

"Oh, God, she'll get past my station and out into the main complex. Lansing will kill me."

He really did think Lansing would kill him. The guard's fear came through so loud that it was like a scream inside her head. With the scream came a mental image of his guard station, including the image of a door that led to the outer complex. If she could get into the main part of the Resource, she might escape, or at least find Alec.

She skidded to a stop at a turn. Her trail of blood drops gave her away like a blinking neon sign. She had to bandage the hand, somehow. She looked around the corridor in front of her. It seemed just the same as the last one, all white walls and fluorescent lighting, but there was a half-open door at the far end that looked exactly like the image in the guard's thoughts.

She dashed into the guard station and shut the door behind her. If nothing else, she could barricade herself in here for a while and try to use the telepathy to reach Alec.

Monitors covered one wall. On the desk below sat several computers and other electronic equipment. On one of the monitors, the one that received images from the camera in her room, the guard banged on the door, yelling for help. Damn. Her command had worn off fast.

There was a red light blinking above the monitors. That couldn't be good. She flexed her hand and winced but the pain was not as bad as before. She could have laughed. She was lost somewhere in this complex, she was naked, her hand throbbed and yet she felt more alive than in years. No wonder Alec got a charge out of running into battle.

She turned around and noticed a heavy green jacket hanging on the back of the chair in front of a second group of monitors. She snagged it with greedy hands and slipped it on. It was too big, it was made from some scratchy synthetic blend, and it was an awful shade of puke green but it was warm, the sleeves covered her bloody hand, and it was so big that it went down past her butt.

I'll take it.

Now if only she get into the rest of the complex without bleeding all over the place. She walked around the corner at the end of the station and found another door with a small window cut in the middle. She went up on tiptoes and peered through it. The corridors seemed bigger out there and the ceilings higher. She pushed down on the door handle. It didn't move. *Locked.* She settled back on her feet and saw an electronic code box on the wall to the right. It would need a code that she didn't have.

She pounded the wall. What a stupid way to be stopped.

She walked back to the monitor, staring at the guard in her room. He'd given away the location of his station by his thoughts a few minutes ago. He might think about the alarm code she needed. She closed her eyes.

At first, she heard nothing but her heart pounding in her ears and the quiet hum of the computers. Then semi-incoherent rage started to come through. When the guard's words made sense, she knew she'd been right.

"She'll never get out, she can't get out, she doesn't know the code. I know the code. 1078. She'll never get it, they'll trap her in there soon."

Not only had he given away the code, he'd also thought about the exit from this floor out to the grounds. Now she knew which direction to go. She blew a kiss to the monitor.

She ran back to the alarm box, punched in 1078, took a deep breath and hit enter. This time, when she turned the handle, the door swung open.

She ran down the corridor. Just before an intersection with a second hallway, she heard quiet footsteps. She stopped and flattened herself against the wall, like they did in movies. Maybe it would work. She closed her eyes and tried to listen. The telepathy seemed to work better if she closed her eyes.

"I am going to rip Lansing to shreds if I don't find her soon. Let's see him heal that."

"Philip!"

He came around the corner. She threw herself into his arms with a quiet squeal. Her bare cheek scraped against his scruffy chin. He hugged her back so hard that she was hardly able to breathe. *"Thank God. Beth. Daughter. Beth."*

"Smart girl, to save us the trouble of finding you." His eyes were full of tears.

Tears sprang to her own eyes. She *felt* his relief and joy inside her head. But underneath that was something else: pain. His shoulder was on fire, pain flowing from it in never-ending waves. How was he even standing?

She backed away, easing the pressure against his arm sling. He held her a few inches from him and smiled, which brought some life to his haggard face. He cleared his throat and wiped away the tears with a sleeve. There were dark circles under his eyes and his jaw seemed permanently clenched, either in pain or anger. She hugged him again, not so hard this time. He kissed the top of her head. *"I love you, daughter."*

"I love you too." She swallowed, a lump in her throat.

He blinked. "I think that might take a little getting used to." He studied her. "What are you wearing?"

"It's a guard's jacket."

He took her wrist and exposed the bloody hand. "What happened?"

She raised it to him. "I pulled out an IV needle. I'm okay." Compared to his shoulder agony, her hand was a paper cut. "But I think I set off an alarm when I escaped."

He looked down at her feet. "Do you want my shoes?"

"They're too big."

"All right. Then we should move." He pointed down the left hallway. "Stay close."

She followed, trying to ignore the pain he was broadcasting and instead listen for anyone else who might be close. Footsteps sounded behind them. Philip spun around, gun ready, and pushed her behind him. Whatever the pain, he was clearly able to ignore it. Though for how long?

She shivered. All the euphoria from her escape vanished. Someone appeared at the opposite end of the hallway. The thoughts, loud as a scream, blasted at her.

"Beth!"

"Alec."

She put her hand on Philip's shoulder. "It's Alec."

Philip lowered his gun. Alec skidded to a halt. He scooped her up in his arms and twirled her around, hugging her close, tighter than Philip had held her, squeezing the breath from her. He smelled of cigarette smoke and alcohol, though he seemed completely sober.

"Beth, Beth, Beth, Drake told the truth, Lansing lied, he had you, but you're safe now. I'll keep you safe. Beth, Beth, Beth."

"I'm getting dizzy. Stop!"

She closed her eyes and covered her ears. He was so loud, much louder than Philip or the guard, like a continuous high-volume stereo. And Philip's thoughts mixed in now too, intruding with his wariness of Alec, worry about them, worry about escape and more of that pounding pain. She dropped to one knee. Loud, so loud.

"Beth?" Philip put a hand on her shoulder.

She took her hands off her ears and stared at Alec, who'd lost his grin. *"What the hell is wrong, Beth?"*

"You're thinking so loud it hurts. Think softer."

"How do I do that?"

"I don't know! Think like you whisper."

"Okay."

That did feel much more like a whisper than a scream.

Philip helped her to her feet. He stared at Alec. Philip hadn't put away his gun.

"I'm okay. Alec is setting off my telepathy. I can't control it. It hurts."

Alec reached out to touch her and stopped when she waved his hand away.

"Not having control sucks. Are you okay?"

"I will be when I'm out of here."

"Follow me," Philip said. "And, you—" he pointed at Alec, "—don't touch her again."

They fell in behind Philip. "Where are your clothes?" Alec asked.

"This is the best I could find." She swallowed. Even talking seemed to cause difficulty. She'd hit overload.

Philip started back down the corridor. She stayed a step behind them. Damn, all those sexy dreams she'd had about Alec to distract her from what the scientists were doing and now she couldn't even touch him.

192

"Alec, I am glad to see you. Really, really glad."

"I'm sorry, I should have figured out you were here sooner. You were trying to talk to me, weren't you?"

"You heard me? Good. I tried. I thought I wasn't getting through because of the drugs."

"Lansing drugged you? I'll kill him."

"Let's just get out of here."

At the end of the corridor, they stopped at the bottom of a metal stairwell that led to an oversized metal door with locks at the top and bottom. "It leads to the ground floor," Philip said.

"Can we get through it?" she asked.

"The door is not the problem," Philip said. "The question is what's on the other side. I don't want to walk into an ambush. You said you set off an alarm?"

She turned around. "There was a red blinking light in the guard station."

"It might be a localized alarm," Alec said. "Anyway, I can take care of whatever or whoever is on the other side."

"Like you did in Maine? I don't think so," Philip said.

"You didn't do any better."

"Tone it down," she said. Their angry thoughts felt like hornets buzzing in her head. She stepped between them. "We have to get out, so we have to go through the door."

Philip nodded. He pulled a small revolver from inside his sling and handed it to her. "Point and shoot. It's a close-range weapon. You may need it. And stay behind your firestarter. He can stop bullets."

She nodded, her throat dry, and slipped the gun into the pocket of the guard's jacket. No, definitely not fun anymore.

"I told you, I can take care of her," Alec said.

"Oh, you've done a lovely job so far," Philip said.

"Hello. I got *myself* out."

Philip started up the steps. "Stay behind me. And if we're separated, you both do whatever you have to do to get out of here."

"I'm not leaving you, Philip."

"You may have to. I'm not healing as fast as I should. I should not be in this much pain."

"What do you mean?"

"It's not healing right. I must be getting old."

She closed her eyes for a second against his frustration and the agony centered on his shoulder.

"If her power's out of control, that's got to be awful. I'll show her, I'll work on it with her, we'll fix that."

Alec's thoughts crowded out Philip. So very Alec too. No worries, just go forward and fix whatever was wrong. But if he was contributing to the problem, if she couldn't even touch him, how could she fix it?

The metal mesh on the steps cut into her feet. It was just as well that they were almost numb from the cold. Alec's thoughts kept running a mile a minute, worried about her, worried about what was at the top of the steps, anger with Lansing, worry that Daz wouldn't hold up his end.

"Daz is helping you? He's the one who took me in Maine, Alec."

"I know. And that's eating at him. He thought you messed me up. Now he doesn't."

"Just that simple?"

"I think so. We're team. A unit."

"I don't understand that, Alec."

"I do. At least, I hope I do."

Meaning that Alec wasn't sure of Daz. Fantastic. Philip stopped at the top of the stairs and spun around.

"There's a crowd coming." He pointed in the direction where they'd just come.

She heard the now-familiar thud of military boots. Alec put his arm around her shoulders. Everything got loud again. Not only from Alec and Philip but from the men running toward them.

"Alec, I can hear who's coming. It's Daz. And please get your arm off me. Every time you do that, I hear everything all at once."

He removed his arm. *"That should be cool."*

"Would you like a crowd screaming at you all at once?"

"No. Sorry."

She grabbed the stair rail for balance. Philip slipped an arm around her waist. "Stay the hell away from her and go make sure your team isn't going to turn on us." He pointed to the soldiers now visible in the corridor.

Alec bounded down the steps.

"Easy," Philip whispered to her. "Stay on guard."

"You don't trust Alec's team?"

"Beth, I don't trust *Alec*. That's why I'm here..."

"*...which may have been a mistake if I can't stay on my feet.*"

"Oh."

She didn't think that Philip had wanted her to hear that last part. She reached out past him to hear Alec instead. She expected his thoughts to center on F-Team. Instead, his thoughts were a running commentary on her legs and her breasts and her butt. At least it was complimentary. Men.

"*Thank you.*"

He glanced up at her in response. "*I didn't know you could hear all that.*"

Alec tensed and raised a hand as the soldiers drew closer. Marshalling his TK or fire, she thought. Daz was carrying a big rifle and there was a handgun holstered at his side. He was flanked by a soldier she didn't know and by a tall man who was so skinny that he almost seemed like a scarecrow. Gabe, she remembered, the electronics specialist, the second in command of the unit. The one who'd played sniper during the drill and had nearly been burnt up for the effort.

"We got her," Alec said.

Daz held the rifle easily at his waist. "You and Drake were supposed to stay with us."

Alec lowered his hand. "What matters is that we got her."

"No, what matters is we were supposed to do this together. We agreed. How did you get her?"

"She escaped by herself," Alec said. "And quit your stupid hissy fit long enough for us to get out of here."

Daz pointed at Alec. "The next time you have to deal with an underground complex, a telepath, a spook and a lovesick firestarter, let's see how pissed you get."

Beth ignored the headache and tried to make sense of all the voices demanding to be heard. Daz didn't trust Philip or her and he wasn't completely sure about Alec. Neither Philip nor Alec was sure if Daz could be trusted.

This is my rescue team?

Her headache grew worse. Like a sinus headache, it pounded behind her eyes, almost as if her skull would explode. Lesson one: Don't read so many people at the same time—just shut them out.

Gabe tapped some sort of device strapped to his wrist. "We're in trouble. I bypassed the alarms but one of them went off about five minutes ago anyway. We're running out of time."

"Commander," Philip said, voice as sharp as a slap. Everyone stared up at him. "What are the odds of an ambush on the other side of this door?"

Daz frowned. "The alarm's down here. That's where they'll send the goon squad first. Well, some of them."

"So we assume there's an army out there. Battle ready through the door," Philip said. "Commander, if you're going to back us up, get up here."

Daz scowled but walked up the flight of steps and stopped next to her. Beth shrank back against Philip. Daz scared her. Why? He gestured with his hand to Alec and her memory flashed on the night she'd been taken, when he'd gestured just like that to another soldier. Daz had picked her up off the floor in Maine.

"Let's go, Drake," Alec said.

Philip nodded. "I go, then you, then the team, protecting Beth..."

"...And if they fail, they won't live long enough to regret it."

Beth winced at the intensity of Philip's thought and caught an image of two Resource guards shot in the back of the head. *I don't want to see that.* She imagined a wall around her. She blinked. That worked. She imagined opening a door to Alec and only Alec. That worked too. The pounding in her head eased.

"Alec, you'll protect Philip? He's in bad shape."

"I will. Trust me."

"I do."

She gritted her teeth, bit her lip and let Daz and the other two soldiers surround her. They were careful not to brush against her and she realized they were as afraid of her as she was of them.

Philip pushed down the metal handle of the steel door and released the bolts at the top and bottom. He punched in a code and turned the handle again. The door opened and he dashed through. Alec followed, one step behind.

She held her breath. Alec reappeared almost immediately. "Clear."

She rushed out from behind F-Team and raced through the door. Alec grabbed her hand as she entered the hallway, and the walls inside her mind came tumbling down.

"Alec, let go of my hand, dammit."

He dropped it. *"Sorry. Forgot again. You're just irresistible, counselor."*

"That's not funny. Do you have any idea how much that hurts?"

"Sorry."

"At least I know there's no one else in this hallway, so it accomplished something. And you can trust Daz. But your team doesn't like risking a fight."

She imagined the walls around her brain again and the headache lessened. She recognized this as the ground floor of the Resource where she'd met with Alec. Unlike below, the walls on this floor were pastel-colored and decorated with classic art prints. She sighed as her feet sank into the carpet. The rough fibers felt like silk after all that cold linoleum and sharp metal.

Philip opened his mouth to speak and was instantly drowned out by a blaring alarm. The lights went out.

Shit.

Chapter Nineteen

Red lights flickered above them. They appeared on the ceiling tiles in a straight line, casting everyone in an eerie glow. Shit had really hit the fan.

But we're together. I can protect her now.

"Nearest exit," Alec said in a low voice. "Go."

They ran, passing Beth's old office. She kept close behind him. Drake brought up the rear, behind Daz and the other two soldiers. They stopped for a second at an intersection with the second hallway. One more, and they'd be out on the grounds.

Alec sent the TK ahead, searching for anything moving. Nothing. "Let's go."

"Philip," Beth said.

Alec turned. Drake was leaning against the wall, hardly able to stand.

"Go ahead," Drake said through gritted teeth. "Now."

"Not without you," she said.

"Support him," Alec ordered Daz and the others, "Beth, you stay with me."

Daz put his arm around Drake's waist and took his weight. "Watch when we get to the door, Firefly. They've got gas pressure-rigged to go off."

Shit. "I'll handle it."

"Better or we'll all end up in the brig or worse," Gabe muttered.

Slowed by Drake, they moved more at a walk than run. This was not the rescue Alec had envisioned. He doubted Drake had expected it either.

"It's better than being a prisoner, trust me, Alec."

He could have kissed her. And he would, soon as they were out of here. The sound of boots thudding against carpet grew louder.

A group of Resource soldiers rounded the turn behind them. The guards wore body armor and helmets with dark shields that covered their faces. They raised their rifles. Two of them had tranq guns. *Fuck.*

"Total fucking mess," Daz muttered, bringing his rifle to his shoulder.

Alec flexed his hands, marshaling his fire.

"Stand down, now," the guard in the middle said. "Do what I say and no one gets hurt."

"No way." Alec lifted a hand. He felt the fire close, coiled, ready to be set loose. He was almost glad. No more skulking, no more waiting.

Beth stepped to his side, right into the line of fire.

What the hell? He tried to grab her shoulder and missed. "What are you doing?"

"Keeping *anyone* from getting shot, even them." She grabbed his hand.

His head snapped back as pain slashed at him, like a spike right between his eyes. He blinked and it was gone. He was left with feeling liked he had double vision. In a way, he did. He was linked to Beth's mind and seeing through her eyes as well as his own.

"Lower your guns. You don't see us, you don't see anything wrong. You heard noise down the other end of the complex. You have to go check it out."

Alec felt the power behind her thoughts but they didn't affect him, just as he couldn't feel the pain of her headache anymore. He was a spectator. She expected the guards to do as she commanded. Beth could do *that?* Cool.

Sweat dripped down her face. Her skin felt ice cold. She squeezed his hand tighter. Her eyes had a vacant, unfocused look. Drake slid closer, to stand at her other side. Maybe not so cool, if using her power cost her that much.

Alec kept himself ready to act but the guards stood still, frozen in place. He would have given a lot to see the expressions behind their face shields. Inside his head, he heard Beth sending out the same message, again and again.

After a silent moment, the lead guard raised his visor and waved a hand at the others.

"Okay, nothing here," he said. "I think I heard something down the other way."

The other guards nodded and lowered their rifles.

"So, let's go!" said the one in charge.

They ran off in a controlled jog.

Beth crumpled to her knees.

Alec scooped her up. She moaned and let her head drop against his shoulder. She'd bitten through her lip. Blood trickled down her chin. People said he was brave, but she'd just risked herself for people who wanted to make her a prisoner.

"What the hell just happened?" Daz asked.

Beth moaned again. "It won't last long," she whispered.

"She told them to go away telepathically," Alec said. "Let's not waste it."

"A real life Jedi mind trick. Shit," Gabe said.

They only got a hundred feet before the sound of booted footsteps echoed again, this time in front of them. Another squad.

"Damn," Daz muttered.

They ducked into a dead-end hallway. Drake collapsed to one knee.

"Now what?" Gabe asked.

Alec took a deep breath. Beth was defenseless now. Drake was hardly better. He looked down at her pale face. Through the telepathic link with her, he caught echoes of intense pain spiking in her head.

Two down. Bad odds in a fight.

"Firefly, we have to move," Daz said.

"Not without Philip."

Even her mental voice was weak and dripping with pain. Alec looked up at the water lily painting and realized they were right on top of Lansing's elevator. He turned to Daz. "Here, hold her a minute."

Daz blinked. "Are you kidding? I—"

Alec handed Beth to him. Daz had no choice but to grab her. Gabe took the rifle from Daz, so he could get a more secure grip. Daz looked at Beth as if she was some sort of bomb that might go off. Beth opened her eyes and stared back at him.

"Boo."

Daz half-smiled.

Alec pushed aside the painting and punched the code on the alarm pad. Nothing happened. *Fuck*. Lansing had changed the pass code already.

Gabe tapped the device on his wrist. The small screen was completely red. "Whatever you're doing, Alec, do it fast. Cameras are going to come back on soon and we'll be sitting ducks."

Alec started tapping on the wall, desperately trying to find the seam that hid the elevator entrance. The TK could slip into the smallest crack and push the door open by force. If not, he could try melting the wall.

Whoa.

His TK slipped inside *something*. At first, he thought he'd found an empty space behind the wall. But that wasn't it. Nothing pushed back at his TK, nothing stopped it. He felt like he was swimming underwater. All that space and no end to it. He reached out with the TK and felt tiny balls and thin strands.

Shit, he hadn't just slipped *inside* the wall, he'd slipped inside the *molecules* of the wall. It felt like the time he'd taken the fence apart and put it back together, except it had taken him hours to peel back the fence molecules from each other and he'd never slipped *inside* the steel fence. He'd no idea his TK could do this.

"What's taking so long?" Daz said.

Alec opened his eyes and he was back in the regular world again. He stepped back, blinking, still overcome with the sensation of feeling as if nothing in the world was solid. That was damn disconcerting.

"I'm going to open the code box from the inside," Alec said. "Just a few more seconds."

If he could slip through the molecules of the wall, then he could find the mechanism behind the code box and manipulate it to open the elevator door. Alec put his hand on the code box and closed his eyes. He fumbled around, looking for wires, and grasped them. Whew. He'd done it right this time.

He followed the wires up to a square panel. He tested, pushing gently at the panel. It had give behind it. If he pushed harder, he'd either set off a local alarm or he'd open the door.

What the hell.

He pushed hard. Something clicked. The wall started sliding.

He took Beth back from Daz. The other three helped Drake into the elevator and the doors closed shut behind them.

"Where does this lead?" Daz asked.

"Lansing's penthouse," Alec said. "Last place they'll look."

Drake snorted. "I could get to like you, boy."

The elevator doors opened. They exited onto the top floor, into the hallway where he'd stood only hours ago with Lansing.

Alec rushed to the penthouse door and punched in the alarm code from earlier that night. This time, it worked. The locks clicked open and they all hurried inside. Daz closed the door behind them.

"You bought us time. But I don't like this." Daz circled around the room, weapon ready. "Feels boxed in."

Drake collapsed into one of the sitting couches in Lansing's living room. Alec set Beth down on the couch next to Drake. She opened her eyes.

"Thank you for watching out for Philip," she whispered.

"Save the thanks for when I know I didn't trap us."

"You two, go check if we're secure," Daz said to the other team members. "Alec, we're sitting ducks, unless you know of another exit?"

"The roof."

"That's not going to do us any good unless we can fly." Daz scanned the ceiling and the walls. "Where are the cameras?"

"Lansing wouldn't have them in his home," Drake whispered.

"Yeah?" Daz said. "Since you know so much about him, where would he hide a secret exit?"

Drake shook his head, tried to stand and collapsed to the floor.

"Philip!"

Beth knelt down over her father and laid a hand to his neck. She couldn't feel any pulse. She put her hands on his face. His skin was cold and clammy and his breathing was shallow.

"You can't die, Philip!"

"It is what it is."

She saw memory flashes in Philip's mind: him putting a gun to the back of the head of two Resource guards and pulling the trigger; a younger Philip tracking down one of her kidnappers and slitting his throat; a confrontation with Lansing from years ago, where Lansing called Philip "son" and Philip knocked him down with one punch; and a last one of Philip as a boy, confronting another man, a towering red-haired man calling him bastard and no son of his. The man backhanded Philip into a wall. A young girl rushed to the boy Philip's side.

More memories flew at her, too fast for her to sort. The pressure inside her head became worse, pulsating. Her skull felt like it might explode.

Philip was dying and there was nothing she could do.

"You have to get better, Philip, you have to get better, you have to heal, I won't let you die. You have to heal."

Philip's head snapped back. His face flushed. Inside her head, she felt something click, like when she'd accidentally turned off Alec's fire. The intense pressure against her skull eased to a dull roar. What had she done now? Killed her father?

Philip opened his eyes. He blinked and coughed.

"Daz, help me get him on the couch," Alec said.

Philip coughed again as he was moved. After they settled him, she felt for the pulse at his neck again and found it. His breathing seemed less shallow.

"Alec." Philip took a long, labored breath. "Get Beth some clothes and treat her hand. Fast."

Beth grabbed his hand. "I don't want to leave you."

"Momentary collapse. Not my time."

"Bullshit. What happened, Philip?"

"You saw way too much of my life. But you gave me more of it."

Daz placed himself in front of the door. One of the soldiers rushed back into the room. "Found the roof exit," he said. "But that's it."

"Jackpot here," Gabe said from the kitchen. He'd opened the double doors of what Beth had thought was the pantry. "Full security setup. Monitors, alarms, the whole shebang." Gabe rubbed his hands together. "I can see everything they're doing down there from here. And maybe screw with them."

"Do what you can," Daz said. "If Drake's better, get the girl ready to move, Firefly. Fast."

Alec scooped Beth up again. She let him carry her but avoided touching his hand. She'd no idea what happened with Philip and she didn't want to repeat it. Alec leaned down to kiss her forehead. She turned her face away. What if she accidentally messed with his fire again?

Alec frowned. He'd wanted to kiss her. He didn't like that she'd turned away.

Her head pounded as Alec strode down the hallway. Somehow, the burgundy wallpaper seemed more blood-red. She squinted to shut out the color. That seemed to help the pain. As a bonus, it kept her from seeing many of the garish cherubs that lined the tables in the hallway.

When they were out of Daz's hearing, she spoke. "Alec. I'm scared to touch you. My telepathy is—well, I did something to Philip, I think. I don't know what the hell it was. I don't know if it hurt him."

"He seemed better."

"The last time I felt something like that in my head, I took away your fire."

A long pause. "Okay, that would be bad."

Alec stopped at the last door in the hallway, opened the door and set her gently on the bed. He clicked on the desk light. At the base of the light, a little train moved around a tunnel.

A red and black flannel comforter covered the twin bed. The shelves were filled with books on military tactics and biographies. The only fiction she noticed was the Harry Potter series.

"This was your room." She wished she could curl up on the soft bed and sleep for days.

"Until I was twelve." He started digging through one of the bureau drawers.

The train lamp began playing "I've Been Working on the Railroad." He jabbed at a button and the song stopped. She collapsed on the bed, eyes closed, rubbing her temples, wondering if her headache would ever end. Alec had run from a fight because of her. If they were trapped, it was her fault. She was useless. So much for the great escape.

She heard Alec rifling through the drawers, throwing clothes every which way, taking his frustration out on them. Her feet throbbed, reminding her of the cuts and bruises on her soles.

"I hope these fit." Alec placed sweatpants and a black T-shirt in her lap.

"They look the right size, thank you."

He kissed her forehead. "Want these?" He dangled socks in front of her.

She grabbed them out of his hands. "Yes!"

He smiled. "Shoes next."

He opened the closet door and shifted through the stuff at the bottom. She put the socks on while he searched the bottom of the closet, taking a second to enjoy the soft cotton against her cuts. Socks were highly underrated. She slipped on the sweatpants but hesitated over the shirt. The blood from her hand was sticking to the jacket. She'd rip open the needle wound when she took it off.

Alec moved aside Lego blocks and black dress shoes, found sneakers and knelt in front of her.

"I think these should be okay." Alec slipped the sneakers over her feet. "They fit me when I was twelve."

She put her hands on his shoulders. He was so strong. "They're as good as any glass slipper, Alec."

And he was the closest thing to a Prince Charming that she'd ever find in real life. *I won't let anything hurt him, ever.*

He rose and kissed her cheek, a soft brush of lips against skin. "You're welcome, counselor."

Happily, his touch didn't send off more waves of pain in her head. She wiggled her feet, the comfort almost compensation for the headache. "This is wonderful. I felt a little too Bruce Willis there for a second."

Alec smiled again. "Yippee kai yay. You didn't need a machine gun either."

"We're not out of the building yet."

"If you're on your feet, it should be no problem to smash our way out."

"My feet aren't the problem. My head is." She let him tie the shoes. Taking care of her seemed to calm him. It sure as hell calmed *her.*

"Why didn't you ditch the jacket for the T-shirt?"

"The sleeve is stuck to all the blood seeping from my hand."

He winced. "I'll get bandages. One second."

As soon as he left, she unbuttoned the jacket and slid out her good arm. This was going to hurt. Ah, well, next to her headache, it was a pinprick. She gritted her teeth and pulled off the other sleeve with a jerk.

"Ouch!" She clutched the hand to her chest and doubled over. Fresh blood trickled down her wrist and arm.

Alec rushed back in and dumped some bandages on the bed. "I told you to wait for me." He sat and pulled her against him. Their telepathic connection clicked into place without effort.

"I thought it was better to do it myself."

"Let me see, Beth."

She let him take her hand and shivered, cold again. The pounding increased. Alec's thoughts came through loud and clear. He wanted to fix her hand. He was also noticing her breasts. She sighed. A headache. Couldn't she have a better excuse to be not in the mood than that stupid cliché? Of course, there was also the bleeding and the men with guns wanting to take them prisoner.

She reached for the T-shirt. "Let me get the shirt on first, Alec. Please. I'm cold."

He flushed. "Right."

He protected her hand as she slipped it through the sleeve. She fell back on the bed, dizzy.

"It hurts that much?" he asked. "The headache?"

"The headache's worse but I'm a wuss. It's the bleeding that is making my head spin."

"You bandaged *my* bloody hands, remember? You're not that much of a wuss." He smiled, trying to relax her.

"It's different when it's your own blood."

"Easy, counselor. You'll be fixed up in a minute."

She suspected it would take her much longer than a minute to recover from today. If they got out of here. He took a warm, wet cloth and wiped away the blood. How had he gotten it that warm? Oh. Duh. Firestarter.

She looked away from what he was doing so she couldn't see the blood. Alec discarded the washcloth on the floor.

"How's the headache?"

"The same. Let's go."

He slathered antibiotic lotion on her hand. "Can you walk now? Run?"

She hissed at the cold ointment against the gash. "I'll have to."

"Not good enough." He ripped open a sterile bandage packet. "You need control. We'll start now. Help me."

"Excuse me?" She tried to grab her hand back. He kept it tight in his grip.

"Stay in my head and think of amping up my TK."

"Why?"

He grinned. "There's flap of skin on your hand that I want to reattach. That'll stop the bleeding without stitches."

"What?" She sat up. "Are you kidding?"

"I can fix your hand. And maybe if you see what I do, you'll see how to control your headache."

"Um, excuse me, but have you done anything like this before?"

"First time." He grinned.

"That's not funny. What if it doesn't work?"

He pointed to the bandages. "Then I'll do it the usual way."

She grabbed his wrist. "What if instead of reattaching the skin, you do something else, like make half my hand disappear?"

He blinked. "C'mon. I wouldn't do that."

"How do you know? You said it was your first time."

"You don't trust me, counselor?"

"This is not a game!"

He sat next to her on the bed. "No, it's not. We're in trouble. You can't leave a blood trail and we might need your telepathy. So let me fix your hand then the headache, if I can."

She took a deep breath and closed her eyes. "Okay, give it your best shot."

"I won't hurt you."

"What if my gift does something strange to yours again?"

"You mean like give me greater molecular control and hotter fire?"

He brought her hand to his lips and kissed her fingertips. "I can take care of you."

She was about to protest that she didn't need him to take care of

207

her but realized that was not true. She *needed* him.

"Fine. But if you break my hand, you're creating me a new one."

"Deal."

She closed her eyes and concentrated on her telepathic connection with Alec. Something shifted in his head. Her hand tingled, like when it fell asleep. She resisted the urge to shake it and instead focused on what Alec was doing with his TK.

She didn't have words to describe it. There seemed to be movement coming from his mind but she couldn't see anything. She felt a force flowing out and figuratively stepped out of the way. Her hand was engulfed in that strange energy. She winced, gritted her teeth and lost the connection to Alec. She gnawed at the place where she'd bitten her lip earlier. Coward, that's what she was.

She took a deep breath and thought about getting back to Alec's mind. Her telepathy instantly made her wish a reality. Through his eyes, she saw images that looked like slides under a microscopic lens: long, green, furry strings.

It took her a moment to realize that the strings were threads from the green guard jacket. Alec was picking them out of her hand before he resealed the wound. His TK flicked the fibers aside like brushing away lint. When he finished, he paused and put the flap of skin in place with his thumb.

"Ready for this?"

"Wouldn't miss it."

She closed her eyes.

He held her hand tight, holding down her wrist and her fingers. She clutched his shoulder. His shirt was hot and sweaty. Pain jabbed into her hand. She jerked. Alec held the hand fast for a second, then let it go.

"Should I look?"

"Damn right, you should look."

She opened her eyes and brought her hand to her face. She couldn't see the wound. She brought it closer to her eyes. All that was left was a thin white line where the gash had been.

"Not perfect but damn good, right?"

"Damn good, Dr. Farley." She flexed her hand. It didn't hurt. Her head still did, unfortunately. "You were right, I saw what you did with the TK. But I still couldn't tell how you did it. I felt you imagining walls and a door but I've done that and it doesn't work for very long."

"You need practice."

"Yeah." She stood. "There's no time."

He stroked her hair. "We fix the headache, you're an asset. If we don't, you're a liability. You want that?"

"How?"

"Watch."

"Watch what—"

He kissed her lips.

Heat passed between them, a coiled desire, waiting to envelop both of them. It flowed from his mouth to hers, binding them together. She dug her fingers into his shoulder. He wrapped his arm around her waist. She should break this kiss. She didn't want to.

"There's no time for this, Alec!"

"It's the quickest way to get our powers to work together. Pay attention to what's going on in your head while we're connected."

Right, as if it would be easy to concentrate on her mind and not her body, with him kissing her like this. He deepened the kiss. Oh, hell. She couldn't imagine not wanting him when he touched her like this. She let herself hug him tighter and imagined opening a door and letting him in.

"Wall off the headache, counselor. Think of it being gone and it will be. Visualize. Wish for it."

"Trying."

He pushed her down on the bed. She tried to ignore his hands on her because if she focused on that, she wouldn't be able to concentrate on anything else. He showed her the images he used in his mind to control his fire: walls, doors and windows that kept the fire and TK locked up when he wanted and let them out when he wanted. She caught glimpses of metaphorical fire dancing behind his walls.

"Try it!"

She imagined sweeping up her telepathy and sealing it in a closet.

"That's it, that's right. Now lock the door. Imagine a key and put it in your pocket. You can do this."

He stopped kissing her. She cuddled against him, imagined a key and put it away in a pocket.

"Wow."

Her head cleared, the pain and fuzziness gone. She sat up, rubbing her temples.

He hugged her. "It worked, right?"

"The headache's gone. Just like that." She felt only a vague ache. All the pressure behind her eyes had vanished. "How can it be that simple?"

"I told you it would be easy." He grinned.

The door to the room opened wide. "Easy isn't a word I'd use for this situation."

Her father stood there, glaring at them.

"You've been in here ten minutes." Philip was gruff and accusing. "Too long. We have to move."

Alec stood. "We needed that time."

Philip raised his eyebrows. "I see."

Oh, they were going to take time to fight over her again, were they? Great. "Stop it. My headache's gone thanks to him."

"Usually headaches prevent what you were just doing." Philip sighed and reached into his pocket. "Here." He tossed a small, shiny black cube at Alec. Alec caught it, frowning.

"It's a jammer for the tracking device that Lansing implanted inside you," Philip said. "In case we're separated when we're out, you'll have it."

"I have a tracking device *inside* me?" Alec started looking over his arms.

"How do you think Lansing found you in Maine?" Philip turned to her. "Where's the gun I gave you?"

She tapped the pocket of the sweatpants. She'd moved it there from a pocket in the guard's jacket.

"Good. Let's go."

"Wait, how do I get the tracking device out?" Alec asked.

"You're the one with TK," Philip said. "When we have time, stop, search for it inside your thigh and get it out. The jammer will work until then."

They followed her father down the hallway. It was just like him to have some sort of tech device just when it was needed. His steps were now brisk and light, his shoulders straighter, and she no longer picked up continual pain from him. He'd healed, as she'd wished him to heal. *How?*

"What happened to you, Philip?"

"No time to explain."

And she sensed he didn't want to talk about it in front of Alec. He still didn't trust anyone but her. *"You better explain to me, Philip. Now."*

"Fine. I have an unconscious healing power, something akin to internal telekinesis, that fixes my body when I'm hurt. When you touched my mind and ordered me to get better, you clicked my power up to a conscious level. So I fixed the artery where the stitches had ripped open."

That was too much to absorb in one chunk. Healing powers. Dying. To say nothing of the earlier memories, with Lansing calling Philip "son".

"You have a healing power?"

"Yes, and you used it to save my life."

She flushed. She'd saved his *life*. She'd done something right with her telepathy. And she'd made him more powerful, just the way she'd increased Alec's fire. Was she some sort of catalyst? If so, she had no control over it. *I better be very careful what I wish for.*

She tensed as they entered the living room but relaxed when the headache didn't start up again and the soldiers' thoughts didn't crowd her. But she didn't need telepathy to read Gabe's grim mood as he looked over the bank of monitors.

"They got past my blocks down there," Gabe said. "Cameras are back on. I've tapped into their audio feed from here. They're on full alert now and reviewing the video feed. They'll know where we've gone soon."

Daz looked over his shoulder. "Where are the guards?"

"Stationed right outside the hallway that dead-ends to Lansing's elevator."

Alec walked over to them. "They coming up here?"

Gabe shook his head. "Soon. But if we go back down there, we walk into a trap."

"No, we don't. We go down and I blast out the back of the elevator. Brand new exit." Alec waved a hand at the coffee table. One of the legs crumbled. The table tipped over, spilling the gargoyle on it to the floor.

The ceramic shattered into pieces.

Beth thought back to how easily Alec had fixed her hand. What were his limits now?

"Good enough," Daz resettled his gun against his shoulder. "Let's move."

Her father hung back as they gathered to leave. She opened her mind and read Philip's intent. Dammit. He was planning on staying behind to kill Lansing. No time to argue with him. She sent a telepathic order to Philip to come with her and prayed it would work on him. He stepped close and shot her a nasty look.

"We are going to have a long talk after this, young lady."

Alec reached to open the door. Beth caught a flash of thought just behind it.

"Wait, Alec!"

He turned to her. "Why?"

"Lansing's on the other side."

Chapter Twenty

"Daz," Alec said. "Cover the door."

Alec stepped to the side. He let his fire gather inside him and uncoil inside his brain, ready to strike.

The door opened. Lansing closed it behind him. Alec stepped into the open, raised his hand and used the TK to slam his supposed father into the door.

Lansing hit with a thud and fell to his knees with a grunt. "You're pathetic, Alec."

"Search him."

Daz pulled him upright. Gabe found a handgun in an ankle holster and a knife in a forearm sheath. Daz took out a smart phone from Lansing's pocket.

"I'll take that," Drake said.

Daz tossed it. Drake put it in his sling.

Lansing glared at Alec, who glared back. The director's tweed jacket started to smoke. Beth grabbed Alec's hand.

"That's enough."

"Not nearly," Alec said.

"You're a soldier, not a murderer." She gripped his hand tight.

Drake grabbed Lansing by the front of his shirt and slammed him into the wall again. "What, nothing to say?"

"Not to you, mongrel," Lansing said through clenched teeth.

Alec squeezed Beth's hand, thinking of the gash he'd healed and how pale she had been. This bastard deserved to die. Maybe he should let Drake do what he obviously wanted to do.

"Please, Alec."

It was her mental voice, so worried, that reached him, not the words.

"We'll take him with us and use him to get out of here."

"Can you get him to call off the goons down there first?" Daz asked.

Drake wrenched one of Lansing's arms behind him and jabbed the barrel of a small .22 into the thick hair of his captive's skull. "Do it."

"Not a chance, boy."

"We don't need him," Beth said. "All we need to do is punch in the code on the security setup in the kitchen."

"If we knew the code," Gabe said.

Beth smiled. "I know it."

"Not possible," Lansing hissed.

Beth crossed her arms over her chest and smiled. "I'm a telepath, remember?"

Lansing scowled.

"Show Gabe," Alec said.

It took about thirty seconds while Gabe punched in the code into the main computer. He counted seconds until the computer beeped and reported it had given a coded stand-down order to the Resource guards.

Drake kept the .22 on his prisoner while they waited. Given that Drake was several inches shorter and had to wrench Lansing lower to keep the gun against his temple, that had to be uncomfortable. Good. Let Lansing suffer.

"Nothing more to say?" Alec said to him.

"Nothing that you'll hear, since Drake and the girl got to you. What a pathetic waste of time you were."

The tweed jacket started to smoke again. "Don't push it," Alec said.

"Alarm's off, back to normal down there," Gabe said.

"The goons?"

"Returning to their quarters," Gabe said.

"That fast? Gotta be a trick," Daz said.

"It's not," Beth said. "The director's word is law around here. Unlike all of you, his security force was brought in to take orders. And they follow those orders without question."

Alec didn't look back as they left the penthouse and all Lansing's crazy plans for him behind them. Lansing had sounded utterly serious about the idea of tracking down and taking out Putin and other world leaders. And he'd nearly bought into it.

Drake kept a close hold on his captive in the elevator, probably cutting off circulation in that arm.

They hated each other, that was clear. Why?

"You don't want to know." Beth slipped her hand into his grasp and squeezed against him. Her mental voice sounded not so much angry as depressed. He put his arm around her. She shivered, so he concentrated for a second and warmed her clothes. She sighed happily.

They'd had hardly any time to really be with each other. The beach in Maine, that kiss that healed her headache. First chance, as soon as they got out of here, they'd take the time to really be together.

"Yes, soon, Alec."

On the ground floor, they stepped out of the elevator. He kept hold of Beth's hand. Even when she wasn't speaking telepathically, he could *feel* her in the back of his mind, a soft caress at some deep mental level. It didn't feel the least bit intrusive.

Beth gave him the telepathic equivalent of a hug.

Daz pulled an iPhone from his pocket and they walked down the hallway, to the exit.

"I'm going to text the rest of the team, have them meet us outside," Daz said. "We'll leave together."

"You have a contract, Commander," Lansing said.

"Yeah, and it didn't include kidnapping a woman and helping to keep Alec a prisoner," Daz said. "Sue me. See how far you get in court."

They stepped outside. The lights were on in the parking lot but the full moon made them almost unnecessary. "We'll take the van," Alec said.

"What about him?" Daz pointed at Lansing.

Drake moved the muzzle of the .22 from his captive's head to his heart. "Alive, he'll always be a threat to both of you."

"No," Beth said.

Alec squeezed her hand, torn.

"Your father's right," he said. "Lansing's got some wacked-out plan to use psychics to control the world. And he's got the money and

215

power to back it up."

"We can't help any of that right this second."

"You want him to take other kids and do to them what he did to me?"

"You can't save children by staining your own hands with blood..."

"...*Look what murder has done to Philip. You see what he is. Do you want to be like him? He doesn't want that for you or me, I know it.*"

"Let the bastard go." Alec flicked his fingers, calling the TK, and knocked Drake back from his prisoner.

Drake scowled. "This is a mistake."

"Team's coming," Daz said. "Fast."

Alec nodded.

"You'll come back, Alec. This is what you are," Lansing said. "You'll be lost without it."

Alec shook his head. For the first time, the man who had controlled his life seemed old, shrunken in size. Irrelevant.

"I'll decide what I am."

"Not with the girl controlling you. Obviously, she has more power than you know. And Drake has an agenda."

"He wanted to save his daughter," Alec said. "Simple."

"You're the simple one, being led around by what's below your waist. She wants you to be some fool with a house and a job. You'll hate it."

"Team's assembling." Daz pointed to the other nine members of F-Team, in full battle gear, headed in their direction.

Alec turned to Lansing. "You blew it, old man. You had a chance with me. You could have been a real father to me, like Drake is to his daughter. You could have put my safety and my life above all. Instead you shoved me into war games before I was twelve, drugged me and lied through your teeth when it suited you."

"It was necessary. You'll realize that."

Alec jabbed a finger into Lansing's breastbone. "I could have cared about you. Now, we're done. Come near me after this and I'll cremate you."

Alec's impulse to kill the man faded. Lansing had no power over him anymore.

Beth tugged at his elbow. "I want to get the hell out of here. *Now.*"

The sound of chopper blades cutting through air stopped the conversation. Alec looked up. Lights shone down overhead from an approaching helicopter.

Not just a chopper, a Blackhawk and probably armed. And they had no place to run in the open air.

"You did this." Alec grabbed Lansing by the shirt.

Lansing shook his head. "It's not mine."

"Bullshit." Alec had to yell over the sound of copter blades.

"He's telling the truth, Alec. Whoever is inside is thinking about Lansing, something urgent, but he doesn't work for Lansing."

Alec let go of the shirt and raised his hands, marshaling the TK. He tried to grab the chopper blades but they moved too fast and had too much power behind them. He could break them but not control them. He could knock the copter from the sky or blow up the gas tank but that would destroy it and everyone on board.

"Don't. I'm not sure that's an enemy."

"If they're trying to save Lansing, they are. How many inside?"

"Three. Two pilots and someone else. They're not thinking about attacking us. They want to talk to Lansing."

With his TK, Alec nudged Daz to get his attention. Daz turned. Alec held up three fingers and pointed to the Blackhawk. Daz nodded. F-Team surrounded Lansing, preventing escape. Drake had once again moved to Beth's side. He moved pretty damn fast for someone who'd been almost dead fifteen minutes ago. That needed an explanation. Soon.

The Blackhawk touched down. The blades stopped rotating.

A man dressed in a suit stepped out of a side door. Kowalski, the Resource's CIA contact. "Lansing, what the hell kind of show are you running? You have your men ready but—"

"The Resource is busy right now, Kowalski," Drake said. "Leave a message and we'll get back to you."

Alec grinned.

Kowalski turned on Drake. "You're not supposed to be here, asshole." He looked them over. "Forget it. I don't want to know what's going on. What I want is F-Team deployed. We've located Demeter's group. They're close to Manhattan and probably ready to detonate the bomb. We need to hit them first."

"Bullshit," Alec said.

Beth grabbed his forearm. "He's telling the truth. Demeter has his group on a container ship just outside New York harbor. They could detonate the bomb anytime now." Her face grew paler.

"Straight dope?" Daz stepped forward, looking at Beth. She nodded.

Daz took a deep breath and lowered his rifle. "Shit." He looked around and shrugged. "Demeter has lousy timing." He pointed to several team members. "You three, get our ship assault gear, including grappling hooks." He turned to Alec and tossed him a set of keys. "You take the girl and Drake and get the hell out of here. Nice knowing you, Firefly."

Alec caught the keys. For all the weight they carried, they shouldn't have felt so light. He put them in Beth's hand. "Take your father and go."

"Because you're going with F-Team."

"I have to," he said. "I'll find you after. Or have your father find me. He's good at that."

She shook her head. He felt her mood telepathically: resigned, worried and determined.

"No."

He set his hands on her shoulders and searched her face. "What did you say?"

She tossed the keys to the ground. "I'm going with you."

Chapter Twenty-One

"No," Alec and Philip said in unison.

"Yes." She shut out their mental cries. "I have to go. Every time Alec and I touch, he has access to more power. I don't want him to fail because I'm not there. And I can help with my telepathy."

"You're not trained," Alec said.

"I did fine just now. I'm going." Beth crossed her arms over her chest. It was a good thing he couldn't read her mind because he would never agree if he knew how scared she was.

Their thoughts battered her, angry and insistent. Philip was ready to knock her out and take her to safety. She was tempted to let him. The gun fight in Maine had been enough battle for a lifetime.

"I'm going." She pushed down her fear. "You either take me or I'm going to make you stay behind, Alec."

"You can't—"

"I can. Remember what I did to the guards?"

Alec swore. The blacktop at his feet started to melt. He stepped to the side.

"If you're coming, Firefly, we need to go, fast," Daz said.

Alec clenched his teeth. "She's coming with us."

Daz raised his eyebrows. "Are you nuts? I'm not taking a civilian on this."

"Yes, you are, Commander Montoya." She stared at him, sending the command to him, telepathically, several times over.

"Fuck, back off, shrink." Daz shook his head, as if trying to clear his brain. "You want in so bad, you win. You better be up to it." Daz spoke into his phone, calling for another set of body armor.

"I'm glad she's your girl, not mine, Firefly," Daz said.

"Why?"

"Because she's going to win every argument you ever have."

She smiled. Alec scowled.

"Make that two sets of body armor." Philip took off his sling. "Stop looking shocked, Commander. I'm no civilian."

"You're a liability," Daz said. "We could have gotten out of that shithole much faster if you hadn't collapsed."

"I got better," Philip said, face blank.

Daz turned to Alec, questioning. "I'm not risking our people unless he's good to go."

"Beth?" Alec looked at her. "He's hurt. You could order him to stay."

If she lied, Philip would have to stay here. He'd be safe. And that would be as wrong as Philip forcing her to stay.

"He's okay now," she said. "He's healed. Side effect of my telepathy."

Daz shrugged. "All right, but it's your funeral, Drake. We're not taking time to babysit you."

Beth turned to her father. "You *should* stay."

"If you can make a choice to risk your life, then I can make the same choice to protect you."

Which she knew. She hugged him and he squeezed back so tightly it took her breath away. He understood why she had to go. He hated it, but he understood. And she knew why *he* had to come. She'd known for years that she was one of Philip's few holds on sanity. If she was gone, she suspected he wouldn't live long after her death, even with his healing ability.

A soldier arrived with a smaller version of Alec's body armor. She let Philip put it on her, knowing she'd fumble with the Velcro straps. It was heavier than she'd expected, and she fought to keep her knees from knocking together. It covered her butt like the guard's jacket had. Alec hovered, worried, and she hoped she looked calm.

"I'm also coming," Lansing announced.

That brought everyone to silence for a few seconds. Gabe, who'd been discreetly covering Lansing with a rifle, muttered a curse.

"I'd as soon take you into battle as a snake into my bed," Daz said.

"No," Philip said, "let him come."

Alec frowned, looking between Daz and Philip. "Why?"

"We bring him, we can watch him," Philip said. "We let him stay, he'll have an army of goons and government backing to arrest us once this is over. Behind our backs, he's a serious threat. With us, we watch him."

"Point," Daz said. "But he could fuck up the mission."

"Then he'd die and he doesn't want that, do you, Richard?" Philip said Lansing's first name like a curse word.

Alec stared at Lansing. His foster father stared back, not flinching this time from the anger.

Beth tried to read Lansing's thoughts but all she got was determination to come on the mission. He did want to help, for some reason.

"Alec, I can control him, if necessary."

"You sure? We could be getting shot at when you try."

"My father is right. If we leave him behind, we could stop the bomb and then find ourselves massacred or imprisoned by government troops. Anyway, Lansing doesn't want to die on this mission. He won't act against us until he's out of danger. That, I can read clearly."

What she didn't tell Alec was that Philip would be waiting for just the right moment to put a bullet in Lansing's skull. It was part of the reason Philip wanted to take him along. Lansing must guess that. It would be something else to keep him in line.

Alec nodded. "All right. Get him gear but no weapons."

"I'm not fighting without weapons," Lansing said.

"When we get there."

They finished with the body armor and everyone clambered aboard the helicopter. She'd never ridden in a helicopter to a battle before. She'd never used telepathy this way before, either. She could have happily replaced those firsts with, say, first time making love to Alec in a real bed.

She tucked her head into her knees, concentrating, trying not to think about copter crashes that she'd seen on the news. In the body of the Blackhawk, Philip sat across from her. Alec sat next to her. The noise from the copter blades was overwhelming, the air practically pounding in her ears. She tried to huddle against Alec as best she could, wishing for the lost cabin in Maine. *Soon*, he'd said in the elevator. So much for that.

I hate this.

Lansing boarded the Blackhawk, with Gabe shadowing him. Philip pointed and Gabe settled his captive next to her father. Lansing scowled at Philip. Her father grinned menacingly.

She'd read Lansing's sincerity at wanting to come. But she didn't know *why*. She had to know why.

Once again, the telepathy made her wish real. Lansing's surface thoughts were swirling, angry, making them difficult to comprehend. Wait, he was Philip's *father*?

The helicopter jerked, taking off, and it broke her concentration. She braced her back against the metal wall and held on to Alec. He clasped her hand. She squeezed it tight. The body armor felt heavier now, more of a burden, bringing home the realization that she had no idea what she was getting into.

She glanced from her father to the Resource Director and back. There was some physical resemblance between them, mostly around the eyes and chin but they seemed too close in age to be father and son. Oh, screw it. Instead of guessing, she could find out everything.

She closed her eyes and dug deep for answers in Lansing's mind. She wondered if he knew she was doing it. She decided she didn't give a damn.

Images flooded her. Lansing as a soldier in the Queen's Army— Queen *Victoria's* army. Battles raged around him, friends fell and died. Images of his family, a wife and children, growing older while he remained the same age. Other images that covered the years between but they zipped by too fast for her to read carefully. She caught a glimpse of a young woman with brunette hair and high cheekbones telling Lansing that he was going to be a father and Lansing's utter dismissal of that announcement. *Damn you, Lansing.* Philip hadn't even seen his father until he'd been a full adult.

The strongest recent memory was the day Lansing had taken toddler Alec into his arms, full of optimism and plans for the future. That was normal enough, given Lansing was Alec's father in all but name. What was abnormal were his plans for Alec. Lansing's immortality had effectively driven him insane. The Resource Director was tired of taking orders, of hiding his true self, of other men running everything. He'd looked at Alec as the first step on the road to eventually controlling the world. Those plans started with molding Alec into a weapon without peer, one that could be pointed at heads of state or terrorists or whoever didn't take orders from Lansing. And the Resource Director had plans to locate others with powers and train them like Alec.

Philip had been far better off without this man in his life.

What was truly creepy about Lansing was that with the mercenary and research branches of the Resource, he had enough power and influence to make his insane dreams real. Or at least real enough to cause a lot of death and destruction. Philip was right. Lansing would never give up trying to control her or Alec.

Should she let her father kill Lansing? She suspected that she couldn't stop him. Eventually, Philip would do it, whether she approved or not.

She opened her eyes and rested her head on Alec's shoulder, taking a shuddering breath. Reading all that made her feel sick, almost nauseous. *Mental note: Stay out of the heads of crazy people.* Alec squeezed her hand. He had his head tilted to the side, looking over a report on the CIA agent's laptop. The laptop had been set at their feet, in the space between the two rows of men.

Philip, Lansing and Daz also leaned forward, studying the same thing. They made hand gestures but how they could communicate in this noise, she had no idea. Lansing tapped his helmet and frowned, protesting something. Oh. The rest of them were listening via radios in their helmets but Lansing's wasn't working. She moved her head a little but couldn't figure out how to turn her radio on.

She clutched Alec's arm as the helicopter banked right. She could feel the vibrations down to her bones. The straps of the body armor dug into her shoulders. The metal of the floor felt cold under her butt. She must had made some sign of her discomfort because Philip raised his head and met her gaze.

"Philip, you should have told me what Lansing was to you."

"He's no father to me. But yes, I should have told you."

"Are you immortal, like he is?"

"God, I hope not."

"Why didn't he want to train you like he trained Alec?"

"You heard him, I'm a mongrel. Not fully white. Bad blood from my mother."

"But he was going to use me and I'm Japanese."

"You have abilities he can use. As far as he knew then, I was powerless. Nothing to train, nothing to exploit, unlike you or Alec. He offered me a job once. But that's different from acknowledging me as his son and giving a damn."

"Blood doesn't make a father. I learned that from my father."

Philip smiled. She felt the affection pouring from him.

She smiled back. What else was there to say? She couldn't change the past for Philip. He went back to reading the intelligence report. She connected telepathically with Alec and attempted to read the report through his eyes. The military jargon made it difficult to follow, but she tried.

It seemed this Demeter and his group planned to get close enough to Manhattan to cause maximum destruction. They had a dirty bomb, a conventional explosive laced with radioactive materials that would not only kill hundreds of people but contaminate the entire area for decades. It explained the hurry. They had to get to the container ship before it was within close range of Manhattan.

In Alec's memory, she saw some of the previous battle on the docks: the incineration of the sniper, the death of Hans, the co-leader of this group and how the cell had escaped with the bomb. She also received Alec's memory of that fuzziness he'd sensed before the explosion. Damn. Clearly, the unknown bothered Alec. But there was nothing to be done about it now.

She gathered that Hans had been the brains behind the organization and that Demeter was the fanatic. Without Hans, Demeter had bullied the entire cell into a suicidal assault.

Someone like that would set off the bomb at the first sign of attack, which was why F-Team needed to approach the container ship in stealth. That explained why the Blackhawk would land at the Newark docks. There would be no way to hide its approach. Instead, they were going to board a Coast Guard patrol boat and conduct a sea attack.

Well, at least she knew how to swim.

But how would that work? Even a Coast Guard patrol boat would be seen. She sank deeper into Alec's thoughts, reading the plan. Right. The patrol boat was a fixture in the shipping lanes. Its appearance would cause no alarm, at least until they got close. The big problem was how they'd get on board the container ship without being discovered. She "listened" in on the radio conversation through her connection with Alec.

"We need to get right next to the hull," Daz said on his radio. "Then you do your stuff, Firefly."

"No problem."

"Trickiest part will be while we're boarding. Odds are they'll spot us."

"Alec, I can help with that." In fact, she might be invaluable. She could broadcast a general telepathic call that would cause the crew to ignore a boarding party. She explained to Alec, who relayed it to Daz.

Daz tapped her foot and gave her a thumbs-up. Great. She'd just taken on responsibility for the success of this whole thing. Beth Nakamora, savior of the free world. She felt sick.

She tucked her knees closer to her body, swallowing back bile and fear. The left side of her was toasty warm. Alec had warmed her up. He brought up her hand to his mouth and kissed it, sending that familiar tingle of power up her arm. He trusted that she could do this.

Should she tell him the truth about Lansing? No, that was a distraction that he didn't need right now. Time enough to tell him later. And if they failed, it wouldn't matter.

Alec turned to her and rubbed her cheek with his fingertips.

"I'm sorry," he mouthed.

"Don't be sorry. All my life, I've been afraid of people finding out about my telepathy. I've been afraid of myself too, of what my telepathy could do. I've been running or hiding since I was eight. I'm glad not to run anymore."

"You hate that I'm a soldier. You must hate this."

"No, I hate that you were given no choice about becoming a soldier."

"I thought I could walk away from this. But it wouldn't be right."

"I know. You're a hero. It's part of why I love you."

Alec took a sharp breath. He brushed the back of his hand

against her cheeks, enveloping her whole face in that energy. So warm. She closed her eyes. She probably shouldn't have said that. She didn't even realize how she felt herself until it had slipped out.

But it was true.

Alec leaned over and kissed her softly on the lips. His TK slipped under her clothes, copping a psychic feel. She sank into the kiss, not caring about whoever was watching them.

"I love you too, counselor."

Alec put his arm around Beth's shoulders after the kiss, wishing he could have left her behind. In the Kevlar vest, black jacket and helmet, she looked like a child playing war games. No child could have done what she'd done to escape, but that didn't mean she was ready for full combat. Drake would be better protection than the Kevlar but neither would save her from the bomb if he failed, like on the docks.

Drake gestured with his hand to Beth. She smiled. Her father actually smiled back. It seemed strange to see a smile on the man's face. Hell, it seemed strange to see Drake *alive*. He'd have sworn the man had no pulse when he'd collapsed earlier.

"He has a low-level internal TK, Alec. It heals him when he's injured, exactly as you healed my hand. Don't worry, he's fine."

"Drake has some sort of TK?"

"It's a different kind of TK than yours. It knits him back together inside."

"How long has he been able to do that?"

"I'm not sure. Most of his life, I think, but the healing happened instinctively, whenever he was truly in danger of dying. When I ordered him to get better, Philip gained conscious control of it. And, I think, it increased the overall healing ability."

"You're a catalyst. You upped his power like you did mine. You saved his life, Beth. When you're doubting your telepathy, think about that."

The Blackhawk jolted as they landed, cutting short his question about where Drake had gotten his power. Later. Now they had to move.

The Coast Guard vessel was one of the regular harbor patrol boats, sturdy but small. It was watertight, designed to pop back to the surface even if monster waves swamped it. It wasn't truly suited for an armed group of eighteen but it was their best bet to get close to the container ship without causing suspicion. With the other small blips on radar from all the patrol boats and smaller vessels in the shipping lanes, the navigators on the container ship would never give it a second glance.

He and Beth went to the bow. For the first time since the helicopter, she let go of his hand and instead clutched the railing. F-Team assembled on the stern. Daz, Drake and Lansing gathered on the small bridge, presumably to talk strategy. It'd be easier to hear on the bridge.

Alec went with Beth. He knew what to do. Use his TK to get them on the ship, then let F-Team guard him while he took out the bomb. The problem was finding the damn thing. It had to be either in the front or rear of the rows of containers, for easy access, but that still left a lot of them to search. The longer the op lasted, the riskier it was.

"You're going to board the ship, then search around for the bomb, hoping you wouldn't be spotted? That's insane."

"Hey!" Of course, she'd just echoed his own worry. "You make it sound like we're being stupid. We're good at this."

"But it's practically suicidal."

"It would be for a regular unit. Not us." Besides, if their chances were slim, a regular ops team wouldn't have any chance at all. It was all on them.

She stared off into the morning fog. "You know how my telepathy works as well as anyone. Tell me what to do to help, Alec."

He took a deep breath. Yes, let the others worry about protecting him. He needed a strategy for Beth.

The boat's engine revved up, filling his ears, making it impossible to talk.

"Tell me."

Her mental voice was insistent.

"Here's what we need. The bomb is guarded. Can you listen once we get on board and tell where the guards are?"

"How many men?"

"Over twenty, at least. It's not clear if the regular crew is part of the plot or was coerced into it. All we really need is to find that bomb and get it out of their hands. Once we secure the bomb, we can call in

reinforcements from the regular military units."

"Will the guards be thinking differently from the rest of the crew?"

"Yeah. They'll be the most suicidal crazy ones."

"Very comforting." A pause. "I think that should make it easier to find them. They'll be getting ready to die, focused on the task. Anything else?"

The most risky part was the actual boarding. They'd be sitting ducks during it and they could only speed it up so much.

"How long do you think your Jedi mind trick will last while we get aboard?"

"I have no idea. I haven't had a stopwatch the last two times, I was just glad it worked." Another pause. "Maybe five minutes?"

"How close do you need to be?"

"I was able to hear the man who guarded my cell from about two hundred yards away."

"That'd be enough. Be right back."

He walked to the bridge and slipped inside. Daz looked up from a drawing of the container ship. He pointed to the sides, showing Alec how little room there was between the deck rail and the stacked containers. Once they got on board, it would be close quarters.

"There's only enough room to walk in pairs," Daz said. "You and the girl stick in the middle of our line, Firefly, until we're at the target."

Alec nodded.

Daz pointed at Drake. "You and Lansing make another pair. Stay in the middle, just ahead of Alec and Beth. And play nice until we've secured the target."

Lansing smiled, a creepy grin. "Certainly."

Drake only nodded.

Alec explained their timeframe and Beth's telepathic range. Daz looked out the window of the bridge at Beth, smiled and gave a thumbs-up.

"Once we hit the open deck at the bow, Drake's going to shadow her." Daz pointed at Beth's father. "You hear me, Firefly? Do what needs to be done and don't worry about the girl. You screw this up, everybody's dead."

Alec nodded. Beth would tell him the same. Besides, Drake was more than capable, especially if he could heal.

"She needs to close her eyes to sort out thoughts, Drake. Watch for it."

"I'll protect her." Drake glared at Lansing.

Now why did Alec get the impression that protecting Beth might somehow result in Lansing's death? If so, he wasn't about to argue.

Beth looked small and lonely at the bow. The best thing he could do now was soothe her nerves. Alec walked back, put his arms around her and wondered why the hell Lansing had wanted to come. Presumably, he had soldier's training but he was too old. This made no sense, especially since Lansing had to guess that Drake was waiting for the right moment to kill him.

Maybe Lansing was waiting for the right moment to kill Drake.

"No, that's not it. He knows that he's safe until the bomb is dealt with. They both won't make a move until that's over. I read that from them clearly." Beth leaned against the rail and looked out over the water as they pulled away from the docks. *"More than anything, Lansing wanted to stay close to you, even at the risk of his life."*

"Don't tell me he gives a damn about me."

"In his way, he does. His feelings are so wrapped up in his crazy dreams that it's hard to separate them. He cares about you but mostly because he views you as part of him, as belonging to him. Obsessive and warped but sadly more common among parents than you'd think."

"I'm done with him." Alec wrapped his arms around her from behind, using his TK to keep himself stable as the boat bounced in the waves.

"I know."

He felt her relax against him.

"Alec, I have a question. Let me know if it's stupid."

"It won't be stupid."

"I understand what you want me to do. But how can we board a container ship from this boat? They're not going to send down a ladder."

He grinned. *"That's my job and that's what the grappling hooks are for. You just do the telepathy thing and stay with me and your father. We'll protect you."*

As they left the docks behind, the fog rolled in. In a few moments, it was difficult to see more than five feet past the edge of the bow. Alec turned his head. Lansing and Drake stood on the bridge, locked in deep conversation with the boat's captain. But then Drake scowled, left the wheelhouse and walked toward them.

"*What was that about?*" Alec said.

"*Philip wanted the running lights off. The captain disagreed,*" she said. "*The idea is that they need to blend in with the other small boats. Philip argued that the fog offered enough concealment that getting close without being seen from the bridge was more important.*"

"*He's been living in the shadows too long,*" Alec said.

"*Yes.*"

They picked up speed. Alec hugged her tighter. Spray washed over them. He inhaled the smell of the sea, thinking of the beach in Maine. He'd take her back there when this was done, rebuild that cabin, start a new life.

Drake grabbed the rail and turned to Beth. He touched his stomach, then his mouth, asking Beth wordlessly if she was hungry.

She nodded so vigorously that Alec realized *he* should have thought about that. She'd just escaped from a prison. He had no idea when her last meal had been.

Drake fumbled in the pocket of his jacket and pulled out a small bag of M&Ms. The boat slowed as it went over the wash from the ships coming into the harbor. The noise died down.

Beth laughed at Drake's offer. "First a handgun, now M&Ms. What else were you hiding in that sling?"

Drake smiled. "A portable bazooka, a jetpack and a kitchen sink."

He handled her the M&Ms but the boat rolled and the bag slipped from her hand. Before it could go overboard, Alec grabbed it with his TK and settled it in her hands.

"Thank you." She ripped the bag open.

"Maybe I should have let it go overboard. That bag looks kinda grungy."

"It is not! I want them. Philip always brought M&Ms for me when I was little."

And he'd brought them with him while going to rescue her, a little gesture but one that said everything about their relationship and told Alec everything he needed to know about where Lansing had utterly failed as a father.

Alec kissed the top of her head and began scanning the fog with his TK. The ship's radar would probably spot their quarry first but it gave him something to do. Almost immediately, he ran into that fuzzy feeling he'd first sensed the night on the docks. Damn. But it was moving away from them at a high speed. He tried to follow but lost it after a few seconds. When he scanned again, it was completely gone.

"That was strange, Alec. Almost like your TK encountered some sort of sponge."

"I know." He sent the memory from the docks. *"But it's gone now. Maybe it's something connected with the ocean. I don't have time to worry about it now."*

She nodded and munched on the M&Ms. "One fight at a time."

"Exactly."

She'd called him a hero. But this was his job; it was what he trained for. It was what he did.

He could feel her still in the back of his head. He couldn't read her thoughts but he could read a little of her mood. She was scared. This was the last thing she'd wanted to do. But she was risking her life because it was the right thing, because she could help.

So who was the real hero here?

Chapter Twenty-Two

The waves grew higher as they moved into the shipping lanes, ocean swells mixed with wash from the mammoth tankers, freighters and container ships heading into Newark harbor. The patrol boat bounced around as it maneuvered closer to their target.

Two miles to target.

Beth closed her eyes and concentrated on absorbing the calm she felt emanating from Alec and Philip. She looked over at Philip, checking the various guns he'd strapped to his body and realized they'd done *this* together before. The day he rescued her. He'd told her to stay quiet, to listen for anyone coming, to follow him. They'd both escaped, mission accomplished. If she could do it when she was eight, she could do it now.

Daz stepped up to the bow and tapped Alec on the shoulder. "Almost there."

"Direction? I'm hitting several ships that size out there," Alec said.

"East, twenty degrees."

Alec closed his eyes and she followed his mind as he searched with the TK. She felt his satisfaction as he locked on to something big and moving. There was no sign of that spongy stuff he'd encountered several minutes ago. A mystery to solve later.

"You sure they won't be alarmed if they spot us close by?" Alec said to Daz.

"Nah. A patrol boat getting caught in the wash from their ship shouldn't faze them. Is your girl ready for her part?"

"You could talk *to* me instead of around me," she said.

Daz scowled. "Okay, you ready?"

"I have a name."

"Okay, Beth Nakamora, are you *ready*?"

And the last word indicated he thought she was anything but ready. He might be right. "Let me know when we're about two hundred yards away and I can start projecting to the people on board."

"You sure about those five minutes?" Daz said.

"No. I only know what I did to the Resource guards lasted about that long. It depends on how many there are and how much work it is to think at them."

Daz stared at her for a minute. "Okay, fair assessment. We work with what we have. Firefly, you give us a boost to cut the time."

"No problem," Alec said.

Daz reached out and awkwardly patted her shoulder. "You're okay, Nakamora."

She wanted to make a sarcastic remark but felt the overwhelming sense of approval behind Daz's curt words. *"You're okay too, Daz."*

Daz blinked, stepped back and she thought he was angry for a second but he smiled and gave her a thumbs-up. "That's the sign. Watch for it."

She nodded and reached out to Alec. "Hold my hand. Whatever we're doing to each other's abilities, I need it."

He clasped her hand and she felt the familiar energy flow between them. No sparks, like the first time but more like a hum, warm, glowing and comforting. Maybe they were learning to control this.

Philip slipped an arm around her waist to steady her as the boat lurched back and forth in the water. To steady himself too, she decided. He wasn't nervous about going into battle. He was terrified at the idea of *her* going into battle.

Daz whistled and gave her the thumbs-up.

She stood rigid, her eyes closed, head down in concentration, opening her telepathy. At first, she heard only vague thoughts. As the patrol boat moved closer and the massive shape of the container ship loomed over them in the mist, the thoughts became more distinct.

Lookouts on the bow and stern, annoyed with the fog...someone on radar, checking for unusual contacts, they'd seen the patrol boat but decided it was a routine patrol...the captain, worried about collisions, pacing on the bridge...

"I have been used. Now I will be the avenger."

Intense determination. That had to be one of the bomb's triggermen. She could easily zero in on him and order him to stand down. But that might take all her power and leave the others on board free of her influence.

She looked around at F-Team, checking their weapons. No, too big a risk to control one person. She had to get the team on board first. She took another deep breath and started projecting a general message to every mind she could reach.

"Nothing unusual. Just a patrol boat, regular crew on board, following in the wash. Nothing to be alarmed about."

Alec waved a hand, signaling his team. Daz and Gabe knelt on the deck, grappling hook guns pointed straight up.

She felt Alec tense beside her. Energy flowed through him, then her, as he summoned the TK. She swallowed and heat soared through her body. If only she could lose herself in that. Tomorrow, perhaps, if there was one for them.

Daz and Gabe fired the grappling hooks. The hooks, ropes trailing behind, flew up the side of the container ship. Alec launched his TK. She felt the moment when he grabbed the hooks, helping them over the rail of the ship. He used the TK to secure the hooks to the rail, pleased at doing so easily what would once have taken him minutes, not seconds.

She reduced her mental suggestion to a simple "everything is normal" and tried not to think about how the hell she was going to climb those lines in heavy body armor.

Alec tapped her on the shoulder. She opened her eyes and saw the lines were, in fact, two sides of a large net with rungs like a ladder.

The patrol boat veered left, narrowly missing the massive hull of the container ship. She grabbed the railing for balance. Water slapped over the edge of the bow. She saw the captain's face go white at the near collision.

"Too close," Philip muttered.

Daz waved his hand and F-Team swarmed onto the net. Philip warily watched Lansing grab hold, though she doubted there was any way for Lansing to escape this mission now.

Alec picked her up and steadied her on the rail. She leapt and snagged the net with both hands. It swayed from the movement of everyone climbing and she held on for dear life. The rough, wet line dug into her palms. She looked up and swallowed, feeling so very small against the mammoth steel of the hull. Only Alec at her side prevented her panic.

Philip appeared at her other side and steadied her as F-Team clambered up the ladder, silent and efficient. She closed her eyes and kept concentrating on sending her mental orders to those on board the ship: *"Nothing unusual. Nothing unusual."*

Sweat and sea spray mingled on her face, dripping into her eyes, making it difficult to see. The weight of the body armor pressed down on her. She groped ahead blindly, rung by rung, deciding it was better not to look down, wishing she'd lifted more weights at the gym. Alec and Philip stayed with her as she climbed in case she faltered.

She bit her lip and tried to push away her panic. She'd no idea what would happen if her broadcast to the ship's crew included fear. Boom? Everybody dead because of her?

Alec's mental voice was exhilarated. That made no sense to her.

"I'm terrified and you think this is fun?*"*

"Not fun, Beth. But intense. Hang on. We'll be up in just a sec."

She felt a lurch, like an elevator beginning to move. She opened her eyes. They were speeding up the side of the container ship.

They were quite literally flying.

Alec was pushing the net and everyone on it with his TK. When they reached the railing, she clutched it and swung over with immense relief. She went down on one knee to practice deep breathing, sending out her broadcast to the crew, over and over. Once this is done, she thought, I am going to practice pull-ups. Lots of them. Wearing body armor. Just in case.

Philip helped her to her feet but half his attention was on Lansing, who'd made the climb easily and had his rifle at the ready. But Lansing made no threatening moves.

It was close quarters. As Daz had warned, there was only room for two people between the rail and massive containers looming over them. She looked up. The top rows of the containers were lost in the fog, giving them the appearance of going on forever.

Daz clapped Alec on the back and smiled. She didn't need

telepathy to interpret that thanks. She wondered how many missions it would take before exhilaration replaced nerves, like with Alec. She didn't want to find out.

F-Team formed up. As directed, Philip and Lansing took the row in front of her and Alec. She steadied herself by setting her right hand on the containers. This ship seemed as stable as dry land. No rocking or bouncing in the waves. It was too big for that.

Big was their problem. Where now?

Alec leaned over and whispered. "Time to pinpoint the guards for the bomb."

She nodded. *"Right, but I have to give up telling them they don't see anything."*

"Do it. We can't afford to go in the wrong direction and waste time. I'm taking care of concealment."

She blinked her eyes and let go of her broadcast. Her head felt immediately lighter and her eyesight grew clearer. It was easy now to hear the fanatic.

"Forward."

"Gotcha."

They started walking. She let Alec lead her as she closed her eyes again and listened, searching for the person who'd had such clear thoughts about death earlier.

She hit a churning mess.

At least five people, all agitated and ready to die.

One determined not to be a coward, to follow his leader and his God into the promised heaven. Another terrified but too much of a coward to go against the others. A third lost in some happy dream, avoiding facing his imminent death. Another sad about what the news would do to his family but uncaring about his own fate.

The last was the leader. His thoughts roiled together, a maelstrom of euphoria and madness. *"Glorious death!"* Rewards in the afterlife for delivery of his people from evil—*"glorious death!"*—the faces of those he'd trained as suicide bombers in years past—*"glorious death!"*—now he'd join them, now he'd live forever, be remembered for this strike against those who tortured and bombed children and didn't recognize the true God—*"glorious death!"*—satisfaction that an entire city would be vaporized for the hubris of these evil people.

What? *An entire city vaporized?* A dirty bomb didn't have that much power. She zeroed in again, searching deeper into the fanatic's mind, as she'd done to Lansing.

"Oh, shit! Alec! They don't have a dirty bomb. It's a nuke!"

Alec wrapped his arms around her.

"It's-a-nuke-a-nuke-a-nuke. Holy-ancestors-protect-me, entire city destroyed, burned, all those people, buildings melted. Jesus Tap-Dancing Christ, a-nuke-a-nuke-a-nuke."

He grabbed her by the shoulders. *"Enough!"*

"So many could die."

"They won't, because we're going to stop it. Together." The solider behind them tapped Alec on the shoulder, and he started walking again, pulling Beth with him. Millions dead. He couldn't wrap his mind around that. Better not to try.

"We're going to win, counselor. Trust me. Where are they?"

"In the bottom row of the first set of the containers. I'm not sure which one exactly."

Damn. That row was about ten across. That meant they'd have to spread out on the forward deck and risk being seen. *"Stay with me. I'm pulling in the fog around us."*

He'd had practice with air molecules now, so it worked better than the tear gas in the cabin. The problem was that holding the fog took a hell of a lot of concentration. Once he started using the TK for fighting, he'd lose the fog and their cover. And once they were spotted, they would have only a few seconds before everything went *boom*.

Daz, at the front of the line, turned to him, questioning about Beth's temporary stumble. Alec gave a thumbs-up. He'd have to break radio silence to tell him about the nuke and it wasn't worth the risk of their frequency being picked up. They already knew they couldn't afford to alert their targets. Nuke or dirty bomb, it made no difference for the op.

Fuck, Demeter could detonate that nuke now and it'd still be effective. What was stopping them? How much time did he have?

"Alec, I'm locked in on them. They want to see the city in front of them, see it right before it's destroyed."

She'd recovered from the momentary panic. Good. Now if only he could erase the image of millions of people melted and the seas boiling from his own mind.

"*Beth, order them out of the container and away from the bomb.*"

Long pause. "*I tried. But I couldn't get into his head deep enough. He's so focused and intent that I'm skipping off. I didn't realize that could happen. I could try harder but what if it somehow alarms him?*"

"*Shit. No, don't do that.*"

The sun rose higher in the sky and the fog grew harder to hold down on the deck. They halted. Daz held up a hand with two fingers, signaling them to take the turn onto the bow in stealth. He counted the pairs ahead as they turned. One, two, three, four, *now.*

He and Beth turned the corner.

Two shapes appeared out of the fog.

"*Fuck.*"

Lansing grabbed one man from behind and twisted his neck. Alec heard a sickening snap. Daz punched the other in the throat and knocked him to the deck. The man started to gurgle, metal flashed in Daz's hand and the gurgling stopped.

Alec took a deep breath. They'd both reacted faster than he could have, especially when holding on to the fog. Lansing hadn't been kidding about being a soldier once.

Daz pointed with his thumb and F-Team dragged the bodies to the side of the deck and tossed them over the railing. Alec kept them enveloped in fog. The splash of the bodies was barely audible. Alec took a deep breath. So fucking close, either to death or victory. Just like Lansing's "death or glory" motto.

Beth stumbled. Drake slipped to her side. Alec grabbed her forearm. Had she been hit?

"*I felt them die. The deaths got through the mental shield you taught me. I felt exactly what that man felt when his neck snapped. Hurts. Now I know why my telepathy went latent. I felt my captors die during the escape.*"

"*I'm sorry.*" He squeezed her arm. "*But we have to keep going.*"

"*I know.*" A pause. "*I'm locked in to the leader again. He's getting impatient. Maybe he got some of my overflow from the deaths I felt. I'm sorry.*"

"*Not something you could anticipate. Send him soothing thoughts, if you can. Trust yourself.*"

The containers were stacked ten across and six high on the deck. They all looked the same. *"Which one, counselor?"*

"Middle. But that's as close as I can get."

Drake tapped Alec on the shoulder and pointed at one of the middle containers. Paint had been scraped off of the side of that one, exposing bare metal. It'd been opened. Drake had a good eye.

Target sighted.

His show, now.

Beth slipped her hand into his. *"I'm coming with you. You need me to keep them calm and you need me to amp up your fire."*

"Dammit, Beth. That's not the plan."

But what she said was true. He pulled Beth with him, sliding past Daz. Daz gave him a nod, ceding control of the op. Beth clutched his hand so tight that Alec's fingers went numb. The grip loosened. She must have read his complaint. He hated that she had to do this. She'd never have come except for him.

"I did it to myself. And I trust you. Let's go."

F-Team surrounded them in a protective half circle. Alec crept forward to the container and stopped right next to the scraped paint Drake had spotted.

He took a deep breath, wishing he knew the layout inside. He wanted to rip the door right off the hinges, reach inside and knock them away from the bomb. But what would Demeter do?

"I've been working on him. He's calmer. It should buy a few seconds."

"Excellent, counselor."

He could cut loose.

Alec flung out his hand and pulled back, releasing all his power. It rose out of him like an unseen hand. The metal creaked, he concentrated harder and ripped the entire front of the container off the hinges. The metal door flew over the edge of the deck and disappeared.

He rushed inside, Beth behind him, their hands still clasped.

Four men started shooting at them. He waved his hand and the bullets dropped in midair. He pushed hard and the attackers slammed into the sides of the container.

Drake fired, finishing off two of them. F-Team rushed inside. The bomb was the key. But the container was empty, save for the men firing at them. Where the hell was the bomb?

"They've connected this to another container. It's through the door on the left. Hurry-hurry-hurry, he's trying to detonate it. I'm ordering him to not move but it's hard. He's so focused."

Alec flung the door to the side container open.

"I lost him, Alec!"

Alec stepped into a maelstrom, heat and light and molecules bouncing, dancing, free...

He was too late.

Chapter Twenty-Three

He'd *failed.*

Desperate, Alec flung his TK into the explosion. The TK zoomed past the fire and found something intact. Yes! The conventional explosives had detonated but the nuke hadn't gone off yet.

Alec threw up a TK wall between the nuke and explosion.

So many molecules, spinning so fast. It reminded him of a dust storm that he'd created as a training exercise, except these tiny particles were more agitated, hotter, more demanding, buzzing around him like angry bees. They bashed at his TK wall and demanded more space, somewhere to spread out, building up more force and gaining strength.

The pain lashed into his head, a parallel to the battering by the explosion. He lost balance and crumpled to the floor, unable to see, everything focused onto holding the wall steady.

"Don't fight it, give it somewhere to go, Alec."

Beth. Her mental voice was steady and this time she calmed him. He wrapped his arms around her to protect her from the explosion. Her psychic strength roared into him. The pain loosened its hold and he could see again. He poured the additional power into his TK wall but knew it wouldn't hold for long. Beth was right. It needed an exit.

"Hold on, Beth. It's about to get very hot."

He called to the explosion just as he did when he called fire.

"Come to me, come to me."

It roared to him, a living being of heat and light. He stumbled to his feet, holding Beth. The fire enveloped them, encircled them. Yellow flames cast shadows in the container, making it a mythic hell.

"Come to me."

He grinned as the flames wrapped around their bodies, swirling from his head to his toes, heat licking at him, power demanding release. He raised his hands over his head, urging the fire upward. It melted the metal roof, hissing, sending molten steel hurtling to the floor of the container. Nothing could stop it, nothing could stop *him*. He lifted Beth up, she wrapped her legs around his waist, and heat surged around him and in him.

"Come to me."

Impact after impact as the explosion slammed upward, through container after container, seeking escape, seeking to be free, seeking the sky.

He went with it and Beth with him, hot, burning, on fire. Together.

"Free!"

Air, beautiful sky. The explosion roared into the open, expanding out, higher, farther, faster. He flew with it, exulting in the power, one with it, letting all the angry molecules roll around him, caressing him.

He kissed Beth. She moaned. Her mind flowed into his and he felt her arousal, felt her body shiver, waiting for him, wanting him. He pulled her closer, clothes ceased to exist, and he was inside her.

They joined inside a cocoon, safe, the power a living thing between them. His TK flowed into her, covering her skin, touching everything, her neck, her breasts and inside her. He felt everything that she was, and she felt him. They were one person.

They were a glorious fiery being.

The explosion roiled around them, blotting out the sky, and yet it had no effect on them. It was nothing, no threat. The union with Beth built, his erection feeling just like the explosion, ready to go off at any second.

He released the fire. The explosion burst outward with a huge clap of thunder, the molecules spreading out as his essence spread out within Beth. He threw back his head, lost in his orgasm, lost in *her* orgasm, until they melded together.

"I am fire. We are fire."

The sky cleared. The explosion vanished. They floated in the soft, morning air.

Beth's head rested on his shoulder. He felt the weight of his body armor again. Their clothes were back but not the helmets.

They'd made love inside the fire. Physically, mentally, hell, even molecularly. That *had* happened, right?

"Oh, yes." She raised her head.

He kissed her. A warm hum spread through him. Her shivering quieted.

"Alec?"

"Yes?"

"Can we get down now?"

"Down?"

He looked below and the container ship was a speck in the ocean below them.

He was flying.

Okay, not exactly flying. His TK was pushing against the ground and holding them up. Or maybe it was pushing against the air molecules. He wasn't sure. It didn't matter right this second. It was just *cool.*

"Funny, it seemed hot to me," she said, her voice muffled against his chest. "But can we get down now?"

"You don't like heights, counselor?"

"Not when nothing is holding me up, no."

He grinned. "I've got you."

She started to laugh. "Yeah, but who's got you, Superman?"

"Okay, okay. Here goes."

He thought about going down. They started falling.

Fast.

Beth said something that was stolen away by the wind but he was pretty sure it was a curse. He smiled, thought about going slower, and they began floating softly.

"I can *fly!* Damn. I can do so much with this."

"Start with putting me down."

"Killjoy. For now. But we're going to try this again."

"Oh, goody."

He would have smiled again but his limbs started to feel heavy. Exhaustion was creeping in. A sure warning sign he was almost out of juice. She was right. They needed to land, now. There was a clear space to land on the bow of the ship. At a hundred feet up, he could see F-Team. At twenty feet, he picked out individual members, including Drake and Lansing.

They landed with a quiet thump. *Perfect.* He let go of the TK and his limbs turned to jelly. Yep, definitely out of juice. He lost his grip on Beth and he went down to one knee.

Drake scooped Beth into his arms.

"Firefly?"

Weird. Daz's voice sounded strange, almost shaky.

"Firefly? You okay?"

"I'm okay but out of juice."

"Fuck, no wonder after that," Daz said. "I thought you'd been burned up in it."

In a way, he had. He took a deep breath, trying to draw breath to stand. "We good, Daz?"

"Nuke's secure but the ship isn't."

Daz's voice sounded normal again. He turned to F-Team, some of whom were staring, their mouths open in shock.

"Hey!" Daz ordered. "Get your eyeballs back in their sockets, surround them and get them out of the open."

Lansing offered Alec a hand. He hesitated a second, then took it. When Alec was on his feet, Lansing leaned over and whispered in his ear. "You see what you can be, Alec? And you'd give that up for a *girl?*"

"Fuck you. Beth is the reason I could do it."

Gunshots thudded into the deck near their feet.

Chapter Twenty-Four

Lansing grabbed Alec and pulled him toward cover. Alec went along, closed his eyes and tried to reach for the bullets with TK.

Nothing. Fuck.

Daz shouted again but his voice was fainter. Lansing had splintered them off from the main group with Beth.

"I need to get to Beth," Alec said.

Lansing pushed Alec so hard that his head smashed into the metal wall of a container.

"*Shit!* That's enough, Lansing." The old bastard couldn't wait to get his knocks in, could he?

The gunshots stopped. Alec raised his head and blinked, trying to focus. He flung his arms out. Solid metal on one side. At first, his other hand found nothing but open space but then his knuckles hit the railing. They were on the side of the ship's deck. Not the most secure place but better than in the open space of the bow.

"We need to get inside the container I ripped open." Alec struggled to his feet. He wiped sweat away from his face from the back of his hand. "Coverage on three sides. Safer there."

"Safer for you. Not for me, not with Drake there." Lansing grabbed the straps of Alec's body armor and used the leverage to slam him against the container again. "And why waste this quiet moment between us?"

Alec's vision went fuzzy again. He tried to lift his arm to hit back but lacked the energy. Fuck. Stopping the explosion and flying had taken everything he had.

"Uh, what moment?"

"It's past time." Lansing's face came into clear focus. His pupils were wide, his stare unblinking.

And I thought he was crazy before.

Alec took a deep breath, remembering how easily the old man had snapped someone's neck only minutes ago. *I need to buy time.*

"People are shooting at us and you want to have a *chat?*"

"Yes." Lansing jabbed his forearm into Alec's throat.

Alec choked and clawed Lansing's body armor with his hands but it had no effect. He fought for breath, trying to stay calm. His legs felt like lead. His vision blurred. Lansing spun them and pushed him backward, halfway over the rail. Fuck, he'd just flown into the air, controlled an explosion and saved Manhattan from a nuke. Now he couldn't deal with one crazy old man?

"Can't have a talk if I'm dead," Alec whispered, using all his breath. All he needed was a few minutes, then his energy would come back.

"That's the idea."

Lansing wanted to kill him. No surprise. But why hadn't he shot him or tossed him overboard already?

"You are giving up what you are for a *girl*. You belong with me."

Lansing's hold relaxed. Fresh air flowed into Alec's lungs but the spots before his eyes didn't go away.

"Answer me," Lansing said.

"Was there a question?"

"Why would you give this up for the girl?"

"Why do I have to choose?"

"Because she's afraid of what she is. She always will be."

Alec thought of being with Beth, in the fire, making love thousands of feet in the air. *That* was what he was, what *they* were.

"She's not afraid of her power. She only wants to use it the right way."

"The right way is to protect yourself and take control."

"You can protect yourself without becoming, uh, consumed by it." He wanted to call Lansing "crazy" but that didn't seem like a good idea just now.

Lansing's forearm bit into his throat again, cutting off air. "Power is control. There is nothing else."

The spots in front of Alec's eyes grew bigger and brighter. *Nothing else but power? So I can look forward to becoming a crazed lunatic, pushing his foster son over a railing in the middle of a gunfight?*

Alec opened his mouth but he had no breath to talk. Lansing eased the pressure once more.

"If there was nothing but power, you would have killed me already."

"Killing you is wasteful. I wanted to give you another chance."

"You keep telling yourself that. Truth is, you don't *want* to kill me."

"Of course, I don't *want* to kill you. It's a regrettable necessity."

"That's not why you haven't shot me."

Lansing bashed his elbow into the side of Alec's face. Pain blossomed and spread over his cheek. Alec spat at Lansing. The old man jerked back and Alec bull-rushed him into the metal wall of the container. Lansing hit with a thud that echoed around them.

Alec grabbed at the rifle barrel. Lansing smashed the rifle butt into Alec's face, knocking him down to his knees. Alec gripped the rail for balance, gritting his teeth. Stupid fight move. Daz would not approve. What good was all his training if he didn't have the energy to use it? And Lansing was an old guy. Where the *hell* had he gotten that kind of strength?

Lansing aimed the rifle at Alec. Point blank range. A red dot appeared in the middle of his chest. The body armor wouldn't hold up to a shot that close.

"You made your choice, Alec. I'm sorry. I really am."

"I believe you." Alec reached out and closed his hand around the rifle barrel. "But I still don't think you can kill me."

"It's a waste, true. But rabid dogs have to be put down."

"You raised me like your son. Remember the chess games, teaching me to play piano, all the time you spent showing me proper manners, and those hours in the lab teaching me to control the fire? You put your life at risk." Alec smiled. "You give a damn about me, old man. Admit it."

Lansing's face lost all expression. "That doesn't matter. I have to pull out the weed and start over."

"The weed's too strong now. Besides, Beth's not the problem. You

247

think it's a coincidence that I'm more powerful with her around?"

Lansing took a deep breath, understanding. Finally. "She's a catalyst."

Keep him talking. Lansing couldn't kill him because he cared, despite himself. Alec almost felt sorry for the old bastard.

"We increase each other's abilities."

"You'd never have lived long enough to be with her if not for me." Lansing jabbed the barrel into Alec's body armor.

"That's true." Alec fought the impulse to take a step back. Instead, he tightened his grip on the rifle barrel. With the TK so weak, the closer he was to the bullet, the better. He'd only get one shot. Shot. Hah. Stupid pun.

"You could have raised me like Demeter, brainwashed beyond all reason, a fanatic who believes in a cause. You could have brought me up without any morals at all. Instead, you raised me like a son and found people like F-Team to fight with me."

"They were the best." Lansing took a step back. "You needed to learn to command men."

"You could have picked any kind of men. You picked Daz—an honorable, decorated Navy Seal commander—to lead them, to be my military mentor. You made it our job to protect people. What does that say about you, Lansing?"

Lansing blinked. "It says I'm a fool. I should have kept better control of you."

"It says you have morals, even if you've hidden them behind bullshit rationalizations," Alec said. "You won't kill me because you damn well don't *want* to kill me."

"You're naïve, boy. My fault. I won't make the same mistake when I do it next time."

Alec tensed. Next time? Did Lansing have a kid in mind? "There won't be a next time."

"No, not for you."

Alec tried to summon the TK. All he got was blurry vision. He'd no idea if he could stop a bullet. *Daz, where the hell are you?*

Lansing narrowed his eyes and his face became a frozen mask.

He was going to pull the trigger.

But a split second later, Lansing blinked and focused on

something past Alec. Alec twisted to look but Lansing knocked him to the deck and fired over his head. Someone fired back.

Lansing fell and his rifle clattered to the deck. Alec saw the attacker out of the corner of his eye. One of the terrorist cell members. *Shit.*

Alec grabbed Lansing's rifle, and rolling to his side, he fired back. The attacker jerked sideways and hit the railing. He hung there, balancing perfectly between rail and ship for a moment, and then fell overboard.

Could have been me, Alec thought. *So damn close.*

Daz rushed into view. "Firefly!"

About time. "Not hit." Alec stumbled to his feet.

Daz knelt over Lansing. "Shit, he's bad. This went into the neck." Daz slapped his hand over the neck wound. It was instantly covered in blood. "Medic's in the wrecked container up front with the rest of the team. Let's go."

Daz grabbed Lansing under the shoulders and dragged him. Alec followed along, rifle at the ready. They turned the corner and F-Team swarmed around them, providing cover. Shots were fired, they pinged off the deck in front of them. Alec fired back with the rest of F-Team.

Alec stumbled into the container and helped Daz pull Lansing inside. Daz's pants were soaked in blood. The medic swore and slapped bulky bandages over Lansing's neck. The patient groaned.

Alec swallowed. Lansing had been shot *protecting* him, only a second after Lansing had been about to *kill* him.

"Alec?"

"Beth?" He turned his head. She sat with her back to the wall. *Safe.* Drake loomed over her, weapon in hand.

"Lansing saved me."

"After he dragged you away from safety," Drake said.

"Beth, what does the medic think?" Alec said.

"The medic's worried," she said, face pale. "He thinks an artery is severed."

Daz lined up F-Team at the opening of their small sanctuary. "No one goes out again. We're secure for now, at least in here. Gabe got radio confirmation that reinforcements are coming. We won't be outnumbered for long."

"Good." Alec knelt next to Lansing. Why would this man take a slug for him?

Lansing moaned and opened his eyes.

Drake knelt on Lansing's other side. "Artery wound?"

The medic nodded. The white bulky bandage had turned blood red.

Lansing had saved his life, he deserved help. Alec summoned the TK. Pain sliced through his mind. He dropped his head between his knees, to stave off fainting. Why fucking now did his TK find its limits?

"I can't help him." He looked over at Beth. "I can't."

"If you hadn't used your power to stop the nuke, he'd be dead already. And he was the one who exposed you both to attack."

"He saved my life," Alec said. *"Of course, he threatened to kill me too."*

"I know. I heard. I tried to get him to stop but my telepathy was too weak."

Lansing rolled his head to the right and stared at Drake. He lifted a hand and curled his fingers on the strap of Drake's Kevlar vest. "This is *it?*"

Drake shook his head. "You've been a damn lucky bastard for two hundred years, Richard. Heal it."

"Too much blood loss," Lansing whispered, his voice a wheeze.

"Two hundred years?" Alec asked.

"I forgive you, Drake," Lansing sputtered.

"Fuck you." Drake scowled.

Blood spilled from Lansing's mouth. He tried to spit it out, couldn't, and crooked a finger at Alec.

Alec leaned over him.

"Alec." Lansing's breath was a painful whisper.

Beth grabbed Alec's hand and he felt that familiar disorienting snap before their connection settled.

"Alec, what he's thinking, you need to hear it, feel it, before he dies."

Alec blinked and he was inside Lansing's head. An image appeared of a beautiful woman, long legs, gorgeous black curls *"...beautiful woman, dark eyes, dark hair, perfect body but unfortunately tainted by mongrel blood. I didn't know her boy would* turn out to be competent and gifted or I would have taken him with me...but then I found you, Alec...and you have no equal..."

Lansing smiled. *"Always paid attention. Always wanted to please me. A good boy. The best. My true son."*

Alec felt *love* coloring Lansing's thoughts about him. *"We'll put things in order, me and you and the others, stop all this mess. Just as soon as you listen to me. We're so much better than they are. We deserve to be in charge."*

Alec met Lansing's gaze. The old bastard's eyes were already glazing over. *"Don't let them make you normal, boy, don't let them do that. You'll take the Resource and have control. Do what you have to do. It's worth the cost."*

"Don't die," Alec whispered.

"Smart boy, don't be a damned follower and die for nothing."

Alec's mind filled with anger, sadness and then pain. Lansing's voice in his head fluttered and abruptly disappeared. Alec slumped back against the wall and dropped his head between his legs.

"He loved me."

"I know." Beth wrapped her arms around him.

Through the blur of tears, Alec saw Drake slump back and rest his hands on his knees, hands that were still covered with Lansing's blood. Beth reached out a hand to her father. He shook his head and refused the comfort.

"Beth, Richard Lansing actually cared. He could have killed me. He kept saying he would kill me but he couldn't."

"He loved you, Alec, as much as he was able."

"He was also fucking insane."

"Oh, yes."

"Alec," Daz tapped him on the back. "Reinforcements are on the bow, unloading from the Blackhawks overhead. That CIA fuck Kowalski's with them. They're looking for the person in charge."

"I'll talk to Kowalski." Drake stood.

"No." Alec struggled to his feet. "I'm in charge now. I'll do it."

Chapter Twenty-Five

Beth rested her head on her father's shoulder as activity swarmed around them. They sat with their backs to the wall in the container that Alec had peeled open like a tin can.

The bodies of four terrorists who'd died in the gunfight had been dragged out to the bow. Lansing's body had been carefully picked up and placed in a body bag. Alec had watched. Philip had not.

The blood remained, splattered on the opposite wall of the container and in a small pool where Lansing had taken his last breath.

Her father looked up at the light streaming in from the hole ripped through the containers by the explosion.

He whistled and shook his head. "How?"

"Alec took control of the explosion and sent it up to the sky."

"And the two of you rode with it?"

"We did." *We did? Yes, we did.*

"That must have been..." Philip shook his head again.

"Yes, exactly." How to describe it? Impossible.

She closed her eyes, trying to recapture the amazement, the ecstasy, the instant where she and Alec and the fire had become all mixed together. His power had made the fire controllable. Her power had linked them together. And then...

She dropped her head to hide the flush from her father. Now she knew why Alec loved his gift.

"And then you came back down to death," Philip said. "I'm sorry."

"You have nothing to be sorry for."

She almost wished that she and Alec had never come down. They could have landed safely somewhere else if she hadn't been so insistent. And then she wouldn't have felt Lansing's pain at dying and heard Alec's grief in her thoughts.

And that was why she didn't love her gift.

It was almost a relief that her telepathy was so weak now, though it prevented her from knowing what Alec and Philip were going through. Alec had the benefit of knowing that Lansing's actions toward him were from love, twisted as it was. Mixed blessing, considering he didn't know if Lansing would have eventually pulled the trigger on that rifle.

Philip, though...Philip's blood father had tossed him aside as unworthy. The father who should have cared for Philip hadn't cared at all save to demand obedience. No wonder Philip had tried so hard to be a good father to her.

Philip had given her what he never had.

"I love you, Dad."

"I'm so proud of you. And don't you ever, ever do this again."

Nuclear airborne sex while saving the world? Well, probably it wouldn't come up again. She smiled. "What happens now?"

He kissed the top of her head. "Mop up. I assume they're posting guards on all parts of the ship. We can expect to see people soon in HazMat suits, taking control of the bomb. They're going to be in for a shock."

"Why?"

"Because they have a bomb where the explosives were detonated but the nuke wasn't." He smiled. "What you and Alec did is impossible. It ought to give scientists sleepless nights."

Impossible. What she and Alec had done together defied reality. Even F-Team had been surprised and they were used to Alec in action. She curled closer into Philip. Fear, death, love and back to death, all in the space of two hours. Philip didn't need to stop her from doing something like this. She didn't think she *could*.

But Alec would, in a heartbeat, if he was needed. Where did that leave them?

"What happens to the Resource, Philip?"

He sighed. "That is a very good question."

"Yeah, I'm wondering that too," Alec stepped back in the container and knelt in front of her. "You still okay?" He brushed her cheek with the back of his hand. Only a small remnant of the connection between them stirred.

"I'm okay," she said. "But I want to get out of here."

"Working on it." Alec nodded. "We're secure now."

"You have everyone in custody?" Philip asked.

"No, there was a member of the cell who jumped off the stern about thirty minutes before we arrived. One of the crew said the other terrorists were pissed but there wasn't much they could do about it."

Beth wondered if the missing terrorist had something to do with that spongy area that Alec felt earlier, before they boarded the container ship. She'd have to ask Philip later.

"Neither can we," Philip said. "He must have drowned."

"Yeah. He's likely dead. They're still sorting out if the crew was in on it or not. Not our job. F-Team is getting the hell out to preserve our part from going public. That's what I came to ask your father about. Kowalski out there is giving them trouble. I don't trust him."

Philip raised an eyebrow. "And you trust me?"

Alec nodded.

Philip shook his head.

Beth nudged her father's shoulder. "Just stop."

Philip shrugged. "I'll take care of Kowalski. He owes me. He's afraid of me."

"Imagine that," Alec said.

Alec offered his hand and she took it. A slow warmth spread into her from his hand, a stronger connection than just a second ago. They belonged together, though she couldn't see how they could combine their worlds. Today's events had proved that Alec and F-Team were needed, but if the Resource was gone, what happened to them?

Alec put his arm around her shoulder. "Let's go."

Philip shook his head. "No."

"It's a little late to object to my being with Alec." Her father certainly picked a strange time to play protector of her virtue.

"It's not that. You don't officially exist, Beth," Philip said. "I'd rather keep it that way."

"It's going to be hard to claim I don't exist when F-Team knows me, plus the guards and scientists at the Resource."

"F-Team won't talk. I can handle the CIA. Alec, I'm going to need your help with the Resource people."

"What do you need?"

"The CIA will go into the facility and clear it out. They'll handle the goon squads and any scientists that live onsite. I need to get into the records and delete anything about Beth. Also, I want to erase other information that the CIA shouldn't have. Two people would be faster than one."

Alec nodded. "We'll take Gabe with us. He's got the tech expertise."

"Good."

"And where am I going to be while you two do this?" She crossed her arms over her chest.

"I have an idea." Alec motioned for someone just out of sight. Daz stepped into the container and took off his helmet.

"Did you convince the CIA agent out there to let us get the hell out?" Alec asked.

"He's an asshole but transpo is finally on the way."

"I want you to take Beth. Pretend she's a team member. Keep her as far away from the spooks and the feds as possible." Alec looked at Philip. "Uh, no offense."

Her father shrugged again. "It's a good plan."

"If you like being sent away like a child," she said.

Alec hugged her. "Mission's over, we won. You won. Your father's right, the less they know about you, the better. Besides, you just escaped from a prison and haven't slept properly in who knows how long. You have to be exhausted."

"So are you."

"But I have to be here. You don't."

She was tired. No, drained was more like it. And she was being petulant for no reason, because the crisis was over and she was so empty of energy there was nothing that she could do, even if she wanted. Bed. Yes. "All right."

"Daz, put your helmet on Beth," Alec said. "It'll hide her face."

Daz took off his helmet and held it out for her inspection. She closed her hands around it but it slipped out of her grasp.

Daz caught it. "Here, I'll do it."

He settled the helmet over her head. That wasn't so bad. He gave

255

it a tap at the top and closed in on her, covering her eyes.

"I can't see a damn thing." She pushed it up so she could have a sliver of light.

Alec laughed. "That's because Daz has such a big head."

"You know it," Daz said.

"It's all sweaty inside," she said.

Daz cleared his throat. "Sorry. But we'll take care of you. You earned it."

She pushed the helmet up an inch more and stared at him. She didn't need telepathy to read the approval there. "Okay."

The smell of breakfast—eggs, bacon, toast—woke her. It took a moment for her to remember that she was finally, against all odds, back in her own bed. Safe. Alive, despite crazed immortals and nuclear bombs.

But who was in her kitchen? Philip? She concentrated, curious if her telepathy had returned with enough strength to pick up thoughts.

It worked. But it wasn't her father in the kitchen.

It was Alec.

She looked down at her filthy clothes—Alec's borrowed clothes—covered in the sweat and grime from yesterday. *I am not going out there to him like this.* Alec might not care. *She* cared. She wasn't going to show her face until she washed up.

The shower felt normal, even down to the lack of water pressure, which made her relax because it was so familiar. Her own shampoos and conditioner, her own body wash. Perfect. She closed her eyes and let the hot water run over her, ignoring the sting of the cuts on her feet from yesterday. She looked at her hand. No sign of the gash that Alec had repaired. No, most of the changes were on the inside. She turned off the water and took time to appreciate the soft towels.

Philip had apologized for not helping her with her telepathy, he'd felt awful that he hadn't given her everything she needed. But she liked this life, she liked her apartment, she liked her work. Her father had given her everything she asked for.

Alec had given her what she hadn't known she wanted.

She kicked the dirty clothes to the side and took care dressing in her favorite pants and blouse. She took out the red patterned scarf that she'd worn during her first meeting with Alec. If she wore it now, what did it mean? Who knew. It matched the blouse. She tied it around her neck.

There, that was more like herself, whoever "herself" was at this point.

She opened the door to her bedroom. Motown music was playing in her living room. *Your love keeps lifting me higher...*

She smiled and bowed in the direction of the Buddha in her cabinet.

Alec was puttering around the kitchen, looking very domestic. All he needed was an apron. Over a bare chest, preferably. Bruises decorated the right side of his face but they didn't seem to be bothering him.

"Hey, counselor." He picked her up and hugged her. He'd cleaned up and shaved, though he was wearing his customary jeans and dark T-shirt. "You look great. You smell great."

She blinked. "So do you. What possessed you to cook breakfast?"

He grinned and put her down. "I watched you in Maine, remember? It didn't look that hard. Sit down and I'll fix you a plate."

She sat in her breakfast nook and watched Alec. He seemed no worse for wear after yesterday. In fact, he seemed energized. He would be. Or maybe he was trying to avoid thinking about Lansing's death. She could read him and find out. She decided not to.

"Where's Daz?" F-Team's leader had driven her home, then insisted on staying to make sure she remained safe.

"Gabe took him home after dropping me off."

"Where's Philip?"

"Off doing whatever he does. Does he vanish like that often?"

"Routinely. When he reappears, he usually has presents for me." There was no sense worrying about her father. She'd hear from him when he was ready.

"So Drake's kinda like Santa Claus."

"If Santa carried daggers and packed heat."

Alec laughed and served her scrambled eggs, bacon and toast with orange juice. He sat across from her.

"Aren't you going to eat?"

"I did, already. Had to make sure the food came out edible."

She took a moderate portion of the egg. Warm. Fluffy. Good! "It's perfect." The bacon especially, crunchy but not burnt.

"Well, I used my TK to get the temp just right."

"Could you do that before?"

"Before us, you mean?" He drank down a full glass of orange juice. "Yeah. But I need you to jack me up to the power level I had yesterday. I tried to fly this morning. I could only hover a few inches above the ground." He put his elbows on the table and leaned forward, close to her. "What about you, counselor? You okay?"

"I don't know." She scraped up the last of the eggs and walked to her counter to measure out loose tea for brewing. "I think I'll be happy if I never have to go on a mission like that again."

"Why? You regret what *we* did?"

She almost rolled her eyes. Of course, he'd focus on their lovemaking. "Alec, I hated seeing anyone die. And with the telepathy, I *felt* them die. Just like I felt you during our, ah, flight."

"I didn't realize the memory would linger."

"Death cries are so potent that they imprint on my memories. I heard my captors dying for years in my sleep after my first kidnapping. I thought I was dying too."

"That sucks. Did you hear them last night?"

"No, I slept like a log."

"Good."

"I think the death memories are why my telepathy went latent after Philip rescued me." She picked up her teakettle and filled it with water. "I was only eight, and I didn't know how to shield my mind from them."

"And it freaked you out." Alec took the kettle from her and put his hand underneath it.

"Freaked out doesn't begin to cover it. So I think my telepathy shut down as a protective measure."

The kettle started whistling.

"Showoff."

"Yep." He poured the boiling water in the teapot for her. "That's why you lost composure yesterday, when those men died during the assault?"

"Exactly. But you were connected to me, then, and your calmness prevented me from shutting down again. At least, that's what I think happened. Maybe their deaths didn't get imprinted in my memories like the ones from my childhood. I hope so. I guess I'll find out. There's so much that I don't understand about my telepathy."

She poured milk in the bottom of a mug, added the tea and cupped her hands tight around the mug, covering the "World's Best Daughter" logo. She drank down a long swallow. "Perfect again. Thank you."

"Just taking care of my girl." He leaned against the counter. "How'd you hook me into Lansing when he was dying?"

She shrugged. "We're connected, as you might have noticed."

He grinned.

"So I wished for you to hear Lansing and you did. And you acted as an anchor for me when he died. Otherwise, I think I might have confused his dying with mine." She shuddered.

He hugged her. "Hey, you could stop thinking about that and go back to the whole making love in the sky thing. Unless you think we shouldn't do it again?"

She smiled. "I didn't say that."

He picked her up. "Good, because I want to try it again."

"Now?"

He kissed her and stroked her hair with his fingers. She wrapped her arms around his neck, and felt his rising excitement. Even more, she could feel his worry and how he'd wanted to fuss over her to make sure she was okay. He'd put on a show for her.

"Did it work, counselor? I never had a girlfriend before."

"You did wonderfully. But how about a simple, normal bed this time?"

"Can I levitate you?"

"If you insist."

He hugged her closer.

Beds. They had their uses after all. Especially one as soft as this one. He hadn't realized some sheets and blankets felt like warm hugs.

"Alec?"

"Yes?"

"TK sex, sex in the sky, and now this," she said. "I'm ruined for other men."

"Good."

"I hope so."

That sounded too tentative for his liking. She was still skittish, even after their melding. Though the mess from yesterday had something to do with it too. Hearing men die inside one's head. He couldn't imagine that and he didn't want to. God knew *he'd* tried not thinking about Lansing's death. All he'd wanted to do was get through the night and get back to her.

Ringing sounded from the pocket of his jeans. His phone. Okay, borrowed from Gabe but it was his, not something given to him by Lansing. Alec waved a hand, the pants floated to him, and he answered the phone.

"Let me speak to my daughter," Drake said.

So much for *his* phone. He handed it to Beth and tried to listen to the conversation through their mental connection. He was getting better at it, though he supposed the downside was that she'd have a stronger connection to his thoughts. Who cared? It made the orgasms better. *Much* better.

All he could tell from this conversation was that Drake was being a concerned dad.

"Yes, my hand's fine. No, no nightmares, Philip, not like before. You're the one who was hurt. How are you?"

A pause. "Oh, like you'd tell me if it was bad." She sighed. "I love you too."

Beth handed the phone to him. "Philip wants to talk you. He's worried, still."

That didn't sound promising. He put the phone to his ear. "What, Drake?"

"You have questions, Alec."

"More than I can count." Starting with Lansing's life, an explanation for that "true son" business, and what the hell he was going to do now. Though he suspected Drake didn't have an answer for the last one. Live with Beth? He didn't want to live without her. But what would he do for money? For a job?

"I have information," Drake said. "We need a debriefing."

"Spill. I'm listening."

"Not over the phone. Meet me at the Resource, Lansing's penthouse, as soon as possible."

"Why would you want me to go *there*?"

"Because the CIA just swept it. It's clean. Beth will be with you, and it's the safest place for her right now because they won't look there again."

He held the phone a few inches from his face. "Beth? You want to come?"

She smiled. "You couldn't keep me away."

Chapter Twenty-Six

The Resource was eerily quiet. Someone had turned off the power generators to the underground levels. Alec had never paid attention to the steady hum before but now that it was gone, it was impossible to ignore the silence.

The first floor looked the same. It was hard to believe they'd been fleeing in these hallways just a day ago.

"I didn't realize until I was held here how big this place is," Beth said. "Why?"

Alec frowned. "Lansing rented out the above-ground space as a conference center, especially for military contractors. He could promise them privacy and security. Most of the rooms on the lower levels were for training me, like the mock warehouse. We couldn't do it in the open most of the time."

"That's a big investment for one person," she said. "And there's the science lab and the quarters for the guards on duty." Beth shook her head. "What did he intend to do with all this space?"

"Rule the world from it, I think. He talked about finding other kids to create a whole team of us, with me as the leader. At least, that's what he said to try to get me to stay." Alec stopped in front of the door that led to the lower level. "My place is down these steps."

"Do you want to go there?"

"No. After seeing what a real home looks like, it would just piss me off."

He turned and caught her staring at him. She was studying him, analyzing him. It reminded him of their sessions together. He didn't like it, it felt like they were going backwards, that she was withdrawing from him.

She shivered and hugged herself. "Good, because I don't want to go down another level, either."

Because it would remind her of being drugged and held captive. Idiot. This wasn't about him. It was impressive that she'd even come back. Drake should have known better than to ask her to.

"Let's go. Your father's waiting."

He put his arm around her, feeling the panic that she was fighting. She'd been analyzing him as a way to push aside her memories as a prisoner. His annoyance vanished.

The elevator doors were open and waiting for them. The front door to Lansing's penthouse was also open. Alec tensed. Drake had thought this was safe. What if it wasn't?

"Stay behind me," he said.

"Philip's the only one inside."

He scowled. "You could have mentioned that."

"Sorry. I was busy checking. I was worried too."

The foyer of the penthouse was empty. "Which way?"

"Toward the back, the opposite way from your room."

The door to Lansing's private study was open. He went inside first, Beth behind him. Drake was standing in front of the wall painting of the siege of Khartoum, arms crossed over his chest, no expression on his face.

"You haven't slept, have you?" Beth asked.

"Later," Drake said.

"Promise you'll rest as soon as we're done?"

"More rest than I've taken in a long time. I promise."

"Okay."

She turned in a circle to take in the whole room, the coat of arms over the fireplace and the tables with all the miniature battles.

Alec pointed to the coat of arms. "Death or glory. Did he get either?"

"He saved your life," Beth said. "More than I ever thought he'd do."

"It's more than I ever thought Richard Lansing would do for anyone," Drake said.

"Yay, the monster loved me." Alec had no idea what to think about that. He wasn't sure that he loved Lansing back or that he would have taken a bullet for him.

"There's nothing wrong with that, Alec."

She'd spoken in his head to protect his privacy from her father. That was nice.

"I think Lansing raised you thinking that he could keep his distance, emotionally. But it became more than just a role," Drake said.

"Was he really your father? That was your mother I saw in his memories, right?"

Drake's face lost all expression. "He was no father to me. He wouldn't allow himself to be." He shook his head. "He left my mother without a second thought because he considered her beneath him."

"You were better off without him."

"Maybe, though my mother's taste in men worsened. But you want answers about your life, not to hear my old grudges."

"They're entwined, aren't they?" Alec said. "When did you figure out Lansing was your father? And that he was immortal?"

Drake collapsed in a chair in front of the fireplace. He didn't look as bad as when he'd almost died but it was close. The dark circles were back under his eyes and so was the weariness, almost like some great weight was crushing him. Seeing his blood father die, Alec guessed, had affected him. He also guessed that Drake would never talk about it.

"I always knew my stepfather wasn't my biological father," Drake said. "But I didn't connect anything with Lansing until just before I rescued Beth, about fifteen years ago. I didn't trust Lansing at all, so I dug deeper in his background."

Drake scowled.

"I discovered that Lansing was the father who'd abandoned me. He already knew. He'd been waiting for me to approach him. He naturally thought his bastard son would join him in this crusade to control events. In a secondary position, of course, because my mother's mixed-race blood and my common upbringing kept me from anything higher."

"Mixed race?" Beth asked.

"My mother was a quarter Lakota and a quarter African-

American," Philip said. "It only takes one drop of the wrong blood to disqualify a person from true nobility." He imitated Lansing's cadence exactly. "I decided he wasn't a suitable father figure for anyone and I made sure Beth was never delivered to him. I should've realized that he already had a child under his control." Drake looked away. "I could have looked deeper and found you then."

"But you decided to protect Beth instead by giving Lansing no reason to look your way." Alec nodded. "I would have done the same."

"No," Drake said. "You would have gone after him with everything you had and dismantled his entire operation. There were reasons for me not to do that, protecting Beth being the primary one. But that's the difference between you and me, Alec. You aren't satisfied unless you have total victory. I value survival above all."

Alec scanned the room again, not certain how to take Drake's comments. Lansing had sat in this place and brooded, reliving his old battles. No, not just battles. Defeats. What was it like, to live so long and have everyone you love die and everything you knew change beyond recognition?

"He never really left the Victorian age, did he?"

"No." Drake cleared his throat.

Alec thought of all the stiff, silent meals with Lansing, the insistence on knowing specific kinds of music and books, the endless academic tests and drills.

"He called me his true son, Drake. Does that mean he was my blood father? Are we brothers?" Alec hoped not. That would make his relationship with Beth more than a little weird.

"No, we're not brothers, for which you should be grateful. I'm not the type of person most people want for a relative."

Beth cleared her throat. Drake smiled. "With one notable exception." He put his feet up on a footstool, allowing more of his fatigue to show. "Your adoption by Lansing was legal and aboveboard, though I suspect he paid off some of the state officials to formalize it, so—"

"Wait a minute. Lansing *adopted* me?"

"He never told you?"

Alec shook his head.

"That would be typical." Drake slapped a hand on the armrest of the chair. "He was probably making you earn the right to be called his son."

"Yeah, that fits." Wait, if Lansing was his adopted father, then— "What about my birth parents?"

"Your birth parents, as far as I can tell, were from a good family but simply not ready to take care of a child."

"You know who they are?" He had family? Relatives?

"Do you want to know?"

"I—uh, I don't know. Are they like me?" Alec took a deep breath and produced a ball of fire above his palm. Beth slipped her arm around his waist.

"Do they have your abilities?" Drake shook his head. "Not as far as I can tell. And I think Lansing would have grabbed them if they had." Philip stared at the fireball and chewed on his lip, as Beth did sometimes. "Do you want to meet them, Alec?"

Meet some strangers who'd given him away? "What would be the point? If they cared, they wouldn't have handed me over to Lansing."

"I'm certain they thought they were giving you a better life. Lansing would have presented a good cover."

Alec shrugged and let his fireball go out. What did it matter, really? Drake himself proved that it was taking care of someone that made you a parent, not blood relationships. Maybe someday he'd look into it, if there was need. But Beth was his family now. And Daz and F-Team. Drake too, by extension, he supposed. Though he didn't know if Drake would like that much. Alec wasn't sure that he liked it either.

"It's probably better that my blood parents didn't raise me. I'd have burned down their house or something. Lansing taught me control. Now I know why he wasn't too worried about getting burned. He could heal it."

Alec put his arm around Beth's shoulders, feeling her mental support to go along with the physical.

"Are you older than you look, Philip?" Beth said. "Are you keeping anything else from me?"

Beth's grip around Alec's waist tightened. He hoped Drake hadn't lied to his daughter the way Lansing had lied to him.

"No, I'm the age I look." Drake opened his eyes and smiled. "Forty-one this year, I think. My birth records are a bit fuzzy on the date. A long story but a very dull one. In any case, I'm surprised I lived this long."

"I could read the long story from your mind," Beth said.

Drake shook his head. "It's an old tale. Timid mother, bad father. You don't need to hear it."

"What else do you know about Lansing?" Alec said. "What the hell did he do after his first life as a soldier in Queen Victoria's army?"

Drake closed his eyes again. "I could only trace his tracks in the modern day. After he left my mother, he next appeared as an undercover operative for the CIA, specializing in investigating psychic weapons. He spent some time undercover in the Soviet unit that studied psychic abilities. He set up his network of military and CIA contacts during that time.

"Once back in the States, he resigned from the CIA and built the Resource, setting himself up as an independent contractor specializing in psychic research. Beth supposedly was going to be the first long-term study subject under a contract from the Company. He said he had Beth's mother's consent. He didn't. And then Beth was grabbed by the others, I rescued her and Lansing was left in the lurch." Drake stared up at the coat of arms above the fireplace and smiled.

"It wasn't until recently that I realized Lansing also had you under wraps, Alec. It came as an unpleasant shock. And I told Beth, and she wanted to help you and here we are."

"Yeah, here we are." He was trained as a weapon. He was good at it. He'd saved *millions* of people. But with the Resource finished, what did he do? "Now what?"

"Whatever you want, Alec," Beth said. "All the choices are yours."

He walked away from her. "Counselor, I don't even know what the choices *are*."

"I do." Drake snapped to his feet.

"You want me to work for the CIA?"

"No one in their right mind should."

Left unspoken was Drake's implication that he wasn't in his right mind.

"Though I have no doubt they'll approach you," Drake said. "After what I saw yesterday, I'm assuming you can handle them."

"He's not in danger from them any longer?" Beth asked.

"I think it's safe to say that after his heroism yesterday, they view him as more useful alive." Drake walked over to Lansing's massive black oak desk in the corner and tapped a foot-high stack of papers.

"Here are your real choices. It's all yours, Alec. Lansing left the Resource to you, along with all his other holdings, which are run by several different shell companies."

"*What?*" He was Lansing's heir? "He owned this place outright?"

"Not outright. Through several holding companies that look like they hold leases on it. But he's the ultimate owner."

"How did he get that kind of money?"

"He seeded it with his savings. But the vast bulk of the money is more recent, as he acquired government and military contracts. If you know the right general with Pentagon insider experience, and you hire him to lobby for your new military consulting company, well, money piles up fast. He used that to pay off the original loans and to set up the other holdings."

"What other holdings?" Beth asked.

"The mercenary operation centered in upstate New York, for one. Most of the guards here were originally with that division. Lansing used it as a way to vet them and he picked the guards from the most reliable soldiers."

Beth whistled. "What about the science lab where I was held? Are there more of them?"

"Yes. Several research facilities specializing in genetics. They're scattered across the world. I think we can guess what type of research it was."

"Why would he leave things to me?" Alec put his hand on the stack of papers and spread out his fingers. He was tempted to burn the whole pile into ashes. Was Lansing reaching out to him from the grave? Take the Resource, that's what Lansing had said. Is this what he meant?

"This is a quick summary." Drake picked up a portable hard drive next to the papers. "I assume everything was left to you because he knew he had to fade into the background at some point as people started to wonder about his age. He certainly didn't expect to be dead. It probably never crossed his mind."

"He thought he'd have control of me."

"Yes, of course."

"Did the genetic research facilities find other children?" Alec said.

Drake winced. "Not as far as I know. But—" he sighed, "—I haven't looked into them as deeply as could have, as I said." He looked at Beth. "There's also one other element to consider."

Beth frowned. "Now what?"

"After Alec left last night, I searched the records further. I found some of Lansing's personal notes." He set a black leather journal on the desk. "Alec, you reported something unusual that night on the docks. You said you encountered a 'spongy' feeling with your TK just before the tug exploded."

Alec nodded. "That's right. I also felt it just before we assaulted the container ship. But it was moving away. Lansing told me it was nothing after the first incident."

"He lied." Philip tapped the book. "He's concerned that someone else, another party other than the terrorists, was watching you. Or him. He's not certain which. He was worried these people would take you from him. Maybe that's part of why he came on the final mission with us."

"How much did Lansing know about these watchers?" Beth asked.

"I don't know, and that worries me. I'm guessing they have abilities like you or Alec. The implication from the notes is that Lansing knew about them but didn't completely trust them. Perhaps they were behind the operation to take Beth all those years ago."

Alec picked up the notebook. "So if these guys were watching me or involved in the terrorist plot as a way to get me to show off what I can do, does that mean Putin wasn't behind the bomb plot after all?"

"He certainly allowed some radioactive materials to slip through the cracks but that appears to be the end of his involvement," Philip said. "It's the CIA's judgment that even Putin wouldn't risk being connected to blowing up New York City. Also, the United States does unpredictable things after an attack like this. Putin would be wary of that."

"So the ones that Lansing was worried about might be behind the attack," Alec said.

"Yes." Philip ground his teeth. "And I don't know anything about them, either."

Alec paced the study, furious. How did this all land on him? He stopped, faced the wall behind the desk and waved his hand.

The wall vanished and there was only open sky in front of him.

Wind blew in, sending some of the papers flying. Alec closed his eyes and imagined a big picture window like in the Maine cottage. When he opened his eyes, the wall had been replaced by three of those windows.

Drake's mouth was hanging open. He shut it quickly and flushed, probably mortified he'd been caught surprised. "Molecular re-arrangement. That will be handy for redecorating."

Beth touched the windows. "Alchemy of a sort." She smiled. "Is that what happened to our helmets up there in the sky, Alec? They just vanished."

"I think so. That's a bit blurry. I was focused on other things." He took a deep breath. His knees felt week. He joined Beth at the window and put his hand on the glass for support. *Note: Don't do this every day.*

"Does this facility all fall apart without Lansing?"

Drake ran a hand over the windows, as if to double check if the glass was real. "There are people who'll continue to run the other operations for the Resource on a day-to-day basis. The general who heads the military consulting firm, for instance, and the CEO of the mercenary company. Lansing's attorney has the will, it'll be filed, and then you'll have legal control of it all. And very full bank accounts."

Drake sat on the edge of the desk. "I can dismantle the Resource for you."

"I bet you could." But was that really the best course? To throw it all away? There might be something salvageable from this. "But it looks like I'm the one with the power to play God now."

"Or Lucifer," Drake said. "Best to get rid of it all, start fresh."

"Maybe." Alec stared at Philip. "That's what you'd do?"

"Yes. Liquidate everything. Put aside enough money to support yourself and my daughter for the rest of your lives. Donate the rest of the funds to a well-run charity. Make a clean break."

"You mean run and hide," Alec said. "You're offering to help Beth and me start fresh and have a normal life. And it would also keep us safe from these people watching me."

"Just so. Beth's safety has always been my first priority."

"And this all turns to ashes?" But there had been something valuable about being raised to control his power. Doing so had saved his life, and yesterday, he'd saved a lot of other lives as a result. "All my skills, all that I've learned, all that F-Team can do and we just let it go? Like it was nothing?"

Drake glared. "Now you sound like Lansing."

Alec glared back. "I won't put the responsibility off on someone else. Who says I can't take this place and make it what it should be?"

"And what should it be?"

"A chance to make a difference."

Drake snorted and looked out the new windows. "People seemed damned set on killing each other. The best that can be done is to protect your own."

"Protect your own. Now *you* sound like Lansing."

Drake slapped the window. His face lost all expression. "Watch it, boy."

"Yeah, Lansing called me that too."

Drake took a step toward him, his hand hovering near the gun holstered at his waist. Beth grabbed her father from behind.

"Stop it. Neither one of you is like Lansing, deep down, and you both know it."

Drake scowled. "You don't know all the consequences of the decision you're making. You've no idea who your opponents might be."

"And you're convinced that I can't make a difference because you couldn't," Alec said.

"Philip did make a difference. He saved me," Beth said. "And without my father, I wouldn't be with you. And you wouldn't have been able to stop the nuke."

Drake shook off Beth and paced away. Alec took a deep breath. Beth knew her father. There had to be something underneath that he didn't see, something kinder. But that didn't make Philip Drake any less dangerous.

Alec flexed his hand, summoning the TK. "Will you stop me if I don't liquidate the Resource?"

Drake turned around and faced him, his mouth set. For a moment, it was eerily like that moment where Lansing had been about

271

to kill him.

Beth stood behind her father, eyes wide, her face pale.

Drake shook his head and broke eye contact. "If I wanted to stop you, Alec Farley, I wouldn't have given you all this information," he said, his voice hoarse. "I'm not Richard Lansing." He tapped the papers on the desk again. "But, dammit, be aware what you're getting into. And leave my daughter out of it."

Drake turned around to look at Beth. "You're with him on this?"

"That's between us, Dad."

"I've taken you out of the line of fire. Stay with him and you'll be right back in it."

She nodded. "I know."

"This is not what I wanted for you."

"I know." She kissed his cheek.

He hugged her, nearly pulling her off her feet. Beth had said that she was more than a daughter to Drake, that she was his hold on sanity. The man was completely different with her than with anyone else.

"If he hurts you, the gloves are off."

"Oh, stop growling, Dad." She let go of him. "Are you going to get that rest?"

"Yes." He handed her a smart phone. "It is customized for top security. You can reach me at speed dial one." He glared at Alec. "Good luck. You're damn well going to need it."

Drake closed the door behind him so quietly that it didn't make a noise.

Beth walked back to the window and stood beside him.

"Do you want me to do what your father said? Take the money and run?"

"You're not Philip. There's something very damaged in him that's not damaged in you."

"Sounds like you spent a lot of time figuring him out."

"Sometimes I think I went into psychology just to understand Philip better. But I never doubt that he loves me." She shook her head. "And even he doesn't believe all of what he says."

"What do you mean?"

"If my safety was Philip's first priority, he would never have arranged for me to get inside the Resource to help you. He also wouldn't have let me go on the mission to the container ship. And he certainly wouldn't let me decide to stay with you now. Whatever else he's done, he's tried hard to be a good parent."

"You love him very much," Alec said.

"Of course."

"Even though you don't approve of what he does for the CIA?"

"It's hard to pass judgment when what he does saved my life."

"Beth, would you pass judgment on me if I took control of the Resource?"

She flinched. "I won't answer that. Don't ask me to. I made my mistake already, by kidnapping you, which led to my accidentally taking away your abilities, which led to an entire mess." She shook her head. "I'm not your counselor anymore. I never should have been. You have to decide what you want. You wanted to be in charge. You are."

"But if I choose wrong, I'll lose you."

"And you may choose wrong, if I tell you to jump one way or the other. This can't be my choice. And you can't do it to please me."

"You're still being a counselor."

She shook her head. "You won't provoke an answer from me."

It felt like his insides were vibrating, excitement and nerves and fear all at once. He put arm around her shoulders, thought of lying in bed with her. "I love you."

"I love you too."

That was all the answer he would get from her.

He could take days, maybe weeks to decide about the Resource. But he knew what he wanted. No, what he had to do. He wasn't normal, he never would be. But that didn't mean he couldn't do what was right. If whoever was out there wanted to stop him, well, let them try.

He could accomplish anything with Beth's help.

"I'm not Lansing. I can't continue it his way. But I can continue it. My way."

She stepped away from him. "I thought so." She spoke so low it was nearly a whisper. "And not because I can read your mind."

He put his hands on her shoulders. "The Resource doesn't have to be the way it was."

"I know you think that." She shook her head. "It wouldn't start that way, true. But my father had a point."

"That people want to kill each other?"

"No, that helping people isn't simple. For instance, Lansing wanted to train other kids into weapons. Is that what you want too? Do you want them to eventually join some version of F-Team?"

He frowned. "I want to show them how to use their gifts."

"How? Will you just put up a billboard advertising your services? Psychic School, telepaths, telekinetics and firestarters welcome."

She really sounded like her father when she was angry, especially that dry tone.

"These kids will have parents. I'll talk to the parents, let them decide what's best."

"And if they don't want their children trained?"

Alec frowned. "Why wouldn't they?"

Beth shook her head. "People are naturally afraid. How are you going to convince parents to trust you?"

"I'll show them what I am. What their children can be."

She walked out of his hold. "Parents aren't going to want to see problems with their children or think they're different. I know. I've seen it with parents of my gifted patients."

"I'll figure it out." *Stop asking questions.*

"To know the answers, you have to ask the right questions and I don't think you know them yet." She crossed her arms over her chest.

"You're creating problems before they are even here. You make everything sound so wrong."

"Because it came from something wrong. This place has a black soul. Take the Resource, that's what Lansing said. You're doing exactly what he wants."

No. "Lansing felt love too, even if he hid it from himself. Does that make love all wrong? So why can't he have been partially right about this?" Alec put his hand on the paper stack and sat on the edge of the massive oak desk. "You said you trusted me."

"You don't—" She stared out the windows. "You don't know what this can cost you."

"Maybe not. But I can't sit by idly. It's not in me."

"Yes, I know that."

"It's not in you, either."

"What?"

He wrapped his arms around her from behind. They both stared out the windows that he'd created with a wave of his hand.

"When you demanded that your father get you in to see me, you didn't know what you were getting into either. You only knew I needed help. You didn't let the problems stop you."

"I couldn't let you—"

"Exactly. And you kidnapped me to show me the way," he said.

"See, that's what I mean. Good intentions go awry." She twisted to face him. "I'm sorry. I've apologi—"

"No, listen. I meant you did something a little wrong to make sure I was okay and it worked." He kissed her cheek, feeling that current between them again. She'd opened up to him. She was wavering.

"You're looking at doing nothing as the right thing and doing something as all wrong. It's not. Look at your father—he's a walking mess of contradictions. You haven't given up on him. And you won't, either."

"What will you do?" she asked.

"I'll go through the whole thing, company by company, program by program, person by person, rip up what's rotted and keep the rest. Lansing thought people needed someone in charge. Hell, he wanted supermen in charge. More, I think he wanted to make sure no one could lord it over him. Someone must have ground him into dust at one point."

He took a deep breath and held Beth at arm's length. "But it's undeniable that because I could control my abilities, millions of people are still alive. Don't you think other people deserve the right to be heroes too?"

"You're all alone in this, there's someone unknown watching you and you don't know who you can trust. Not to mention that you lack experience in the corporate and political worlds."

"That's why I need you, counselor."

Her face went deathly white. "No."

"You can tell me who's trustworthy. You can separate the guilty from people like Daz and F-Team."

Her eyes went wide. "Alec until a week ago, I had no idea how I still had my telepathy. I'm barely controlling it now. And now you want me to manipulate people at the highest levels? I can order people around just by wishing it. Do you know how dangerous that is?"

He stepped back and shrugged. "I know how dangerous it could be if you don't train it. What if there's someone else out there with this ability? You might be the only one who could help them."

"Oh, that's not fair." She dropped her head and stared at the floor. "I was captured and my mother was killed by people who wanted to use me. By making these kids known, we're exposing them to danger."

"I don't think your mother would want you to stay afraid."

Beth smiled, closed her eyes, and shook her head. "A catalyst, that's what my father said I am. I did what I did to you and Philip without knowing. How do I know I might not do the same to a child, even with good intentions?"

"That's bullshit. I'm sure your father regrets being able to heal himself. I sure as hell know I regret riding an explosion into the sky. You're afraid, counselor."

"Maybe." She sighed. "All right—hell, yes."

"You keep saying I'm a hero, but you helped find the bomb and save everyone."

He grabbed her hand and entwined their fingers, pushing his power into hers until he could feel their telepathic bond again, until their bodies started humming along the same frequency. "You can't put the genie back in the bottle and have everything the way it was."

"There's a thought."

She huddled into his shoulder.

"Remember you said I couldn't conceive of a normal life because I hadn't seen it? Like a fish couldn't envision being outside of water? Maybe you're refusing to consider this because you can't imagine a world where your telepathy is part of your normal life."

"But I knew you could learn to drive or shop at Wal-Mart. I don't know if I can do this."

"I know you can."

She let more spill into their link, he saw the images of her late mother and her kidnapping, of the abuse that she'd suffered from her captors. He fought the anger at the men who'd hurt her, the men who'd made her afraid of her gift.

"*We'll* protect other kids from that."

"You picked that up, did you?"

"No, you let me see. Admit it. You want this."

He sent everything he felt about her through the link. Love, support, joy, desire.

She raised her head. "I love you, Alec."

He grinned, lifted her off her feet and twirled her around. She laughed. "Put me down."

"Only for now." He looked at the coat of arms over the fireplace. "I think that the Resource needs a new name if we're going to take over, something that signifies the new start. Glory or death are extremes. I want choices."

"Are you really going to make this a school? Do you have any idea what that entails, logistically?"

"Maybe not a school. A training facility or something. Have some extracurricular activities. Like, you know, Quiddich or something."

She blinked. "Well. That would be interesting."

"Yep." He looked at his handiwork, out to the sky. "And we need more windows, to let in the light."

About the Author

Corrina Lawson is former newspaper reporter with a degree in journalism from Boston University. She turned to writing fiction after her twins were born (they were kids three and four) to save her sanity. She naturally filled her books with the kinds of stories she loved as a kid: superheroes, alternate history and the connections people make in the midst of all that chaos.

Corrina is currently an editor of www.GeekMom.com and a core contributor to its brother site, GeekDad on www.Wired.com. She also writes for Sequential Tart, a webzine about comics and pop culture written solely by women. Often you can find her hanging out on comic book writer Gail Simone's forum on Jinxworld.

Her published works include the novellas, *Freya's Gift*, *Luminous*, a Phoenix Institute series story, and the upcoming *Phoenix Legacy*, book two of the Phoenix Institute series, all from Samhain Publishing. She has two alternate history romance novels, *Dinah of Seneca* and *Eagle of Seneca*, and is the co-author of *The GeekMom Book*. You can find her website at www.corrina-lawson.com.

SAMHAIN
PUBLISHING

It's all about the story...

Romance

HORROR

www.samhainpublishing.com

CPSIA information can be obtained at www.ICGtesting.com
Printed in the USA
BVOW030900100912

300028BV00002B/3/P